FLOWERS BY NIGHT

FLOWERS BY NIGHT

LUCY MAY LENNOX

Contents

haru no yo no
yami wa ayanashi
ume no hana
iro koso miene
ka ya wa kakururu
In the darkness of a spring night,
I may not see the alluring plum blossoms,
yet how could I fail to notice their scent?

poem by Ōshikōchi no Mitsune in the *Kokinshū* collection

c. 920

Pronunciation Guide

a – ah
i – ee
u – oo
e – eh
o – oh

Vowels in Japanese always retain the same pronunciation no matter where they occur, and each vowel is always pronounced, including final e. The only exception is u, which is often elided following some consonants, especially s. All consonants are more or less as in English, although the g is always hard. A macron (ō or ū) indicates a vowel held for slightly longer, but the pronunciation remains the same.

All syllables receive equal stress.

For example:

Ichi: ee-chee
Tomonosuke: to-mo-no-skay
Kiyochika: ki-yo-chi-ka
Matsudaira: matsu-dai-ra
Sadahide: sa-da-hee-day
Gonzaemon: gon-za-eh-mon
Tōdōza: tohh-dohh-za
Tone: toh-nay
Toride: toh-ree-day
gidayū: ghee-dah-yuu
Edo: Eh-doh

I

The Beauty Contest

According to the almanac for the eighth year of Bunsei (1825) in the reign of the Emperor Ninkō, the third day of the month of Yayoi was to be set aside for the changing of winter to summer clothes. Once that arduous task was completed, men and women were free to return to carnal pursuits. No less an authority than that old lecher, Ihara Saikaku, stated that in ancient times, the wag-tail bird taught humans the ways of lust, and since then there has been no end to the mischief it has caused.

On that day in question, a group of gaudily dressed young women lounged indolently outside a teahouse called the Peony Pavilion. Like all fashionable ladies, they had blackened their teeth, painted their skin white, and shaved their eyebrows, replaced with two black smudges high on their foreheads. Their long, thick, oiled hair was held up with an elaborate series of combs in the high shimada chignon, and the brocade sashes of their kimono tied in front announced to the world that they were ladies of easy virtue. But as this was not the great Yoshiwara pleasure district, but merely the town of Sawara, several days' travel north and east of Edo, they could not aspire to the lofty ranks of oiran or courtesan. In short, they were common whores, although like their betters in Edo, they had styled themselves with poetic names: Tsunehachi, Konoito, and Agemaki.

As these three ladies sat drinking tea and eating mochi with sweet bean jam, they amused themselves by evaluating the men who passed by, ranking the relative merits of each and commenting loudly on their appearance.

"Look, that one's not bad at all," said Agemaki. A young man in a striped kimono, leggings, and straw sandals strode by, clearly a commoner but with an air of refinement about him. "A fine high forehead and soft hands," she continued. "He must be the first son of a wealthy merchant. Never had to do a day of work in his life." They all laughed as the man hurried away, ignoring them.

"Now that one is more to my liking," said Konoito. She pointed with her round fan at a young man across the way. His forehead had not yet been fully shaved; he still had the forelocks of a boy, which gave him a delightfully innocent look.

"What? That child?" Tsunehachi burst out laughing. "Come back in a year or two!" she shouted at him, and the boy turned his face in embarrassment as he passed them by.

Agemaki had already turned her attention elsewhere. "Oho, what have we here?" she exclaimed, pointing to a tall, broad-shouldered man approaching from the other end of the street. Although the road was crowded with people hurrying every which way, darting children and dogs, laborers pulling heavy carts, the man looked neither right nor left but strode forward, his high wooden sandals striking the road purposefully. The crowd parted deferentially before him, eying his katana and wakizashi, the two swords at his side that were the marks of his station, along with the clan insignia on the back of his black kimono. He was wearing a black lacquered hat with a curved brim that partially concealed his face, but they could clearly see his square jaw and smooth, even features. He appeared to be about thirty years of age.

"Oi! Samurai-san!" Konoito called to him. "Come sit here with us!" Without so much as a glance their way, the samurai ducked under the noren curtain and into the teahouse.

"Well, I never!" sniffed Tsunehachi. "Thinks he's too good for us! But he's not too good to have a drink on the sly." As befit the dignity of their office, samurai were not allowed to frequent houses of resort like the Peony Pavilion, but in the latter years of the Tokugawa shogunate when the government had grown bloated and flabby, these laws were more often honored in the breach. Inside they could hear him shouting for sake in a deep, powerful voice.

"Look, that's the best one so far!" Agemaki said excitedly, pointing to a figure approaching from the opposite direction. A young man of perhaps twenty, he was wearing the plain indigo kimono of a commoner, hiked up at the waistband to reveal tight-fitting trousers. On his head was a wide-brimmed conical sedge hat and dangling from the fingers of one hand he carried a thin bamboo staff. He walked with a sinuous grace, slow but sensuous. Beneath the hat, they could make out a slender face with skin as pale as moonlight, and a curving red mouth. He was by far the prettiest boy they had seen so far, the winner for certain. They speculated wildly on his identity—could he be an actor or a dancer? Perhaps a famous musician from Edo or the far away capital?

He too approached the door of the teahouse, then paused for a moment and removed his hat. For the first time the women could see he had the shaved head of a monk, but it was not that which made them shrink back in disgust. His eyes were only half open, scarred over and greyish white—the man was blind. More's the pity; they could see now even more clearly his graceful, delicate features, sadly disfigured by his ruined eyes. It was plain that he was no actor, but merely an anma, or masseur.

"Excuse me, but is this the Peony Pavilion?" the young man asked in a light, boyish voice.

"Yes, anma-san," Agemaki replied coldly.

"But not for you," Konoito added, curling her lip in contempt.

Ignoring this last slight, the young man nodded and thanked them politely, then groped for the sliding door and let himself in.

Ichi, for that was the young man's name, was indeed an anma, a member of the Tōdōza, the guild of blind men. There he had been granted the lowest rank of zatō and trained as a masseur so that he might earn his living, but as anma did not belong to the four official classes of samurai, farmer, merchant, or craftsman, he was considered an outcaste or hinin, a non-person.

Ichi slid open the door to the teahouse, ducking reflexively as the noren curtain brushed across his bare head. He listened to the clink of dishes and chatter of the crowd for a moment before realizing he had no way to determine where there might be an empty seat.

"Excuse me," he said. No one answered. "Excuse me!" he repeated, more loudly. The noise around him stopped for a moment. "I'd like a bottle of sake and a place to sit and enjoy it." His request was a bold one, but he kept a smile on his face.

No one answered.

"Hello?" he asked, the smile faltering slightly.

A maid carrying a tray paused to glance up at him. "We didn't call for a masseur," she said curtly. At the same moment, the proprietor swaggered out from behind a partition.

"We don't serve such as you here, anma-san," he drawled.

Ichi's ears reddened. "I have good money," he protested. "Look!" He brandished an oblong silver coin.

"Where did an anma get so much money?" someone muttered.

"Probably stole it from a customer," the proprietor sneered. He approached Ichi and speaking slowly and loudly told him, "This is no place for you or your stolen cash." He batted the coin Ichi still held aloft out of his hand. Ichi gave a yelp of dismay. The coin barely made a clink as it struck the packed earth floor.

The tall samurai who had entered just before him looked up sharply from his corner seat, a frown on his even features. "What is this?" he demanded.

No one dared reply. The samurai strode over to the entrance, looking the proprietor up and down in contempt.

"What kind of man strikes one who is unable to strike back?" Without awaiting an answer, he retrieved the silver coin from the ground and pressed it into the masseur's hand, clasping it with both of his.

For a moment, they both paused, as if taken by surprise. For the first time, the samurai looked at the masseur, taking in his elegant hands and long fingers, his pale skin and curving red lips.

"Anma-san!" the samurai declared suddenly. "I, Uchida Tomonosuke, wish to engage your services. Come to my house at the hour of the dog," he commanded. The proprietor stared at them, dumbstruck.

In a softer, kinder voice the samurai added, "Best not to linger here. I'll see you later tonight." He gave the startled masseur a gentle push in the direction of the door. Ichi gathered his wits, bowed deeply, and departed. The samurai returned to his table, his face wiped free of all expression.

* * *

Later that evening, back at home, Uchida Tomonosuke sat staring at the scroll hanging in the alcove. The stark black characters proclaimed, "In the void there is no form," a line from the Heart Sutra. The calligraphy was by his mother, the Lady Chacha. A stern composition for a lady, perhaps, but his mother was a formidable woman.

The youngest maid, no more than a child, removed the tray with the remains of Tomonosuke's evening meal. With a deep three-finger bow, she snapped the shōji shut crisply. Tomonosuke drew his tobacco pouch from his waistband, filled the tiny bowl of a long thin pipe, and lit it from the andon or oil lamp. With a barely audible sigh, he shifted his legs to a more comfortable cross-legged position.

Tomonosuke was a member of the Uchida clan and indeed a direct relation to the daimyō of Omigawa domain in Shimōsa province, Uchida Masakata, styled Ise-no-kami. Still, the higher ranking positions had gone to Tomonosuke's two elder brothers. Officially Tomonosuke was a hatamoto or bannerman, but in reality he was merely a retainer of the third rank employed in the daimyō's office of the exchequer. From this position he was painfully aware of the sad state of the domain's finances. A small holding far enough from Edo to be considered provincial, yet close enough to still be under direct control of the shogunate, Omigawa domain provided an income of only ten thousand koku of rice per annum, the bare minimum for the rank of daimyō. Of that, Tomonosuke's personal income was a mere five koku a year. It was just enough to maintain his small household, or rather his small rooms within the narrow row house that accommodated other low ranking retainers and their families. The house was one of many clustered along the banks of the Tone River in Sawara, a few hours' walk to the daimyō's seat.

Five days each month, Tomonosuke made the long trip on foot to the office of the exchequer for his work rota. He undertook this wearisome journey, as he did everything else, without reflection or complaint, has he had been taught by his mother. If he excelled in his work, she often reminded him, he might aspire to be promoted from clerk to supervisor, but despite his dogged efforts, thus far this had not happened. The promotion had gone to men more skilled than he at flattery, their words as unctuous and sticky as ground sesame seeds. Even if his direct superiors were not worthy of their rank, still it never occurred to Tomonosuke to doubt the decisions of the daimyō or the senior counsellor. Surely if he continued to serve faithfully, they would at least increase his stipend at some point. If there was enough rice to do so, that is. Each month, Tomonosuke watched the lists of figures pile up in the domain account books. If the rice harvest this year was good, they might scrape by, but if not, well, they would all be staring into the void.

The maid slid open the shōji again. "A masseur is here to see you, my lord," she announced timidly.

It took Tomonosuke a moment to recall the incident earlier in the teahouse. He did not think to wonder how the masseur had found him, as he had given no more direction than simply stating his name. Whatever lengths the man might have gone to were none of his concern.

"Very well, show him in," he said.

The maid disappeared and in her place the blind man knelt in the doorway, bowing stiffly.

"Ichi, masseur of the rank of zatō, at your service, my lord," he said.

Tomonosuke was struck by how boyish his voice sounded. "Come in," he grunted.

Feeling ahead of him with careful fingers, Ichi pulled himself over the threshold without standing and bowed again, seated directly before the samurai in the tiny room.

Tomonosuke stared at him. How absurd that one so lowly should be possessed of such beauty and grace. His tonsure, the mark of his station as a lay monk, had grown out slightly, and his black hair stood up stiffly away from his head, but the effect was charming. A single petal of a cherry blossom, which just now were falling, clung to the shoulder of his indigo kimono. Tomonosuke stared at the contrast between the pale petal and the deep blue of the rough fabric. Without thinking, softly he recited,

> *yuki to nomi*
> *furudani aru o*
> *sakurabana*
> *ika ni chire to ka*
> *kaze no fukuramu*
> Like snow in the valley
> the cherry blossoms
> sad enough that they scatter,
> must the wind attack them so?

Ichi bowed his head and murmured,

> *hana no iro wa*
> *kasumi ni komete*
> *misezu tomo*
> I can't even see
> the color of the flowers
> shrouded in mist

His voice was so low it could barely be heard.

"What did you say?" Tomonosuke demanded. Ichi sat up straight, his face paled.

"I apologize—"

Tomonosuke cut him off. "Recite the whole thing," he demanded.

Ichi repeated the poem and added the final lines,

ka o dani nusume
haru no yamakaze
I only steal their scent
on the spring mountain breeze

It was a poem from the classic collection, the *Kokinshū*, a companion poem to the one Tomonosuke had recited. In these degenerate times, one was more apt to hear satiric comic verses or the wooden recitation of the sutras; how unexpected to hear the elegant lines of an ancient aristocratic age from the mouth of an anma.

"Most impressive! How do you come to know such a verse?" Tomonosuke inquired.

"My lord, I was trained by the Tōdōza. I can play the shamisen and biwa, recite any poem or song, old or new. I can chant the entire *Tale of the Heike* from the sounding of the Gion bell to the battle of Dan-no-ura—"

"That won't be necessary," Tomonosuke cut in. Impulsively, he reached out and brushed the petal away; it fluttered down to the rush matting laid on the polished wood floor. Sensing the movement of Tomonosuke's hand, Ichi flinched and drew back in surprise. Instantly Tomonosuke regretted frightening him. The brief look of confusion and fear that flitted across Ichi's mobile features reminded Tomonosuke of the earlier incident at the teahouse.

Quickly regaining his composure, Ichi bowed again and said, "Will your lordship allow me to begin the massage?"

Tomonosuke grunted in assent, and with a sharp rap, emptied the ashes from his pipe into the hibachi brazier. Ichi felt his way along the floor until he was kneeling behind him. With expert hands, he began kneading the samurai's shoulders. As he worked, Tomonosuke felt a slow, languorous heat rise to his head. It was pleasant.

"Lie on your side, please," Ichi requested. Tomonosuke complied, and as he lay there he found himself wondering about this strange masseur.

"So tell me, what made you decide to go for a drink at the Peony Pavilion?"

"No reason in particular. I received a generous payment from a grateful customer, and I thought I should celebrate."

"But surely you knew they would not serve an anma in such a place?"

Ichi paused the vigorous action of his hands. "Money is money, isn't that so?" He rolled Tomonosuke onto his other side and began massaging his back again.

"You know very well it isn't," Tomonosuke said. "The Peony Pavilion aspires to be the finest establishment in Sawara, and those women who hang about there, well, they are looking for a wealthy patron. Is there not some other place you usually go for a drink?"

"No, this was the first time."

Tomonosuke was surprised. "Is that so? But you do drink, right?"

"I have had amazake on festival days."

Tomonosuke snorted. Amazake, a sweet, thick, barely alcoholic drink made from the lees of fermented rice, was for women and children.

"Would you like to try it now?"

Ichi was speechless. It was beyond fortuitous that the samurai had returned to him the fallen coin, saving him the indignity of crawling about on the earthen floor to find it, and furthermore given him an hour's employment. That they should sit and drink together as if they were equals was unthinkable. But before he could answer, Tomonosuke had already called for the maid to heat up a bottle and bring two cups. The sharp scent of heated sake filled the air.

"Your cup," Tomonosuke prompted.

Ichi reached out and Tomonosuke place a tiny porcelain cup in his hand.

"It's so small!" he exclaimed without thinking.

Tomonosuke laughed. "It will be enough." With a clink, he filled the cup. Ichi held it up before him with a word of thanks, then drained it all with one gulp. Tomonosuke watched as Ichi's face contorted with confused emotions.

"Well?"

It was a strange sensation, hot and cold at the same time. Ichi could feel it burning all the way from his mouth to his stomach. Already he could feel the warmth radiating through him.

"It's good!" A grin split his face.

Tomonosuke regarded him curiously. Ichi maintained an air of studied, detached professionalism, but every so often, the mask slipped, and revealed his true feelings. Seeing that sudden smile was like seeing the sun peek out from behind the clouds, then disappear again a moment later. Tomonosuke found in himself a strong urge to find out more about him, to see behind the mask again.

"Have you always been a member of the Tōdōza?" he asked, as he poured another cup for both of them.

"Yes, my lord."

"Really? So you have been blind since birth?"

"No, my lord," Ichi replied, seeming uncomfortable with such personal questions. "I lost my sight as a child."

"Well then, you were not always a member of the Tōdōza. Who were you before that? What of your family?"

To Tomonosuke's dismay, the mask snapped back in place. Ichi dropped his head down and to one side, turned away from him. "It's better not to remember," he said shortly. "It was over twelve years ago. Whatever life I had before is gone now. There is only Ichi of the Tōdōza."

"I see." Tomonosuke coughed to hide his embarrassment at having upset the young man. He plucked the empty sake cup from Ichi's fingers. "Perhaps we should continue the massage," he suggested.

He lay down again on his side, and Ichi kneeled over him, slightly unsteadily. The young man was flushed red from the drink, two crimson splotches on his pale cheeks. Tomonosuke felt the sake coursing through his veins as well. It was pleasing to lie there with Ichi's strong, sure hands on his back. He turned his head so he could look up at Ichi's face as he worked. Up close, the contrast of his finely shaped face, high nose and curving red mouth with his scarred eyes was even more striking. His eyes had lost their roundness, and the asymmetrical shape caused his eyelashes to point in various directions. Yet Tomonosuke was not repulsed, quite the opposite...

"So handsome," Tomonosuke murmured, putting a hand to Ichi's cheek.

Ichi froze.

They were interrupted by the loud clattering of the outside door, followed by a confusion of voices from the entryway calling the servants. A moment later the shōji opened with a bang and a woman stood in the doorway. Young and fashionable, she had a shawl draped over her shoulders and a kerchief on her head, protecting her elaborate chignon, with the sides standing out stiffly above her ears in the lantern side-locks style and the intricate coil called marumage at the back. It was Tomonosuke's wife, Okyō.

"What's going on here?" Pulling off the shawl and kerchief in one smooth motion with a snap, she stepped up into the room, followed by a girl with a sharp, pointed face: her maid, Rin. Okyō's gaze flicked over the recumbent Tomonosuke, with Ichi hovering just behind him.

"Ah, I see you've hired a masseur for me. How thoughtful," she declared coldly. "This way, if you please, anma-san." Without turning to see if he followed, she swept through the tiny room and into the larger inner room that also served as their sleeping quarters. Ichi followed after her obediently without a word.

Rin closed the sliding door behind them with a snap. Tomonosuke listened as Okyō barked orders at Ichi, who murmured assent. He felt unreasonably annoyed with his wife, although he was unsure exactly why. Why should he care if she enjoyed the services of a masseur? Tomonosuke rarely cared to touch her himself; their failure to produce children after five years of marriage was the chief cause of irritation between them. So why did he feel as if she were intruding on a private moment?

2

The Plum Rains

It was three months later, in the rainy season, before Tomonosuke thought to engage Ichi's services again. The hydrangea by the front door was in bloom, the bunches of purple flowers standing out against the large green leaves, but the hot, humid air, drizzling rain, and endless cloudy skies were depressing. Sitting home alone one evening, he heard the distinctive sound of a small bamboo whistle—a masseur passing by in the street advertising his services. Suddenly, the image of the graceful young man's features appeared in his mind's eye, and he felt a sudden desire to see him again.

He called for the maid to go fetch the masseur and bring him in. But as soon as the girl tripped out the door, he felt a stab of regret. What if it were someone else? There were other masseurs in Sawara. It would be cruel to deny employment to them just because they were not young and attractive, but he had no desire to be massaged by an old man.

Tomonosuke sighed with relief to see Ichi appear kneeling at the sliding door and give a low bow. His features were as fine and beautiful as Tomonosuke remembered. His hair had grown out even further, two fingers-width or so, standing straight up all around his head. His pale skin contrasted with the deep blue of his homespun kimono.

"Oh, it's you again," Tomonosuke grunted as Ichi announced himself and knelt before him.

If Tomonosuke was hoping for a sign of acknowledgement from the masseur, he was disappointed, although surely the young man remembered him?

Ichi asked in a neutral tone if he might begin the massage.

"Yes, begin," Tomonosuke ordered, stretching out on his side. As Ichi's fingers began rubbing his back, he added in a rough voice, "I am glad to see you doing well."

"And you, my lord."

As the massage continued and he relaxed under Ichi's expert fingers, Tomonosuke realized that it had not occurred to him to send for Ichi directly. Why not?

"Do you live in Sawara?"

Ichi rolled him onto the other side before answering. "Yes, my lord."

"By yourself?"

"No, my lord, I live with four other members of the Tōdōza."

"And have you always lived there?"

"Yes, my lord."

"So you were born in Sawara?"

"No my lord, I was born in a village in Shimōsa province."

"Then you haven't always lived in there."

Ichi pulled his hands back and frowned uncertainly. He had answered without reflection, meaning that since he had settled in Sawara, he had been living in the same house, but he had no intention of explaining himself. Instead, he replied, "You seem to enjoy teasing me, sir."

Tomonosuke again felt a stab of regret. It was unseemly for him to harass the anma like this. What was it about the young man that made him want to grasp and pry him open? He wanted to share the deepest intimacy with this strangely graceful zatō.

"I apologize," he said, sitting up abruptly and allowing Ichi to rub his shoulders. "But you are an educated man, correct? You should be able to follow a logical statement."

Ichi attacked his shoulders vigorously, continuing the massage. "I attended a temple school until I was eight years old."

"So you learned to read and write?"

"Yes, my lord."

"And then the Tōdōza, after...?" Out of the corner of his eye, he saw Ichi nod, but realized by his silence and troubled frown that he had already pushed the anma too far. He tried a different topic. "You are educated in the classics but do you know of any modern works? Have you read *The Legend of Eight Dogs*?"

Ichi had not heard of it.

"Most modern literature is trash, but *The Legend of Eight Dogs* is a shining example of moral righteousness," Tomonosuke intoned solemnly, then added, "and thrilling adventure. If you call on me again I will read it to you."

Ichi ran his hands down Tomonosuke's arms on either side, completing his usual massage routine. "You may send for me at any time, my lord."

As he was departing the row house with payment in hand, Ichi heard two sets of footsteps approaching and caught the heavy scent of hair oil. Not wanting to risk another encounter with Tomonosuke's wife, he bowed low with a murmured greeting and set off hastily down the street, using his bamboo cane to find his way.

Okyō watched him go with narrowed eyes and pursed lips. "Follow him," she ordered Rin, who was standing by her side. "Find out everything you can about that anma."

"Yes, my lady."

Rin tucked up the skirts of her striped cotton kimono and hurried down the muddy street. At least the rain had stopped for the moment. Ichi walked along in a curious posture, his head flung back and to one side, his entire body leaning back, only one arm reaching forward with his long thin bamboo cane dangling loosely from his fingers. He kept up a smart pace, tapping with the cane, checking for features along the way that he evidently knew—the stone foundation of a house, a post, a mile marker set in the road. At the end of the street he turned carefully to the left and away from the district where the low-ranking retainers lived, across a busy neighborhood filled with shops, around several open-air food stalls, and finally to the poorer section of town. Rin followed him to a set of row houses, in truth not that different from the one in which Tomonosuke lived, although somewhat smaller and more run down. In the alley between the houses, the roofs of each tenement were so close together that they touched, keeping the entryway in perpetual twilight.

Ichi felt his way carefully with the tip of the cane to the third entrance in the alley, then paused before the sliding door and turned to face the maid.

"You are Rin, correct?"

Rin staggered back and gasped in surprise. "How did you know?"

"You've been following me all the way from Uchida-dono's house. I guessed it might be you. So Okyō-dono has sent you to spy on me?"

"Ye-e-s..."

"Then you'd better come in before it starts to rain again." Ichi slid open the door and called out lightly, "I'm ho-ome!" No one answered. "See? Everyone else is out. No need to feel shy." He left his straw sandals and cane in the entryway and stepped up into the house.

The step from the entryway into the house was unusually steep, so Ichi turned and offered Rin his hand as she kicked off her wooden sandals. She stepped up awkwardly, twisting to prevent the front of her kimono from gaping open.

Her hand was small and bony. Her fingers grasped his tightly for a moment then pulled away hastily once she was inside. She reminded Ichi of a kitten, tiny but with sharp, fierce claws.

The entryway led directly to an open, unadorned front room, the only furnishings worn cushions on the rough wood floor. Ichi gestured towards the floor before sitting with his legs neatly folded under him.

"Please, be seated. What does your lady wish to know about me?"

Rin sat down carefully, hardly making a sound. "She wants to know why Uchida-dono is interested in you."

"I don't know," Ichi replied truthfully. "He only hired me twice. Is that so unusual?"

"It is," Rin said sharply. "And I know the reason already, even if you don't. My lord is fond of young men. He sometimes sees the male prostitutes in the pleasure quarters. You're young and very handsome. Has he propositioned you yet?"

"No." Ichi's startled face told her that he spoke the truth. "If you know all this already, why question me like this?"

Rin gave a tiny sigh, her rigid posture relaxing slightly. "My lady gave me an order and I followed it."

Ichi laughed. "You are very loyal to her."

Rin sat up straight again, her eyes snapping. "Yes! I owe her my life."

"I meant no offense, miss. Such loyalty is admirable. I would not send you back empty-handed. Is there anything else you wish to know?"

"My lady would know everything that Uchida-dono does, all of his associates, and anyone he is intimate with."

"I understand. I'm an anma, nothing more. But you're welcome to call on me whenever you like. Your master is an honest man and I think he would not employ anyone in his household who is not also honest."

Rin arched an eyebrow at him. "How do you know?"

Ichi gave a broad smile. "When you have touched as many human bodies as I have, you come to know a person's character immediately," he said, flexing his fingers as if giving a massage. "Uchida-dono is stiff and formal but his body is lean. In these hard times, only dishonest men grow fat."

3

The Summer Festival

Uchida Tomonosuke was a follower of the way of young men, a lover of what was called male color. This was not at all unusual; the manliest of warriors naturally would not debase himself with affection for women, but seek the favors of other men. For two men to pledge their love formally as brothers was considered the height of chivalry. Indeed, the most exalted samurai in history, including Oda Nobunaga, Tokugawa Ieyasu, and Miyamoto Musashi all had well-known male lovers, and who would not seek to emulate them?

As a youth, Tomonosuke had been inducted into the ways of male color by older samurai in the domain. Now that he was an adult, it was expected that he would pursue younger men. Some of his colleagues had "younger brothers" who lived with them, even while they were also married to women, but Tomonosuke had not yet formed such an attachment.

Tomonosuke occasionally visited the pleasure quarters to hire kagema or male prostitutes, sometimes with his colleagues, sometimes alone. The boys in such places wore women's clothes, painted their faces, and arranged their hair like women, growing out their forelocks and covering their shaved crowns with a purple kerchief. Many of them looked and sounded just like girls, but while Tomonosuke would buy their favor, he never felt a strong attachment to them. As soon as they were in the private chamber, he ordered them to strip off the women's clothes and speak in their male voices, which did not endear him to the denizens of such places. Moreover, it troubled him that the boys there did not give themselves willingly but were forced by the brothel owners. Tomonosuke longed for something different, even if he could not say exactly what.

Although he had promised to call for Ichi again, he could not quite bring himself to do so. If Tomonosuke were to take a male lover, it must be a page or apprentice, that is, a young man of the samurai class. Or at least someone who could be adopted into a samurai family. Certainly not an anma of the very lowest class, a hinin or non-person. The Buddha taught compassion for all people, but non-persons were exempt from such consideration.

* * *

The rainy season ended, bringing in the stifling summer heat, long sunny days and short humid nights. The loud buzzing of the cicadas only increased the sense of oppressive heat, but the rice grew tall and food was plentiful.

High summer brought the Obon festival, and Tomonosuke and Okyō dutifully accompanied his mother and brothers to make offerings of food at the family grave. After this, they returned with them to the family residence, far larger and more impressive than their rented row house rooms. He and Okyō endured a nearly silent evening meal with them, lit sticks of incense on the ancestral altar, and departed as soon as possible.

The commoners celebrated Obon in a much more lively fashion, with dancing, fireworks, and hundreds of small paper lanterns floating down the river. Tomonosuke saw these festivities from a distance as he and Okyō walked home together. They paused for a moment at a crossroads as fireworks lit up the sky, both of them turning their faces skyward, illuminated by the multicolored lights.

Okyō glanced at him. "You want to go see the dancing," she observed.

"Of course, don't you?"

"So why don't we ever go? I know where they have set up the stage. It's at the Benzaiten Shrine, just down the road." She pointed away from the river.

Tomonosuke sighed. "I don't know. My mother would be angry if she got word that we had been seen mingling with the townspeople."

Rather than replying, Okyō gave a dissatisfied sniff, and began walking again in the direction of their house. Tomonosuke followed after, feeling equally dissatisfied.

Some few days later, as if to make up for this disappointment, Tomonosuke suddenly announced one morning that they would visit the Benzaiten Shrine. They had missed the dancing, of course, but the festival was still ongoing. The priest would be offering blessings, and no one could think it improper if they went to pray.

Okyō kept Rin bustling about all morning, dressing in an elaborate brocade kimono and obi despite the heat. Tomonosuke as usual wore his formal kimono with the round stylized horse-bit crest of the Uchida clan on the back, and hakama trousers, his katana and wakizashi at his side. His topknot was freshly washed and tied, with the ends splayed out above his shaved crown in the ginkgo leaf style.

Okyō fanned herself vigorously, complaining of the heat as they strolled along the road by the shrine, crowded with stalls selling charms and mochi on skewers dipped in sticky syrup. Further along the road, somewhat removed from the bustle of the stalls, Tomonosuke was surprised to see Ichi sitting cross-legged on a straw mat spread on the grass. He was playing the shamisen for a small group of children and young women, his face turned up towards the sky and brow wrinkled in concentration. He beat the buzzing strings with the triangular plectrum vigorously as he sang a popular ballad about lost love. His light tenor voice tripped up and down the scale skillfully.

The song ended, and a few of the women threw small coins onto the mat. Ichi thanked them with a sunny smile then launched into a series of comic linked verses about a pair of hapless travelers on the road to Edo. The children laughed with delight as he altered his voice to imitate the various people they met along the way.

Tomonosuke lingered at the edge of the crowd, watching diffidently, trying to look as if he were not staring. The young man had skill, no question. It was not a polished performance, but his voice was strong and true, and he had a way of engaging the audience even though he could not see them. Ichi paused at just the right moment then continued in an even more comically exaggerated voice, drawing peals of laughter from the children. As Tomonosuke watched, Okyō and Rin watched him.

They waited until Ichi finished his performance and gathered up the coins, feeling methodically along the mat to be sure he had them all. Tomonosuke stepped forward as the crowd dispersed.

"Ichi!" he commanded, "It is I, Uchida Tomonosuke."

Ichi nearly dropped the coins in surprise.

"T-thank you for listening," he stammered.

Tomonosuke startled him again by grasping his hand and pressing a few small coins into his palm. Ichi pressed his palms together, his hands before his face, and bowed low, thanking him again.

"I believe the prayers and dancing are about to start," Tomonosuke said. "Come with us up to the shrine."

"Oh no, I wouldn't presume..."

"Nonsense, you must receive the blessing of the priest to ward off illness in the hot season," Tomonosuke insisted. He strode off in the direction of the shrine, without looking to see if the others were following, leaving them to scramble behind him.

Ichi hastily wrapped the shamisen in a cloth and slung it on his back. Rin offered to guide him by taking one end of his cane. Just as they were about to set off, he felt her duck down again. As she rose, she whispered to him.

"You missed one of the coins."

Ichi smiled. "That's all right. You keep it."

Rin had taken up his offer to visit, and from time to time had stopped by his dwelling when she had a few moments free while running errands. Their conversation had not progressed much beyond exchanging greetings, but a wordless friendship was growing between them.

Now, she thanked him for the coin and tucked it in her obi as they hastened to catch up to Okyō and Tomonosuke.

The sliding doors of the shrine had been removed on three sides, to create a large open stage. The priest in his white jōe robe and tall black eboshi hat intoned the incomprehensible ancient lines in a deep rumbling monotone, while shaking the ceremonial bells and staff with folded paper and sacred leaves, banishing evil spirits that might cause disease. Behind him, the drums beat and shrill flutes whistled. He was followed by three miko or shrine maidens, in their white jōe robes over red hakama, their long hair tied simply with a paper twist, hanging down their backs. They performed a slow, deliberate dance, stamping their feet and ringing clusters of small bells as they turned in circles, calling in good luck for the coming harvest.

As the people thronged about the shrine, Ichi found himself jostled repeatedly by the crowd, until he was pressed right up next to Tomonosuke. Although he had already massaged him twice, somehow Ichi felt this was a more intimate position, and he shifted nervously, holding the shamisen awkwardly in front of himself to protect it.

The music droned on and on as the miko made their ponderous gyrations.

"Is it very dull to only listen to the music and not see the dancers?" Tomonosuke asked him in an undertone. "I apologize, I did not think through my invitation to you. I didn't mean to take you away from your work."

"No, my lord, it's quite all right," Ichi lied. In truth, he had planned to continue playing for coins, and the shrine music was indeed dull and repetitive. Ichi did not understand why this samurai took such an interest in him, and he found the attention somewhat unnerving. Rin had said her master desired sexual favors from him, but if this was so, why had he not demanded it already? In Ichi's experience, men of privilege did not hesitate to act on their desires. What else could he possibly want from an anma?

Ichi knew he should have refused the samurai's invitation, and yet here he was, pressed up against him. He had to admit he felt a physical attraction as well. Due to the nature of his profession, Ichi had detailed knowledge of the great variety of human forms, yet there was something about this man that intrigued him. The man was so controlled, as taut as a string, yet Ichi felt there was the capacity for great passion in him.

Propriety demanded that Ichi keep his true feelings hidden, and long experience had taught him to maintain a mask of cheerful neutrality with customers. He did not betray any of his confusion of wariness and attraction.

He jumped again as he felt a heavy hand thump him on the shoulder.

"So have you thought on my invitation to read *The Legend of Eight Dogs*?" Tomonosuke asked, still speaking softly.

"My lord, I asked the other Tōdōza members I live with if they knew how to recite *The Legend of Eight Dogs*, but none of them knew it."

"Of course not. *The Legend of Eight Dogs* is not an epic poem to be recited like *The Tale of the Heike*. It's a novel."

"A what?"

"A book for reading. It's still being published in installments by Kyokutei Bakin, a great man living in Edo."

Before he could extend a more specific invitation, Tomonosuke was interrupted by an ear-piercing flourish of the flutes as the miko finished their dance.

The crowd shifted and they were compelled to follow along as everyone took a turn to throw coins in the offertory box, with a brief prayer.

"Come, we must buy omikuji," Tomonosuke ordered. Rin again took hold of Ichi's cane as they went to one of the other buildings along the side of the shrine courtyard. Tomonosuke purchased omikuji fortunes for all of them.

Ichi unfolded the small slip of paper that Tomonosuke thrust in his hand. "What does it say?"

"Great happiness—that's the best one," Rin said, looking over his shoulder.

Ichi turned to her in surprise. "Rin-san, you can read?"

"My lady taught me how," she whispered.

Ichi heard a grunt of dissatisfaction beside him. "Uchida-dono drew misfortune," Rin explained.

Tomonosuke strode off to tie his paper fortune to a small tree in the courtyard, so that the bad luck might be left behind. When he came back, he had charms for all of them, small brocade bags containing a prayer on a slip of paper.

"For you, anma-san," he said, tying the bag to the neck of the shamisen. The instrument did not belong to Ichi; he had borrowed it from one of the senior Tōdōza members he lived with, but he did not say as much to Tomonosuke. As the samurai tied the charm to the shamisen, he whispered in his ear, "Come to my house at the hour of the snake tomorrow, and I will read you that worthy novel."

4

The Hour of the Snake

At first, Ichi was not taken with *The Legend of Eight Dogs*. Set in the distant past age of heroes, the stiff, classical phrases describing the siege of the Satomi clan were tedious. He found the scene in which the last of the Satomi, Princess Fusehime, agrees to marry a dog utterly ridiculous. To someone like Ichi, who had memorized thousands of lines of real poetry of the Warring States era and earlier, it seemed like a false copy, although not difficult to understand.

"That's enough for today," Tomonosuke said. "The beginning is a bit slow, but I promise it gets better. If you come again tomorrow, you'll see."

Ichi had not disguised his boredom as well has he had imagined.

But Tomonosuke was right—by the next chapters, Ichi found himself completely gripped. He was deeply moved by the story of the boy Shino, given a girl's name and made to wear girl's clothing until he turned fifteen, due to a prophecy. Ichi leaned forward, listening intently as Tomonosuke read the lines about Shino's loss of his parents, the abuse he suffered from his evil aunt and uncle, and how they plotted to trick him out of his inheritance.

Ichi was even more entranced when Shino met Gakuzo, and they discovered that they shared the peony birthmark that marked them both as dog warriors, the spiritual children of Princess Fusehime. How wonderful, Ichi thought, to meet a stranger, a powerful warrior, and discover a hidden connection, a secret brotherhood.

But the love story between Shino and his arranged bride Hamaji displeased him.

"Well?" Tomonosuke asked, setting the string-bound volume aside.

Ichi frowned, his head cocked to the side. "It was wrong of Hamaji to come into Shino's room at night to try to seduce him," he burst out. "Shino's karma is to partner with Gakuzo! Why must Hamaji interfere between them?"

Tomonosuke smirked. "Shino and Hamaji are both young and beautiful. It's the way of the world for men and women to marry."

"Why? I will never marry."

"Do you want me to tell you if Shino and Hamaji will marry, or if Shino goes off with Gakuzo to avenge the Satomi clan?"

"No! I want to be surprised."

"Very well, then come again tomorrow."

* * *

Ichi visited nearly every day through the month of Minazuki. Tomonosuke still could not bring himself to send for Ichi directly. But Ichi found that if he walked through Tomonosuke's neighborhood blowing on his bamboo whistle, the samurai would send a maid out to fetch him in. While Ichi massaged him, Tomonosuke read aloud from *The Legend of Eight Dogs*. As the novel had nearly a hundred chapters and was still being published, they were in no danger of running out of reading material.

Ichi was morbidly delighted to hear of Hamaji's sudden death; indeed, it seemed as if she simply vanished to allow Shino to fulfill his destiny in the company of Gakuzo and the other dog warriors.

It was stiflingly hot and humid in the airless row house, which shared walls with the neighbors and was only open to the outdoors along one long side, but neither man noticed or cared. They were transported to a virtuous age three hundred years prior, entranced by the manly devotion the dog warriors shared with each other.

Ichi heard a shuffle of paper as Tomonosuke set the book aside. Ichi took this as his signal to end the massage. Bowing low, he thanked the samurai for his kindness. As Ichi raised his head, he was startled to feel the brush of fingertips along his cheek. He jerked his head back in surprise, his heart hammering. Had he misjudged the distance when he bowed? Was this some accident? But as he moved his head back, the hand cupped his lower jaw even more firmly, the thumb stroking his lower lip with unexpected gentleness. A tiny gasp escaped his lips.

So it was true, Tomonosuke did desire him. His heart hammered wildly. He had occasionally been solicited by clients during or after a massage—usually men, but sometimes women as well. If the client was not too odious, he almost always acquiesced, with varying degrees of pleasure. But he had never before felt himself to be so desired. He could sense the passion of the other man emanating from his body in hot waves, and it stirred his own feelings in return.

Tomonosuke's mouth crushed his in a long, hot kiss. Ichi found the kiss surprisingly sweet, even as he reminded himself not to form an attachment to this strange samurai. Surely the man was only toying with him.

"You are so very beautiful," Tomonosuke breathed in a low whisper.

"So I've been told," Ichi said in a carefully neutral tone. Too often this kind of praise from a customer preceded rough usage. He wanted to trust the samurai, but he could not be certain.

"Do you want to know what I look like?"

Ichi bit back a reply. He wanted to say he already knew what the samurai looked like, or at least the form of his body, what really mattered. The face was irrelevant; Ichi had long since ceased to rely on any visual memory. But before he could think of a polite refusal, already he felt the other man take his two hands and place them on either side of his face.

With the lightest touch, Ichi allowed his fingers to explore Tomonosuke's face, at first just to oblige him but then with increasing interest.

He had a smooth, high forehead, and the bridge of his nose was flat. Smooth cheeks sloped down to a strong jaw, giving his face a squarish shape. Along his jaw was the faintest hint of stubble, carefully shaved. His lips were thin but his mouth was open slightly, his hot breath panting against Ichi's sensitive fingers.

There was no question the samurai desired him. If it was sex he wanted, well, it was a pleasant way to pass an afternoon. Tomonosuke's form was pleasing, and his touch was gentle, almost hesitant. Ichi found himself more aroused than he had expected.

Impulsively, Ichi leaned forward and kissed him, pulling at his shoulders and grasping his kimono. Tomonosuke tumbled him backward, pushing his hips insistently against Ichi's.

"Your wife...?" Ichi whispered.

"She'll be home soon," Tomonosuke confirmed flatly. "We'll have to be quick."

Ichi pulled open the front of his kimono, loosening his obi, as Tomonosuke leaned over him, running his hands over his smooth chest. Ichi's arms were strong from years of massage, but he felt slight in comparison to the tall samurai. Suddenly Tomonosuke disappeared from his arms. Ichi could hear rustling about in a drawer, then smelled the sharp scent of clove oil.

"May I—?" Tomonosuke asked with surprising solicitude.

"Yes!" Ichi frowned impatiently. Most men did not bother to ask in this way.

Still Tomonosuke hesitated. "It's not your first time...?"

"Do I look like a blushing virgin to you? No, it's not my first time! Come on, you said we have to hurry. Or do you plan to leave me in the lurch halfway through?"

Ichi again was surprised at how much Tomonosuke was holding back. It was kind of the samurai to be so concerned for his comfort, but Ichi hated being thought of as an inexperienced child.

"All right, all right," Tomonosuke grunted.

Ichi unwound his fundoshi loincloth, and he could hear the unmistakable sound of Tomonosuke doing the same. Ichi found himself warming towards this strange samurai, despite himself. This unwonted solicitude somehow made him feel like he was the one in charge of this encounter. He was more determined than ever to show that he knew what he was doing.

"I await your pleasure, my lord," Ichi said with playful, exaggerated formality, drawing his legs up and exposing his bottom.

The samurai must have liked what he saw, because Ichi heard him draw his breath in sharply as he squeezed his bottom with both hands. A moment later, Ichi felt the slick, warm, slightly numbing sensation of clove oil rubbed on his entrance.

Ichi reached forward with insistent fingers until he found Tomonosuke's smooth chest before him, then trailed down, following the curve of lean muscles, and over the rise of his hips. Then he grasped Tomonosuke's cock in his hand, pleased to hear the other man's gasp as he did so, and guided him into position. Breathing deeply through his nose, Ichi relaxed and opened as Tomonosuke slid inside him, pausing for a moment at the tight spot halfway, then with a deep sigh of satisfaction, all the way deeply inside.

Tomonosuke thrust slowly at first, then more vigorously. At last Ichi felt Tomonosuke give full reign to his passion and take him without hesitation. It was glorious to be the recipient of such unbridled desire. Most people treated him as if he were invisible, insignificant. Feeling the full force of Tomonosuke's regard for him was intoxicating.

Ichi bit his lower lip and arched his neck back as Tomonosuke grasped his cock and rubbed it, still thrusting. With loud groans, they finished at nearly the same moment.

There was no time to lie about affectionately, however. Tomonosuke pulled away and Ichi felt tissue papers placed in his hand.

"Sorry," Tomonosuke said gruffly. "Next time will be better, I promise."

Ichi could hardly imagine how this might be so.

5

The Procession

"Oi, zatō! Have you heard the news?"

Ichi raised his head, his chopsticks halfway to his mouth. He was eating his evening meal, a bowl of unpolished rice mixed with barley in his hand. On the tray before him were a small piece of grilled fish and slices of daikon pickled in rice bran—something from the sea and something from the mountains. Times were good, and they had hired an old woman to cook and clean for them.

"No, what news, kōtō-san?" The four other Tōdōza members with whom Ichi lived were all higher in rank than he, although only the highest ranked, Matsuura bettō, had been allowed to keep his own name. The others had all been renamed Ichi, distinguished by rank. As zatō of the fourth rank, Ichi was the lowest. The man speaking to him now was a kōtō of the third rank.

"The Omigawa daimyō is going to Edo this month for his alternate attendance," the kōtō explained.

The shogun required all daimyō to reside in Edo every other year, as a means of controlling them. The daimyō of Omigawa ought to have departed for Edo in the spring, but had been granted dispensation as he had been ill. But now that news of his recovery had reached Edo, the shogun sent down orders that he depart immediately. His household, and indeed the entire town of Sawara, was thrown into a frenzy over the hasty departure.

"Well?" drawled the kōtō. "Will you join the procession?"

The daimyō's procession to Edo was always a grand affair, with over two hundred attendants, not including any hangers-on who might choose to follow behind them.

Ichi made a noncommittal noise as he crunched his pickled daikon.

"I've heard that Uchida Tomonosuke-dono is among those ordered to accompany the daimyō," the kōtō said slyly.

Ichi lowered his chopsticks slowly and leaned back on his heels. The samurai had continued to invite him in from time to time and read to him, although as his wife was about, they had not repeated their intimacy. Ichi had often reminded himself not to form an attachment, yet he found he would miss this companionship if Tomonosuke departed for Edo.

When Ichi did not reply, the kōtō snickered lewdly, as if he had discovered a great secret. But in fact, Ichi's thoughts were running in a different direction. He disliked the men he lived with. Although they had all trained in the arts of massage, acupuncture, and music, only Ichi made his living in that way. The other men had all lost their sight as adults, and their wealthy families had purchased higher ranks in the Tōdōza for them. They did not walk the streets whistling for customers or play by the side of the road for coins, but instead served as unofficial but sanctioned moneylenders, making loans at ruinous rates, which in no way endeared the Tōdōza to sighted people. Ichi dressed like a laborer, with his cotton kimono tucked up in the back over tight-fitting peasant trousers called momohiki, for ease of movement while working. But the others wore lavish, loose-fitting kimono with skirts that reached nearly to the ground, like men of leisure.

Furthermore, one of the older men, a kōtō of the second rank, had been pestering Ichi for sexual favors. While so far he had taken no for an answer, Ichi was not sure how much longer the man would suffer his refusals.

Ichi finished the last of his rice and barley, feeling about carefully in the bowl with his chopsticks to be sure he had found every last grain. He set down his chopsticks on top of the empty bowl with a decisive clink.

"I shall follow the procession to Edo," he declared.

* * *

The procession of the Omigawa daimyō departed on the first day of Fumizuki. The aged daimyō rode in a palanquin, accompanied by a small army of retainers in matching outfits of lustrous black silk, marching in ordered rows. Some carried banners, spears, or staves, while others rode on horseback, led ox-carts laden with supplies, or toted boxes. Every object bore the Uchida clan crest, a cross in a circle, representing a stylized horse bit. It was an impressive sight, all the samurai turned out in their finery, marching in silent, perfect formation, and as they passed through the streets of Sawara, the commoners were obliged to bow down before them.

Tomonosuke was not among those lucky enough to ride on horseback. He had to walk in formation with the other lower-ranked retainers, carrying a box on a pole balanced over his shoulder. The box was crammed with account books and ink stones, the instruments of his office, and was very heavy. The hot sun beat down on his black lacquered helmet, and he was already bathed in sweat before they even left the town.

Far behind the official procession came a small number of wives and servants, among them Okyō, with Rin walking along beside. The women were expected to keep themselves out of the way, so as not to mar the display of masculine strength. Okyō wore a large sedge hat with a round brim, a veil attached all the way around reaching nearly to the ground, to protect her white skin from the sun, as well as cotton gaiters and arm protectors. Rin wore a curved sedge hat like a farm girl, the ends of her striped kimono tucked up in her obi.

Neither of them had made the trip to Edo before. They both came from Echigo, the snowy land far to the north, and Okyō had brought

Rin with her when she married into the Uchida clan. This was the first time since their marriage that Tomonosuke had been ordered to join the daimyō in the alternate attendance in Edo. Ordinarily wives stayed at home, but Tomonosuke was to be posted to Edo semi-permanently, and so his wife was allowed to relocate with him. She insisted on bringing Rin, but the other servants she had dismissed. As they walked along, Okyō counted up their household accounts in her head and tried to estimate how many kimono she might have made in the latest styles.

Even further back, straggling along behind the official procession was a motley collection of itinerant musicians, monks, miko, and masseurs, all those who made their living traveling from place to place, accompanied to the edge of town by laughing children and barking dogs. Among these was Ichi, tapping along the road with his bamboo cane, his few possessions tied in a cloth on his back, his conical sedge hat protecting his freshly shaved head from the summer sun.

At first, Ichi felt elated to be leaving the city behind, striking out on his own. The other vagabonds around him on the road were likewise in high spirits, calling out folk songs and comic verses as they walked along, and he felt buoyed by their chatter. He could also be assured as he followed their voices that he had not wandered from the road. But the weather was hot, and as they walked mile after mile, the crowd grew weary. Soon Ichi had only the tramp of other feet around him to guide him. Sweat trickled down his neck and even the small bundle on his back felt heavy. Yet pride spurred him on—he would not fall behind the sighted travelers. He willed himself to keep pace with the briskest of the footfalls beside him.

The procession followed the Tone River, heading for the Mito Road that connected Edo with the eastern provinces. It would have been much faster to float down the river in a barge, but there was no glory in traveling like a shipment of goods. No, the procession was obliged to go on foot along a path by the river so that all the commoners they passed along the way would be forced to fall to their knees and tremble before the might of the Omigawa daimyō and his retainers.

After a day of walking, the procession stopped for the night at the town of Kōzaki where the samurai commandeered all the inns and even private houses when the rooms were not enough.

Rin quietly excused herself from her lady and walked away from the town to the riverbank where the hangers-on had gathered. While the samurai would sleep indoors, the beggars following them would be given no accommodation. But already the crowd had lit camp fires and broken out bottles of homebrew sake and were singing and dancing in a lively manner, flinging their hands up in the air and shouting out the beat.

Rin dodged uncomfortably through the crowd until she found Ichi crouched by the fire. She plucked at his sleeve nervously.

Ichi raised his head at her touch. "Is that you, Rin?"

"Here," she said, thrusting a rice ball in his hand.

He thanked her warmly with a smile.

"Shall I take you to Uchida-dono?" she asked woodenly.

"No!" Ichi replied with some alarm. "He doesn't know that I'm following the procession. Please don't tell him."

Rin regarded him through narrowed eyes. "All right. I won't say anything."

Ichi sighed. "I don't want to make trouble for you. Your lady will be angry when she hears to whom you have given your rice."

"Okyō-dono is a fine lady," Rin said defensively. "If she's sometimes difficult, it's only because she's had a hard life. You mustn't think less of her."

Ichi did not reply, but privately he wondered what a high-born lady could know of hardship. It was well-known in Sawara that Okyō had come from a very wealthy family, a match intended to bring more money to the Uchida clan.

"Promise you won't tell your lord," Ichi repeated, and Rin promised.

The revels along the riverbank continued late into the night, even after the hour of the ox. At last the noisiest of the monks fell into a drunken stupor, but Ichi still found it difficult to sleep. The riverbank was more pebbly than sandy and he had no mat to lie upon, but neither did he wish to wander off and risk losing his way. As he tossed and turned on the hard ground, tiny insects crawled inside his clothing and bit him, and the damp of the river seeped into his bones.

Ichi was exhausted from the long day of walking, his mind even more so than his body. While he knew his way around the streets of Sawara like the inside of his own house, they had soon left that behind. He was too proud to ask a stranger to guide him, and in any case there was no one in the band of stragglers whom he trusted. Listening to the calls and footfalls of those around him and feeling with the tip of his cane to be sure he did not wander off the road or trip over a stone took all of his concentration.

Ichi sighed and rolled over, swatting at the mosquitoes that whined around his face. He should not have joined the procession to Edo. Tomonosuke would not thank him for it, and Okyō certainly would be angry when she noticed. Perhaps in the morning he should turn back, but the thought of returning to the narrow house he shared with those hateful men was even more unappealing. Shino and Gakuzo and the other dog warriors would never complain of having to sleep on the ground, he told himself.

There was nothing for it but to carry on and see what fortune Edo might bring him.

6

At Toride-juku

The procession continued at a stately pace through the villages along the Tone River, heading slowly west. Up at the head of the procession, Tomonosuke was not having an easier time of it than those at the back. Not only did he have to walk in formation carrying the heavy box attached to a pole on his shoulder, but as the procession began, he found it was his misfortune to be in line beside Matsudaira Sadahide, his direct superior in the office of the exchequer.

A direct descendant of the clan that had held the title of Omigawa daimyō over a hundred years previously, Sadahide felt very keenly the injustice that had led the shogun to dissolve his great-great-grandfather's claim and give the domain to the Uchida clan. He never missed a chance to take out this resentment on Tomonosuke. It did no good to remind Sadahide that he was in fact Tomonosuke's superior, a vassal of the Uchida clan of a much higher income and rank. Sadahide was nursing a century-old family grudge and Tomonosuke was a direct relation to the usurper daimyō.

"Posted to Edo, eh?" Sadahide drawled as they marched along. The easy way he hefted his box suggested it was much lighter than Tomonosuke's.

"Indeed." Tomonosuke agreed. He had not been ordered to Edo since he was a youth, and felt very lucky to have been chosen. His two elder brothers as senior retainers remained in Omigawa, along with their mother, to help oversee the domain in the daimyō's absence. In truth, he was glad to be away from them. Already he felt his spirits lift as the miles separated him from their oppressive propriety. In Sawara, his mother might forbid him to indulge in low-class entertainment, but he knew that in Edo, even samurai attended the theater, and he was alive with curiosity to see it.

"How lucky for you. And not a moment too soon." Sadahide gave him a sly glance out of the corner of his eye. He had a lean face with a pointed, high-bridged nose that gave him an air of perpetual suspicion.

Tomonosuke only grunted. He had no idea what this was about. He hoped the other man would read the air and cease his talk, but Sadahide was not to be discouraged.

"Everyone knows you've been spending too much time with that anma," Sadahide continued. "It really is best to put some distance between you."

Still Tomonosuke did not reply. He kept his eyes pinned to the dusty road ahead of them.

"He is handsome, despite his disfigurement, I grant you that," Sadahide said in a tone of false concern. "But isn't he a bit old? You know, they say a boy's beauty is in full flower at the age of sixteen. By nineteen, he's already a flower about to fall. That anma must be over twenty, hardly a youth anymore. Although since he doesn't wear a topknot, you can't even tell if he's old enough to be declared an adult."

Tomonosuke willed himself to remain silent.

"I'm sure you understand how inappropriate it is to form an attachment to a non-person," Sadahide rattled on.

Tomonosuke could not help coloring at that last comment. Seeing the flush spread across his cheeks, Sadahide dove in for the kill. "Really, sir? A member of the Tōdōza? You know they are vile moneylenders, dishonest and grasping men, every last one of them."

"Ichi is not a moneylender," Tomonosuke replied angrily.

Sadahide gave an insinuating laugh. "Oh no? Well, it doesn't matter what he does for a living, like all blind men he envies the sighted. His heart must be full of evil and resentment. I'm surprised that someone from such an exalted family as yours would fall for his beguiling ways."

"I have nothing more to say on this matter," Tomonosuke insisted, trying his best to keep the emotion from his voice.

"Really? Do you deny that his blindness is a judgment from heaven for some sin in this life or a previous one?"

Tomonosuke gave an impatient snort. "How can anyone know that?"

"So the Buddha teaches," Sadahide intoned with false piety. "If you wish to live a virtuous life, you should avoid those who are blighted by evil karma. Come now, once we reach Edo, I, Matsudaira Sadahide, will personally accompany you to the kagema tea houses in Yoshichō where you will meet enough beautiful boys to banish all thought of that lowly anma from your heart forever. And you know, the pleasure with a kagema is much sweeter than with any other companion because he does not give himself willingly."

Tomonosuke shuddered inwardly. Among his acquaintances who were the most devoted to the way of male color, some treated their "younger brothers" with great solicitude and even lived together. Others, like Sadahide, did not pledge a bond with one brother, but thought of all young men as conquests, the more unwilling the better. Knowing this about him, Tomonosuke had avoided visiting a brothel with Sadahide, and had no intention of doing so in Edo either.

When Tomonosuke did not reply to this invitation, at last Sadahide fell mercifully silent.

By the third day on the road, Sadahide managed to avoid carrying the box by trading places in the procession with a lower-ranking retainer, who nonetheless carried a much lighter banner closer to the front of the procession. Tomonosuke noted bitterly that it was just like Sadahide to shirk his duty, but he was glad that he would not have to spend every day of the journey listening to his prattle.

* * *

On the sixth day, the procession forded the Tone River in order to reach the post town of Toride, where they would meet the Mito Road to Edo. As it was summer, the river was low enough to walk across, but still the water reached above the waist at the deepest part. The aged daimyō was carried across in his palanquin balanced on the shoulders of his attendants, but everyone else was forced to become wet.

Toward the rear of the procession, Okyō set her foot in the cold water distastefully. The river swirled around her wooden sandals, making them so slippery she could barely keep them on her feet. Rin held her hand, urging her across. Okyō had removed her veil reluctantly, not wanting it to be spoiled by river water. She was proud of her pale northern complexion and was loath to expose her skin to the sun.

All around her, the other samurai wives and maids marched into the water as impassively as if they were walking down a city street. As Okyō reached the middle of the river, the skirts of her kimono and under-kimono wrapped around her legs and billowed out in the water.

"Oh my!" She heard a startled cry and titters of laughter behind her. Okyō glanced behind her to see streams of blood blooming to the surface of the water as she walked, like red flowers. Blushing furiously, Okyō turned her face resolutely forward, not meeting the mocking gazes of the women around her.

"My lady!" Rin gasped, but Okyō did not answer. What was there to say? There was nothing she could do about it.

When they reached the opposite shore, Rin tried to find a discreet bush or tall grasses where she might help Okyō rinse out her skirts and apply fresh rags, but there was no privacy to be had on the sandy bank.

"It's hateful! Hateful!" Okyō cried in a passion, grinding her teeth and beating her thigh with her fist. Rin tried to soothe her but she was not having it. "Every month, a cruel reminder of my failure as a wife," she muttered. "But does anyone blame *him* for failing to lie with me? Oh no, the blame must all be heaped on *my* head. And now I am made a laughingstock to the other wives, my shame exposed for all to see."

"There, there, my lady," Rin said. "I see the men are lighting some camp fires. Let's go dry off."

Okyō ignored her. "I thought there might be a change when we reached Edo, but I have seen that masseur is following us there." Seeing Rin's stricken face, Okyō continued, "Oh yes, I know that you have been giving half of your portion of rice to him. Look, there he is on the far side of the river right now, preparing to cross. Do you take me for a fool?"

"My lady, I apologize," Rin whispered.

Okyō locked eyes with her. Although her face went pale, Rin could not look away.

"You of all people I thought I could trust," Okyō said in an angry undertone.

"I'm sorry!" Rin said miserably. "You can trust me, you know that!"

"Then why have you joined my husband in befriending that anma?"

"He's a good person, and very kind. Would it really be so terrible if Uchida-dono took a younger brother? It might make things easier for us—"

"Hush," Okyō hissed at her, glancing about uneasily. "I see Edo shall be no different than Sawara," she predicted. "I should have stayed in Omigawa."

* * *

After crossing the river and walking several more weary miles inland, before the procession could enter the post town or juku of Toride, first the entire party was required to stop at the check station where every single person from the daimyō to the lowliest beggar had to present traveling papers. And not only the people but everything they carried with them had to be inspected, all the boxes opened and the contents displayed. This process took several days.

Ichi lay in the tall pampas grass outside the check station, listening to the buzzing of the dragonflies and the cries of the cicadas in the trees overhead. He had heard that the song of the cicadas varied with the temperature, their chirps coming faster as the weather got hotter. The day was very hot, and their cries blurred together into a single high-pitched scream, so loud as to nearly blot out any other noise.

He fingered his traveling papers tucked into the front of his kimono. He counted himself lucky to have a passport provided by the Tōdōza allowing him to travel wherever he wished, to any province in any of the three islands of Japan. He might be considered a non-person, but even samurai did not have that privilege. It pleased him to think that in this regard, he had greater liberty than most sighted people.

Suddenly he felt a light touch on his sleeve and jerked upright.

"Who is that?" He reached out but the hand had disappeared.

"It is I, Rin."

Ichi could barely hear her timid voice over the sound of the cicadas.

"You startled me! I didn't hear you approach. What is it?"

"I'm sorry." She crouched down next to him and pushed a flat, papery piece of dried squid into his hand. There would be no more rice until they reached Toride.

"Okyō-dono knows you're here," she said laconically as they munched the squid together.

"And?"

Rin shrugged. "Try to stay away from her as we pass through the post towns."

Ichi nodded. "I'm sorry to have made trouble for you, Rin. Please don't tell Uchida-dono."

"I already promised, didn't I?" she said irritably, pulling at the grass at her feet. "You needn't worry. I never speak to him at all."

Ichi cocked an ear towards her. "Rin, are you afraid of your master?"

"No, it's not just him..."

"Are you afraid of men?" Ichi asked gently. There was a moment of silence as the cicadas paused for a second, then resumed their screeching.

"With good reason," Rin muttered defensively, looking away. Ichi felt a pang of sympathy at the note of anger and bitterness in her voice. He could well imagine what she meant by that.

"Even me?"

"No, not you."

"Why, because I'm blind? I tell you, blind men are still men, and can be just as evil as sighted men. I know from personal experience." He thought of the kōtō in Sawara who had tried to kiss him. He was lucky to have escaped without further assault.

"No. I don't know. It's just... you have an air of kindness about you."

Despite himself, Ichi laughed. "What does that mean?"

She puffed out her cheeks and frowned in annoyance at being laughed at. When Rin did not answer, he said, "I'm sorry, I didn't mean to make fun of you. Thank you for the compliment. You have been very kind too, to share your food with me. Once we reach the post town, I will earn some money and treat you."

He heard the crunch of her sandals in the grass as she stood up. "Promise?"

Ichi nodded seriously.

"Do you think they have toasted mochi in Toride?" Rin asked, and he was glad to hear a note of hopefulness in her voice.

"I'm certain we can find some," he replied with a smile.

* * *

The daimyō's retinue arrived at last in Toride-juku, weary and disheveled, their kimono caked with dust from the road and reeking of sweat and river water. Tomonosuke was glad for the chance to bathe, change clothes and have his face and crown shaved and topknot retied, even if the bath house was crowded and he had to wait in a long queue at the barber, as all the other members of the procession sought the same services.

Toride boasted many inns specifically for traveling daimyō and their retinue. There would be soft futons for all the retainers and hot meals at last. As part of the official procession, Tomonosuke would be housed separately from Okyō and Rin until they reached Edo. But no matter, at least Matsudaira Sadahide had pushed his way even further up the line and secured a private room for himself, so Tomonosuke was spared having to bunk with him.

Late that night, Tomonosuke walked slowly down the street. The sake he had just drunk warmed his belly, and he felt refreshed after the wearisome days of walking. Although it was late, nearly the hour of the ox, laughter, singing and the twang of many shamisen rang out from the taverns that lined the road. The round paper lanterns suspended from the eaves cast a warm glow. A full moon shone overhead.

Just then, Tomonosuke caught sight of a familiar figure further down the road.

"Ichi?"

The anma was tapping along the road with his cane, blowing his whistle to announce his business. On hearing Tomonosuke's voice, he froze for a second, then hurried along his way, tucking the whistle into his waistband.

"Wait!" Tomonosuke ran after him, his large rectangular wooden sandals slapping his feet. Ichi increased his pace, but Tomonosuke easily caught up with him just past the row of taverns, where the street widened out to fields. He grasped Ichi's arm, bringing him up short.

"What are you doing here? I thought you were in Sawara. And why are you running from me?"

Ichi ducked his head, pulling his arm free of Tomonosuke's grasp. "I'm following the procession to Edo, my lord. But I shan't bother you. I'll just be on my way..."

"Don't be ridiculous." Tomonosuke took his hand, gazing at Ichi in the moonlight. Ichi's head had been shaved recently and was only just beginning to grow out, making him look somehow fresh and clean. Despite the days on the road, his face was only lightly tanned, and his curving red mouth and high cheekbones glowed in the moonlight. As ever, his eyes were half closed, only a line of white visible between the uneven black lashes, but even this Tomonosuke found attractive.

Tomonosuke had been thinking of Ichi during the journey, regretting that he had to leave after only one night of passion. Seeing him now unexpectedly, looking so lovely in the moonlight, Tomonosuke felt his desire stir more powerfully than before. Even the way Ichi shifted from foot to foot, fingering his cane nervously was charming.

"But my lord..." Ichi protested.

"Come with me," Tomonosuke commanded, dragging him by the

hand behind one of the outbuildings of the last tavern on the street. Ichi stumbled behind him. Tomonosuke pushed him up against the wall and kissed him hungrily.

The vertical wooden beams on the outside wall of the outbuilding still retained the heat of the day and gave off a pleasant scent of cypress. Despite the late hour, the air had not cooled much, but only seemed even more humid. Tomonosuke ignored the trickle of sweat that dripped down his back.

"But what will people say?" Ichi whispered.

"No one can see us," Tomonosuke assured him, cupping his cheek and running his thumb along his lower lip. Ichi gave a low moan, his eyelids fluttering helplessly.

The sight of this drove Tomonosuke to even greater heights of passion. He pressed his body against Ichi's, moving his hands to grasp his buttocks through his kimono and squeeze. He pulled open Ichi's kimono, grateful that he was not wearing the momohiki trousers, but only a fundoshi underneath. He pulled away the twisted cloth, and Ichi's cock sprang up, eager and hard. Ichi grasped him around the shoulders, pulling him closer.

Yet Tomonosuke hesitated. He regretted the tiny bottle of clove oil that he had left behind in Sawara, never imagining that he might need it on the road, of all places. As amorous as he was, he had no desire to cause Ichi pain. Many men, he knew, did not spare a thought for the comfort or pleasure of the youths they lay with, and a few even preferred to cause pain or injury. Tomonosuke found this callous attitude distasteful. Besides, it only increased his pleasure to see his partner enjoying himself.

Ichi relaxed his grip and shifted back against the wall, confused as to why Tomonosuke suddenly stopped moving.

"My lord? Is something wrong?"

"No, not at all. It's just...I don't have any oil here, and I don't wish to cause you pain by entering you dry."

"Oh." His eyes opened wide in surprise for a moment before drifting half closed again, sorely testing Tomonosuke's restraint. "Ah...you're right. That would hurt... So what do we do?" There was a sweetly plaintive note in his voice.

Rather than answering, Tomonosuke wrapped his fingers around Ichi's cock, causing him to sigh and lean back against the wall with his eyes closed, his head tipped back. He rubbed rhythmically, enjoying the sound of Ichi's increasingly ragged, panting breath.

Ichi reached out boldly and grasped him in the same way. With a growl, Tomonosuke leaned forward and buried his face in Ichi's shoulder, kissing his neck and nipping at him playfully.

Ordinarily, Tomonosuke might have found this kind of thing childish, what boys might do with each other before being tutored in the ways of sex by an older man. But somehow, being out in the open, with the risk of discovery, and being denied the usual pleasures, his arousal was at a high pitch.

For a time they leaned together, both transported in waves of ecstasy, then finished far sooner than he would have guessed. He stood there in wonder, panting, staring at the graceful anma. Why was he so beguiling?

For his part, Ichi leaned back against the wall, his legs still trembling slightly, awash in conflicted emotions. He had told himself he was only going to Edo to avoid the kōtō who had been pursuing him and not to be with Tomonosuke. But encountering him like this, he had to admit he found the samurai's attentions seductive. It was so tempting to give himself up to pleasure in the arms of the older man, to imagine him as an elder brother.

Earlier in the day, Ichi had found some massage customers at the bath house and earned a few copper coins. As he walked the streets by the inns, Rin had come running up to him, as he hoped she might. He did not mind when she grasped his hand without saying a word. Ordinarily he hated when sighted people did this, but he had come to recognize her small bony hand, and understood her shyness.

Rin led them to a yatai where Ichi bought them toasted mochi slathered in soy sauce and wrapped in nori seaweed.

As they ate together, Rin commented in her low, small voice, "You know, Uchida-dono might make a good elder brother."

"Rin!" Ichi choked slightly in surprise, his ears reddening.

"I mean it," she insisted. "You could do worse."

"You just told me you never even speak to him! Besides, I'm certain he is not in earnest with me. Once he has satisfied his curiosity, his passion will wane."

Rin gulped down her mochi. "No, I don't think so. He's not like that."

Ichi was still not convinced. "In any case, I doubt your lady would appreciate you talking to me in this way. She's jealous, and wishes me away."

"No. You misunderstand her. Her bad temper isn't from jealousy."

"What then?" But Rin refused to say more, and Ichi did not want to press her to gossip about her mistress, to whom she was clearly deeply attached.

Despite Rin's encouragement, Ichi had thought to stay away from Tomonosuke. And yet the moment he heard the samurai call his name, his resolve proved as insubstantial as dust before the wind, and he had given in to lust without hesitation.

Ichi found he could not resist the touch of the samurai's large hands, so strong and assured, yet gentle. The feel of that hand on his cock transported him with ecstasy, and for a few moments, all he was conscious of was that throbbing heat and the sound of their panting breath. But as he gradually returned to himself, Ichi again felt unsure.

As he leaned against the wall, Ichi could hear the slight rustling as Tomonosuke rearranged his clothes. A samurai would never take an anma as a younger brother, Ichi reminded himself sternly. And yet Tomonosuke had shown him nothing but solicitude. Ichi resolved to enjoy this pleasure, even if it was only fleeting.

7

Edo

The hardest part of the journey now past, the procession continued in high style through the post towns on the Mito Road. After Toride-juku, they stopped at Abiko-juku, then Kogane-juku, Matsudo-juku, Nii-juku and Senju-juku. At each post town, they stayed several nights, and Tomonosuke managed to find Ichi wandering the streets late at night.

After the first night of passion up against a wall out in the street, Ichi had vowed no more, but as soon as he heard Tomonosuke's deep voice and felt his large hand on his arm, he could not resist.

At Abiko-juku, late at night they stole away down to the banks of the river where Tomonosuke pulled a dried gourd filled with sake from his kimono and they shared it, drinking straight from the flask.

Tomonosuke took a long swallow and gasped a bit at the harshness. "It's not very good," he admitted. "When we get to Edo, the sake will be much better."

Ichi nodded politely. Mistaking his reticence for shyness rather than lack of interest, Tomonosuke went on at length about the delights of Edo, the various neighborhoods, the delicacies they would eat, the music, the late summer festivals, and of course the kabuki theater. Samurai were forbidden to attend kabuki but there were ways to get a ticket if one knew where to ask.

Ichi listened silently, not adding anything, until at last Tomonosuke worried that he seemed uninterested. "Is there anything you look forward to in Edo?" he asked.

"Yes, do you think we might find the latest volumes of *The Legend of Eight Dogs*?" Ichi asked hopefully.

"Of course. We might even call on Bakin himself, haha!" Tomonosuke promised rashly, not reflecting on how this might be at all possible.

"I should like that very much," Ichi said softly. But to him this seemed as improbable as the idea that Tomonosuke would continue to meet with him like this once they reached Edo. The city was so large; surely they would go their separate ways upon arrival.

It will be for the best, Ichi reminded himself. Besides, he disliked the way Tomonosuke spoke to him of the pleasures of Edo, as if he were a child who knew nothing of the world. He had already told Tomonosuke that he had not lived his entire life in Sawara. What did Tomonosuke imagine he had been doing before that? But Ichi knew that Tomonosuke, like all sighted people, had not imagined anything at all about his life, how he got about or where he had been. It was pointless to try to make him understand. As always, Ichi assumed his mask of neutrality that did not betray his inner thoughts.

* * *

After what felt like an interminably slow journey, at length the procession crossed the Nihonbashi Bridge into Edo. The wooden sandals of the retinue boomed loudly against the curving boards of the bridge as they all marched in formation, and again the commoners in the street were compelled to bow down before them.

Tomonosuke joined the official retinue delivering the daimyō to the kami-yashiki or upper residence in Yotsuya, at the very edge of what might be considered the prestigious neighborhood of Marunouchi, inside the moat of Edo Castle. But Tomonosuke was not of high enough rank to stay there. With the other lower-ranking retainers and their wives and servants, he slowly made his way across the city to the shimo-yashiki or lower residence at the far western suburb of Takadanobaba.

The city was just as lively and bustling as Tomonosuke recalled from his youth, but somehow in his memory he had omitted the filth, the noise, and the hauteur of the locals, who called themselves Edokko, the children of Edo. The Edokko were well accustomed to recognizing those of the highest status at a glance, and were not to be awed by low-rank-ing country samurai. They might bow down, but their sneering looks were unmistakable. Tomonosuke tried his best to ignore them, but it was hard not to feel like a bumpkin, outclassed even by the townspeo-ple in the great city.

Upon their arrival, they discovered that the lower residence had been shut up for over two years, and their quarters were musty and cramped.

"This must be repaired," Okyō ordered, opening and closing the fusuma that divided their quarters from the others. The sliding doors were warped from disuse and stuck in the frame.

"My lady?" Rin looked at her uncertainly. She was the only one to whom Okyō could issue orders, and she was no carpenter, nor did she know where to purchase replacements.

"Never mind, I'll see to it myself," Okyō snapped irritably. She turned her attention to the tatami mats, which were lumpy and mildewed, then opened the closet and threw all the bedding on the floor in disgust.

"Ugh, it stinks! Who can sleep on this!"

Rin looked at her sorrowfully and did not reply.

"Take all of this and throw it away," Okyō continued. "Then go out and buy new futons." She reached into her waistband to withdraw her purse. "I will see about finding someone to repair the fusuma and re-place the tatami."

"Yes, my lady," Rin whispered. She looked the coins Okyō placed in her hand. "And for me...?" In their row house in Sawara, most nights Okyō chose not to sleep next to her husband, but banished him to the outer room and let Rin stay in the main room with her. But here in the lower residence, the servants had separate quarters, and Tomonosuke had been allotted just one room.

"I'm sorry," Okyō said kindly, squeezing her hand. "But remember we're only staying here temporarily, until the daimyō returns to Omigawa." Rin still looked unhappy, and Okyō added, "Take some of the money and buy yourself new bedding as well. It will not be so very long before we move into a row house, then things will be as they were before, I promise."

* * *

Tomonosuke was also kept busy at first settling paperwork in the transplanted office of exchequer. Unpacking all the accounts they had brought with them and reconciling the domain's ledgers with those in the Edo residence took quite some time. Mercifully, even Matsudaira Sadahide was too distracted with work to pry into Tomonosuke's personal life or invite him to a kagema brothel.

But as they gradually settled into a routine, Tomonosuke found his thoughts turning to entertainment. He visited the booksellers in Kanda and purchased the latest chapter of *The Legend of Eight Dogs*, as well as some satirical books by Shikitei Sanba and Hiraga Gennai. This last he bought thinking it was essays in praise of male color, and was surprised to find it included a treatise on farting. He had to admit it was rather amusing, if a bit vulgar.

Next he began making discreet inquiries among his lower-ranking colleagues on how a samurai might purchase theater tickets on the sly. This, it seemed, was easily done through a go-between, but to his dismay the kabuki season had not yet begun, so he would have to wait.

With one thing and another, Tomonosuke did not think to call on Ichi or wonder where he was. But one evening, as he was making the long walk from the upper residence back to Takadanobaba, at the sight of the yellow moon full once more, he suddenly recalled those nights of passion in the post towns. He had not seen Ichi since the last night in Senju-juku, nor had he inquired into his plans in Edo. Where was

Ichi staying? Did he have any place to go, or was he homeless? And how would Tomonosuke ever find him in this teeming city?

For the first time in his life, Tomonosuke thought of something besides himself or his duty to the daimyō. But as for how to turn those thoughts into actions, he had no idea.

The more he puzzled over Ichi's whereabouts, the more worried Tomonosuke became. Ichi was an innocent young man, barely more than a youth. And he couldn't even see! What was he thinking, walking into Edo all by himself? How would he know where to go? He could be picked up by the police and arrested for loitering. Or worse, trampled by a horse! He could be lying dead by the side of the road and Tomonosuke would never know.

Even while at work, these thoughts intruded in his mind, terrible images floating in his imagination with alarming vividness. He sighed and stared at the column of numbers before him. This would never do. He could not make the sums come out correctly no matter what he did. He clacked the beads of his abacus impatiently but it was no good.

Reluctantly, he showed the list to Matsudaira Sadahide, sitting before him at a low table in the cramped office.

"Forgive me, my lord, but I'm having some difficulty."

Sadahide glanced over the account book with a sneer. "I'll take that," he declared, snatching it quickly out of Tomonosuke's hand. "You seem distracted lately. Is something troubling you?"

"No, my lord."

To Tomonosuke's relief, Sadahide did not inquire further into his affairs. But the next day, Tomonosuke found himself summoned to the kami-yashiki in Yotsuya.

Tomonosuke was sweating and his heart pounding as he waited kneeling on the tatami mat in the antechamber, but to his vast relief, he was shown in to an audience with the young lord, Uchida Kiyochika, the son and heir, rather than the daimyō himself. Kiyochika was called the young lord by courtesy, but in fact he was slightly older than Tomonosuke, in his mid thirties.

Kiyochika greeted Tomonosuke with a warm smile and inquired after the health of Tomonosuke's brothers and mother. He had a round, kind face and quiet manners, very different from his crotchety father. As the daimyō grew older and his health declined, Kiyochika, who resided year round in Edo, was slowly taking on more of the responsibilities of running the domain, and he made it his duty to know the particulars of each of his retainers.

"By your leave, my lord, my family is all very well," Tomonosuke replied stiffly, his nose nearly touching the crisp tatami as he kneeled and executed a three-finger bow, the first two fingers and thumb of each hand pressed together to form a triangle on the mat before him. The mats were so new that they were still greenish and gave off a slight scent of grass.

"Very good. Please be easy."

Tomonosuke raised his head, sitting back on his heels with his arms planted on his thighs, his elbows out, his back straight as a board.

Kiyochika continued, "Now what's this I hear from Matsudaira Sadahide about you seeming unwell and behaving strangely at work? Do you suffer from piles? My honored father has been sorely afflicted by piles."

"No, my lord." Tomonosuke felt his cheeks burning.

"Are you ill? I have heard there is cholera in Edo. We must be on guard against pestilence in the hot season."

"No my lord, I am quite healthy."

"Good, good. I know Sadahide can be difficult, but my father trusts his judgment. Please try not to antagonize him."

"I understand, my lord."

"Perhaps it is a personal matter that oppresses your spirits? You must be troubled that your wife has not yet produced an heir. Tell her to go pray to Kannon at the Sensōji Temple in Asakusa. That's what worked for my wife."

Tomonosuke wanted to sink beneath the floor in shame at hearing of his personal affairs from the mouth of the young lord. With great effort, he kept his expression neutral, although his face burned even redder.

"As you command, my lord. My deepest apology for my lapse in duty."

Kiyochika waved a hand. "Think nothing of it. Good luck to you, and please come see me again if you have any difficulties."

Tomonosuke staggered out of the dim mansion, squinting in the bright sunlight reflected against the white gravel of the courtyard and shaking his head in disbelief. He was grateful to Kiyochika for his concern, but he feared for the future of the domain. The father could be a harsh taskmaster, but the son was entirely too soft. Is this what a lifetime of being cosseted in a mansion in Edo did to a man?

He snorted with laughter at the thought of going to Kiyochika with his troubles. As if he would ask the daimyō's son to help him locate an anma, only to satisfy his lust, to his shame. Sadahide was right, he needed to forget about Ichi.

As he strode away from the mansion and down the wide boulevard, Tomonosuke vowed to himself that he would lie with Okyō that very night. No more excuses or distractions, he would perform his duty as a husband. Once he got a child on her, all this muttering and restlessness would cease.

But the walk back from Yotsuya to Takadanobaba was very long, and as he went, he reflected on his past attempts to get Okyō with child. Objectively, he could recognize that she was very beautiful, with her pale white skin and full red lips, her brows perfectly arched like two pine boughs. The sharp point of her chin was quite alluring, and her long black hair was lustrous and thick. But he could feel no desire for her at all. To the contrary, her soft womanly curves and feminine scent filled him with revulsion. His failure to perform the deed to completion frustrated and humiliated them both.

No matter, he told himself, he must succeed this time. He just needed to put himself in an amorous frame of mind. Immediately, Ichi's face appeared his mind's eye, Ichi with his face contorted in pleasure, his soft mouth open and panting, his pale cheeks flushed... no no, that would never do.

Perhaps he should buy an erotic woodblock print. Tomonosuke was just passing through Shinjuku where the streets were lined with shops selling prints of all kinds—images of kabuki actors, sumo wrestlers, ornately attired oiran, famous scenes around Edo. He loitered for some time before one shop specializing in erotic prints featuring beautiful young men, but he could not bring himself to go in and make a purchase from such a low establishment. It was beneath his dignity as a samurai.

Tomonosuke shook himself and set off again down the road. Of course he would not buy a print like a commoner or a merchant. What would his mother, the Lady Chacha, say?

He knew very well what she would say. The entire rest of the way to Takadanobaba he could hear Lady Chacha's iron tones ringing in his ears: he must not neglect his duty. Human emotion led to carnal attachment, and that was a sin. The word samurai meant to serve, and he served his lord by having many children and making the clan prosperous. Okyō was from a clan much wealthier than their own, and they were lucky her family had deigned to give her to him, and with a generous dowry for a younger son.

Thoughts of his mother did nothing to incite Tomonosuke's desire for his wife, quite the opposite, but even in his imagination, once Lady Chacha started lecturing, there was no stopping her. Tomonosuke returned to the lower residence late that night, weary, dusty and sweaty but with a sense of grim determination.

"I'm home!" he shouted, pushing open the sliding door to their quarters. The fusuma had been repaired and now slid nearly silently. The room was already darkened, the futon spread on the floor with just a single guttering candle set in a corner. But even in the dimness, he could clearly see the frantic shuffling under the light summer blanket and hear the squeals of dismay. He crossed the room in two strides and flipped the cover back to reveal Rin lying naked on top of Okyō. Rin gasped and hid her face in shame on her lady's shoulder, but Okyō merely stared back at him in silent defiance, her black hair disheveled on the pillow behind her and her black eyes glinting angrily in the candle light.

Tomonosuke sniffed. "Madam, forgive my lateness. I came to do my duty as a husband, but I see you are already occupied."

He turned and left, banging the fusuma shut behind him and making it jump in the frame. Tomonosuke stalked about the darkened mansion until he found a small unoccupied room and flung himself down on the bare floor.

Really, it was not such a surprise. He had long suspected there was some deeper bond between his wife and her maid. After all, they had been together since before the marriage; Okyō had brought Rin with her from Echigo. But to have it confirmed in this way wounded his pride. He felt foolish for not realizing why she insisted he sleep in the other room in the row house; he had simply gone along with her request without reflecting on it. Men might lie with other men as they pleased, but for a woman to lie with a woman was a bit perverse, although not unheard of. And here he had been feeling guilty for desiring someone else and neglecting her, when all this time Okyō was the one with another in her heart.

He ought to be angrier, but instead he felt strangely relieved. Now Okyō had no grounds to object to him bringing Ichi to their household. Ichi! But where was he? How would he ever find him again?

Tomonosuke was exhausted but still sleep would not come.

8

The Six-Mat Room

Tomonosuke passed the greater part of a month in the same uneasy routine. He wished he could request a separate room for himself, but to do so would give rise to gossip. He and Okyō slept on opposite sides of the room and did not speak to each other at all.

At work he still could not make his sums come out correctly. Although Sadahide grumbled about his incompetence, he did not report Tomonosuke to the daimyō again. Unlike in Sawara where he had to walk a long distance for his work rota, here in Edo the office of the exchequer was temporarily located within the walls of the shimo-yashiki, the same sprawling complex in which Tomonosuke was quartered, so days might pass without him ever leaving the gates.

The summer turned to autumn, bringing days and days of heavy rain, making him even more reluctant to venture out into the city. One rare clear evening when the rains stopped, he went out for a drink, and as he was returning to the lower residence, there tapping along the road and blowing his anma's whistle was Ichi.

Tomonosuke could scarcely believe his eyes. Glancing quickly up and down the road to be sure there was no one else about, he abandoned all propriety and ran after him.

"Ichi!"

This time the young masseur did not run away, but his face remained an impassive mask as he waited for Tomonosuke to catch up to him.

"Oh thank goodness! Are you well? I'm so relieved!" Tomonosuke grappled him in a tight embrace.

"Of course I'm well," Ichi said, nonplussed, extricating himself from the samurai's arms. "How is Edo treating you, my lord?"

"Well enough. But there's no reason to stand about in the street. Please come in."

"Thank you, my lord. But the way is unfamiliar to me. If I might ask you to guide me..."

"Of course," he said gruffly, pushing at Ichi's elbow. But that seemed to make the young man uncomfortable, for he pulled his arm away awkwardly. Tomonosuke realized with a start that he had never had to lead Ichi anywhere before; he always seemed to know somehow where he was going on his own. Or perhaps someone else had helped him. Tomonosuke had never noticed.

"Most people just take the end of my cane," Ichi suggested, holding out the slender bamboo staff.

"Oh yes, I see," Tomonosuke said in embarrassment, taking one end of the cane. He had a vague memory of seeing Rin do the same. Ichi followed along behind him through the gates of the lower residence.

Anyone seeing them would just think that the anma was visiting the mansion to give a massage, but still Ichi seemed uneasy.

"Sir, I don't wish to cause trouble. Your wife..." ...Ichi mumbled as he removed his straw sandals and stepped up into the foyer.

"Don't worry, we needn't see her at all," Tomonosuke said as he led him down the polished hardwood hallway. "This mansion was built in a time when the domain was much more prosperous and many more people stayed here. There are so many empty rooms. Come, be easy, I assure you no one will notice you."

They crossed through a series of low buildings connected by raised floors, all of the same highly polished dark wood. Tomonosuke slid open the door to an unused six-mat room and set down the andon he carried in a corner. The tatami was rather musty, but at least it was soft and no one would bother them. Having tatami at all was a luxury he could not afford at home in Sawara, where there were only portable rush mats to cover the wood floors.

The two men knelt on the tatami rather self-consciously. Ichi sat on his knees with his back straight as a rod, as if waiting to find out what the samurai might do.

Tomonosuke had imagined that he would be so consumed by desire on finding Ichi again that he would take him in a carnal embrace without even speaking, but suddenly he found himself strangely overcome. And he could not tell if Ichi was pleased to meet him again or not.

"I was so worried about you!" Tomonosuke exclaimed. "Tell me, do you have a place to stay? Where are you living? Do you have enough to eat? How do you know where to go?"

The mask slipped very slightly as Ichi's eyebrows raised in surprise. "You were worried about me? Whatever for?"

"But I thought..." Tomonosuke suddenly did not wish to put his thoughts into words, to admit he did not think Ichi could take care of himself. "In any case, where are you staying?"

"At the Sōroku yashiki, of course. Where else?"

"The what...?"

"The main residence of the Tōdōza. It's on the banks of the Sumida River near the Ryōgoku neighborhood."

"Ryōgoku! That's very far from here. How did you find your way all the way here to Takadanobaba?"

"My lord, I know my way around Edo very well. After all, I lived in the Sōroku yashiki for eight years before I moved to Sawara."

"You what...? Eight years...?" Tomonosuke was dumbstruck. And here he thought this was Ichi's first trip to the great city, when in fact Ichi knew Edo better, and had lived here longer than Tomonosuke himself. "But I thought you said you were from Shimōsa province?"

"Well, yes, I was born in Shimōsa, but after I lost my sight I was sent to the Tōdōza in Edo for training, and I remained there until I achieved the rank of zatō and became an adult, then I returned to my home province. But business wasn't good in the countryside so I moved to Sawara. Still, I have traveled back to Edo a few times since then."

"By yourself?"

"Yes, of course," Ichi replied, a hint of annoyance creeping into his voice. "The Mito Road is very well traveled. It's perfectly safe."

"Huh. I'm astonished. And yet that night in Abiko you let me prate on and on about Edo as if you had never been here before."

"I never said..."

"It's all right, I didn't ask. I just assumed." Tomonosuke fell silent, realizing how thoroughly he had misjudged the young man. Of course the sort of education Ichi had received was only available in Edo, not in a provincial town like Sawara. Tomonosuke knew the head of the Tōdōza was located in Edo. He should have realized that Ichi had spent time there, and as a member would be entitled to seek lodging there whenever he pleased.

Yet the thought of Ichi lodging at the guild of blind men filled him with unease the more he thought of it.

"I'm glad you have safe lodging but I do wish you had a better place to stay," Tomonosuke said with concern.

"What do you mean? What's wrong with the Tōdōza?"

"It's a corrupt organization built on envy and spite of the sighted."

The mask now slipped entirely as Ichi's face was suddenly transformed with anger. He stood up, his cheeks flushed and brow knitted in a frown. "My lord, you are mistaken. If you have such a low opinion of me and the guild to which I belong, then I will take my leave of you." He stepped forward with a hand extended, searching for the door.

Tomonosuke caught his hand, filled with remorse. He had not realized Ichi would take his words as a personal insult, and he regretted speaking without reflection. "I apologize. Please don't go."

Ichi hesitated, his face still angry. "Admit you know nothing of the Tōdōza. It's an honorable, upstanding guild that has done much good in the world. I owe them my livelihood, and my very life." As he spoke, Ichi allowed himself to be pulled back down to sit on the floor, but his voice shook with emotion. Tomonosuke had never seen him so worked up. And yet he still could not comprehend the full meaning of what Ichi was saying.

"What do you mean you owe them your life?"

Ichi's frown deepened and he spoke reluctantly. "I was not always Ichi, a zatō in the Tōdōza. I was the only son and heir of a wealthy landowner with a large estate in Shimōsa. I had three sisters, and we were all raised gently and sent to a temple school to learn to read and write. When I was eight years old, all of us were struck with a fever and a terrible rash, the illness they call hashika. My parents made offerings to Kosodate Kannon at the Kampuku temple, but their prayers were only partially answered. My two eldest sisters recovered quickly, but Saya, the sister only one year older than I, she died, and the fever took my sight. I was disinherited and a new heir was adopted in my place. If there were no such place as the Tōdōza for me to go, what would have become of me? I would have starved to death as a beggar in the street."

Tomonosuke blinked in surprise, shocked at this confession. He was about to say, what sort of parents banish their only son to starve? And yet he knew very well. His own mother would certainly have done the same without turning a hair if such misfortune had befallen him.

"The Tōdōza is not corrupt anymore," Ichi continued defensively. "In the past there were some unfortunate practices but Hanawa Hokiichi sōkengyō has made admirable reforms. If you meet him, you'll understand. He's a man of great learning and virtue."

"Hmmm." Tomonosuke made a noncommittal noise. The idea of visiting the Tōdōza made him feel uneasy. Countless blind men creeping about in the dark like moles—what sort of lives did they lead there? He could hardly imagine.

"Still, they should not be acting as moneylenders," Tomonosuke insisted.

Ichi sighed and his rigid posture deflated somewhat. "It is unfortunate that the sōkengyō has not been able to put a stop to that evil practice. But please do not judge the Tōdōza solely on that account."

"Yes, well, I suppose it's all right. In any case, you are not like the rest of them. You're different."

"I tell you, I am not. I'm a blind man like all the other Tōdōza members, and of the lowest rank at that. Have you met any others besides me? You're always teasing me about logic, but now you have made an illogical statement." Ichi crossed his arms and sat back on his heels, still frowning.

Tomonosuke stared at him, at a loss for how to proceed. For so many days, he had dreamed of meeting with Ichi again. How had it gone wrong so quickly? Even now, he ached with desire for Ichi, despite their argument. He wanted nothing more than to tackle him, push him to the floor and have his way with him. But he could not. It was not just that Ichi was angry. The room was completely bare, without even a cushion to sit upon. Even when Tomonosuke had visited the cheapest brothel in Sawara, there was always sake and tobacco to share first, futons to lie upon, and tissue paper to clean up after. Somehow, taking Ichi in this bare room, little more than a closet, felt even more sordid than up against a wall in a post town. That had been an exigency of the road. Now Ichi was in his home, but he could hardly call a servant to bring drinks. Why, why did Ichi have to be an anma? If he was only of slightly higher status, there would be no trouble at all.

"I apologize. I did not mean to offend you," Tomonosuke said carefully, casting about for a way to make things right between them. "I'm glad I ran into you. It's very lucky you happened to be passing that way."

"Lucky? Luck had nothing to do with it!"

"What?"

"I've been waiting for you to call on me for days and days! It wasn't hard to find out the address of the lower residence of the Omigawa daimyō. I knew you were staying here so I've been walking these streets every night blowing my whistle, hoping you would see me."

"You did that for me?" Tomonosuke raised his eyebrows in disbelief. To think, all this time he was worrying about Ichi and here he was just outside the gate. He had never felt so foolish.

"What else could I do? I tried to enter the residence but I was turned away at the gate. That night in Abiko you made all sorts of promises of the things we would do together in Edo, but if you weren't in earnest, I won't trouble you again." He made as if to get up.

"No!" Tomonosuke took his hand and pulled him back down to the floor. "I was in earnest. I apologize for not seeking you out myself. I'm grateful it was you who came to me," he said, hoping Ichi could hear the emotion in his voice. He had wanted to peek behind the mask Ichi habitually wore, yet seeing the anma's true feelings filled him with unease. Did Ichi really assume Tomonosuke was only trifling with him?

Ichi allowed Tomonosuke to hold his hand, but he still did not conceal his displeasure. "Coming all the way out here has been very bad for business, I tell you. This is a very remote area and I've hardly had any customers."

"I'll try to make it up to you," Tomonosuke said in a low voice. Rather than risk saying the wrong thing again, Tomonosuke leaned forward and kissed him. To his delight, Ichi leaned into the kiss, wrapping his arms around his shoulders.

"I've been thinking of you every day," Tomonosuke whispered in his ear.

"And I, you," Ichi replied, with a trace of reluctance.

Tomonosuke burned with desire, yet still he was not prepared. He was troubled by the hesitation in Ichi's voice, their bare surroundings, and not least that he did not have clove oil or anything else in this room. Not even tissue paper.

Suddenly, he saw in his mind's eye himself and Ichi, sneaking from the room, trying in vain to hide the tell-tale stains on their clothing. The idea of leaving Ichi to make his way home with marks of shame on his kimono caused him to wither.

"On second thought," he said, "this room is not suitable. I think I hear someone coming down the hall. Come back again, and I will prepare more carefully for you, I promise."

9

Okyō

After the encounter in the storeroom, Ichi swore to himself that he would not return to the lower residence. Tomonosuke might claim to want more than a casual dalliance, but his prejudice against the Tōdōza showed how little he understood of Ichi's world. How could they pledge to each other as brothers?

Even knowing this, Ichi still found his feet taking him on the long walk to Takadanobaba. Twice he turned back, but the third evening found him blowing his whistle hopefully along the quiet streets near the lower residence once again.

He was relieved to hear Rin calling his name as he tapped along. With only a single word of greeting, she took hold of his cane and led him into the mansion.

Ichi could not be sure, but he felt as if Rin led him down a different hall than he had gone before. They entered a room he sensed was somewhat larger, and he caught the scent of charcoal in a lit hibachi, as the weather was turning cool at last. Rin dropped the end of his cane, which he took as his cue to sit formally with his legs folded under him.

"I'm sorry," Rin whispered as she stepped out of the room and snapped the fusuma shut.

"Uchida-dono?" Ichi's head jerked up in alarm.

But instead of Tomonosuke's deep voice, it was Okyō who greeted him from beside the hibachi.

"Surprised?" she said acerbically, rattling the long metal tongs as she poked at the ash in the hibachi.

"My lady, I thought..."

"I know what you thought," she snapped. "You think I don't know that you followed us to Edo, that you have been loitering about the lower residence for days, and that you visited my husband here a few nights ago?"

Ichi's mouth gaped open, unable to answer. Okyō terrified him.

"I know everything that goes on in my household!" Okyō's voice rose in anger. "Do you think I don't know about my husband's attachment to you? I make it my business to know everything he does. How can I do otherwise? You may come and go as you please but my life is tied to that man, like it or not."

"My lady, I meant no harm..."

Okyō gave a very high-bred snort. "Lucky for you, Rin says you're not a bad person, and I trust her judgment, or I would have turned you out before now. But ill-intentioned or not, you are meddling in affairs you know nothing about."

"I.... what...?" Ichi was at a loss.

"Men! You're all the same, blind or sighted, only thinking of yourselves and your own pleasure. I swear, you are the most selfish person I have ever met. Do you have any idea what will happen to me if my husband doesn't produce any children?"

"No, my lady."

"My father will divorce us and take me back to Echigo to find me a richer, more virile husband, that's what, and I won't have it. I'm never going back to Echigo, never!"

It was true, a bride's family had the right to dissolve her marriage if they saw fit, but Ichi did not want to inquire into the reason for her desire never to return home. He felt very uneasy; he had heard too much of Okyō's private affairs already.

"So I have a proposal for you, anma-san," Okyō continued in a tone that was slightly softer but still brooked no controversy. "I will allow you to visit my husband whenever you like, but in return you must get me with child. What do you say? You're young and handsome. Or are you a woman-hater like my husband?"

"I—no, I mean..."

"Come now, you can come visit my husband freely. I will send Rin to fetch you, and you may use our quarters here. No more sneaking about in unused rooms like criminals. We'll say you're giving the master a massage, and no one will bother you. In return, you must lie with me once a month until I conceive. Do you agree?"

"My lady, this is a very unexpected request. If I might have time to think it over..."

Ichi heard a shuffle of paper, the soft scrape of Okyō's socks, and the train of her kimono dragging as she walked across the tatami. With sinuous grace she sat down beside him, so close he could smell her hair oil and feel the hot puff of her breath on his cheek as she spoke.

"Don't think of my request as a chore," she said in a low, suggestive voice. "I know how to please a man. What do you think this is?"

Without waiting for permission, she grasped his hand and pulled it into her lap, forcing his fingers onto the object she held there. He felt the slightly rough, soft surface of papers bound together with string at one end.

"It appears to be a book, my lady," he answered, wondering where this was going. Sighted people were so strange. Why bother to make him touch the flat pages, instead of simply reading it aloud?

"It's a sex manual," she said without a trace of shame. "All the positions, fully illustrated, with instructions on reaching the highest planes of pleasure. And this is not the only one I own. I've been sending Rin to the booksellers in Kanda every day to buy the most interesting volumes. Not just the sort that a young woman might be given on her wedding night, oh no, the ones with perversions you can hardly imagine." She grasped his hand tighter and brought it to her breast.

"I'll make you howl," she whispered in his ear, her lips brushing his skin as she spoke.

Ichi's heart pounded in his chest. This was not at all what he thought Okyō would say to him. She pulled him closer, her hand around his wrist so tight it almost hurt. This was not right. He had never met a woman like this before. Despite himself, he felt a stab of arousal. Her aggressive pursuit of him, her shamelessness, all bespoke a great passion within her. The idea of giving himself up to her, allowing himself to be borne along on the stream of her desires was not unappealing. But it was all so sudden. Even though he had not yet exchanged vows with Tomonosuke, he felt this might betray their friendship, or whatever it was.

"I will...I will consider it..." he gasped.

As soon as he spoke, Okyō dropped his hand and stood up with a rustle of heavy, thick silk. "Good. I take that as your assent. Lucky for you, today is not the right time. I will summon you here in ten days. In the meantime, do as you please."

Ichi found himself out in the hallway, summarily dismissed.

* * *

True to her word, a few days later, Okyō sent Rin to bring Ichi to the shimo-yashiki.

"Rin-san, you set a trap for me," Ichi said as she led him into the courtyard, holding the end of his cane, but his tone was good-natured, more teasing than resentful.

"I'm sorry. My lady gave an order and I had to follow it. But please don't think badly of her. If you knew what she has suffered, you would understand why she behaves this way."

Their straw sandals crunched along the gravel in tandem. Without thinking, they had fallen into step together. Ichi's mouth turned up in a half smile.

"You're very loyal to your mistress," he commented. "You must care for her very deeply."

"Yes. You may laugh, but before she was married, we pledged to each other over cups of sake, like men do. I know such a thing is not for women, but she said it didn't matter, it was just between us. Please don't tell her I told you."

"I promise," Ichi said seriously. "I think it's quite noble." He paused, then asked in a lower voice, "Does she really have a collection of erotic books? Does she send you every day to buy more?"

Rin laughed. "She has a few, but mostly they're books of kimono patterns."

"Oh, indeed? So she was just trying to shock me."

"Yes. Please, I told her she could trust you. Promise me you won't do anything to hurt her."

Rin led him up into the mansion and down the hall to their quarters. Ichi was bemused by the thought that he might be at all capable of doing anything to hurt Okyō. If anything, the opposite seemed more likely to him. But Rin's comment made him realize how much Okyō had put herself in a precarious situation with her unusual proposal to him. Was she merely toying with him, or driven by real desperation?

Ichi crossed the threshold to their quarters with some trepidation, sinking to the floor in relief when he heard Tomonosuke's masculine voice grunt out a single word of greeting.

Ichi gave a formal bow. "My lord."

Behind him, he heard Rin snap the door shut. It was as Okyō promised, they were alone. He could smell the pleasantly acrid scent of charcoal from the lit hibachi, as well as tobacco smoke and a bottle of sake heating over the coals. Tomonosuke emptied the tiny brass bowl of the long thin tobacco pipe with a sharp rap on the edge of the hibachi.

"There's a cushion to your left if you want to sit on it," Tomonosuke said. Ichi swept his fingers along the tatami until he found it, then bowed again.

"Please be easy," Tomonosuke told him. "You needn't worry about my wife any longer. We have come to an agreement."

Ichi was startled. Had Okyō told Tomonosuke? He thought their arrangement was a secret. "Yes, I know..."

"Oh, so she spoke to you?"

Now Ichi was not sure they were talking about the same thing but he could not bring himself to speak aloud her brazen words, nor admit that he had not only agreed, but was secretly aroused by her aggression. It seemed disloyal to Tomonosuke, and now that he was before the stern samurai, he was afraid to say anything that might prevent them from meeting again like this.

"She...requested my services..." he said vaguely.

Tomonosuke grunted, and Ichi still could not be certain if he knew of Okyō's plan or not. He knew he should say something more, but he did not want to risk Tomonosuke's anger or resentment. He drank the hot sake offered to him; the warm tendrils snaking from his mouth to his belly filled him with lust and he felt even less like speaking. Rin had said not to embarrass Okyō. Well then, he ought to be discreet and not mention their conversation.

Tomonosuke drained his sake cup and leaned forward with a growl, plucking the empty cup from Ichi's fingers. Ichi allowed him to yank open the front of his kimono, loosening the obi.

In the moment, Ichi forgot his lingering hesitation, about Tomonosuke and about Okyō's proposition. He longed to become Tomonosuke's younger brother, to visit freely and allow the samurai to do to him whatever he wished. The flat, hard planes of his muscled chest, the strong arms gripping him, the masculine scent of cypress and tobacco, all inflamed his desire almost beyond bearing.

Tomonosuke pulled open the strings of his momohiki trousers, and Ichi gasped with pleasure, his cock stiffening.

This time, Tomonosuke assured him, he was fully prepared with bedding, tissues, and clove oil. Okyō was out, and no one would disturb them. Somewhat roughly and awkwardly, Tomonosuke pushed his shoulders forward.

"Lie down here," he ordered.

Ichi felt about until he found the edge of the futon, already laid out on the floor at the opposite end of the room. He didn't like being pushed, and he wished Tomonosuke might guide him more gently, but he didn't say anything, not wanting to spoil the moment as he had before. Lying back on the futon, he removed the kimono, trousers, and fundoshi that Tomonosuke had loosened. Sprawling naked on the futon, he felt rather exposed, but tried his best to pose confidently.

"So beautiful," Tomonosuke murmured.

Ichi was pleased beyond measure at the way the samurai always admired his beauty. Not that he was vain, but Ichi was accustomed to the fact that sighted people's comments on his appearance were always tinged with pity or regret: So beautiful, what a shame he's disfigured. Was the appearance of his blind eyes really so hideous? Tomonosuke might sometimes frustrate him with his lack of understanding, yet the samurai was the only sighted person Ichi had ever met who took his appearance just as it was, without qualification. It was intoxicating to be so desired.

Ichi lay with his legs drawn up, and as Tomonosuke entered him, their foreheads pressed together. He could feel the samurai's hot breath on his face as he thrust. It was exquisitely intimate.

As he reached the heights of pleasure, Ichi felt he would do anything to remain like this in Tomonosuke's arms.

10

Sukeroku

In Shimotsuki, the month of frost, the first performances of the new kabuki season began, and Tomonosuke was determined to attend in style. While officially samurai were not allowed to mingle at the theater with commoners, in practice there were few among them who could resist the allure of the pageantry and excitement of the performances.

Tomonosuke secured tickets for a box for all four of them. Okyō was resplendent in a dark purple kimono of stiff silk adorned with a peony pattern, tied with a contrasting brocade obi in dark orange and a brightly patterned red under-kimono peeking out at her collar and sleeves. Rin was dressed in a much more subdued cotton kimono with dark red stripes, but her mistress had purchased for her a new black velvet collar that she could not resist fingering. Tomonosuke as always wore a simple black silk kimono with the Uchida clan crest on the back.

They joined the crowd thronging in front of the theater, under the fluttering banners advertising the names of famous actors written in bold characters.

"Look, there's Ichi!" Rin called, and pushed her way through the crowd to fetch him.

Ichi was standing diffidently on the other side of the street, rattling his cane nervously, his head tilting down and to the left as he waited, listening to the crowd, but when he heard Rin calling him, he lifted his head and smiled.

Rin grasped his cane and led him over to where Tomonosuke and Okyō waited.

"It's very kind of you to allow me to join you, my lord," Ichi said, bowing especially low. Tomonosuke grunted a greeting and left Rin to guide Ichi inside, through the boisterous crowd.

The box, marked off with low wooden dividers about a foot off the floor, was not large. Ichi found himself squeezed between Tomonosuke and Okyō as they all sat on cushions on the floor. The entire floor of the theater was taken up with these boxes, people crammed in against the low dividers.

As they sat through the prologue, Ichi could hear the rustle and creak of Okyō's rich silk kimono and he imagined that everyone was dressed very finely. He felt self-conscious of his plain indigo cotton outfit, which was all he could afford. He had let down the skirts of his kimono, but he knew he still cut a poor figure. He shrank down in the box, trying to be inconspicuous.

"Stop fidgeting!" Okyō hissed at him, and he snapped to attention, sitting with his back straight as a rod.

Okyō still terrified him, although he really didn't know what to make of her. She had called for him as promised, but she did not force herself on him as he had expected. Instead, she toyed with him, making him kiss her and pinching his cheek, while keeping up a stream of the most shocking erotic talk, mingled with threats and promises.

Ichi had sat there sweating, his heart pounding, but in the end she sent him away without taking him in a carnal embrace, saying she was not in the mood. Ichi was relieved to have escaped without compromising his loyalty to Tomonosuke, but he was more puzzled than ever over Okyō's actions.

At the intermission, Rin served them food from the lacquer boxes that had been prepared at home: grilled fish, fried burdock root, braised daikon, sticky rice with red beans. Vendors walked up and down the aisles with hot sake and hot tea. Ichi sat stiffly, holding the heavy lacquer box awkwardly right under his chin, feeling about carefully in each compartment with his chopsticks and conveying each bite to his mouth very slowly. He did not want to embarrass himself by dropping food on his clothes or on the floor.

"Well, what do you think?" Tomonosuke asked conversationally as they ate their lunch.

"It's rather sedate so far," Okyō sniffed. "I had hoped there would be more action."

"What do you think, Ichi?" Tomonosuke asked. "Is this your first time at the theater?"

"No, my master, Matsuichi kengyō, is a great lover of kabuki, so he took me often when I was a boy," Ichi answered truthfully, although he felt a twinge of annoyance as he heard Tomonosuke give an impatient sigh and did not continue the conversation further. It had not escaped Ichi's notice that Tomonosuke seemed eager to act as his guide and mentor to the entertainment and pleasures of Edo, and was disappointed to learn that Ichi in fact knew more than he did. But what was he to do, lie and feign ignorance? Ichi could not think Tomonosuke would respect him if he did so. It still irritated him that Tomonosuke thought of him as a child who knew nothing of the world.

The main attraction that afternoon was a performance of the play *Sukeroku*, with the famous actor Ichikawa Danjūrō VII in the title role. At last Okyō had her fill of excitement as they watched Sukeroku provoke duels with various men, trying to force them to draw their katana so he could find the treasured family sword stolen from his father. His lover, the oiran Agemaki, was bedecked in such an elaborate wig and headdress that the man playing the role could barely walk across the stage. Her obi, tied in front, was like a waterfall of brocade.

Rin leaned over Ichi's shoulder, narrating the action in his ear in a whisper, describing the sword fights and quick costume changes in breathless tones. Ichi enjoyed the performance, and was grateful to Rin for her effort, although he wished it were Tomonosuke sitting so close beside him, breathing in his ear. Reciting poetry together or listening to Tomonosuke read aloud to him gave him the liveliest pleasure, and Ichi had hoped the same might be true at the theater. Was it propriety that kept Tomonosuke aloof, or had it just not occurred to him to share the experience with Ichi in this way?

The play ended with Sukeroku at last taking revenge for his father by killing the villain Ikyū in a dramatic scene, with much shouting and posturing. He then escaped the police by jumping into a giant vat of real water, right on the stage. Ichi laughed to hear the water cascading over the boards, and the audience erupted in cheers and shouts.

This was still not the end of the performance, however, as it was followed by more dances and short scenes from other plays. All the while the vendors continued walking up and down. Tomonosuke knocked back more sake as the crowd grew ever rowdier. After they had been sitting for more than three hours, Okyō announced that she needed to visit the facilities, a rather refined term for what was no more than a row of buckets behind the theater.

She was gone a very long time. As the next dance started, then the next, Ichi began to feel uneasy.

"My lord, shall we search for Okyō-dono?" he whispered, leaning forward anxiously.

"What? No, why?" Tomonosuke was unconcerned, but Rin seemed to share Ichi's concern, for she picked her way through the crowd and out of the theater in search of Okyō.

In the middle of the next scene, Rin reappeared with Okyō behind her.

"I want to go home now," Okyō demanded.

Tomonosuke did not even turn around. "No, why? I want to stay to the end."

"But that's another two hours at least! I want to leave." She stood beside him, even though the people behind them grumbled and shouted at her to sit down.

"Leave and do what?" Tomonosuke asked, clearly with no intention of shifting.

Okyō did not answer but at last Rin whispered, "My lord, the facilities are, ah, rather too public and, um, dirty for my lady's liking."

"So?"

"So there's piss all over, the buckets are overflowing, and drunk men were leering at me," Okyō burst out angrily. "Would you have me soil my new kimono, or expose myself to a drunkard? I'm leaving now!"

Tomonosuke shrugged. "Do what you like."

Ichi shifted uncomfortably, pained to be overhearing this exchange. "I will accompany you back to the shimo-yashiki, my lady," he offered hesitantly.

"You?" she snorted derisively. "That won't be necessary. Come Rin, let's go. We shall hire a palanquin," she said and swept out of the box, as Rin hastily gathered up the lacquer boxes and dashed after her. Tomonosuke sat unmoving.

For the first time, Ichi felt a pang of sympathy for Okyō. Why couldn't Tomonosuke treat her a bit more kindly?

* * *

This was the first incident that changed Ichi's opinion of Okyō. The second occurred the next time she called on him to attend her. Apparently Rin was busy because a different servant showed him in. As he sat in the main room awaiting Okyō, he heard a harsh voice he did not know raised in anger in the hallway, on the other side of the closed fusuma. It was a woman's voice, speaking in a high-class accent—it must be another retainer's wife. The unknown woman was scolding someone for some perceived infraction.

Suddenly, Ichi heard a slap and a cry of pain. Was that Rin's voice?

"How dare you lay hands on my maid!" Ichi heard Okyō shout angrily.

"She deserved it," the other woman shot back in a sneering tone, "and you are not permitted to talk to me like that. You're nothing more than the wife of a third son. Now apologize or I'll report you to the head of the household and get your good-for-nothing maid turned out in the street."

Ichi was shocked to hear Okyō mumble a formal apology. The other woman stalked away with a sniff and a rustle of expensive silk. Okyō and Rin remained in the hallway. He could hear Rin crying softly.

"There, there, darling, don't worry. It'll be all right," he heard Okyō say. He had never heard her speak in such tender tones before.

"But she said I'll be turned out!" Rin wailed.

"No, I swear, I will never let that happen," Okyō assured her. "Didn't I promise to protect you always? I won't let anything happen to you."

There was more shuffling and murmuring, but at last Rin seemed to recover.

"Ichi-san is waiting for you," Rin said, her voice still quavering a bit.

"I don't care. Send him away."

"No, he came all this way. Don't spoil your fun on my account. Please, enjoy yourself," Rin said, a hint of teasing in her voice.

A moment later, Ichi sat up straight as he heard Okyō slide the fusuma open then shut it behind her with a snap.

"Did you hear any of that?" she demanded.

"Any of what?" Ichi let his blank mask fall into place.

"Hm." Okyō seemed to take possession of herself, her mood shifting suddenly. "Well!" she said imperiously. "That was a private matter, not for the ears of a lowly anma. If you had heard, I should have to beat you."

All of a sudden, Ichi felt he understood Okyō—she was acting, playing a game with him. Rin had often said how Okyō suffered, but now he was beginning to see it.

Theirs was not a society that allowed for personal freedoms; they all led lives constrained by duty and obligation, even him. But it seemed Okyō had even less freedom than most. Ichi was low in status, but he was his own master. Tomonosuke might be bound to his lord, but he was the head of his household. Even Rin could leave and seek employment elsewhere if she wanted. But Okyō had no choice about anything in her life. Given by a family she seemed to despise to a man who did not care for her, teased by the other wives, humiliated as a matter of course, it was little wonder she was always so bad-tempered. Lording over the poor anma was her one way of taking control, of feeling powerful, yet he could not feel there was evil in her. If she truly wanted to hurt him, she would have done so already. No, he felt she was actually quite tender-hearted, but it pleased her to pretend to threaten him.

"Oh no," he said, playing along, making a show of cringing from her. "I am, as you say, a lowly anma. Please don't beat me!" He flung himself to the floor at her feet, wondering if perhaps he was overplaying his role, but she seemed to enjoy it.

She placed her foot on his forehead. "Vile worm!"

Ichi squirmed obligingly. To his surprise he found he enjoyed giving her pleasure in this strange way. The hardest part was to prevent himself from bursting out laughing.

As before, she kissed him and teased him but made no move toward any further intimacy. This he still did not understand. Was her plan to have Ichi impregnate her merely a ruse to save face, so that she could tolerate Ichi's presence in her household? Or was she shy? For all her suggestive talk and perverse posturing, did she still scruple to break her marriage vows with another man? Whatever the reason, he was glad that their play did not go any further.

11

Onna Gidayū

Tomonosuke rolled his neck, trying in vain to release the stiff muscles as he stared at the columns of figures in the account book. Try as he might, he still could not make the numbers add up correctly. Ever since the move to Edo, he felt slow and unfocused in his work. Every so often, the sums would not come out right no matter how many times he tallied each line. He set down his brush and shook his hands, trying to warm his stiff fingers. There was no hibachi in the office of the exchequer, and the weather was growing very cold, although at least the rains had lifted recently.

He was just considering whether or not to mention this problem with the figures to Matsudaira Sadahide when slowly the room began to shake. He looked up sharply, meeting the alarmed gaze of the man beside him. They each clutched the edge of their low tables as the floor swayed gently back and forth.

"Earthquake!" someone whispered, earning a brisk reprimand from Sadahide.

Tomonosuke held his breath, waiting to see if the shaking would get worse. A moment later, it stopped. With a shuffle of paper, the activity in the office resumed as if nothing had happened. This sort of tremor was so common in Edo that it was considered bad form to comment on it, especially for the impassive, dignified samurai.

He decided not to mention the errors just yet. He was beginning to wonder if perhaps the cause was not a problem with his arithmetic but some larger issue. It would be best to be sure before bringing it to Sadahide's attention.

Feeling dissatisfied and uncertain, when he returned to his quarters after work, he had no desire to stay in. Finding Okyō unexpectedly at home as well, he suggested they go again to the kabuki. It would be pleasant to take his mind off things by escaping to the fantasy world of the theater.

Okyō had been unusually good-natured lately, but to his surprise, she had other ideas.

"I'm so tired of the same old plays," she declared. "We've been many times now and it's always the same. You know, I've heard that the Edokko prefer the variety shows at the downtown theaters. That's where the real action is." From within the spacious rectangular sleeve of her kimono, she pulled out a handbill announcing a theater troupe called Katsumata, performing at an address in Kanda. It was decorated with an image of a woman striking a heroic pose, with a staff in her hand held aloft.

At home in Sawara, Tomonosuke tended to live as frugally as possible, but here in the city he had taken to heart the Edokko saying, "Money should not be kept overnight." They had all been going out to the theater together regularly, although he had to agree with Okyō that the charm of the officially sanctioned kabuki theater was beginning to wane. Many of his colleagues were very taken with the onnagata, the male kabuki actors who specialized in women's roles, and a few had even purchased the favors of these actors after the show, but Tomonosuke did not find them to his taste.

He looked at the handbill, with its image of a rather rakish woman and florid promises along the side of wonders never before seen this age.

"Let us go tonight."

* * *

The performance was not at a proper theater like where they had watched the kabuki, but instead at a yose, a large hall used for various community events. The yose seemed to be owned and run by a gang of firefighters, for they were all running about in their matching happi jackets, hustling in the audience and trying to pack as many people as possible into the hall.

The firefighter gang boss, a burly man who called himself Heihachirō, ambled up and down the narrow walkways of the yose, making sure that everyone had a paid ticket. His jacket strained at the seams over his thick shoulders and elaborate tattoos were visible on his arms just below his sleeves. His topknot sat at a jaunty angle.

Fires in the city were so common they were called "flowers of Edo" and the Edokko rather perversely almost enjoyed the frequent conflagrations. As firefighters employed by the government only protected the shogun's residence, the townspeople organized their own gangs of firefighters. They ran about in flashy happi jackets adorned with their gang name, showing off their muscles and acrobatic skills, but when it came to actually fighting fires, their only strategies were to climb up to the roof with a flag of streamers called a matoi to act as a warning, and to tear down the surrounding houses to try to stop the fire from spreading. Most of them had sidelines in building construction, sleazy entertainment, and organized crime.

Tomonosuke eyed Heihachirō uneasily. He hadn't realized this would be such a low-class establishment. Kabuki was bad enough, but he could be fined or even arrested if he was caught here.

"Oi, samurai-san!" Heihachirō laid a heavy hand on his shoulder as he strolled by. "Enjoy the show!"

Tomonosuke tried not to flinch. Okyō shrank back behind him, uncharacteristically timid. She seemed to realize as well that they were the only ones of samurai rank in the audience.

"We should not have come," he said in an undertone.

A moment later, Rin pushed her way through the crowd to join them. Ichi followed her with his hand on her shoulder.

"Why shouldn't we have come?" Ichi asked. "I'm so glad you invited me! The Katsumata troupe has been the talk of the town for months. There's an onna gidayū who's supposed to be spectacular. I'm longing to hear her."

"Yes, me too," added Okyō, reasserting her natural boldness now that Ichi had arrived. "Danna, you worry too much. Let's enjoy the show."

A child of indeterminate gender with a painted face like a kabuki actor, wearing a flashy kimono and pantaloons, walked out on stage and announced the troupe in a shrill piping voice, while striking a pair of wooden clappers. A man and woman leapt onto the stage, followed by five young people also in the same striking green and red patterned kimono and loose pantaloons, fastened at the ankle. As the child beat on a small drum, they began a tumbling routine.

Ichi slumped back on his heels. So he would have to wait through the opening act for the main attraction, he realized. He tried not to show how bored he was by the acrobats. Evidently they were quite skilled, for he could hear the oohs and aahs of the crowd, but it was not a pleasure he could partake in, as there was not even a musical accompaniment.

Rin occasionally whispered in his ear, but her narration was not particularly skillful. "Oh, they are standing on each other's shoulders—and, oh my! They just...oh...now they are...um...I don't know what to call it..." He appreciated her effort, but he did not attend to her words, not bothering to try to follow the performance.

Instead, Ichi listened to the crowd. They were a rowdy bunch and the firefighters were still packing in more people at the back, as many as could squeeze in while sitting on the floor. The yose made the kabuki theater look downright respectable by comparison—here there were no railings separating the seating areas, nor fancy lacquer boxes with food, nor vendors. Most of the people in attendance seemed to have brought their own liquor with them.

Ichi could understand Tomonosuke's unease. This was obviously an unlicensed theater, and it was illegal for women to appear on stage. The shogun's police could raid them at any moment, shut down the show and arrest everyone. His mentor, Matsuichi kengyō, had often taken him to concerts and theater performances, but never one as low-class as this. The samurai might be worried, but for his part, Ichi found it rather exciting, this feeling that anything could happen.

At last the opening act ended and the man stood up with a flourish.

"Welcome one and all!" he proclaimed in a commanding voice of surprising volume. He was rather stocky, with a big barrel chest and a round, ruddy face. "I, Katsumata Gonzaemon, welcome you to our troupe of wonders and amazement! We have come from the far north all the way to Edo for your amusement and edification!" He continued on in this vein for some time, in increasingly flowery and exaggerated terms, until the crowd began to grow restless.

"Oi, enough already, uncle! Bring out the dame!" someone shouted.

"Yeah, show us the girl!"

Gonzaemon smiled good-naturedly and assured the crowd that they would now see the main act, the greatest chanter of this age, the onna gidayū Shirataki Gen. As the crowd roared in approval, the child beat the clappers frantically, and the tumblers left the stage.

A tall woman in a man's formal kimono with kataginu and hakama swaggered onto the stage. She had a lean, angular face and wore her hair pulled back in a simple queue, almost like a miko, but with her forelocks tied in front like a boy. She grinned confidently at the noisy crowd, gesturing for them to applaud even louder. This was the woman performing illegally under the ambiguously masculine stage name of Shirataki (waterfall) Gen.

She sat herself down on a cushion in the middle of the stage with practiced grace, greeting the crowd casually. Another woman sat beside her, holding a shamisen, and Gen announced her as Katsumata Oboro. The accompanist kept her eyes trained straight at the back of the theater, unlike Gen, not engaging with the crowd at all, her expression completely blank. She was slight and dressed in more typical women's clothes, a plain blue kimono of rough silk, but her features were even and pleasing, with a sprinkling of freckles across her cheeks.

Oboro struck the first twanging, buzzing notes on the shamisen, and Gen began to chant in a low, rough, masculine voice. This variety of narrative chanting, called gidayū, was the most exciting but also the most taxing—thrilling tales of ancient warfare, of heroism and high drama, almost always sung by men in hours-long epic performances. It was rare for a woman to attempt it, and even more rare for one person to do a solo performance.

The piece Shirataki Gen chose for her performance was a well-known scene from the epic poem *The Tale of the Heike*, describing the death of Atsumori. In the battle of Ichi-no-tani, the Minamoto, the rough warriors of the east, trapped the Taira, the aristocrats of the capital, in between the cliff and the beach. The grizzled old Minamoto warrior Kumagai challenged the Taira commander Atsumori, and easily overpowered him. But as Kumagai prepared to deliver the fatal blow, he realized that Atsumori was no more than a youth, a handsome, cultured young man, and that he had even brought a flute with him to the battlefield. Although he had no choice but to kill him, Kumagai wept for the beautiful boy who was too refined for battle, but who died bravely and without flinching.

Ichi knew this scene very well. For centuries, blind monks called biwa hōshi had performed *The Tale of the Heike*, commemorating the civil war of the Jishō era (1180). He too had been required to learn to recite *The Tale of the Heike*, a performance of many, many hours.

But in Shirataki Gen's chanting, it became something entirely new. This was not the heavy, old-fashioned, obscure poetry that Ichi had long ago memorized. Gen somehow made each line a living, breathing scene, with language that was contemporary but still elegant. She gave voice to both the sweet, brave Atsumori and the tough, grief-stricken Kumagai, her tone perfectly capturing their personalities and emotions. She knew just when to pause and when to speed up, and Oboro accompanied her without hesitation, the two of them perfectly in rhythm together.

Even though the audience already knew the story, everyone was captivated, the more so as the chanting went on and on for over two hours. Still Gen carried on, her voice never wavering or tiring, until the final lines when Kumagai renounced the world and became a priest to atone for the death of Atsumori. Ichi was surprised to feel his own cheeks wet with tears for the beautiful young warrior and the sad karma that brought the older man to kill him. As the final notes of the shamisen rang out, accompanied by the sharp strike of the wooden clappers, the crowd erupted in cheers and applause.

After the show, Ichi held tightly to Rin's sleeve as they joined the throng jostling along slowly to the one small exit. He was still moved beyond words by the performance, but suddenly he lifted his head when he overheard a strong voice carrying over the din of the crowd.

"Is that Shirataki Gen?" he asked, swiveling his head about to hear her more clearly.

"Yes," replied Tomonosuke from behind him. "She's thanking the audience for coming."

Apparently the yose was far more informal than the kabuki theater, and the performers mingled with the crowd after the performance.

Ichi's face shone with excitement. "We must speak with her!"

Tomonosuke agreed. But as they neared her, to their surprise it was Gen herself who pushed through the crowd to accost them.

"You, sir!" she cried, her voice hoarse and rasping after her long performance, but still strong and carrying. As she spoke, she touched Ichi lightly on the shoulder. "You're a biwa hōshi, ain't you? Tell me honestly, what did you think?"

Ichi blushed deeply, his pale skin turned dark red. "I'm only a zatō," he mumbled, surprised and embarrassed by this unexpected attention.

"But you can chant *The Tale of the Heike*, can't you?" she demanded with a grin.

Ichi nodded, rubbing the back of his head shyly. "Well, yes..."

Gen clapped her hands. "Of course! What do these townspeople know about music? Yours is the only opinion that matters. What did you think?"

"It was the finest chanting I've ever heard," Ichi replied fervently.

"Why thank you! In repayment for your kindness, you must let us treat you to a drink. Let's all of us go together," she specified, gesturing to Tomonosuke, Rin, and Okyō with one hand, while her other arm rested on the shoulders of Oboro. "Is this samurai here your patron?"

Ichi blushed even redder. "No, I'm just an anma. I don't have a patron."

Gen cocked a suggestive eyebrow at Tomonosuke, but his face remained blank. "Well, whatever," she shrugged. "Samurai-san, will you accompany a lowly musician for a drink?"

Tomonosuke nodded seriously. "Of course, sensei. I would be honored to accompany artists of such skill."

Gen gave a sharp bark of laughter and clapped him on the shoulder, making Tomonosuke's eyes open wide in surprise. "I'm no sensei! Just call me Gen."

Gen and Oboro led them away from the theater down a warren of tiny winding side streets, until they came to small open-air stall or yatai serving hot sake. They all squeezed onto the stools set out in front, as Gen greeted the owner in a familiar tone. When the owner brought out the ceramic sake bottles, Gen poured the drinks herself, even for Rin.

Tomonosuke formally introduced himself and Okyō, and to their surprise Gen introduced Oboro as her wife, but they were all too polite to comment on it or ask more questions. Of course it could not be a legal marriage, but actors and musicians were allowed their eccentric affectations. If a kabuki onnagata could live as a woman offstage, why could an onna gidayū not live as a man?

"If I may, where did you learn to chant like that?" Ichi asked.

Gen's eyes sparkled mischievously. "From Tokuichi kengyō in the capital."

"The Tōdōza?" Ichi asked in surprise. "But how?" The Tōdōza jealously guarded their preferred occupations. Ichi had never heard of a Tōdōza member agreeing to take a sighted apprentice.

"I had special dispensation," Gen explained with a smile. "My mother was a goze, and she introduced me to Tokuichi kengyō." Goze were blind women who worked as itinerant musicians and masseurs.

"So that's why," Gen continued in her rasping, masculine voice, "I grew up in the company of blind people. I spent my childhood following my mother all over the provinces of Echigo and Dewa, going from door to door, singing so the mistress of the house would come out and put a measure of uncooked rice in the cup she wore tied to her waist." Gen threw her head back, screwed her eyes shut and belted out a few lines of nagauta ballad, while pretending to pluck a shamisen, in imitation of a goze performance. Her voice was powerful and carrying, pitched to summon the members of the household from outside on the stoop. She continued, "I know the inner world of the Tōdōza like it was my own family. Tokuichi kengyō taught me twelve secret songs. That's why I said, zatō-san, that yours is the only opinion that matters to me." She completed her tale with a grin, lifting her chin as if she were on stage, expecting applause.

Before Ichi could respond, Okyō jumped in. "You're from Echigo? I as well, and Rin too," she said, allowing her northern dialect to show for the first time since Ichi had met her.

Gen turned to her with a smoldering look and answered also in dialect. "I should have known. The women of Echigo are the most beautiful."

Okyō stared down at her sake cup, suddenly flustered. Beside her, Tomonosuke made a wheezing, rasping sound. Okyō looked up to see him laughing. Oboro rolled her eyes.

"I thought it was a heroic performance," Ichi said earnestly, feeling the need to bring the conversation back on course.

"Ha! You'll give her a swelled head," said Oboro. "She's insufferable enough already." Despite her teasing words, Ichi did not need to see the look of deep affection in Oboro's eyes; it was evident enough from the tone of her voice.

They drank more rounds, and soon Gen was belting out popular ballads, with the others joining in here and there. Then she prevailed on Ichi to sing something for them, and he found Oboro's shamisen shoved into his hands. He felt rather bashful to perform before two professionals of such talent and acclaim, but emboldened by drink, he plucked out a few nagauta standards. Gen applauded heartily, but Ichi only hung his head, painfully aware of the gap in skill between them. To his own ears, his performance felt plodding and rote, where she had leavened the well-worn tunes with dash and originality.

"Don't be embarrassed." He felt an arm around his shoulders and the hot, sake-scented breath of Oboro on his neck as she whispered in his ear, a bit drunkenly. "You have talent. You just need to train more."

He could only shake his head and pass the shamisen back to her.

Gen sang a few more tunes, but as she paused at the end of the last song, they were surprised to hear the temple bells ringing the hour of the ox.

"My goodness, is that the time?" Okyō exclaimed sleepily, her northern accent showing even more. "We still have to walk all the way back to Takadanobaba."

"What?! But that's much too far," Gen insisted. "Come, stay at the inn with us and go back in the morning. It's just down this street here."

Tomonosuke gave a short laugh. "Impossible!" Then in a politer tone, he added, "It's very kind of you, sensei, but it would not do to be absent from the lower residence come morning. There are penalties for taking leave without permission."

"How annoying," Gen teased him as they all stood from the benches and began their farewells.

Ichi found himself less steady on his feet than he had expected. How many rounds had they drunk? He couldn't recall. Gen made her offer again, and he was happy to accept. The Sōroku yashiki was much closer than Takadanobaba, but still he was grateful not to have to find his way back on his own, with the sake making his head spin and confounding his sense of direction.

He bid goodnight to Tomonosuke, entreating him to take care on the long walk home, then allowed Gen and Oboro to guide him to their inn, where they all promptly fell into an exhausted sleep.

* * *

Propriety and fear of arrest prevented Tomonosuke from visiting the yose again to hear Gen's performance, but Ichi was under no such constraints. Despite the risk of losing customers, rather than walking along the streets in the evening blowing his whistle, many nights found him in the front row listening with rapt attention to Gen's dynamic chanting, perfectly in time with Oboro's shamisen. Gen introduced him to the Katsumata troupe and Heihachirō's gang of firefighters, who took him on as a kind of mascot, brought him backstage to greet the performers, and assured him the best seat even if he came late, skipping the acrobats.

"Oi, Ichi-san! Thanks for coming." Gen greeted him in her rough, masculine voice as one of Heihachirō's men guided Ichi to where Gen stood offstage, awaiting her entrance. "I've got something special for you tonight—I'm going to do the famous scene from *The Subscription List*," she said exuberantly, naming a popular kabuki play.

Ichi bowed low. "Good evening, Gen-san," he greeted her formally. "I'm looking forward to it. Is Oboro-san here?"

"No, she's with her elder brother on the other side of the stage handing props to the tumblers right now. Come, there's still time to greet her before we start."

She took his hand but before they could move, they both heard a loud crash, the stamping of many feet and shouts from the front of the theater. The drumming onstage abruptly ceased, giving way to general confusion.

Among the shouts and screams from the audience, Ichi distinctly heard someone cry, "It's a raid!"

A moment later, a strong, authoritative voice rang out over the crowd.

"This theater is in violation of the shogun's decree prohibiting public performances by women. Shirataki Gen, you're under arrest!"

"Shit!" Gen's grip on Ichi's hand tightened reflexively.

"Where is that bitch?" the same voice shouted. The sound of running and scuffling at the front of the stage increased as the frightened crowd attempted to flee.

Ichi tugged at her hand. "Come with me out the back."

"No, you'll be arrested too." He could hear the fear in her voice.

"They won't arrest me. I promise I'll protect you. Let's go!"

There was no time for further debate. As the police reached the stage, Gen led Ichi down the narrow passageway and out the back entrance to the theater. Luckily there were no guards at the back door, but just as they emerged from the alley onto the main road, a harsh voice shouted, "You there! Stop!"

They were brought up short by a samurai wearing a black lacquer helmet emblazoned the chrysanthemum crest of the Tokugawa shogunate.

"Where do you think you're going?"

Ichi stepped forward half a pace, placing himself in between Gen and the policeman.

"Excuse me sir, but we're just heading home to the Sōroku yashiki."

"You're not going anywhere. You're under arrest for attending an illegal performance."

All around them, Ichi could hear screams and sobs as the shogun's men grabbed people and dragged them off. There were more shouted orders to find Shirataki Gen. It seemed the police knew of the inn where the troupe was staying and were sending men there too. A chill ran down his spine, but Ichi willed his face to remain as blank as possible.

"We were not at the performance, sir. I was with a customer and now I'm returning home."

"Don't lie to me! You came out of the theater."

"Begging your pardon, sir, but we did not. And in any case, as you know, members of the Tōdōza who break the law are not to be tried in the shogun's court but by the Tōdōza itself."

At this, Ichi heard the man shift his stance, and he knew he had won the argument. He could only imagine the sour expression the man must be making.

"If you'll excuse us..." Ichi said, attempting to step around him, but the man seized his arm.

"Not so fast! Who is this woman with you?"

"Why, my elder sister, of course, who serves as my guide. It's very difficult for me to find my way on my own, not to mention dangerous. She takes very good care of me." He bowed with an obsequious smile.

"All right, go on."

Ichi felt nearly dizzy with relief as the man stood aside. As they hurried past him, the man spat on the ground behind them, muttering, "Blind scum, moneylending bastards."

There was no time for anger over this insult, nor regret over the necessity of pretending to be less capable than he was. They hurried along the streets as fast as they dared to walk without arousing suspicion, Ichi's hand on Gen's elbow. He appreciated how skillfully she guided him as they wove through narrow streets crowded with pedestrians, oxen pulling carts, and whatever unknown obstacles shopkeepers had set out—barrels of water, stacks of boxes, or lanterns and curtains hanging from low eaves, not to mention stalls suddenly set up in the middle of the road. With Gen leading the way, he could walk much faster than usual, and no one stopped him to ask for a massage or to share the latest gossip.

"Now what?" Gen paused when they came to the Kanda Bridge.

"You can't go back to the inn. They're looking for you there. Come with me to Ryōgoku."

"Are you sure? I don't want to get you in trouble."

"You saw what just happened. They can't touch us in the Tōdōza. Come, we can hide you in the Sōroku yashiki."

Still Gen hesitated. "Oboro..."

"We can't do anything for her right now, but if she was arrested, we can ask Matsuichi kengyō to help get her out."

"All right." With a surer step, Gen led him over the bridge and south to the Ryōgoku district, to the Tōdōza residence where Ichi was staying. Now that they were far from the theater, they slowed to a more comfortable pace.

"Thank you for rescuing me, Ichi-san," Gen said seriously.

He only ducked his head shyly.

"It was nothing."

"I wouldn't say that!" Her customary jocular tone returned. "That was quite a clever performance! I didn't know you had it in you, hahaha! Elder sister indeed!"

Ichi blushed. "It was the only thing I could think of."

"Well, you can call me elder sister anytime." Gen squeezed his hand affectionately.

* * *

As Ichi promised, Gen was welcomed at the Tōdōza residence by his former master, Matsuichi kengyō. The old man had not met Shirataki Gen before, but greeted her warmly as a disciple of Tokuichi kengyō and offered to let her stay as long as she wished.

A few days later, they discovered that Oboro had indeed been arrested, but as she could show on her traveling papers that her name was not Shirataki Gen, and as her name did not appear on the handbill, the police could not prove that she had taken part in an illegal performance, so she was let go. The Katsumata troupe found a new inn to stay at, and as the yose was shut down, Heihachirō arranged for them to give private performances in teahouses instead.

Although the raid had left her rather shaken for a short time, Gen soon returned to her usual boisterous self. As repayment for rescuing her, Gen offered to take Ichi on a tour of the floating world: the backstage of the theaters, the inside of the brothels, the teahouses of the pleasure quarters, all the places where people of fashion went to show off their wit, style and dash.

"Come, it'll be fun!" she offered. "You can take along your aniki if you like."

Ichi blushed. "He's not my 'elder brother.' We haven't formally pledged each other as brothers."

"Why not? Hurry up and do it already before some other handsome young man catches his eye."

Ichi only hung his head and could not answer.

"Who cares what people think! That's what I always say. So what if you're a zatō, or too old, or whatever. Well, in any case, bring him along and make sure he brings his pretty wife too."

12

Yoshiwara

Tomonosuke strode stiffly along the sloping, curved avenue lined with teahouses. He was self-conscious to be entering the famed Yoshiwara, the largest licensed prostitution district in Edo. He felt conspicuous wearing his black silk kimono with the Uchida clan crest, with his katana and wakizashi at his side, but he had no other formal attire. He had at least purchased fashionable striped hakama, and had his hair dressed in the ginkgo leaf style. Beside him, Okyō hurried to keep up with his long strides, her high wooden sandals flapping somewhat anxiously. As the weather had turned cold, she was wearing a silk haori jacket, but under that was her latest purchase, a purple kimono with a gold ginkgo leaf pattern, and a flashy brocade obi in contrasting crimson, tied so tightly she could barely draw a deep breath.

As they neared the great gateway to the Yoshiwara, they could see Shirataki Gen waiting for them, her hair parted in the middle and tied high in back in a jaunty queue like a boy. She also wore men's hakama, decorated with vivid orange maple leaves, but paired with a girl's kimono with long, fluttering sleeves that draped down to her knees, emblazoned with a phoenix pattern. Ichi stood beside her, as ever in his plain cotton kimono of indigo blue, although he had let the skirts down. He leaned on his staff, his head hanging down and to the right, although he jerked upwards when Gen called out.

"Uchida-dono!"

Tomonosuke greeted them with a grunt, and Ichi bowed low.

"Kyō-chan! I'm so glad you could join us." Gen squeezed Okyō's hand, leering at her. Ichi was scandalized by this overly familiar mode of address, but did not say anything.

"Well, what are we waiting for!" Gen gestured inside with a flourish. The four of them stepped through the gate, past the weeping willow that marked the entrance to the floating world of pleasure. On either side of the gate were enormous paper lanterns painted with the kanji characters for "magnificent entertainment."

Gen led them down the main street lined with brothels three stories high, the eaves festooned with lanterns shaped like morning glories. Tomonosuke found the scene imposingly grand, as most buildings in Edo were only one or two stories high. Although it was only dusk, already the street was jammed with people, men ogling the girls who sat arrayed behind the lattice on the ground floor, waiting to be chosen.

Ignoring these lower-class prostitutes, Gen led them down the street and around to the right, to the shrine to Inari-sama, the Shinto fox deity. A minor festival was going on, and the small courtyard was filled not only with men on their way to the brothels, but also women and children, people of the neighborhood, come to pray for prosperity and protection from fire. After throwing a few copper coins in the offertory box and shaking the long braided rope to ring the large, rattling bell, Tomonosuke turned to buy a bear-claw charm made of bamboo and decorated with paper images of the seven gods of good luck. Then he purchased four large rice crackers dipped in soy sauce and shared them out among the four of them.

Tomonosuke, Ichi, and Okyō stood silently crunching their crackers. Gen was the only one who did not seem stiff and ill at ease. Indeed, she was evidently well known in the quarter, as both men and women greeted her familiarly. The other three stood in a group behind her, waiting as she chatted with first one passerby then another. Around them vendors cried their wares while dancers and musicians performed for small crowds.

"Oh, I see a procession!" Okyō exclaimed, pushing through the crowd towards the street to get a better look.

Tomonosuke followed her, taking up Ichi's staff as he went, not wanting to leave him behind. He immediately felt uncomfortable that he made Ichi jump by pulling so roughly on his cane without warning. Feeling vaguely that he needed to do something more, he muttered, "The procession," as he pulled Ichi behind him.

"The what?" Ichi gamely attempted to keep up.

"One of the oiran has been summoned from the brothel to meet a customer at a teahouse," he explained. "Now she's parading down the street with her girl attendants and a man holding a big parasol over her head." They could hear the sound of drums and flutes accompanying the procession, and the shouts of the crowd admiring the oiran.

Okyō glanced at them as they came up behind her. "My goodness, but you paint a poor picture, danna," she snapped. "Ichi-san, the oiran is wearing the most outlandish black lacquered sandals, more than seven inches high. She can barely walk in them, but drags them slowly along behind her with each step and keeps one hand on the shoulder of a manservant just so she won't fall over." Ichi smiled, and Okyō continued her description. "She's wearing at least ten tortoiseshell combs in her hair, splayed out like a halo around her head. Her kimono is padded out with rolls of wadding at the bottom, and her obi is tied in front, so indecent! I declare, it's the biggest padded obi I have ever seen, with a pattern of a golden tortoise in front, and the ends hanging down to her feet."

"Why is she barefoot?" Tomonosuke wondered, noting that she was wearing her sandals without socks.

"It's sexier that way!" Gen came up behind them unexpectedly, thumping him on the back. "Of course! Look at those white little feet! Have you ever seen such refinement!"

Tomonosuke looked away at her salacious comments. He was not even supposed to be in the licensed quarter, but so many samurai visited anyway, the police had all but given up trying to keep them out. He glanced down the street to the great gate at the entrance, with the tall willow tree beside it, wondering for a moment if it would be better to save his dignity and leave. People called it the "looking back willow," marking the spot where visitors returning home heaved a sad sigh and looked back in regret at having to leave the pleasures of the Yoshiwara behind to return to the workaday world of obligation. Somehow he felt that if he were to leave now, he would feel double that regret.

He turned to Gen with an air of command, trying to salvage his pride as much as possible. "Very well then, sensei, let us proceed to the teahouse."

Gen only laughed. "My my, samurai-san, aren't you a stick in the mud! I didn't bring you all this way just to show you a shrine festival or an oiran walking down the street. You can see that here any time. No, tonight is the Niwaka dancing. There'll be plenty of time for the teahouse later, but first we need to see the geisha doing the lion dance. Come on, we have to get a good spot!"

The street was becoming even more crowded, and Gen dragged and prodded them through the throng to a choice spot at the corner, not a moment too soon. With great shouts and whoops, banging on drums and shrill whistles, the parade appeared from within the quarter, the colorful floats passing directly in front of them. Each float, pulled by young men, was decorated with rich brocade cloth and strung with lanterns, with elegant calligraphy announcing the names of the geisha and their patrons. The geisha stood on the floats in groups of three or four, dressed as men. They all wore their hair tied in topknots like men, and their kimono decorated with a knotted rope pattern were tucked up at the waist and pulled down over the shoulders, their arms and chests tied with cloth covering like laborers. One girl at the head of the line held up a lion mask, while the rest brandished black lacquered fans painted with peony flowers as they danced vigorously to the beating of the drums, wooden clappers and gongs, their wrists snapping smartly to the beat and feet stamping. The incongruity of the girls was utterly enchanting: their painted faces and colorful, girlish kimono with sleeves draping to their knees contrasting with their masculine hairstyle and undergarments, their sweet little faces and their rough, rowdy dancing. A few were even wearing eboshi, the black lacquered hats of noblemen.

Tomonosuke tore his gaze away from the parade to glance at Ichi, standing patiently beside him. Surely this must be boring for him, Tomonosuke fretted. The music was loud and vigorous but not what one might call high quality. It was the dancing, not the music that was the attraction. He longed to share the scene with Ichi, but again found that words failed him.

"The geisha are dancing, but dressed as men..." he began, although he had to shout to be heard over the din.

Okyō gave him a withering look and bent her head to Ichi's ear, providing him a much more vivid description. Seeing Ichi's face light up with excitement, Tomonosuke could not but share his enjoyment, even if the words were not his.

One by one the floats all passed by, followed by comical male dancers, wearing caricature masks and mugging for the audience, and those were followed by laughing, shrieking children and barking dogs running behind them, their curled tails wagging in excitement. As the parade trailed off, Gen led her guests through the crowd, now breaking up, down the main street then down another street to the left, and at last to the entrance to a small house that Gen explained was a go-between, that is, where their entertainment for the evening would be arranged.

Here there were no girls sitting out front behind a lattice, but instead maids who greeted them with low bows and flowery phrases. With the utmost polite language, the maids insisted that Tomonosuke surrender his two swords before he could be allowed to enter, and all four were required to leave their sandals in small lockers by the entrance. He felt a bit anxious about this requirement, but did not want to be taken for an unsophisticated country samurai, so hid his surprise and discomfort as best he could.

The head go-between assigned to them was a sharp-eyed middle-aged woman, no doubt a retired oiran, dressed in luxurious grey silk crepe. With every elegant step, the skirts of her kimono fluttered, revealing a lining of red sateen, flouting the sumptuary laws that allowed only samurai to wear the finest fabrics. She led them to a zashiki, or large sitting room with fresh tatami mats, the tightly woven rushes smooth and slightly fragrant beneath their feet.

"The fusuma are all covered in gold leaf and painted with lilies and cranes in the Rinpa style," Okyō whispered to Ichi as they sat down on cushions of damask and velvet. Ichi ran his sensitive fingers delicately over the lavish fabric, nodding his head as if he understood. Again, Tomonosuke felt vaguely frustrated that he was not the one describing the scene. Did Ichi know what she meant by Rinpa style? Tomonosuke was not certain he knew himself, although he had heard the term before.

"The alcove is bordered with a pillar of polished rosewood," Okyō continued, "and displays a vase of pampas grass. A very tasteful arrangement, I might add."

Again Ichi nodded. "A good choice for late autumn," he concurred.

"This room is more luxurious than even the Omigawa daimyō's upper residence," Tomonosuke added, rather over-loudly. His attempt to join the conversation earned him a disparaging look from Okyō, who clearly thought he sounded like a bumpkin.

As soon as they were seated, Gen began issuing her orders. She was hungry, she declared, and ordered stir-fried burdock root, dried sardines, roasted tofu, fish cake on skewers, scrambled egg over rice, pickled lotus root, clams boiled with vegetables, and of course hot sake. For singing and dancing, she called for hōkan and geisha, naming each one by their stage names. Now came the more delicate negotiation of engaging the carnal entertainment.

Gen turned to Tomonosuke. "Well, samurai-san? Shall we bring you a kagema, a beautiful boy? There are not so many in Yoshiwara but I think onēsan here could find you one," indicating the go-between.

Ichi made a strangled sound halfway between a laugh and a cough. Tomonosuke said with embarrassment, "No, that won't be necessary."

"What then?" demanded the go-between. "We can call in girls of every description, from seasoned experts to fresh-faced beauties just arrived from the north, girls skilled in dancing or shamisen or composing comic verse, only state your preference."

Tomonosuke suppressed the urge to squirm under her calculating gaze, and glanced at Okyō, who remained impassive. The go-between ignored her. Men did not ordinarily bring their wives to such a place; the go-between seemed to assume she was a maid or concubine.

"I leave it to you, sensei," Tomonosuke addressed Gen stiffly.

"Hmmm." Gen smiled, looking Okyō in the eye as she addressed the go-between. "Bring us Hana-ogi, if she isn't already engaged for the evening. Tell her Shirataki Gen sends her regards."

The go-between bowed low as the other maids shuffled about on their knees, bringing them bowls of water to wash their hands and brightly patterned hand towels. The go-between produced a ledger from inside the fold of her kimono, and calling for ink stone and brush, proceeded to make a detailed record of all four of them, what they were wearing and their physical description.

This close examination made them uneasy, but Gen assured them it was only to fulfill the letter of the law and nothing would come of it. The teahouses of the pleasure quarters did not discriminate—samurai or townsmen, men or women, members of the Tōdōza, everyone was welcome as long as they had money to pay.

"We are all alike in desiring the pleasures of the flesh," Gen declared.

The maids brought in plate after plate of food, and Gen tipped them lavishly, making them simper and smile. A moment later, the door slid open again and a man in gaudy pantaloons over a richly patterned kimono entered, brandishing a folding fan with the studied air of a professional dancer.

"Who's this?" Tomonosuke blurted out in surprise. He had been expecting female geisha, and was mildly apprehensive that this man was intended for him. Although elegant, the man was far from young and not what one might call attractive.

"Why, it's the hōkan, of course!" Gen laughed, clapping him on the shoulder as Okyō again looked daggers at him for embarrassing her.

"He's a kind of buffoon or entertainer," Gen added kindly, seeing his confusion.

The hōkan glided into the room, never lifting his feet from the mats. He paused before Gen and closed his fan with a snap then bowed so low he was bent at a right angle.

"Thank you for your patronage, my lady," he intoned, using the ritual phrase.

The maids returned bearing more trays of hot sake and food, followed by five geisha, or dancing girls. They were dressed in plain black crested kimono with their hair tied in a simple chignon without ornament, so as not to outshine the oiran who would arrive later. Two carried shamisen and one brought a small drum.

As the maids served the sake, the three geisha set up their instruments while the other two prepared to dance. Meanwhile, the hōkan, with mock formality, greeted and bowed not only to the customers but also to each of the maids and the geisha.

After they all drank a toast, one geisha beat the small drum balanced on her shoulder, the two geisha on the shamisen strummed a jangling chord and the other two began their dance, turning about and flicking their fans in unison. The hōkan jumped up in front of them, making lewd gestures until even the geisha were laughing so hard they could barely continue with their movements. Meanwhile, the maids kept refilling the tiny sake cups so fast, the four customers barely knew how many rounds they had sunk. Before long they all had flushed red cheeks, and Okyō had turned a vivid purple from the tips of her ears to the ends of her fingers. At some point, the elegant sake was replaced with the more plebeian shōchū, a stronger liquor distilled from sweet potatoes.

"And now, the foot dance!" the hōkan proclaimed. He lay on his back with his legs in the air, a lion mask affixed to his feet, and shook it about in imitation of the Niwaka dance they had just seen out in the street.

Ichi listened to all this politely. The jokes were rather crude, and of course the dances were lost on him. The geisha performed more songs and dances, while the hōkan cracked dirty jokes and urged everyone to drink more. Ichi found the geisha adequate musicians, their fingers nimble enough on the shamisen, although their chanting lacked the vigor and dramatic depth of a truly talented professional. He felt his feet begin to cramp and tried to shift his weight discreetly, stifling a yawn, but this did not escape the attention of the hōkan, whose job it was to ensure all the customers were fully entertained.

"You call that singing?" The hōkan berated the geisha with feigned outrage. "Do you realize who you're playing for? You should be ashamed to show your face before the great Shirataki Gen! Why, even this zatō here can play better than you, probably."

"Very well, then let him try," said one of the geisha with a saucy grin.

Ichi found a shamisen thrust into his hands. Taking up the plectrum, he tested the strings, adjusted the tuning pegs, then with a confident twanging chord, sang out a popular love ballad about partings at dawn. The others joined in, clapping and singing along, as the other two geisha played and beat the drum. When he finished, he was pleased to hear Gen applaud enthusiastically. He played another ballad, then another, as Gen joined in with her expressive, somewhat masculine voice.

Suddenly, the door to the zashiki slid open with a bang. "Ageha! Yonehachi! For shame! Letting the guests provide the entertainment! You should be the ones paying them!"

A young woman stood in the doorway, posing imperiously as if for a woodblock print of famous beauties of the pleasure quarter. Her face was painted white, with red eyeliner and green lipstick, the very height of fashion. The high bridge of her nose gave her a sophisticated air. But unlike the oiran they had seen processing in the street, she was dressed as man, with hakama over her kimono and her hair in a boyish topknot.

"Hana-ogi!" Gen leapt up and embraced her with rough affection, planting a sloppy, drunken kiss on her lips and at the same time groping her breast through her kimono.

The oiran laughed, returning her affection, then sat down beside them cross-legged like a man. She grabbed the big ceramic jug of shōchū off the table, drinking a swig directly from the bottle without using a cup and smacking her lips in satisfaction.

"Gen!" Hana-ogi exclaimed. "Long time no see! How ya been? Why ain't I seen you here lately? Forgotten me already?" Like Gen, she spoke in a rough, masculine voice.

Ichi had heard there were oiran in the Yoshiwara who were specially trained to dress and act like men for the benefit of female customers, but he had never met one in person before. He had to admit the effect was rather fascinating.

"Gimme a break, I've been busy," Gen protested, and they immediately fell to gossip about mutual acquaintances, of which they seemed to have many.

Just as Ichi felt himself starting to nod off, Hana-ogi smacked the low rosewood table with her hand, making the dishes jump. "Gen! What kind of business is this!" she demanded. "Why did you call only for me? There are four of you! Do you take me for a common nighthawk who sees four customers in a night?"

"Of course not, my darling!" Gen kissed her hand, then gave Okyō a broad wink. "You're here for one customer only, and there she sits. Ain't she lovely? Haven't you always wanted to do it with a proper samurai daughter? I bet she knows all kinds of perverse tricks. Just look at her."

Okyō, who had been uncharacteristically restrained so far, now leaned forward, her cheeks even redder if possible, her eyes huge. Hana-ogi gave her a smoldering look, but then with professional grace turned to Tomonosuke.

"All right, but what about the samurai and the zatō? The owner will be angry if he hears we have freeloaders."

Gen shrugged. "I don't know, can't you find them a kagema?"

"Yes, yes!" cackled the hōkan. "A girl dressed as a boy for the wife, and a boy dressed as a girl for the husband! Just as nature intended! What a pleasing, harmonious household!"

"Tsk, you're in the wrong neighborhood for a kagema," said Hana-ogi. "But anything for a customer, right? Kichi here will take you to a room and we'll see what we can do."

Ichi felt Tomonosuke beside him arise rather unsteadily then put a hand on his shoulder. He stood, leaning heavily on Tomonosuke as the floor slid under his feet and the room seemed to spin. The hōkan laughed as he guided the two of them through another sliding door, down a hallway with a polished wood floor, and into a smaller room.

Ichi and Tomonosuke sank down to the floor together gratefully. Ichi realized they were sitting on a futon, no, three futons piled up, very soft and inviting. The tatami under his feet smelled fresh, like grass, and there was a lingering scent of incense in the air, cassia and aloeswood. All at once, Ichi felt his head was unbearably heavy, and he leaned back, stretching out on the futon with a happy sigh.

The hōkan hovered in the doorway, rubbing his hands together. "Well, my lord? Whom shall I summon? A girl in boy's clothes? A kagema? If you don't mind waiting, we can send to the Kabuki-za for an onnagata. Or is it me you desire?" That last comment was a joke, as Kichi would not be employed as a buffoon if he were young or handsome enough to command a higher price for his favors.

Tomonosuke smiled wanly. He knew he was once again appearing utterly unsophisticated, but none of the companions offered sounded at all appealing. Without answering, he looked down at Ichi lying on the bed beside him, his eyes closed and his cheeks flushed with drink. There was no one else he desired—not one even came close.

Reading this look in an instant, the hōkan backed out of the room with many obsequious bows and reassurances that he would find just the right companion.

Once they were alone, Tomonosuke stretched out beside Ichi, embracing him tightly. Ichi snuggled happily in his arms, pressing his face up against his neck.

"Are you enjoying yourself?" Tomonosuke asked hesitantly. "It isn't too dull, with the dancing and all?"

Ichi shook his head, still pressed up against him. "No, I'm just happy to be here with you."

"I'm sorry I'm not more skilled at describing things."

Ichi gave a muffled laugh. "I'm sorry too. Can't you at least try?"

Tomonosuke felt unexpectedly stung by this. Yes, he promised himself, he should try harder. He didn't want Ichi to feel left out. He put a finger under Ichi's chin and tilted his face up to kiss him. Ichi's eyelids fluttered briefly then shut even tighter as he returned the kiss sleepily.

They embraced tightly, pressed cheek to cheek, but before long the alcohol got the better of them. By the time the hōkan returned, bringing with him a fresh-faced girl with a boy's haircut, they had fallen asleep in each other's arms. Kichi observed the two of them snoring away with a smirk.

"Sit down," he instructed the girl, indicating a cushion next to a small table. "Stay here for two hours, then dishevel your clothes and hair, smear your lipstick, and head back to the brothel. Tell everyone what a heroic lover this samurai is, and that you are pining with love for him. Understand?"

The girl laughed and nodded, pleased to be paid so well for doing nothing at all.

* * *

Meanwhile, things were proceeding very differently for Okyō, who had drunk much less and remained in control of her faculties. She had sampled the fine sake, to be sure, but she knew much better how to toast each round while only sipping moderately. She watched with disdain as her husband and his lover staggered drunkenly off, relieved that they were at last gone, and marveling at her good fortune.

She knew that Gen had been flirting with her since they first met, but in truth she was rather in awe of the famous singer and hesitated to approach her. This oiran, however, was another story entirely. Her smooth cheeks and easy, boyish manner were utterly captivating. Okyō had heard tales of the Yoshiwara all her life, but never dreamed she might experience its pleasures for herself, nor that she might be offered a companion so singularly chosen to please her. Already she felt a burning between her thighs.

Hana-ogi knew her business very well, and there was no mistaking the look Okyō gave her. Taking one last swig directly from the bottle, she stood from the table and set off down the hallway with Okyō and Gen trailing behind her. She led them to another lavishly appointed room, with expensive bedding spread on the floor, the andon already lit, an elegant tea service on a small table, and a box of polished cherry bark containing tissues placed discreetly beside the futon. The heady scent of sandalwood hung in the air.

Okyō did not wait for the oiran to speak, but the moment they entered the room, she flung her arm around her neck, locked her in a deep embrace and kissed her hard. Hana-ogi returned her advance with equal roughness and a low throaty laugh. Okyō yanked off the oiran's obi, pulling open her hakama and kimono, and was delighted to see that Hana-ogi was wearing a belly band and fundoshi loincloth like a man.

As Okyō pulled away her kimono, Gen came up behind Hana-ogi and placed her hands on her breasts. The three of them sank down onto the futon together.

From an ornately carved rosewood stand in the decorative alcove, Hana-ogi retrieved a large harikata fashioned from tortoise shell, realistically embellished with glans, folds of flesh and even the hint of veins. This she tied on with a red cord and swaggered back over to the futon where Okyō lay sprawled, awaiting her.

With a grin, Hana-ogi recited a well-known lewd verse:

Haru kaze ni haru mizu o dasu nyogashima
On the Isle of Women, the spring breeze makes the waters gush

Gen supplied the next verse:

Nyogashima sokaicho wa minami kaze
The south wind on the Isle of Women blows open the treasure chest

Okyō laughed and jumped up. "No!" She recited another line:

Oku naka no sure-sure e kono ippon nari
Rubbing hard with one rod deep in the chamber

"Give it to me!" Okyō demanded, untying the harikata. As the other two women watched, laughing, she poured hot sake into the tortoise-shell appendage to warm it, then locking eyes with Hana-ogi, drank it all out again. Tying the harikata around her own waist, Okyō grappled the oiran and pushed her back onto the futon.

Kneeling over her, Okyō stared into Hana-ogi's flashing black eyes as she entered her. The oiran, ever the professional, contorted her face in amorous delight. Whether real or feigned, that look made Okyō burn with desire. She thrust harder, reveling in way Hana-ogi moaned and shuddered beneath her.

When at last it seemed that Hana-ogi had crested the peaks of plea-sure, Okyō flung herself down to the futon beside her. Gen planted her face between Okyō's thighs without even untying the harikata. With her expert tongue, Gen soon had Okyō also panting and writhing as Hana-ogi leaned over and kissed her mouth and caressed her breasts.

Okyō dug her fingers into Hana-ogi's glossy black hair, returning the kisses greedily. This was a pleasure for her alone, and after all she had endured, she felt she had earned it. For just a moment, she set aside thoughts of her husband and his unusual companion, and even of Rin, and gave herself over to ecstasy.

13

The Tōdōza

Tomonosuke hesitated at the gate of the Sōroku yashiki. The wooden doors stood open to the street, but he could not bring himself to step inside. He glanced behind him at the Sumida River. The water was low and slow-moving, the grasses on the bank dry and brown in the cold weather. A white stork waded methodically through the reeds.

Ichi had invited him to call at the Tōdōza residence in Ryōgoku. The highest ranked members of the Tōdōza were equal to a hatamoto or bannerman like himself so Tomonosuke thought none could find fault with him for accepting the invitation. Yet the thought of a house full of blind men made him uneasy.

Chiding himself for his want of courage, Tomonosuke sighed and stepped over the threshold of the front gate, following the short stone path to the front door of the residence. It was an impressively large structure, with wood roof shingles instead of thatch, the many overlapping eaves suggesting a large complex with inner courtyards.

The sliding door at the main entrance also stood open, and he stepped into the entryway, calling out, "Hello! Excuse me!"

A servant boy with a shaved head came running out with a bucket to wash his feet. Tomonosuke noted as he removed his sandals that the boy did not appear to be blind. Or maybe he was? It was hard to tell.

A moment later, Ichi came hurrying from the interior of the residence and kneeled down to greet him with a low bow. "Sir, you honor us with your visit. Please come in."

Tomonosuke stepped up into the house. "Thank you. It's good to see you again." He did not add that the last time they saw each other was at the Yoshiwara, but the blush that crept over Ichi's pale skin betrayed the fact that their thoughts seemed to be running in a similar direction.

Attempting to hide his embarrassment, Ichi rose gracefully to his feet in one smooth movement.

"This way if you please, my lord," he said, leading Tomonosuke down a hallway with a polished wood floor to an inner sitting room. This room was as grand as any samurai mansion, with its carved wood transom, fresh tatami mats and decorative alcove with a tasteful arrangement of chrysanthemum flowers. A tea service sat beside a rectangular hibachi. Despite the cool weather, one side of the room stood open to an inner courtyard with a small rock garden and koi pond. Tomonosuke wondered at how ordinary it all was. Why did they indulge in these decorations that they could not see? He could only conclude it was vanity. For Ichi's sake, he was trying to keep an open mind about the Tōdōza, but he could not forget that all this was paid for with usury.

Tomonosuke sat down cross-legged, not bothering with a formal posture, as Ichi ran off to call for servants. On the other side of the courtyard, Tomonosuke could see into a large room where a group of five youths with shaved heads sat listening to an older man lecture. From deep within the residence, he could hear the sounds of apprentices practicing the shamisen, the strings twanging together then stopping at intervals and repeating the same line over again.

Ichi returned with a sighted servant girl who put a cast iron kettle on the hibachi to boil water for tea. A few moments later, they were joined by an elderly man in priestly robes of yellow silk with a soft round silk cap on his shaved head. Ichi introduced him as Matsuichi kengyō, his master. His face was soft and round, his sagging cheeks lined with age. His eyelids remained closed although he moved with slow but unerring, deliberate steps.

Ichi leapt up to assist him, holding the old man's arm as he sank stiffly to the floor.

"Kengyō-sama, Uchida-dono is here," Ichi said in a low, polite tone. He bowed from his seated position.

Remembering his manners with a start, Tomonosuke also bowed, his hands on his thighs. "It is I, Uchida Tomonosuke, kengyō-sama. You honor me with this invitation."

Matsuichi kengyō smiled warmly, nodding to the girl who placed a hot cup of tea before him, announcing its position in a low murmur. "Welcome, Uchida-sama. Please be easy. I have heard so much about you from Ichi here. It's a pleasure to meet you at last."

Tomonosuke blushed slightly, glad that the kengyō could not see it. Had Ichi really said so much about him? It was embarrassing but also somehow pleasing. He felt tongue-tied.

"You know, it's such a pleasant day, rather warm for this time of year, I find," the kengyō continued, his grin broadening as if he knew exactly how Tomonosuke had reacted to the décor of the room. "How lovely to sit with the shōji open to the garden, enjoying the breeze. I should like to hear some music as we sit here. Ichi, go fetch your shakuhachi."

"My shakuhachi, sir?" Ichi's voice faltered slightly in surprise. "I haven't played it in so long. I think I lent it to one of the apprentices but I'm not sure where he put it."

"That's all right, we don't mind waiting, do we Uchida-sama?" Before Tomonosuke could reply, Matsuichi kengyō continued, "Get Sachi here to help you."

Both Ichi and the maid bowed and shuffled from the room, in search of the flute.

When they had gone, the kengyō took a long sip of tea then set it down again, finding the small wooden coaster with his fingers first. Still smiling kindly, he said, "I'm very glad that Ichi has found himself such a worthy elder brother."

Tomonosuke choked slightly on his tea. "We haven't—I mean, not yet—"

The kengyō waved his hand. "I trust you will exchange the vows in time. Ichi is quite alone in the world, you know. His family disowned him, as is often the case, sadly. Such a pity, too, that they refused to purchase a higher rank for him when he joined the Tōdōza. His father is quite a wealthy farmer, you know, owning his own land. He could have set Ichi up with a higher rank, then he would not have to walk the streets with his whistle, calling for customers."

"I didn't know," Tomonosuke murmured.

"Oh indeed. Even now, he could achieve a higher rank if he studied music a bit harder and passed the examination. He certainly has the talent for it. But he says he doesn't want to."

"Sensei, I found it!" Ichi burst back into the room, brandishing a worn shakuhachi, his pale cheeks flushed with exertion. Evidently he had run down the hallway.

"Excellent." Matsuichi kengyō nodded, leaving off his conversation with Tomonosuke and giving his whole attention to Ichi. "Let's have 'Falling Leaves' followed by 'The Fulling Block.' Those are some appropriate tunes for a late autumn day, don't you think?"

"Yes, sensei." Ichi seated himself facing the garden, took a moment to steady his breathing, then blew into the end of the large bamboo flute.

Tomonosuke watched Ichi's profile as he played, his face suffused with concentration. The breathy sound of the flute filled him with melancholy. Silently, he cursed Ichi's father for blighting his prospects in the Tōdōza. As Ichi played on, staccato puffs alternating with long sustained notes, Tomonosuke reflected with surprise that he was now hoping for Ichi to rise in the ranks of the Tōdōza. Was that really the best path for him? If he achieved a higher rank, would he not become a vile moneylender and spend his days harassing poor samurai families?

These thoughts running uneasily around his mind, Tomonosuke shifted his legs slightly with a small sigh. Matsuichi kengyō cocked an ear towards him.

"Sir, are you quite all right? Sachi, bring the samurai more tea, if you please."

Tomonosuke nodded to the maid as she refilled his cup. Ichi began the second piece, his expression unchanged.

"Is there something troubling you?" the kengyō pressed.

Tomonosuke was impressed at his powers of perception. "I hesitate to bring up a delicate matter," he said slowly, "but since you mention it, I must ask, do all the Tōdōza members lend money?"

The kengyō laughed as Ichi played on. Tomonosuke felt a pang of conscience to bring up a topic that he knew would anger Ichi, but he told himself it was for Ichi's own good to expose the corruption at the heart of this organization.

Yet the kengyō's mild good humor never wavered. "You think evil karma compels us to prey on noble samurai who have fallen on hard times, am I correct?"

Tomonosuke gave a noncommittal grunt as Ichi played a sudden loud blast, rather out of keeping with the meditative tune.

"Tell me, sir," the kengyō continued conversationally, "why do you think the shogunate suffers the Tōdōza to lend money? Anyone with a bit of extra cash could do it, so why us?" When Tomonosuke did not reply, the kengyō continued, "The work that those in power do not wish to do is always given to those of the lowest rank, that they may be despised. Disposing of dead animals falls to the outcastes, so that everyone else can think themselves free of pollution. The coffers of the shogun and daimyō are insufficient to support the samurai who serve them, so the ignoble task of lending money is given to the Tōdōza."

"But—"

The kengyō silenced him with a wave. "Of all ailments that might befall a person, the sighted fear blindness the most. Our existence reminds you that but for the benevolence of the bodhisattvas, you too could become blind at any time. This fear is too much to bear, so you tell yourselves that we blind hate the sighted, and the practice of moneylending is the proof, even though this job is given to us so that people of higher status need not do it."

"I don't—"

"Uchida-sama, we are aware what you think of us. I agree with you that moneylending is a cruel, heartless practice. Hanawa Hokiichi sōkengyō has been doing his best to dissuade our members from engaging in it, but please understand that for many of our members who are not skilled at music or massage, it is their only source of income. What else would you have them do?"

"I don't know," Tomonosuke admitted.

"The sighted may scorn us, but they must tolerate us because they never know whose child will be blind next. Peasant, merchant, or samurai, all need us whether they admit it or not. What they don't realize is that we teach much more than music and massage, but also how to navigate in the world without sight. Who else would provide such teaching but other blind people? It is our way, the right way, and that is why we are called the Tōdōza, the guild of the right way."

Ichi reached the end of the song and set aside his flute, but did not arise or turn his head.

Tomonosuke stared into his empty teacup. "I understand there is much I don't know about the Tōdōza. But if the practice of members engaging in moneylending causes such disorder, why does the shogunate not abolish it?"

"Look around you, Uchida-sama! Do you really believe the world is ordered as it should be? The peasants in remote villages are rioting about the rice tax, the Hollanders are pressing the shogun to open the ports, meanwhile the shogun's coffers are nearly empty. Are these the features of a benevolent and well-run government?"

Tomonosuke was aghast. Never before had he heard someone of such high rank speak so openly against the shogun. There was grumbling among the lower-ranking retainers but never anything stated with such authority. Was the shogunate truly bankrupt?

When Tomonosuke did not reply, the kengyō again seemed to sense his mood with uncanny precision. "Come, come!" he declared, clapping his hands. "There is no reason to take the conversation in such an unfortunate direction. You are here as our guest. We would be remiss if we did not provide you with better entertainment."

Matsuichi kengyō called for the apprentices to come in to play for the guest. Five youths were led in by a sighted servant. Each carried a shamisen with one hand, the other hand on the shoulder of the one before him. They were all similarly attired in cotton indigo kimono and momohiki trousers, all with shaved heads, but their faces were like a catalog of various eye ailments.

Tomonosuke noted that none of them moved with the easy grace that Ichi possessed, nor did they have the calm self-assurance of the kengyō. All five were awkward and uncertain, sitting and tuning their instruments with some difficulty. Had Ichi also been like this when he first lost his sight and joined the Tōdōza?

When at last they had settled, Matsuichi kengyō rapped out the beat using the metal tongs on the edge of the hibachi, and the youths began to play in unison. Their playing lacked the confidence and spontaneity of more polished musicians, but they acquitted themselves tolerably well for beginners.

Tomonosuke watched their faces, screwed up in intense concentration as they played, feeling an unexpected wave of empathy for these young men. If the Tōdōza did not exist, what would be their fate? They would certainly be beggars, without any skill in which they could take pride, nor instruction on how to conduct themselves in daily life. He recalled what Ichi had said so vehemently, that the Tōdōza saved his life. He at last felt he was beginning to understand.

* * *

When Tomonosuke took his leave, Ichi accompanied him to the entryway, reciting the usual polite phrases of thanks and bowing low until he heard the door slide shut. With so many others about, Ichi felt too self-conscious for a more intimate farewell.

Straightening again, Ichi walked slowly back down the hall. He loved the Sōroku yashiki; staying here always felt like returning home. Although it was a large, sprawling residence with many rooms and long hallways, his feet knew every inch, from the location of each squeaking floorboard, to which fusuma always caught slightly in the frame. Unlike any other house, he could walk about freely without having to concentrate, certain that the arrangement of the furniture would never alter, that no items would be left on the floor to trip over, and the uses and configuration of the rooms would always be the same.

He had longed to bring Tomonosuke here, to share his real life with him, not just the face he showed his customers. But somehow, the experience was not what he had hoped. The samurai's presence here made everything familiar feel strange and uncomfortable. And not only that, he was mortified that Tomonosuke had argued with his master.

Ichi realized that his feet had unthinkingly carried him back down the hall to the room in which they had received Tomonosuke. He could hear the clink and rustle as the maid cleared away the teacups. The apprentices seemed to have returned to their lesson; they were so loud and ungainly, it was impossible to miss them. His master, however, was more skilled at remaining silent.

"Matsuichi kengyō? Are you there?"

"Yes, I am here." Ichi was pleased to hear his soft, reassuring voice. "What is troubling you?" As usual, his master intuited his mood immediately.

Ichi knelt down and bowed. "I apologize for Uchida-dono's rudeness to you."

There was a shuffling and a faint sigh as the older man shifted to a more comfortable cross-legged position. "Never mind. His arrogance derives, I think, from lack of experience in the world, not from meanness of spirit. He has never had cause to question the order of things. It may take some time, but I think he is willing to learn."

Ichi made a noncommittal sound, indicating that he had heard but had no reply. After a pause, he burst out, "Everyone thinks we have pledged to each other as brothers already, but we have not."

"Well? Is that what you desire?"

Instead of answering, Ichi replied with a question. "Is it truly possible for the blind and the sighted to be brothers?"

The kengyō laughed softly. "Is that what is worrying you?"

"Well?" Ichi prompted.

"That is for you to decide. We have our way, the right way, and the samurai have their own way. You can choose for yourself if you want to remain within the Tōdōza and only treat sighted people as customers, or live among them. What is it you desire?"

"I want him to understand our way," Ichi said, for once not bothering to hide the emotion in his voice.

"I think he will, in time," Matsuichi replied, the sound of a smile evident in his voice. "Perhaps if you take him to meet the sōkengyō, the experience might open his mind a bit more quickly."

14

The Scholars

The last month of the year was called Shiwasu, meaning to run, for the priests running about preparing the rites and ceremonies for the new year. Shirataki Gen was in high demand as a performer at year-end parties, and had no time to spare for her new friends.

Tomonosuke was kept busy at the office of the exchequer every day that month, as the end of the year was when all debts came due, and he and all the other clerks were clacking their abacuses all day long tallying the accounts. At least in the Edo residence, the domain's income exceeded its expenditures, although only very slightly. Yet Tomonosuke could not be easy. Something still felt wrong to him about the accounts, but nothing he could put his finger on exactly. Matsudaira Sadahide kept his head down in the account books at the front of the room. Tomonosuke had no desire to open conversation with him on any topic, so he kept his misgivings to himself.

Ichi called at the lower residence but was disappointed to hear from Rin that the master was still out, working unusually late hours. She delivered this news in clipped tones as they stood in the street, making no move to invite him in.

"And where is Okyō-dono?" he asked hesitantly. Okyō had not sent for him since their trip to the Yoshiwara, and he was not sure why. Had she abandoned her plan? Or found someone else? He was relieved not to be at her beck and call, but he did not want her to change her mind about him calling on her husband.

To his surprise, Rin answered with a snappish, "How should I know!"

"Rin, what's the matter?"

He could hear her scuffing her straw sandal in the dusty road. "I'm not speaking to you either!"

"Wait!" If she walked off, he might not even know it, let alone be able to follow her. She was clearly angry about something, but he could not begin to guess what. "Rin, please tell me what's wrong!"

"As if you don't know." At least her voice was still nearby; she had not left yet. "Men, you're all the same."

"Rin, please—"

"How could you all go to Yoshiwara like it's nothing!" she burst out.

Ichi tried to speak in a gentle tone. "Are you jealous that Okyō-dono enjoyed the favors of the oiran Hana-ogi? I assure you, it was only business, what people call the water trade. There's no reason to be jealous. Men go all the time, and their wives accept it."

"I know what goes on in places like that better than you," Rin sneered. "I'm not a stupid jealous girl. But knowing the abuse that happens there, how could she set foot in such a corrupt, evil place? How could you?" Her voice cracked with anguish.

Ichi was taken aback. The Yoshiwara was the cultural center of Edo. A visit there was the very height of fashion. He had considered himself very lucky to receive a tour, which ordinarily would be far beyond his means. He had to admit he had not thought much about the women who worked there, although everyone they met had seemed cheerful. Of course, Gen had been extraordinarily open-handed, and Ichi himself knew very well how to maintain a cheerful façade for a paying customer.

"I'm sure Gen would never patronize a house that mistreated anyone..." he said hesitantly.

"You don't know what it's like."

"Was your indenture here in Yoshiwara?"

"No, it was in the north, in Echigo, but it's all the same. I never thought my lady would enter such a place."

Privately, Ichi felt that it wasn't all the same, and that an oiran like Hana-ogi in the elegant, refined Yoshiwara would have a much easier time than a poor nighthawk in a provincial brothel, but he did not want to suggest he understood her suffering better than she did. He had never known her to be this upset; ordinarily she was so quiet.

"Please," he said, "tell Okyō-dono how you feel. I'm sure she would never do anything to intentionally hurt you."

* * *

As the last day of the year drew nearer, even Tomonosuke noticed the cooling of affection between his wife and her maid. But the two women rarely spoke of private matters in front of him, and he did not want to pry into their relationship.

Okyō, Rin and all the other wives and servants ran about preparing the New Year's feast called osechi, to be served in special lacquered boxes with many small compartments: daikon and carrots pickled in vinegar, mochi, candied black beans, candied chestnuts, preserved anchovies, konbu seaweed strips soaked in sweet soy sauce, tied in decorative knots. When they were not cooking, they were decorating the house with sacred rope, pine boughs, plum branches, bamboo stalks, and mandarin oranges.

Rin carried out her tasks even more silently than usual, never meeting Okyō's eye. At night, she slept in the servants' quarters, as Okyō had been unable to secure more than one room for them, and in any case they did not want to arouse suspicion.

"In the new year, the daimyō will return to Omigawa domain, and we shall move to a row house. Things can be as they were in Sawara," Okyō said in a discreet undertone as she and Rin sat pulling the stitches out of Tomonosuke's best kimono, separating the silk into strips in preparation for laundering. They were alone in their room, but only the thin paper fusuma separated them from the hallway and the rooms housing other retainers.

"What does it matter!" Rin burst out.

Okyō slowly lowered the fabric in her hand and fixed Rin with her stern gaze. "I'm tired of all this sulking. If you're angry with me about something, just tell me what it is!"

Rin glared back at her. "You know what it is!"

"Oh, that." Okyō scoffed and went back to pulling the seam.

"Yes, 'that'! I never thought you of all people would be so cruel. Ichi was right!"

Again Okyō put aside the kimono and raised her eyes. Rin only rarely showed her emotions like this. "Ichi was right about what?" she asked suspiciously.

"He said that danna-sama is only toying with him to satisfy his curiosity, that samurai would never seriously consider an attachment to someone so low in station. And now I as well—! See how easily you set aside my feelings."

Okyō stared at her pale face, appalled. Rin's words wounded her deeply. "Going to the Yoshiwara means nothing," Okyō insisted defensively. "Everyone does it."

Rin flung aside her half of the kimono in frustration. "Why won't you try to understand? It's not jealousy! Are you jealous of danna-sama and Ichi being together?"

"No!"

"No, of course not! You're angry at him for treating you inconsiderately and neglecting his duties as husband, right?"

Okyō nodded.

"So why won't you consider my feelings?" Rin continued. "I told you about the brothel in Jōetsu, every shameful detail! I don't care if the teahouse you visited seemed respectable. It's an evil practice. For every pampered oiran, there are ten thousand girls treated no better than slaves. Even the oiran are like the frog in the well. No one wants to look at the misery going on around them. But I thought you of all people understood..." she trailed off in a strangled sob.

Okyō embraced her as Rin sobbed harder, her small, thin frame trembling in Okyō's arms. Okyō's heart ached for her, and she regretted her callousness. How could she have so thoroughly disregarded Rin's feelings? It had not always been so.

"I'm sorry," she murmured, rubbing Rin's back. "I'm sorry. I pledged my heart to you, and I meant it sincerely. I should have thought of you before I agreed to go."

Rin gave a hiccupping sigh, her sharp features pale and unhappy, but she seemed reassured.

"I promise. I won't go back again," Okyō said.

* * *

The preparations reached a fever pitch on the last day of the year, until at midnight, everyone rushed out to temples and shrines dressed in their finest kimono to hear the large bronze bell rung one hundred times.

Tomonosuke threw a few coins in the offertory box and clapped his hands, bowing low and making a silent but vehement prayer for prosperity in the coming year. The state of the daimyō's finances was precarious at best, and if the kengyō was to be believed, the shogunate itself fared even worse. The priest shook his haraegushi or lightning wand over the crowd, the zigzag paper streamers rustling loudly as he intoned the incomprehensible sacred words to purify the supplicants. And yet Tomonosuke still did not feel easy in his heart.

With Okyō and Rin trailing silently after him, Tomonosuke purchased a talisman in the shape of a large wooden arrow with a paper charm rolled around the middle. When they returned home, he placed it over the lintel at the door to their quarters, then remained staring at it a long time, after Okyō and Rin bustled away to the kitchen to direct the final preparations for the feast they would eat the next day. The andon in the corner sputtered quietly. It was very late, yet he did not feel like sleeping. He should be feeling grateful, he realized. The domain was solvent this year, at least on paper. He was posted permanently to Edo, the biggest, most entertaining city in the world, and he had a younger brother who brought joy to his heart. Why then this sense of foreboding, as if a dark cloud hung over his household?

They had only a scant few hours' sleep.

The first day of the new year dawned bright and chilly, a cold sun shining in a cloudless sky. The city was at last quiet as families ate osechi at home together, along with mochi in soup with seaweed, and noodles for long life.

"Our first new year in Edo," Tomonosuke observed, as he and Okyō sat side by side, the small trays of osechi before them. "Is all well with you, wife?" He eyed her warily sidelong.

Okyō continued to eat without batting an eye. "Yes." After a long moment, she added, "I have promised never to visit Yoshiwara again."

"Is that so?" Tomonosuke kept his voice purposely neutral, not really understanding what she was talking about. In any case, it seemed unlikely to him that Gen would invite them a second time, and they could not afford to go on their own.

Okyō popped the large sugared beans she had been saving for last in her mouth. "It's a small price to pay." Having finished her meal, she stretched her legs out in an unladylike pose, savoring the prospect of the few days of rest before her.

* * *

After the first quiet day, visiting began in earnest, and the dusty streets were once again clogged with people rushing about to call on friends and relations to greet them in the new year.

On the third day of the new year, Ichi came to call at the lower residence in Takadanobaba. Rin showed him in, informing him in a whisper that her mistress was out visiting, but the master was at home.

Tomonosuke was lounging in the main room, lying on his side near the hibachi with a pipe and a copy of the latest volume of *The Legend of Eight Dogs*, which had just been released.

"Ichi!" Tomonosuke tossed the book aside and stuck his pipe in the cinders as Rin tactfully withdrew. "Happy new year!"

Ichi knelt down and gave a formal bow. "Happy new year, my lord."

There was a pause, and Ichi tried to guess why Tomonosuke did not reply—he sounded happy to see him again, so why this silence now? Had he changed his mind? Was his appearance less than pleasing? Was there a servant in the room? Only the slightest rustle on the tatami warned him of Tomonosuke's approach. Ichi startled slightly to feel a sudden rough embrace.

Tomonosuke's arms dropped away again almost immediately. "I'm sorry. Every time I touch you, I make you jump. It's not my intention. I just...I don't know how not to."

Ichi slid a hand along the mat until he found Tomonosuke's knee, and his hand upon it. Taking Tomonosuke's hand in his, he placed it against his own cheek, drawing the other man nearer again.

"You're so often silent. If you speak, I'll always know where you are," Ichi said in a low voice.

Tomonosuke rubbed his thumb against Ichi's lower lip. "May...may I kiss you?"

"Of course."

The kiss was hot and sweet, and Ichi felt just a tiny sliver of Tomonosuke's passion which he normally kept so tightly hidden away. If only he would express himself more fully. They still had not formally pledged to each other as elder brother and younger brother. Ichi longed to hear these words from Tomonosuke's lips, to know that the attachment was in earnest.

Tomonosuke moved away again and suddenly the pungent scent of clove oil filled the air. Ichi squirmed in anticipation, his bottom hot.

"I—I would kiss you again," Tomonosuke stated awkwardly.

Ichi stretched out a hand in his direction, and finding his face, guided him to his lips.

"I believe you intend to do more than kiss me," Ichi murmured, feeling the blood rush to his cheeks. With the hurry of preparations for the new year, it had been too long since their previous encounter.

Tomonosuke grunted his assent, pushing Ichi down and loosening his fundoshi. He began slowly, methodically massaging with his fingers before entering him. Ichi appreciated his gentleness and consideration, and as ever it was sweet, so sweet. But still Ichi felt Tomonosuke was holding back.

After they had both finished and cleaned up with tissue paper, as he was rearranging his clothes, Ichi remarked with somewhat forced casualness that this was not in fact the reason for his visit.

"I am going to pay my respects in the new year to Hanawa Hokiichi sōkengyō," Ichi said somewhat bashfully. "Since you seemed to find your visit to the Tōdōza edifying, I was wondering if perhaps you might like to accompany me to his residence in Awajicho?" As he spoke, his phrasing became increasingly polite.

"What, now?" Tomonosuke sounded surprised.

"If you're not busy, I mean, if it's not too much trouble..."

Tomonosuke found he could not refuse such a heartfelt entreaty. The sōkengyō was the head of the Tōdōza. Tomonosuke had no idea what sort of man this Hanawa Hokiichi was, but Ichi and all the other Tōdōza members seemed to hold him in very high regard. If the head of the guild of blind men was as percipient as Ichi's former teacher, he might be worth meeting.

As they walked down broad boulevards lined with the walls of daimyō residences, their wooden sandals kicked up clouds of dust. How many days since the last rainfall, Tomonosuke wondered silently. Ten? Or more? The air felt very dry.

He was holding Ichi's bamboo cane, yet Ichi was the one directing their route, as they left behind the samurai residences and passed along more crowded thoroughfares, home to townspeople whose houses were built right up to the edge of the street, without gates or walls. The sliding front doors of most houses stood open, noren curtains fluttering in the chilly breeze.

It was a remarkable feat, Tomonosuke reflected, how well Ichi knew his way around the city. He had seen how Ichi oriented himself with mile markers, gates between neighborhoods, street side shrines, and other landmarks, but still. Even now, after months in Edo, Tomonosuke himself sometimes became lost in the narrow alleys of the townspeople districts.

"The sōkengyō is a very learned man," Ichi was saying rather apprehensively as they walked along. "Did you know he has written a complete history of Japan?"

"Indeed?" Tomonosuke was skeptical. "And how can he do this when he can neither read nor write?"

"He has sighted apprentices, of course, to read to him and to write down his dictation. They say he only needs to hear a book read once and he can remember it forever."

"Huh."

Ichi chattered on excitedly. "I heard the sōkengyō lost his sight to a fever as a child, like I did. But when he came to the Tōdōza, he found he had no talent for massage nor for music, so he decided to become a scholar instead. Isn't that remarkable? He's even been granted an audience with the shogun."

"Is that so?" Tomonosuke's tone was dispassionate, but privately he was bemused by Ichi's enthusiasm. A blind scholar would indeed be remarkable, if it were true.

They came at last to a somewhat large gated residence on the banks of the Kanda River. The large tile roof spread impressively above wide shōji sliding doors. A small vertical plaque at the side of the gate was adorned with the single kanji character for Hanawa, the surname of the sōkengyō. It could have been the residence of a moderately successful merchant, but considering the size and wealth of the Tōdōza, the head of the guild had chosen a relatively modest home for himself.

In the spacious entryway, Ichi called out a greeting, and a maid appeared with a bucket of water to wash their feet. She led them into a large room, appointed with fresh tatami mats. At the far end of the room was a decorative alcove with oranges and small round cakes of mochi displayed for the new year.

Hanawa sōkengyō was seated before the alcove, with an ease that suggested this was his usual spot for receiving visitors or working with his apprentices. He appeared to be in his seventies, a small man with a kindly round face, although his eyes remained closed. He was attired in a manner suggestive of a Buddhist priest, with a scarlet robe over a plain white kimono, and on his head a yellow cloth cap with folds of fabric that draped over his shoulders.

There were already several other guests come to tender new year's greetings. Six young men of the samurai class with eager, intelligent faces sat in an orderly row on the left. Tomonosuke supposed they were the apprentices who assisted the sōkengyō with his reading and writing. An older blind man lounged on the right, sitting with his legs crossed rather than folded under him, and leaning on a rosewood armrest. Tomonosuke guessed that he was another high-ranking member of the Tōdōza, although he was dressed not as a lay monk but as a gentleman of leisure, in a fine black silk haori. He wore no hat on his bald head.

Ichi knelt down and with a three-finger bow delivered a formal new year's greeting. He concluded with the standard polite request for patronage in the new year, then introduced Tomonosuke, who was sitting stiffly beside him.

The sōkengyō smiled. "Welcome, Uchida-dono. We are honored to have a bannerman of the Omigawa domain visit us." He named each of his young apprentices, who bowed in turn, then introduced the older gentleman as Takizawa Okikuni. With a slight smile, the man gave a stately nod, his bald head shining. He had a long, rectangular face and even, patrician features. His eyes appeared clouded over with cataracts, although he held his head steady and pointed his gaze at whoever was speaking, unlike Ichi and the other Tōdōza members whom Tomonosuke had met, who had a tendency to cock an ear instead. He guessed that the man could see, if indistinctly.

Unlike the sōkengyō, who seemed good-natured but retiring, Takizawa had something of the charisma of a performer about him, and a restless, quick wit.

"We were just reciting poems from *The Collection of One Hundred Poets*, although you must forgive us for not using the cards," Hanawa sōkengyō explained affably, referring to a memory card game played at the new year. In a flat, graceless tone, he recited,

asaborake
ariake no tsuki to
miru made ni
at daybreak
looking like
the moon at dawn

"Oh!" Ichi cried, sitting up straighter, his eyebrows raised in excitement. "Poem thirty-one!"

Hanawa smiled indulgently, as they all knew the second verse. "Please, Ichi, let us hear it."

In a more melodious voice, Ichi recited,

Yoshino no sato ni
fureru shirayuki
in a village in Yoshino
the white snow falling

"Very nice," Hanawa said solemnly, but at the same moment, Takizawa offered his own parody of the second verse:

Oyoshi no futon ni
agaru shirashiri
Oyoshi's white ass
rising within the bedding

One of the apprentices guffawed, and the others looked away in embarrassment.

Hanawa sighed. "He's been like this all afternoon."

"And yet you never fail to laugh," Takizawa replied, as a maid entered with a tray of teacups and rice crackers. "Never let it be said that I don't know my audience."

The maid served out the refreshments, murmuring politely, "Tea and crackers, sir," as she served the three blind men, gently nudging their fingers with the side of the dish, so they knew the location as she set it on the floor before them. Tomonosuke wondered admiringly at her consideration. Why had such an action never occurred to him?

"Takizawa-san, please, you'll embarrass our guest," Hanawa protested mildly, still smiling. "We don't want a bannerman of the Omigawa domain to think we in the Tōdōza are so coarse."

The other gentleman laughed. "Of course, I am not a member of the Tōdōza, and am not bound by your rules."

Tomonosuke shifted uneasily, thinking of his recent trip to the Yoshiwara. He was not as upstanding a samurai as they seemed to assume, or was this all in jest?

Ichi leaned forward. "Sōkengyō-sama, Uchida-dono has been very impressed with the reforms you have enacted within the Tōdōza, and with your own scholarly work." He seemed eager to change the subject in a more serious direction, even at the risk of stretching the truth.

"Indeed?" Hanawa said slowly. "Is that so, Uchida-dono?"

"Ah, um, yes," Tomonosuke replied, slightly flustered. "I had the honor of meeting Matsuichi kengyō who told me many interesting facts about the Tōdōza that opened my eyes, I mean..."

Hanawa made a sweeping gesture with his hand. "Come, Uchida-dono, let us thrust directly with the sword point, as they say. We know very well what is our reputation among the samurai and townspeople. And yet they need us, not merely for entertainment and relaxation, but for our medical expertise and to care for their blind sons. I have tried to eliminate the vile practice of moneylending, but to speak plainly, the shogunate will not provide for us otherwise."

"But you have a career as a scholar," Tomonosuke said hesitantly.

"The sōkengyō's omnibus history of Japan is over six hundred volumes," Ichi added in a fervent whisper, attempting to fill in more detail so Tomonosuke might not seem completely uninformed.

Hanawa of course heard him and smiled benevolently. "And have you read any of it, Uchida-dono?"

"Oh, ah, I'm afraid not..."

Tomonosuke felt a pang as the old man appeared genuinely crestfallen. "I expend so much effort to preserve the true history of our country for posterity. And yet I'm certain you have read Takizawa-san's books."

"N-nooo..."

Hanawa's good cheer returned. "Oh but surely you have, although perhaps you know him better by his pen name, Kyokutei Bakin."

Tomonosuke was thunderstruck. This blind man reciting vulgar couplets, this was the exalted author of *The Legend of Eight Dogs*? He turned to Ichi sitting beside him, but Ichi appeared equally as surprised, his mouth hanging open.

"I-I had no idea," Tomonosuke stammered. "Yes, of course I have."

Takizawa laughed. "Of course he has! Who doesn't love a rip-roaring tale of adventure? I'm telling you, Hanawa-san, that's why my books are best-sellers and yours are moldering away on the bookstore shelf even at the price of three mon per volume."

"But my books contain the truth, not fanciful tales," Hanawa insisted somewhat peevishly.

"My books demonstrate Confucian morality, which is also a kind of truth," Takizawa countered, in what was clearly a long-standing debate between them.

"But how—" Tomonosuke burst out.

Takizawa turned his long elegant face in Tomonosuke's direction with an amused expression. "How does a blind man write a book? Is it so very difficult to imagine? Hanawa-san here has his army of apprentices to copy down his words as he recites them. As for me, I have only my daughter-in-law Omichi, but I wager she is faster and writes a more elegant hand than any of these dull fellows."

"Sensei," Ichi ventured in rather star-struck tones. "Uchida-dono has been so kind as to read *The Legend of Eight Dogs* to me, and I have enjoyed it very much, but I had no idea the author was a member of the Tōdōza."

"Takizawa-san is not a member," Hanawa corrected gently. "He is visiting today as a personal friend."

"It's only in the past few years, in my old age, that my eyes have become weak," Takizawa added. "I am indebted to Hanawa-san for his advice and guidance on managing without sight."

"You're too kind, Takizawa-san," the sōkengyō demurred. "It's really very simple. Rather than asking 'Can it be done?' I always ask instead, 'How may it be done?' and the answers become apparent."

"Yes! Thank you, sōkengyō-sama. That is a truly worthy advice, and I shall carry it in my heart always."

Tomonosuke turned to Ichi in surprise. The young man seemed nearly overcome, his cheeks flushed and his hands in fists, gripping the fabric of his kimono against his thighs.

"Zatō-san," the sōkengyō said kindly, "never let anyone tell you what you can and can't do. The Tōdōza is our way, the right way, and that means sometimes you have to make your own path."

"Yes, sōkengyō-sama," Ichi said, bowing again. Tomonosuke watched him, somewhat bewildered at the strength of Ichi's reaction. Was he truly so unaccustomed to words of encouragement? Tomonosuke thought he saw tears drop on the tatami, and felt a strange pain in his breast.

This was forgotten a moment later, as the entire house began to sway gently back and forth. Tomonosuke and Ichi braced themselves against the floor with their hands, while the apprentices stared at each other with wide eyes. As always, time seemed to stop for a moment as everyone waited to see if the shaking would increase. They all breathed a sigh of relief when it stopped.

"Dear me, there have been so many tremors lately," the sōkengyō observed, although as ever in a calm, unworried tone. "We may be due for another big quake."

"I'm afraid you're right," Takizawa concurred, suddenly morose. "In that case, I shall give our guests yet another bit of advice." Turning to Tomonosuke, he said, "Samurai-san, when the disaster strikes, don't expect your status to protect you."

"M-my what?" Tomonosuke stammered, still awestruck by the great author.

Hanawa waved his hand, smiling benevolently. "Don't let him worry you, Uchida-dono. Takizawa-san renounced his samurai status so that he might publish his vulgar novel."

Tomonosuke was about to object that the novel was in no way vulgar, but Takizawa cut him off with a sardonic laugh.

"I did no such thing, as you know very well, Hanawa-san. I renounced my samurai status out of poverty, that I might be allowed to earn a living after my father died and I became a rōnin. The honor and loyalty of the characters in my novel belong to the misty past. Remember, Uchida-san, you will find precious few samurai today who practice those ideals. Renouncing your status is nothing to fear."

Tomonosuke was confounded by this advice. Why should he renounce his status? It was unthinkable that he would ever have occasion to do so. The conversation left him feeling as uncertain as the shaking ground. Neither the head of the Tōdōza nor the great Bakin were at all what he had expected.

15

Fire Season

The dry weather continued throughout Mutsuki, the first month of the year. Day after day, the cold sun shone in a pale, cloudless sky. The earthen roads cracked and split, clouds of dust blowing everywhere.

The people of Edo turned wary eyes to the sky, hoping in vain for a shower. In a city built of sticks and paper, a small fire could quickly turn into a conflagration—the flower of Edo. The first three months of the year were the most dangerous, if no rain fell. On windy days, the public baths closed to lessen the danger that the fires used to heat the water might blow out of control. As the month dragged on, the days without the possibility of bathing increased and on the few open days the baths were unpleasantly crowded. Each night, watchmen patrolled the streets, clapping wooden blocks together and calling out to the neighborhood to be careful of fire.

By the middle of month, the population of Edo declined noticeably as wealthy samurai and merchant families moved the women and children out of the city to the safety of the countryside.

Ichi found his income from massage sadly reduced, as fewer customers called for his services. He passed more than one afternoon walking the streets, blowing his whistle in vain, without being summoned into a single house. Although he was living at the Tōdōza residence, he was still expected to pay his own way.

When Gen invited him out for yet another night of drinking, he was forced to decline. She did not press him, but to his surprise, the following night she invited him to play the shamisen with her in a performance at a private party in Kagurazaka, and afterward shared part of the fee with him.

Late, late at night, after the clients had passed out drunk and the owner of the teahouse had handed over their payment, Ichi and Gen walked home along the gentle slope of the main street, companionably arm in arm, with their shamisen wrapped in cloth and slung over their backs. The air was cold and so dry that Ichi's throat, sore from hours of chanting, ached with each breath. Yet they did not feel the cold, as the clients had shared many bottles of sake with them. Ichi walked with a swaying, rolling gait, but beside him Gen felt solid and reassuring.

Faintly at first, then overwhelmingly his nose burned with the unmistakable acrid scent.

"Fire!" He gripped Gen's elbow more tightly.

Gen craned her neck to see over the roofs of the low buildings on either side of the street. They were still near the top of the slope, heading toward the Kanda River and Iidabashi Bridge.

"Oh yes, I believe I see the smoke," Gen said, unconcerned. A dark smudge stood uncertainly against the black night sky. "Ah, wait, now I see the flames. Looks to be coming from a teahouse near the bottom of the hill. It's not such a large fire, only one building. Come, let's continue."

As they approached the unfortunate teahouse, Ichi heard the steady banging of a hammer on a bronze bell, the fire alarm, bringing the sound of running feet and the rhythmic cries of the firemen as they hefted the matoi standard.

"That voice!" he remarked. "Is it Heihachirō?"

"Why yes," Gen replied in surprise. "I ain't seen him since the new year."

The burly boss loped down the hill, calling out to the members of his gang as he went in his booming voice. They were all clad in heavy padded jackets, elaborately embroidered with fearsome dragons, demons, and warriors. The jackets had all been soaked in water. The youngest member of the gang hefted the matoi, the head of which was decorated with a large white wooden diamond shape, painted with the kanji for five, indicating the block number of the location of their headquarters. The bearer scrambled up a ladder to the roof of a nearby building, shouting and waving the matoi to warn others in the neighborhood. The long white streamers fluttered against the night sky.

The rest of the gang quickly set to work with their hooks and axes, tearing down the buildings on either side of the teahouse. This was the only strategy of firefighters in Edo, to let the fire burn itself out while trying to prevent it from spreading. The owner of the teahouse had already used up the contents of the large water bucket in front, but it was not nearly enough, and there was no means to easily bring more from the well.

Ichi and Gen joined the small group of onlookers gathered before the burning teahouse.

"The fire doesn't look that big," Gen observed. "Too bad for the owner, but the rest of the neighborhood should be safe."

Ichi nodded. He could hear the owner of the teahouse shouting invectives at a maid whom he blamed for not minding the kitchen fire. Beside him, his wife wailed and bemoaned their bad luck. The geisha who had been hired for the evening were entreating the firemen to help them save their instruments, but the firemen were ignoring them.

"Hold this," Gen said, thrusting her shamisen into Ichi's startled hands. Before he realized what was happening, she rushed off.

Ichi shifted from foot to foot anxiously, straining his ears, but he could hear nothing above the shouts of the firemen and the crashing of beams as they tore down the neighboring houses. The owners of the teahouses being demolished stood about muttering philosophically about how many times they had been burned out before. At least this time they would be able to salvage most of their possessions and cash from the wreckage later, if the fire did not spread.

A few minutes later, Ichi heard Gen's voice again, to his vast relief.

"Here!" she said, coughing a bit. "I got three shamisen that were in the front room. Are these yours?"

A chorus of young women's voices thanked her, sobbing with relief. Without their instruments they would have no income at all.

"Sorry I can't go look for more," Gen said gently. "The fire ain't that big but there's a lot of smoke." She coughed again. "Whew! I tell ya, I could barely breathe."

The geisha thanked her again profusely, but she waved them off, clapping an arm around Ichi's shoulders.

"We gotta go! Goodnight! Take care!" Gen called behind her, steering Ichi down the street, away from the fire and toward the bridge.

"My, but that was brave of you," Ichi said in a tone of wonder. As they walked along, he shifted out from under her arm to instead hold her elbow. She was taller than he, and her arms seemed amazingly strong for a woman. "Are you quite all right?"

Gen gave another cough. "I'm fine. I felt sorry for those girls, with no one helping them. But let that be a lesson to both of us, when there is a fire, always be sure to grab the most valuable things before running out the door."

16

The Bath House

The month of Kisaragi brought no relief from the drought and high winds. Day after day the sun shone bright in a cloudless blue sky. Ichi found the skin on the backs of his hands unpleasantly rough and cracked, and his lips chapped and peeled. A feeling of tense unease hung over the city, now more than ever a city of men, with so many of the wives and daughters sent to the countryside. Those who were left were anxious and preoccupied, and he found precious few customers.

The Omigawa daimyō's period of attendance in Edo was drawing to a close and preparations were underway to move back to the domain in Shimōsa province, save for those retainers such as Tomonosuke who were posted permanently to the city. As the lower residence in Takadanobaba would now be shut up again, Tomonosuke was obliged to move his household to a small nagaya or row house located in the Iga-chō neighborhood, close by the Hanzōmon Gate to Edo Castle.

Okyō was greatly relieved for the long-anticipated move, not only because she and Rin could now be together again. It would be good to live in the city center, and to be living near other low-ranking samurai of various domains. Their new quarters were no more than two small rooms, connected by paper-thin walls to the long row of identical rooms, and they were obliged to share the well, outhouse, and shrine with all the other residents. But at least the higher-ranking wives who had been tormenting her at the lower residence would not be living nearby. The new house was not so different from their accommodations in Sawara, and that suited her well enough.

Tomonosuke had no thought to spare for the new housing arrangements, as the daimyō's imminent departure kept him busy all day long, examining and reexamining the financial records. Now he was more certain than ever that there was an error, or rather, a pervasive pattern of errors. The lists of debits and credits balanced out, but somehow it seemed that small amounts were missing here and there. Someone was skimming cash from the accounts, then covering his tracks. Not a large sum all at once, but over time it seemed to be a substantial quantity.

Tomonosuke uneasily eyed Matsudaira Sadahide, who was clacking officiously at his abacus from his seat at the front of the room. It wasn't hard to guess who might be doing this. Tomonosuke did not dare approach him directly, or even discreetly. Such a scheming fellow would be dangerous if confronted.

Pretending to tally a line of sums, Tomonosuke pondered whom he could turn to. The daimyō's son, he thought. Uchida Kiyochika had instructed Tomonosuke to come to him with any difficulty. True, the young lord had been referring to Tomonosuke's personal life, which he had no intention of revealing. But surely this was of far greater importance. If Tomonosuke requested an audience, he was certain it would be granted.

The very next afternoon, Tomonosuke found himself summoned to the upper residence in Yotsuya for an audience with the young lord, less than a day after submitting his request.

Tomonosuke bowed low on the tatami mats, which had lost their greenish tinge. Had it only been a few months since he was here last?

Kiyochika lounged on an armrest and smiled blandly at him. "You're looking well, Tomonosuke. What brings you here? Good news with your wife, I hope?"

Tomonosuke blushed, his heart beating even faster. "No, my lord. It is not a personal matter that brings me here."

"What then?" Kiyochika's smile fell away.

"My lord, it pains me to say it, but I believe there is a discrepancy in the domain's account ledgers."

"A discrepancy?"

"To put it plainly, I have seen signs of embezzlement."

Kiyochika started up in surprise. "Indeed? That's a very serious charge."

"Yes, my lord." Tomonosuke spoke slowly, choosing his words carefully. "It is a delicate matter, calling for the utmost discretion, which is why I have come to you directly, rather than...anyone else." He deliberately emphasized those last two words.

"Hmm, yes, thank you." Kiyochika leaned back again, with a concerned expression. "You did the right thing in coming to me. I shall look into this very carefully, as you say."

"Thank you, my lord." Tomonosuke exhaled the breath he did not realize he had been holding.

He walked home again with a lighter step, congratulating himself on choosing this course of action. Surely the young lord had taken his meaning. Tomonosuke did not dare to accuse Sadahide by name, but what other reason could he have for going over his superior's head? Kiyochika would investigate and set things right, he was certain.

As Tomonosuke walked along the dry street, his wooden sandals kicking up clouds of dust, he heard the temple bells ringing seven times: so, the hour of the monkey already. He scratched at his dusty neck, wondering if the bath house would not be too crowded. Since moving to Iga-chō, Tomonosuke had taken to frequenting the bath house at the end of his block, which while communal, was designated for samurai-class customers only.

Before moving to Edo, Tomonosuke had heard some very shocking tales of the disorder of the city's bath houses: open prostitution, dirty lukewarm water, mixed bathing, or at the most a sheet hung across a single large tub to divide the men from the women, with no separation in the changing area. While that was undoubtedly true in some of the downtown baths for townspeople, he was relieved to find his neighborhood bath was not like that, but kept strictly separate hours for men and women. The water was clean enough, considering it had to be piped in, and very hot.

Just as he rounded the corner and saw the smoke rising from the chimney of the bath house, Tomonosuke spotted a familiar figure clad in indigo cotton tapping down the street. As he watched, Ichi blew the repetitive notes on his whistle, his face turned up slightly to the sky, his eyes half closed. Tomonosuke realized with a jolt that if he never spoke, Ichi, who had doubtless come to this neighborhood in search of him, would pass by without ever knowing he was there. He felt ashamed at his lack of consideration.

"Ichi!" Tomonosuke jogged up to him, heedless of the undignified slapping of his wooden sandals as he hurried up the street.

At the sound of his voice, Ichi was brought up short and turned, his face transformed with a happy smile, although his eyes remained half closed. Tomonosuke felt a stirring at the sight of Ichi's pure, uncomplicated pleasure at hearing his voice.

"Uchida-dono! I was hoping to meet you, but Rin said you were out."

Tomonosuke rubbed the back of his neck. "I was called away unexpectedly, but never mind." He had no desire to go into more detail of his audience with the young lord. "Come, we are standing before the bath house. We're in luck today—it's not too windy. I was about to go in for a dip. Won't you join me?"

Ichi gave him a cheeky grin. "Everyone will think you're my customer."

The bath house might be for samurai only, but an anma would not be out of place there. Feeling suddenly, uncharacteristically lighthearted, Tomonosuke placed his arm around Ichi's shoulders companionably.

"And why not? It's been too long since I had a massage from you. Come, let's go in the water then we can relax over a drink after." The second floor of the bath house was a lounge where customers could enjoy a game of shōgi or a drink or a massage after the bath.

The noren curtain at the entrance bore the kanji for male, indicating that it was the men's time in the bathhouse. The women's hours were earlier in the afternoon and later in the evening. Tomonosuke brushed the curtain aside, carefully holding it out of Ichi's way as they both ducked slightly to enter. He handed over a few small coins to the old hag sitting by the entrance, for himself and Ichi, plus a few more to purchase two small towels and a small bag of rice bran to wash with.

Tomonosuke guided Ichi into the changing room, where they stripped off their kimono and fundoshi and piled them in a basket. Tomonosuke stood his katana and wakizashi along with Ichi's cane in a corner, trusting that no one would disturb them. It was still afternoon, and only a few old men crept about the changing room, slowly rewinding their loincloths.

The entrance to the bath was a door with a very low lintel to keep the steam in, so low they had to bend almost double. Tomonosuke placed Ichi's hand on it so he could find his way. Once inside, he picked up two small wooden buckets and guided Ichi to the edge of the large communal bath. Perhaps it was because they were both naked, but somehow Tomonosuke found the act of taking Ichi's hand to show him about surprisingly intimate.

They dipped water from the bath and sluiced it over themselves, then took turns scrubbing with the bran bag, scraping away the sweat and dust of the day. Usually Tomonosuke visited the bath on his own, but as Ichi vigorously scrubbed his back for him, he reflected on how pleasant it was to have a companion.

As they finished washing, the one other customer exited the bath, nodding silently to Tomonosuke as he departed, so they had the entire bath to themselves.

"Ah, it's so hot!" Ichi exclaimed as he stepped over the ledge and into the wooden tub.

Tomonosuke eased himself in beside him. "I know. I think that old hag keeps it a bit too hot on purpose, so the customers don't linger." The tub could only fit five or six people comfortably. "Be careful not to get light-headed," he added.

Tomonosuke submerged to his shoulders and leaned back against the side of the tub with a sigh, letting his body relax in the hot water. His skin prickled and tingled with the heat, but it was a soothing sensation. The room was densely humid and dim, the only light coming from a small square window near the ceiling. Tendrils of steam curled upwards from the surface of the water. It was like entering another realm—a twilight, water-logged world. The only sounds were the sloshing of the water in the tub, a few tinkling drops falling back in from the ceiling like indoor rain, and distantly, the whoosh of the bellows outside stoking the fire that heated the water.

Tomonosuke stared at Ichi, sitting across from him in the tub. Only the very tops of his shoulders remained above the water, his white skin flushed pink with the heat. His hair had grown out a few inches again and stood at odd angles all around his head, giving him a sweetly boyish appearance. Tomonosuke felt he could never tire of looking into Ichi's face—his full red lips, dewy white cheeks, and those half-closed eyes that never looked back at him. Looking at that white-grey band beneath his uneven lids, Tomonsuke found strangely moving, like beholding a ruined castle or a chipped tea bowl. It made him want to protect Ichi from the unkind world, but even more than that, it stirred him to passion.

Tomonosuke glanced at the low door, but there was no sign of anyone entering from the changing room. Impulsively, he pushed through the water to Ichi's side and embraced him. Ichi's brows shot up in surprise, and his cheeks turned from pink to red.

"My lord—?"

Tomonosuke pressed his body against Ichi's, enjoying the slick sensation of the water between their skin. "Hush, there's no one else here," he whispered huskily in his ear. He leaned down to kiss Ichi firmly on the mouth, and in response, Ichi returned the kiss eagerly, stretching his neck upwards. Their bodies pressed together even closer under water, and Ichi wrapped his legs around his middle. Tomonosuke cupped his rump, enjoying the silky sensation of his skin in the water.

Did he dare enter him in the water? It was certainly not unheard of to enjoy a carnal embrace in the public bath, if a bit unseemly. The thought that someone might walk in at any moment simultaneously stayed him and stoked his desire. As they kissed over and over, their bodies pressed together, Tomonosuke felt Ichi's cock harden and jump urgently. His opening was right there, only a few inches away. They rocked their hips together, slowly moving closer and closer, making small waves and ripples in the bath water.

Suddenly, Tomonosuke realized the rocking sensation was becoming more pronounced, enough to slosh the water out of the tub in waves. The waves were far greater than what they alone were producing.

"Earthquake!" Ichi gasped, now clinging to him with a different sort of urgency. Their erections wilted as the shaking increased, replaced by dread. This was no place to be in an earthquake: stark naked, wet, and sitting atop a large fire that could easily spread. For a breathless moment they both froze, waiting to find out if the shaking would get worse or subside. Could this be the moment the sōkengyō had warned them of? The bath house rocked alarmingly two or three more times, the water cascading out of the tub, then just as suddenly, the shaking stopped as if nothing had happened, the only remaining evidence the slowing eddies in the tub.

Their passion now cooled, Tomonosuke and Ichi silently climbed out of the bath. As he stood, Tomonosuke saw stars and flashes of light for a second, feeling overheated and slightly light-headed from staying the hot water too long. Beside him, Ichi also looked pale and shaky. They crept back to the changing room, Tomonosuke with his arm around Ichi's shoulders. As they dried off with the small towels and dressed, the cool dry air soon restored their senses, although Tomonosuke still felt his spirits oppressed by a heavy foreboding.

Ichi rubbed the towel on his head, making his hair stand out at even crazier angles.

"Is it true that earthquakes are caused by a giant catfish flipping its tail?" he asked.

"I don't know. It sounds like nonsense to me."

"But if not a giant catfish, then what? What force is strong enough to make the earth shake like that?"

"I don't know," Tomonosuke replied shortly, feeling a flash of unreasonable anger and frustration at not being able to reassure Ichi, who still looked pale and anxious. "The gods, probably."

Ichi shuddered as he pulled on his indigo kimono. "There have been so many tremors lately. I hate it! Do you think there will be a big quake as the sōkengyō said?"

"I'm sure it will be all right," Tomonosuke said hollowly, although he was not at all sure. The oppressive sense of foreboding only increased.

17

The Vernal Equinox

The next day was the vernal equinox, as the early cold days of spring gave way to warmer weather. At the last quarter of the hour of the rabbit, the sun rose in a cloudless blue sky. Rin pushed open the sliding doors to the outside, and beyond the low eaves of the row house, skylarks and swallows could be seen flitting through the clear air.

Tomonosuke stretched and rubbed his neck sleepily, while behind him Okyō scooped out his morning rice from a wooden tub into a small chipped bowl. The freshly cooked half-polished rice, mixed with barley, steamed gently in the cool morning air.

"Is that a nightingale?" Tomonosuke asked idly, listening to the sharp, clear notes.

"Yes, there seems to be one nesting in the tree by the well," Okyō observed.

Tomonosuke breathed in the chill air deeply, wondering at hearing such a lovely bird even in the middle of the crowded city.

Just as he sat down before his tray, there was a loud clattering and shouting in the alleyway. A moment later, three guards in curving black lacquer caps with the stylized horse bit crest of the Uchida clan appeared before the open door. Tomonosuke stared at them in surprise, the chopsticks dangling from his fingers. He recognized them as guards posted to the daimyō's upper residence.

"Uchida Tomonosuke, bannerman and clerk of the exchequer!" one of the guards declared in a stentorian voice, brandishing a letter withdrawn from the fold of his kimono. He paused to unfold the letter then continued, "Uchida Tomonosuke, bannerman and clerk of the exchequer, you are hereby placed under arrest for the crime of embezzlement, by order of the Omigawa daimyō!" He waved the letter in Tomonosuke's face, displaying the official seals of the daimyō and the senior counselor, as the other two guards kicked off their sandals and ran into the house to grab him by either arm.

Tomonosuke was so shocked he could not even move. He watched as if from a great distance as the chopsticks and rice bowl fell from his hands to the wood floor. Feeling almost detached from his own body, he put up no resistance as the two guards hustled him out of the house, pausing for a moment to step back into their sandals. Tomonosuke did the same without thinking. They frogmarched him through the alleyway into the street, bareheaded and without his swords at his side. All he could think was that this was the first time in his adult life he had ventured outside without his katana and wakizashi, and he felt strangely light, almost naked without them.

In the main street a horse stood waiting, held by a fourth guard. They manhandled him up into the saddle and tied his hands to the pommel, then set off for the upper residence. He was only vaguely aware of the sound of Okyō's voice, screaming and sobbing behind him as the guard led the horse away. He did not turn around, but stared fixedly at his tied hands.

The guards did not take him directly to an audience with the daimyō, as Tomonosuke expected, but led the horse around to a far distant corner of the upper residence. They pulled him from the horse and threw him in a small jail cell. For domanial matters, daimyō were allowed to mete out their own justice, apart from the shogunal courts. Tomonosuke remained in the cell for a day and a night, during which time his mind at last cleared, blank surprise replaced with frustration.

This must be a mistake, he was sure of it. If only he could explain himself to the daimyō, all would be made right. But the daimyō was not here, he realized. He had gone back to the domain two days previous, along with the senior counselor. It must have been the young lord who placed the seals on the arrest warrant, but no matter. Tomonosuke had already spoken to him—if only he could see him again, surely Kiyochika would realize his error.

The next morning, the guards escorted Tomonosuke around the estate, into the main hall. Feeling disheveled and dusty, Tomonosuke knelt on the tatami and gave the three-finger bow as precisely as he knew how. Hearing a word of approval from the far end of the hall, he raised his head to see with dismay Kiyochika seated on a cushion at the head of the hall with Sadahide at his side, along with several other high ranking bannermen. Tomonosuke tried to keep his face neutral, even as he felt the blood drain from his head, his heart hammering. Why had Sadahide not returned to the domain with the daimyō? And how could Kiyochika have failed to heed his warning?

"Uchida Tomonosuke, bannerman and clerk of the exchequer," Kiyochika said, not unkindly. "I'm very disappointed and concerned that it's come to this. As you know, my honored father the daimyō held your late father in the highest regard. What could have compelled you to bring such shame on your family's good name?"

"My lord..." Tomonosuke choked out, then fell silent. What could he possibly say with Sadahide sitting right there?

"Did I not invite you to come to me with any difficulty?" Kiyochika continued.

Tomonosuke bowed his head in silence, thinking bitterly how little good that had done him.

"My lord, I believe I know what happened," Sadahide offered in a low voice, as if he were unsure if he should speak out.

Kiyochika turned to him in surprise. "Indeed?"

"I hesitate to mention such vulgar matters in the presence of the young lord, but honor compels me to inform you that Tomonosuke has been seen visiting a courtesan in the Yoshiwara pleasure quarters."

"What! But this is very shocking!" Kiyochika turned to Tomonosuke with an appalled expression. "Do you deny it?"

Tomonosuke averted his eyes, his cheeks burning. He could not lie to the young lord. How had Sadahide heard of this? Was he being spied on?

"Oh yes," Sadahide continued in an insinuating tone. "He quite seduced an oiran and made her form an attachment with him. She's been telling tales of what a prodigious lover he is, and how he intends to redeem her contract."

Kiyochika's eyes widened. "Oh my! Well, that explains why you were stealing money from the domain's coffers. Did you really intend to abandon your poor wife to run off with a courtesan? For shame!"

"No!" At last Tomonosuke's control cracked, and the word leapt out unexpectedly. "My lord, I deny it! I did no such thing, and I did not steal the money!"

"Even now, with the sword practically at his neck, see how shamelessly he lies!" Sadahide sneered.

"Yes, I see. When Tomonosuke came to me to warn me of a discrepancy in the accounts, I was so concerned that I went straight to you to inquire, and I am very glad I did. Now I see he was merely attempting to muddy the waters to conceal his own crime, the sly dog. It's really very shocking to think there could be such disloyalty within our own clan."

"Yes, my lord," Sadahide murmured piously.

"Well, in a case such as this it will never do to be lenient. We must send a message not only to our own retainers but to other clans as well, that the Uchida clan will not tolerate such degenerate, wanton behavior. Take him away."

"No, my lord! Please, allow me to explain!" Tomonosuke felt his belly fill with ice, and in a panic he shouted without reserve, even as the guards dragged him out of the hall.

Back in the jail cell, Tomonosuke paced back and forth. Would he truly be executed? It was too horrible to contemplate, yet he could not stop recalling his conversation with Kiyochika over and over, wishing he had said something different, anything that would have saved him from Sadahide's trap. He felt as if he were on fire, expecting at any moment the guards to return with the white kimono and tantō knife, to lead him to the execution ground.

But the only guards who appeared were bearing his meager prison rations, or changing the watch. The hours stretched into days, and it seemed his execution was not imminent.

On the fourth day, the guards allowed Okyō, accompanied by Rin, to speak with him through the barred door. The cell was no more than a shack with a packed earth floor, covered with matting. The windows stood open to the elements, covered only with bamboo bars. It was not particularly secure, but even if he did break out, where would he go? He was still within the daimyō's estate, surrounded by nearly a hundred retainers of various ranks.

Okyō peered in the square window cut in the door, her face partially obscured by the bamboo bars. Her usually lush features were pale and drawn, and Tomonosuke felt a pang of sympathy for her. She had never wanted to be married to him, but now what would become of her?

Without bothering to rise from the rush matting, Tomonosuke bowed his head and muttered, "I hope you will marry again, to a man who can bring you greater happiness than I."

"What?" Okyō squinted irritably into the darkness. "What are you mumbling about? Stand up already! I brought you some food."

Reluctantly, he dragged himself to the door and received the small bundle wrapped in a dried bamboo leaf she shoved between the bars.

"Thank you." He bowed, holding up the bundle to his forehead.

Okyō frowned. "Don't get too excited. It's just okaka." This simple meal of dried seasoned fish in a rice ball seemed to him almost painfully homey.

"I'm still grateful. You didn't have to come at all. Okyō, I'm so sorry."

Okyō snorted dismissively. "Don't be. I know you didn't steal the money, and as for that girl in Yoshiwara, it's laughable. I was there. I know what really happened."

"It doesn't matter. I've brought shame on the family. After I'm gone, I want you to remarry."

"Stop talking like that!"

Tomonosuke leaned his head against the bars. "So when is the execution to be held?"

"I don't know," Okyō replied uneasily. "The young lord had to send to the daimyō for official permission, but the courier hasn't returned yet. There seems to be a delay, but I don't know why."

Tomonosuke sighed. It didn't matter. The courier would arrive any day now, and that would be the end.

"Please say goodbye to Ichi for me."

"Tell him yourself!" she replied tartly.

"What? He's here?" Tomonosuke strained to see out the small window in the door.

Okyō moved aside, and Rin led Ichi forward, placing his hand on the bars.

"My lord!" Ichi reached his fingers through the bars, and Tomonosuke grasped them.

"My lord, please do not lose hope! Okyō-dono has sent a letter to your mother explaining everything."

Tomonosuke sighed. If anyone could intercede on his behalf with the daimyō, it was Lady Chacha. Assuming, of course, that she believed Okyō's account and did not choose to side with Kiyochika in falling for Sadahide's slander. If she thought he had dishonored the family, not only would she not attempt to save him, she would most likely make the trip to Edo to witness his execution herself.

He twined his fingers in Ichi's strong ones regretfully. At least Ichi, unlike Okyō, did not rely on him for his livelihood. He would still have his place in the Tōdōza. With a sudden pang, Tomonosuke felt irrationally sad at not knowing the end of *The Legend of Eight Dogs*, not being able to read it aloud to Ichi and share it with him. He pushed his fingers through the bars and laid them along Ichi's smooth cheek. It would have been better for Ichi if they had never met.

"My lord!" Ichi choked out. Tomonosuke felt tears slip over his fingers, and he was too overcome to speak.

"My lord, this is not the end, I promise you," Ichi said in a fervent whisper. "I have been praying to Kannon-sama every day. The Goddess of Mercy will not neglect one as virtuous as you, I'm sure of it."

Tomonosuke stroked Ichi's cheek tenderly, the tips of his fingers just reaching through the bars. "Ichi, I do not deserve such a loyal brother."

The word just slipped out. Tomonosuke did not realize its import until he heard Ichi's sharply indrawn breath and saw the surprise flit across his features. But just at that moment, the guard called out that their visit was long enough, and hustled them away. Tomonosuke stood at the door, watching Okyō stalk off with her nose in the air, as proud and elegant if she were the daimyō's wife, while Rin hurried behind her, with Ichi's hand on her arm.

Even after they disappeared around a corner, Tomonosuke stood staring at the place they had been. Somehow, witnessing their concern for him only made him feel more dejected. Why had he not formally pledged himself to Ichi as a brother long before now? Why had he not treated Okyō more kindly? He thought he had been leading a virtuous life, but now it all felt as fleeting and insubstantial as bubbles on water.

18

The Catfish

Ichi followed Rin home in a daze, hardly registering the sounds of the city around them as they walked, not noticing where he was. Ever since Rin had run frantically to find him at the Tōdōza residence, to tell him through panicked sobs that her master had been arrested, Ichi had felt as if he were moving slowing through a waking dream.

It was uncommonly kind of Okyō to bring Ichi along when Kiyochika at last granted her repeated requests to visit Tomonosuke in jail. Okyō might have used this crisis as an opportunity to at last rid herself of Ichi's presence in her life, but to the contrary, she seemed to find comfort in having him about. At her request, he had even been staying overnight with them in the row house. If he could do nothing to aid Tomonosuke, he at least could help Rin and Okyō. Not that he could have protected them from anything, but Ichi took it on himself to remain calm and reassuring, even as Rin trembled with fear and Okyō's temper was worse than ever.

This forced hopefulness took a toll on him, however, as internally he was far less certain. The world of the samurai had always seemed distant to him, but he knew enough of their ways to doubt that the daimyō might show mercy. During the day, he showed a cheerful face but at night he lay awake, his heart pounding with anxiety.

When Ichi had first lost his sight as a child, for some time he had been afraid to take a single step. At each moment, he felt as if he were standing at the edge of an abyss. Even in familiar rooms, somehow he could not help imagining that the next step might be into nothingness. As he learned to trust his feet, his cane, and his ears, the sensation faded. Matsuichi kengyō had taught him how to walk confidently, how to let go of fear. And he had. But now the sensation returned—not with each step, but as time passed and they waited, he felt as if they were all about to tumble into the void.

On the way back to Iga-chō from the upper residence, Ichi was so distracted by his racing thoughts that he scarcely noticed where they were going, trusting Rin to guide him. Tomonosuke had called him brother, the word he had longed to hear, although under better circumstances, to be sure. His cheek still glowed with the rough touch of Tomonosuke's fingers, communicating his affection even in this extreme state. This was not a formal pledge, but even so, his loyalty was evident. Ichi felt ashamed to have ever doubted him.

The thought that this pledge might be too late made Ichi's chest and throat contract painfully and his head spin as he stumbled along behind Rin, heedless of the noise and stink of the streets around him. Tales of wild affection between men who were pledged companions so often ended in death—one or both partners dying heroically, selflessly, while others praised their chivalry and virtue. Ichi had thrilled to these stories himself. But now he found it bitter and frustrating. He did not feel like a virtuous hero. It was deeply unfair to lose Tomonosuke to such a petty, fabricated charge.

When they returned to the row house in Iga-chō, Okyō inquired with the neighbors if there had been any messages or letters delivered while they were out, but there were not. She had been asking and asking each day, but the reply from Lady Chacha never came.

Hearing the note of desperation in her voice brought Ichi out of his reverie, and he resumed his role as her protector. At his gentle suggestion, Okyō and Rin went to the bath house, and returned feeling slightly refreshed.

There being nothing else to do, Rin set about preparing the evening meal. Okyō watched her boiling the rice and barley. She had not said anything yet to Rin or Ichi, but with Tomonosuke in jail, his stipend had been stopped. She had a little cash saved up, but not much.

They ate the last of the okaka over the rice and barley, with strips of dried daikon simmered in soy sauce as the only side dish.

"I'm sure we'll hear from Lady Chacha soon," Ichi said quietly, as they crunched the daikon. "Perhaps the reason the daimyō has not replied yet is because she has convinced him not to go ahead with...you know..."

"Or perhaps the courier met with an accident and they will soon send another," Okyō snapped. "We can't know."

They continued eating in silence.

In the next moment, it was as if the world turned upside down. Ichi was just reaching for his tray to set his bowl back down when everything flew up in the air with a tremendous crashing roar, the loudest noise he had ever heard in his life.

"Earthquake!" he heard Rin shriek beside him, and he reached for her. This was not the lurching swaying motion of a few days ago, but instead the house seemed to jump violently up and down, the terrible force of the vibration throwing them to the floor. All around, he could hear crockery breaking, people screaming, and the horrifying sounds of the wooden houses rending apart. All he could think of as he clung to Rin was the giant catfish flipping its tail in the mud, turning the city to flying, crashing chaos.

The unbearable shaking seemed to go on and on. Ichi covered Rin with his arms, expecting at any moment to feel the roof collapse on top of them. But just as suddenly, the earthquake stopped, replaced by eerie silence.

"Okyō-dono?" Ichi called fearfully, but to his relief she answered immediately.

Rin rushed into her arms. "Are you unhurt?"

"I'm fine," Okyō said without reflection.

"But you're bleeding!"

Okyō put a hand to her forehead and stared wonderingly at the red smear on her fingers. She did not feel the gash at all. Rin pressed a folded towel to her brow. The cut was not large or deep, but it bled prodigiously.

"And you?" Okyō asked with concern, staring at Rin.

"Ichi-san protected me," she said in a small voice.

They turned together to look at him. "Ichi-san?" Okyō asked.

Ichi rolled his shoulders and ran a hand over his shaved head. "Something fell on me, but I'm all right." He could feel a knot at the back of his head, and his shoulders were bruised, but his fingers felt dry. If he was not bleeding, he was not seriously hurt, he reasoned, still scarcely comprehending what had happened.

"Part of the ceiling came down, but the greater part of the roof has fallen into the alley, and taken one of the walls with it," Okyō reported stoically.

"Thank the gods it fell away from us," Ichi said in wonderment.

"We can't stay here. There will certainly be aftershocks," Okyō replied.

"Yes, but where do we go? Surely the whole city is affected."

"We must go back to Tomonosuke," she declared in a tone that allowed no argument, as she tied a fresh towel around the gash on her forehead. "Rin, grab whatever clothing you can from the other room."

Ichi listened as they hurriedly pushed aside the jumbled household items and prepared to leave. Just as they were retrieving their sandals from the entryway, he cried out.

"Wait!"

Ichi ran back into the house, thinking of Shirataki Gen's reminder to always grab the most valuable items. With trembling fingers, he groped frantically in the alcove. There, in the corner, were Tomonosuke's katana and wakizashi, where he had left them before his arrest. Grasping the two swords in one hand and his cane in the other, Ichi ran back outside.

The ground lurched again with a sickening jolt, just as he was stepping down into the entryway, sending him tumbling to his knees. Rin shrieked, but the shaking stopped a moment later. With surprisingly sure fingers, Okyō took the swords from him and helped him to his feet. Rin handed him his sandals, and the three of them hurried off to the upper residence again.

When they reached the main street, Rin gasped and began reciting the Buddhist prayer under her breath, "Namu Amida Butsu, Namu Amida Butsu."

"What happened?" Ichi asked, clinging to her arm.

Okyō pressed up close to him on the opposite side. "So many of the houses have fallen down," she said in a stricken tone. "There are roof tiles everywhere, walls have come down, and the people...it's too horrible, I can't..." her voice trailed off. The moans of injured people and wailing of the bereaved were clear enough to him, even without her description.

They hurried along as fast as they could, but with the wreckage in the street their progress was slow. Ichi was ashamed at how often he stumbled, but the familiar streets were utterly transformed, every landmark wiped away, replaced by treacherous, uneven ground strewn with household items and debris from fallen houses. The two women walked on either side of him, steering him around the worst of it. By the time they reached the upper residence it was fully dark.

The kamo-yashiki of the Omigawa daimyō was in disarray. The proud, curving ceramic roof tiles had slid off half of the main hall, and partially collapsed the roof and outside wall at the front left corner. The outbuildings and walls were similarly destroyed, and shouts and cries could be heard from within.

At Okyō's direction, they did not dare to venture in the main gate, but slowly crept around the long, long outer wall to the servants' gate at the back. The gate stood open and unguarded, the door hanging off the hinges at an angle. Rin placed Ichi's hands on the door and they slipped in without being noticed.

Okyō led them around fallen roof tiles to the small shack that served as the daimyō's jail cell.

"Oh no!" she cried in dismay.

"What is it?" Ichi's hand clutched her arm in a sudden surge of fear.

"All the other buildings are damaged, but the jail is still intact and locked," she whispered. "Keep your voice down! The guards might come back at any moment."

It was true, the simple wooden walls of the shack had proved more flexible than the reinforced main buildings around it.

Okyō ran up to the door and peered in the small square window.

"Danna!" she called in an urgent whisper. "Danna! Are you there? Are you unhurt?"

They all breathed a sigh of relief when a dark shadow loomed before the door.

"Yes, I'm fine," Tomonosuke whispered back. "What are you doing here?"

"Breaking you out, obviously! Come on, hurry up!" Okyō snapped back, pulling frantically at the door, but the metal lock was undamaged and would not give.

"What?" Tomonosuke sounded stunned. "Why?"

"Why do you think! Do you want to stay there and wait to be executed? This is your chance, come on!"

"But—"

"But nothing! Were you hit on the head? Come, Ichi is waiting for you!"

Impatiently, Okyō abandoned the door and began searching around the walls of the shack. In the back left corner, she discovered that the two walls had been pulled apart slightly.

"Come here, help me open this!" she called in a low voice. With the three of them pulling from the outside and Tomonosuke pushing from the inside, they were able to wrench the opening wide enough for him to squeeze through.

Tomonosuke stood before them, blinking in surprise. His clothes were dirty and torn. His topknot had come loose and his hair hung about his shoulders in disarray. He looked exactly like what he was, an escaped criminal. His gaze at last focused on Okyō's face.

"Wife! Are you injured?" he asked with concern.

"It's nothing. I'm fine," she said impatiently, handing him his katana and wakizashi. He carefully unwound the cords and tied them securely about his waist, carried on by force of habit. The two of them stared at each other for a long moment, the unspoken question hanging in the air: now what? The guards would be back at any moment, and the whole residence was full of samurai and servants. If anyone spotted them, even in the dark, they would all be arrested again, if they were not cut down on the spot.

After thinking for a moment, Okyō pulled at the bundle of clothing Rin was carrying on her back. Drawing out one of her best kimono, she flung it over his head, somewhat regretfully noticing how the fine silk shone in the moonlight.

"Come, if anyone spots us from a distance, we are injured ladies escaping from the women's quarters. This will do well enough in the dark, and hopefully no one will draw too close."

The four of them huddled together, the two women trying somewhat unsuccessfully to conceal the two men between them. Tomonosuke hunched down with the kimono over his head, trying to be inconspicuous. Ichi caught his breath several times, his heart in his mouth as he heard distant cries and sounds of people digging through the wreckage, but to his relief, no one stopped them before they had squeezed through the broken back gate.

They paused for a moment in the shadow of the gate, all four at a loss now that they had escaped the residence.

Tomonosuke straightened his aching back, but kept the kimono over his head, holding it up with his two hands like a tent.

"I can't go back to Iga-chō. That's the first place they'll search for me," he said in a low voice.

"The row house was damaged anyway," Okyō added.

They were silent for a moment, as the reality of their position as fugitives slowly became apparent.

"What about the Sōroku yashiki?" Rin suggested in a small voice.

Tomonosuke shook his head. "I would never bring misfortune to the Tōdōza in that way. Besides, three sighted people including two women could never hide there for long."

"Shirataki Gen!" Ichi said suddenly, his face lighting up hopefully. "I know the address of the inn in Kanda where the Katsumata troupe is staying. She will shelter us for a few days, I'm sure of it."

19

The Flower of Edo

With no other plan in mind, Tomonosuke, Okyō, and Rin followed Ichi's directions north and east toward Kanda. As they hurried through the ravaged streets, away from the massive samurai estates and into the townspeople's neighborhoods, the scent of smoke hung heavy in the air.

Ichi noticed the acrid odor immediately, but did not say anything, as he was too intent on walking as fast as he could without stumbling. As before, Okyō and Rin supported him on either side, catching him as he tripped over broken roof tiles and fallen beams. Irrationally, he wished he was clinging to Tomonosuke instead, but there was no time for a joyful reunion between them.

As they crossed the Kanda River and entered the tightly-packed downtown, clouds of smoke roiled above the low houses and the dark sky was lit by flames popping up here and there. The earthquake had struck just as most households were preparing the evening meal and the bath houses were open, and now countless fires were spreading from house to house. The paper and stick houses, dried out from months without rain, were bursting into flames one after another, sending showers of sparks up into the night sky. The dreaded flower of Edo was in full bloom.

The streets were clogged with people, some trying to flee with as many of their possessions as possible, others calling in vain for help or simply wailing. The fire alarm bells clanged wildly, and here and there a fireman atop a roof waved a matoi, but the fires were far beyond containment.

At Ichi's direction, they ran east toward Hitotsubashi, but the flames only grew more intense. Soon they were battling against the tide of townspeople fleeing in the opposite direction, and Ichi despaired of ever reaching their destination. Even if they could find the inn, surely by now it would be engulfed in flames.

Among the fleeing crowd were more than a few firefighters, their fine brocade jackets singed. Tomonosuke watched with disgust as they fled their posts. Some of the townspeople they passed clearly felt the same way, and shouted abuse at them. The younger firefighters, looking terrified, did not bother to answer, if they heard at all. One of the older firefighters glanced over his shoulder as he ran, refusing to be shamed.

"It's hopeless!" he shouted. "Save yourselves!"

Two blocks ahead of them was a curtain of flames, sparks shooting up into the sky like fireworks. They came to a halt, stopped by the choking smoke and press of bodies.

Tomonosuke put a hand on Ichi's shoulder. "I don't think we can go any further," he said, trying to be gentle even though he had to shout to be heard above the crowd and the crackling fire.

But Ichi was not paying attention to him, instead swiveling his head around like a cat. "That voice!" he said, clutching at Tomonosuke's sleeve. "It's Heihachirō! Do you see him?"

"No! Where?"

Tomonosuke followed where Ichi was pointing, further down the street, drawing closer to the raging fire. There amid the crowd stood the burly gang boss, his head covered by a padded hood and his face streaked with soot. He was shouting and gesturing at the few remaining firefighters and directing the townspeople to safety. Tomonosuke could hardly believe Ichi had heard his voice above the din.

As they approached, Heihachirō swung around to stare at them in surprise.

"Ichi! What are you doing here! It ain't safe!" He immediately moved to escort them back the way they had come.

"Boss!" Ichi cried, before they could be borne away by the throng. "We're searching for Shirataki Gen! Have you seen her?"

"Yes, the entire Katsumata troupe got out just before the inn went up." Heihachirō jerked a thumb behind him, indicating the massive fire. "They went that way," he said, pointing to the blocks to the east, away from the fire.

Ichi thanked him as Tomonosuke led the four of them in the direction Heihachirō indicated, leaving the firefighters to their futile task. Tomonosuke glanced back just long enough to catch a glimpse of him running back towards the flames to rescue more people, his padded jacket outlined by the unnatural red glow.

They stumbled down the street, grateful for the gusts of clearer air as they headed away from the worst of the fire. They hurried down one block, then two, until Ichi picked his head up hopefully.

"It's Katsumata-san! I can hear his voice!"

In the darkness up ahead, Tomonosuke could just make out a knot of people pulling a handcart, all wearing matching jackets.

"O—iiii!" Tomonosuke shouted as loudly as he could, then began coughing.

Beside him, Ichi called, "Gen-san! Katsumata-san! Gen-saaaaan!" Despite his smaller stature, his voice was surprisingly powerful and carrying.

The troupe paused long enough for them to catch up. Gen rushed over to them with concern.

"Ichi! What are you doing here! Are you unhurt? Uchida-dono! I heard you were arrested..." She trailed off as the situation became apparent.

Ichi reached for her hand. "Please, Gen-san, you've got to help us. We don't have anywhere else to go."

"We're leaving Edo," she said. "The city is done for at least until next year. There's no more money to be made here. We're heading home to try our luck in the countryside."

Katsumata Gonzaemon, the troupe leader, picked up the bars of the cart again. "The fire will be here any minute," he said brusquely. "We're going down to the banks of the Sumida River, that should be safe from the flames. We'll follow the river north out of the city." Without waiting for a reply, he began pulling the cart again, and the rest of the troupe followed.

"Well then," Gen said somewhat sadly, turning to go.

"Take us with you!" It was Okyō, who had been following silently, but now pushed forward past Ichi and Tomonosuke. She stood with her fists balled, her dark eyes sparking in the last remnant of moonlight.

"What?"

"I said, we're going with you," Okyō declared. "I have some cash and some kimono we can sell. Help us get out of the city, so we can flee to the north."

Tomonosuke stared at her in surprise. To the north? Did she mean Omigawa, or back to her home in Echigo?

At last regaining some of her usual swagger, Gen gave her a twisted little smile and a careless shrug. "Very well, then. Let's go."

20

The False Papers

The first night, they slept for a few short hours along the banks of the Sumida River, dotted with the campfires of other groups of refugees. In the disorder, no one questioned who the samurai among the townspeople was. Everyone appeared equally wild and desperate.

The air was still chilly. Ichi curled up next to Tomonosuke, thinking certainly he would not be able to sleep, but the next thing he knew, the samurai was shaking him and saying it was daylight already. Ichi sat up groggily, rubbing his frozen limbs.

"Thank you for coming to get me," Tomonosuke said quietly.

"You should thank Okyō-dono. It was her idea."

Tomonosuke glanced over at Okyō, who was sleeping right next to him with Rin in her arms. As if she could feel the force of his regard, the moment he gazed at her, she rolled over and stared back at him with her glittering black eyes.

He nodded to her. "Wife, I thank you. You rescued me." His voice held a note of wonder, as if he could still scarcely believe what had happened.

Okyō frowned, but when she spoke her voice was kinder than usual.

"It was Ichi who remembered to take your swords as we fled the row house. I would have forgotten them."

Ichi rubbed a hand over his head, making his short hair stand up.

"I owe my life to all of you," Tomonosuke said stiffly.

Okyō sat up and stretched like a cat. Beside her, Rin also arose.

Tomonosuke stood, staring up at the bleak dawn sky, swinging his arms in an attempt to get warm. His hair still hung down around his shoulders.

Okyō frowned at him critically. "You look a sight," she said. "Come, let me tie your hair back. We may be homeless fugitives but we're not barbarians."

She pulled a braided cord from the pack Rin carried. He kneeled obediently before her and allowed her to comb his hair as best she could with her fingers. She could not achieve a topknot with no comb or hair oil, and only a thick braided cord for fastening an obi, so instead she gave him a simple queue high at the back of his head.

"There," she said, surveying her work. "You look very dashing, like a warrior of old."

Ichi perked up for the first time since they awakened. "Like one of the eight dog warriors? Let me see!" He reached out a hand, and Okyō guided it to Tomonosuke's head. "Yes, I believe you look just like Gakuzo!"

Only Rin sat apart, her mood not lightened.

"My lady, do you truly intend to go to the far north?" she whispered.

Okyō looked first at Rin, then at Tomonosuke as she spoke. "What choice do we have? We can't go back to Edo. We dare not go to Sawara. The Katsumata troupe is going north. We'll stay with them as long as we may, then head to Echigo."

"If they allow it," Tomonosuke muttered darkly, shaking himself free of Ichi and Okyō. Just as he stood, Gen strode over from where the troupe was camped a few paces away, her hakama swishing through the tall grass and shaking off the dew.

"They'll allow it," she said, clapping him on the shoulder. He startled at the overly familiar gesture. "I had a word with Gonza and he agreed to let you all come with us."

Tomonosuke blinked at her in surprise. "But that will be very dangerous for you. I don't wish to bring misfortune on the troupe. And none of us have traveling papers."

Gen had shrugged off one of her kimono sleeves like a man, revealing the strips of cloth wound about her chest. She reached her arm up through the middle of the garment to rub her chin thoughtfully. "Well, you'll have to go in disguise, of course. We can forge your papers, but we'll need to think of a plausible alias for you as members of the troupe."

"Forge—?" Tomonosuke stared at her in shock, while Okyō gave a dry laugh from where she still crouched on the ground.

"No one will ever believe this stiff old samurai is a traveling performer," Okyō said.

Gen smirked at her. "We'll need papers for you too, Kyō-chan. I don't suppose you can do the Echigo lion dance?"

Okyō laughed even harder. The lion dance was a daring display of acrobatic skill, usually performed by children, not something to be undertaken by an amateur. "I suppose Rin and I will have to be servants to the troupe," she said.

Gen joined her laughter. "The idea of you passing as a servant, my lady, is even more implausible than your honored husband," she said with mock politesse. "We'll think of something." She turned to Ichi. "Zatō-san, have you your papers?"

Ichi shook his head regretfully. "To my shame, I left them at the Sōroku yashiki."

"Well, no matter, your papers are easily created."

"Do you really think so little of forging official documents?" Tomonosuke burst in suddenly, still staring at the dawn sky abstractedly.

"Of course! Samurai-san, what an innocent you are in the ways of the world! Do you really think the Katsumata troupe would have any papers at all if we didn't create them ourselves?"

"You don't have to do this," Ichi said, frowning. "I'm sorry we're creating so much trouble for you. I should have thought of that before asking for your help."

"Not at all!" Gen crouched down and took his hand, squeezing it gently. "Ichi-san, I owe you a debt, and if I can repay it by helping your elder brother, I'm happy to do so."

"But—"

"Stop! I said it's fine. Please don't worry. Gonza doesn't mind, as long as we can put you all to work in one way or another. Besides, I would never refuse a Tōdōza member who asked for my help, or my mother's ghost would come back and haunt me, haha!" She patted his hand companionably.

* * *

The first day, they took the road very easy, after the alarms of the previous night, keeping to the less populated areas and eating the small amount of food they had brought with them, supplemented with a few sweetfish from the river, spitted on sticks and roasted by the fire. But they would have to go among people, stay in towns and travel on the main roads if they hoped to make any money performing, so on the second day, they made for Sōka-juku, the first post town outside Edo on the Ōshū Road that led to the northern provinces.

After some discussion around the campfire, it was decided that Okyō would be described in her papers as an apprentice shamisen player, with the honorific O dropped from her name. To her chagrin, the other members of the troupe immediately followed Gen's example in calling her Kyō-chan. Oboro took her aside to show her a few basic chords.

Tomonosuke's name was to be shortened to Tomo, with no surname of course, and he would be described as a laborer, engaged to pull the cart and do other menial tasks. Gonza found some indigo trousers and a jacket for him, threadbare and none too clean. Tomonosuke set aside his crested kimono and striped hakama regretfully, then carefully hid his two swords underneath the cart. The contents of the cart would be searched at the checkpoints, but hopefully not the underside.

Rin was made a tumbler, and sent to learn a few moves. Ichi, of course, did not have to change his name nor his occupation.

Standing beside the cart, Oboro drew up all the documents, balancing the rolled paper in one hand and deftly wielding the brush with the other. Her brow furrowed in concentration as she held the brush perpendicular to the page and boldly traced out the angular characters of the passports. It would not do to hesitate, or the uncertainty would show in her calligraphy. These documents were all the same, and she had many years' practice in forging them.

Gen favored her with a look of undisguised affection and admiration. With her freckles and unassuming attire, Oboro was no great beauty, but Gen's regard for her went far deeper than such trifles.

"Lucky for us, we're always ready to leave at a moment's notice," Gen remarked as she watched Oboro endorse the papers with several official-looking seals that had been secreted in their baggage. "Gonza had the cart loaded up a minute after the earthquake, haha!"

Ichi frowned in her direction, listening to the crinkling of paper as Oboro waved it about to dry the ink.

"Will Uchida-dono really pass for a common laborer?" he asked anxiously.

Oboro gave a hoarse laugh. "Well, he never will if you insist on calling him that as if he were a lord and you his vassal. Just say Tomo."

Ichi hung his head. "I...I'll try...but it feels so awkward."

"Gonza gave him a broad sedge hat to hide his face," Gen added, "but there's no disguising the ramrod-stiff way he holds himself. But never mind, it's not so unusual for a traveling band like this to employ a down-on-his-luck rōnin. As long as he has this paper, the officials at the checkpoints won't say anything."

"And Oboro-sama's skill with the brush is really that good?" Ichi asked, still seeming anxious.

Gen draped an arm over his shoulder and said in a conspiratorial tone, "I will tell you a secret: Oboro-chan here and her elder brother

Gonzaemon were low-ranking samurai class until their father gave up his status to try to earn some money as a performer, showing off his quick-draw technique. But before that they both had very good education, far better than I did."

"Oh no, you are very learned as well, Gen-san!"

She released him with an affectionate little shove. "Go on! Anyway it was all by ear. The downside of being educated by the Tōdōza is I never learned to read and write very well."

"Here, Ichi-san, this is yours," Oboro said, pressing the vertically folded papers into his hand. "Keep it on you at all times."

"Oh!" Ichi startled at her touch. "I'm sorry, I didn't mean to gossip about you."

"It's all right," she said kindly. "It's not exactly a secret, but we try not to remark upon it. We're all just commoners now."

Ichi thought of their conversation with Bakin. How many low-ranking samurai had been forced by poverty to renounce their status? Would Tomonosuke do the same eventually? Perhaps then he would truly pledge himself to Ichi as an elder brother.

But as much as he wanted that to happen, Ichi realized he did not want Tomonosuke to abandon Okyō or Rin. If only there were some way the four of them could stay together.

* * *

Oboro's fake papers evidently were good enough, because the officials at the checkpoint outside Sōka post town waved them all through without a second look. Passing through the checkpoint with the small Katsumata troupe took far less time than with the daimyō's retinue, and by late afternoon they were walking into Sōka-juku, with Tomonosuke pulling the cart, hiding his face under the sedge hat.

Sōka was not as badly affected by the earthquake as Edo. Here and there were cracks in the clay walls, or fallen roof tiles, but all the buildings appeared to be standing. Gonzaemon led the troupe to an inn where he greeted the owner as an old friend. They would all have to share one not very large room, but it was better than sleeping outside.

Okyō spent a few of their coins to buy the four of them rice balls with pickled plum for their evening meal, which they ate sitting outside the inn on a narrow bench. Okyō and Rin ate hurriedly then departed for the bath house, that they might wash away the soot and dirt before the women's hour ended. The two men remained behind.

Tomonosuke chewed his rice without thinking, not tasting it at all. Everything felt unreal, as if he were drifting away from himself, watching his body move of its own accord from a great distance. He stared at Ichi sitting beside him, licking the grains of rice from his fingers. Ichi's face bore no expression, and Tomonosuke could not guess what he was thinking. Tomonosuke felt as if he were in a dream, and only Ichi were real. He longed to embrace him, to cling to him, yet the more he stared, the more overwhelmed with guilt he felt.

"Ichi, I'm sorry."

"What?" Ichi tipped his head up in surprise.

"I'm repaying you for saving my life by putting you in greater danger and dragging you on a difficult, uncertain journey." Tomonosuke took Ichi's hand in his, overcome with a strong desire to protect him. While Ichi's face was fair and boyish, his hands were strong and callused. He squeezed back with surprising force.

"No, do not say that," Ichi said, and Tomonosuke was taken aback by the evident frustration and impatience in Ichi's voice. "Why do you always assume I don't know anything? I've spent more time on the road that you have. I've traveled the great roads from Edo to the provinces on my own, all over Sawara, and I've been down and back the entire length of the Tōkaidō Road from Edo to the capital. Have you done the same?"

"No."

"Then stop treating me like a delicate flower just because I can't see. I don't want a caretaker or nursemaid. You said we're brothers, didn't you? Wherever you go, I wish to go with you." As he spoke, he frowned in earnestness, still squeezing his hand.

Still Tomonosuke hesitated. "But—"

"No!" Ichi laid his other hand on Tomonosuke's cheek. "I wish to pledge myself to you as your brother. Why do you deny me? When the earth began to shake, all I could think of was you. Why should we not remain together always, no matter what?"

Ichi's eyes opened wide in surprise as he felt Tomonosuke lean forward suddenly and kiss him hard. He gripped harder at the other, not wanting to let him go.

"Yes," Tomonosuke said at last. "You're right. I've hesitated for far too long. Let us pledge to each other as brothers."

"Our hearts as one, I am honored to find happiness with you in this life and the next," Ichi said fervently, still clutching him. "I swear an oath of loyalty to you, my elder brother."

"And I to you, my younger brother," Tomonosuke replied. "Forevermore in this life and the next, our hearts bound together." He spoke with fervent intensity, then paused and added, "I only regret that we have no sake to drink to each other."

Ichi found Tomonosuke's lips with his fingers and kissed him again. "It doesn't matter. We'll have sake again someday, and we can exchange the three cups then."

"Yes, aniki," Ichi said, savoring the sound of the word.

Tomonosuke wrapped his arms around the smaller man protectively. He doubted they would ever have such a luxury as sake again. Were they really to spend the rest of their days as vagabonds? He could not even imagine a future beyond the next day. But he did not put these thoughts into words. They sat pressed together silently for a long time.

At last, Tomonosuke made to pull away, as he saw Okyō and Rin emerge from the bath house down the street.

"Come, let us take our turn in the bath."

But still Ichi clung to him and said, "Aniki, you must promise me one more thing."

"What?"

"We must never abandon Okyō-dono and Rin. Wherever you go, all four of us go together. Promise me."

Tomonosuke watched his wife and her maid walking hand in hand, looking refreshed after their bath and somehow carefree with their hair hanging loose. Privately, he was not sure Okyō still wanted him as a husband. Had she not said she planned to return to her parents' house? Surely she did not intend to live as a vagabond. But he found Ichi's concern for the two women to be sweetly touching, if surprising.

"Very well. I promise."

21

The Narrow Road to the Deep North

Throughout the spring, as the warm weather slowly crept up even to the northern regions, the Katsumata troupe traveled along the great Ōshū Road, gateway to the north. From Sōka to Shirakawa, at each of the twenty-seven stations, they lingered for several days, performing in the streets or at private banquets, staying at inns along the way. At Shirakawa, they continued north along forty-one stations of the Sendai Road, through country that was increasingly mountainous. For Tomonosuke, who had lived his entire life in the flat reaches of the plains of Musashi, the steep hills clad in lush green pines were both beautiful and intimidating. Okyō only scoffed and said he had not seen anything yet, and the weather was still mild.

The Katsumata troupe consisted of Katsumata Gonzaemon, his wife Osan, their two children, a boy and a girl, and two adolescent boys, all adept at tumbling. Gen and Oboro did their gidayū act for the wealthier audiences, and the goze songs for the commoners. They were pleased to let Ichi join their more informal performances, and his skill increased as he played shamisen and sang alongside them.

Rin and Okyō made themselves useful by assisting the tumblers and mending their costumes, but did not attempt to perform themselves, beyond a few gestures to fool the officials at the checkpoints.

Tomonosuke usually stood stiffly off to the side during performances, but as they traveled from Shirakawa to Sendai, Gonza asked if he might like to add a quick-draw demonstration to their act.

"Plenty of rōnin make ends meet by showing off their skill with the katana," Gonza suggested. "Ain't no shame in it."

"I don't know. It's been years since I practiced, and even then, my draw was never what one might call quick," Tomonosuke replied hesitantly.

"Ah, these yokels won't know the difference," Gonza scoffed. "Just a flash of steel and they're giving up their coppers with their eyes wide, trust me."

Despite his reservations, Tomonosuke was pained to be the only one not contributing to the troupe. Okyō had long ago sold off her all her fine silk kimono, at much-reduced prices, and their store of cash had nearly run out. That evening, he took his katana from its hiding place under the cart and set out by himself to the field of buckwheat behind the inn where they were staying.

Tomonosuke strapped the katana to his waist with a few practiced gestures, his body instantly reverting to the familiar motion. The weight felt strange at his side, especially as he was not wearing hakama and kimono, but the indigo trousers and jacket of a peasant. He had not bothered to have his topknot tied nor the crown of his head shaved, but left his hair in a high queue that hung down his back. The hair on the top of his head grew in haphazardly. He felt unkempt, yet could not summon the wherewithal to groom himself.

With a deep inhalation through the nose, he gripped the hilt of his katana with his right hand, his left steadying the sheath.

"Ya!"

In one motion, he attempted to draw the sword and raise it over his head, as he stepped forward with his left foot. It was a poor performance, to say the least. His draw was painfully slow, and he caught the tip of the sword on the sheath, causing the blade to wobble as he brandished it. This threw off his balance and he staggered slightly on his left leg as he lunged forward.

"Pathetic!" In his head he could hear the voice of his fencing master. "Tomo! What kind of form is that? Remember, by the time your sword is fully drawn, the duel is already over."

He sheathed the katana with a slightly smoother motion, ran through his breathing exercises and tried again. Still slow. His arms felt weak, but at least he completed the form correctly this time, without catching the tip on the sheath. He tried once more with a defensive draw, thrusting upwards from below, rather than raising the sword above his head. Better, but he needed more practice before he dared to let anyone watch.

The next evening, as he prepared to go out to the buckwheat field again, Okyō followed him, dragging a long bamboo pole. He stared at her in surprise.

"Wife, what is this?"

"You can't practice properly without an opponent," she said reasonably, "but as you have no sparring partner here, this will have to do instead."

The pole was the length of a man, and at the top she had wrapped old tatami matting. The end of the pole was sharpened, and she drove it into the ground.

"You were watching me yesterday?" he said in surprise.

She flicked an exasperated glance at him before returning her attention to the pole, ensuring it was securely driven into the soft earth.

"Husband, there is nothing you do that I do not know of. Come now, I've seen my brothers practice fencing often enough. If you can slice the top off the dummy in one quick motion, it might not make a bad show."

"Why are you doing this for me?" Throughout these months on the road, Okyō had barely spoken to him. He kept expecting her to announce she was leaving, even though he would never send her away, in deference to Ichi's wishes.

Okyō walked away from the dummy to stand beside him. "Gonza is correct, it will be good for you to work up your own act. Try it."

Tomonosuke took his stance and breathed deeply, trying to clear his mind of all thoughts, but without success. He relaxed his pose and looked at her again.

"I thought...do you not wish to go home to Echigo?"

She stiffened. "Are you sending me away?"

"Never. Ichi made me promise not to abandon you and Rin."

"Did he?" She gave a sudden snort, halfway to a laugh. "That anma is too tender-hearted." Dropping her gaze to her feet, she added in a slightly softer tone, "I'm in no hurry to return home. As long as Gonza doesn't mind keeping us, we may as well stay with them."

"I'm sorry to bring you such misfortune..."

She cut him off. "It's my karma to share your fate. Our hearts may belong to other people, but you and I are still bound by the red thread of destiny in this life and the next."

He nodded slowly, seeing her with new eyes. She might be short-tempered and quick to criticize, but she was still a samurai daughter, brought up to endure any hardship without complaining. If it was indeed his fate to live the rest of his days as a poor rōnin, he was glad to have her as a willing traveling companion.

"Hurry up," she said impatiently. "The light is fading already. Are you going to practice or not?"

"Hah!" With a grunt, he took his stance and slashed at the dummy, but his katana slid off the matting without slicing it in a weak, awkward blow.

"It's no good," he said, sheathing his sword. "My skill is not that great. I could easily break the blade with this kind of strike, then where would we be?"

"Hmm." Okyō walked to the dummy and loosened the matting she had bound around the top, shaking and pulling at it until the edges stood away, weakening the structure.

"Try again," she suggested, "only this time just try to slice a bit off the top."

It took three tries, but at last Tomonosuke made a clean slash across the top. Ragged edges of the matting drifted down to the ground.

Okyō nodded as he sheathed the sword. "Not bad," she commented. "Keep practicing. If you can do it with a bit more of a flourish, I think people might pay to see it."

* * *

The following evening, Ichi was preparing to walk the streets with his whistle in search of massage customers when he was brought up short by a strange noise. He tapped with his cane around to the back of the inn, following the noise to its source.

"Ichi," Tomonosuke greeted him, having at last learned to always announce himself and not remain silent.

Ichi's head jerked up in surprise. "Aniki, is that you making that noise? What are you doing?"

"Sharpening my katana on a whetstone borrowed from the kitchen." As he spoke, Tomonosuke continued the rhythmic grinding of the blade crosswise against the large flat stone which he had placed on the ground. Sword sharpening was an art best left to the professionals, but he could not afford such a service, even if such an artisan could be found in the tiny post town, so he would just have to make do as best he could on his own.

Ichi cocked his head to the side. "Your katana...?"

Tomonosuke squinted up at him from where he crouched over the whetstone. "Gonza suggested I might add a demonstration of swordsmanship to our act."

"Oh, that would be wonderful! Please, show me!"

Tomonosuke blinked. "Show you how?" He did not want Ichi's precious hands anywhere near the murderous blade.

"I mean, I just want to listen." He smiled eagerly.

Tomonosuke stood carefully, strapped on his sheathed sword and took his stance before the dummy, ensuring that Ichi remained several paces behind him. He breathed deeply several times through his nose, setting his feet apart and letting his gaze go soft. Never stare at your target, his fencing master always said. You can see more with the edges of your vision than the center.

In one fluid movement, he drew the katana and sliced the top of the matting on the dummy, then stepped back and sheathed the sword again. He was acutely aware of the sounds the katana made slithering out and in the sheath, the swish of the curved blade through the air, the very faint crunch of the matting as it was cut, and of course his own shouts with each exhalation, as he had been taught.

As he fully sheathed the sword with a click, Tomonosuke turned to see Ichi's face shining with delight.

"Well? Did that sound like anything at all?"

"Yes, it's magnificent! You really are just like Gakuzo in *The Legend of Eight Dogs*."

"Hardly. I had the slowest draw in the dōjō as a youth, and I haven't practiced at all since then. But if Gonza thinks it will help us earn some money, I supposed I don't mind swinging my katana around in front of a crowd."

* * *

As Gonzaemon predicted, Tomonosuke's display of swordsmanship proved popular enough as a warm-up act, after the tumblers and before Gen's performance. It set the right tone for Gen's recitation of heroic deeds of warriors of old, he said.

Okyō set up the dummy, ensuring that the matting at the top was loose and easy to cut. She soon elaborated the act by fastening flowers or feathers to the top of the dummy, which flew about spectacularly as Tomonosuke cut them. At her suggestion, he added another move, pretending to dodge a strike from his opponent, then lunging in from below with an upward cut to the chest. Okyō affixed a second bouquet to approximate the heart, and the crowd roared with approval as the flowers went flying.

With each performance, his draw became a bit quicker and his slashes steadier. He was still far from a sword master, but at least he no longer felt ashamed of his performance. Tomonosuke was pleased to bring in some cash, enough that they could buy new clothes. Although it was the height of summer, Okyō insisted on laying in a store of padded winter garments, with dire warnings about frostbite.

It was hard to imagine the far-off winter. The days were warm and sunny, clear skies day after day with little rain. Tomonosuke was grateful for the easy traveling conditions, and did not reflect on the lack of rain, even when the dirt roads cracked and clouds of dust followed them as they walked between the post towns. Now that they were no longer in Edo, they did not fear fires, and the state of the rice harvest or the daimyō's treasury was far from his mind.

At the height of summer, they reached the castle town of Sendai, the seat of the powerful Date clan. After the small post towns, the largest city in the northern domains seemed nearly overwhelming. The inn where they stopped was small and crowded, and for the first time in many days they had to share space and compete with other traveling performers.

Gen welcomed the opportunity to play at larger gatherings—shrine festivals, banquets and even theaters, always staying one step ahead of arrest. Ichi was also pleased to find customers more easily, and to sometimes be invited to play shamisen beside Oboro. But Tomonosuke and Okyō felt uneasy in the city, so full of samurai. It was unlikely that the Omigawa daimyō's men would be searching for them here, but they would almost certainly be recognized as samurai class. Tomonosuke had no desire to cross paths with other samurai, much less to perform his quick-draw demonstration where other samurai might watch.

But for the Katsumata troupe, Sendai was a lucrative location and the weather was fine, so they had no intention of leaving anytime soon.

"You're not going to play at the banquet with Gen-san and the others?" Tomonosukue was surprised to find Ichi loitering outside the inn. He had assumed Ichi would have departed already.

Ichi raised his head in surprise at the sound of Tomonosuke's voice. "No...I don't like those drunken parties. I thought I might search for massage customers instead."

"Never mind that. Come have a drink with me."

Ichi's face, still no more than a light gold color, despite their months on the road, lit with delight. "Do we have enough...?"

"Of course. As they say, 'money should not be kept overnight.' It's been too long already."

"Well then, let us go together, aniki." Ichi bowed slightly and held out his bamboo cane.

Tomonosuke considered the proffered stick. Ordinarily people seemed to prefer to guide Ichi by holding it, so as not to have to touch him or stand too close. But now that felt too reserved, as unappealing as watered-down sake. They had already pledged to each other as brothers. Why should they not walk together if they chose?

"Aniki?" Ichi dropped the tip of his cane back to the ground, his smile slipping slightly, unsure why Tomonosuke had not yet taken it.

In the past, Tomonosuke might have simply grabbed Ichi's hand, but now faintly, as if from a great distance, a voice whispered in his heart that perhaps he should ask first.

"May...may I take your hand instead?"

"Of course." Ichi's smile brightened again as he shifted his cane to his left and held out his right hand.

Tomonosuke took Ichi's hand and settled it in the crook of his elbow, enjoying the sensation of Ichi's quick, graceful steps beside him as they walked. Now that they were so close, he felt his passion rise up for the first time since before his arrest. It had been long, too long since they shared a carnal embrace. While the months of travel had dulled the fear and pain of their escape from Edo, there was no privacy on the road. They stayed each night with the entire company in a tiny room, their thin futons laid out nearly on top of one another.

Tomonosuke steered them at a brisk pace away from the inn and towards the licensed quarter.

"Aniki?" Ichi frowned in confusion. "Are we not going for a drink? I believe there is a yatai at the end of the street. I can smell the heating sake."

"I have a better idea," Tomonosuke said. "Let us go find a private room in a teahouse. We can hire a prostitute if we must, and pay her to keep silent."

"What?" Ichi's fair cheeks turned red as he realized what Tomonosuke was suggesting. "Is that not what caused all this trouble for you? That you got caught going to a teahouse?"

"No, that was merely a pretext. Matsudaira Sadahide framed me to cover his own crimes. If it hadn't been that visit to Yoshiwara, it would've been something else. In any case, it doesn't matter now. I may do as I please, and what I want now is a private moment with my beautiful younger brother."

Tomonosuke felt a surge of affection as Ichi squeezed his arm.

The licensed quarter of Sendai was not nearly as large nor as elegant and stylish as the Yoshiwara, but that hardly mattered to them. Tomonosuke led Ichi down the street, past the brothels with the women sitting listlessly behind the bamboo lattice, waiting for customers to select them. None of the women tried to entice them. At the end of the street was a teahouse with a few women lounging in front, the kind of place that did not seem like it stood on ceremony or charged exorbitant rates.

They got no further than the entryway before the madame came out and blocked their path.

"We'd like a drink in a private room and some entertainment," Tomonosuke said in his most commanding voice, drawing himself up to his full height. "One girl is enough."

"One girl, my ass," said the madame, looking them up and down with contempt. "We don't serve hinin here."

Tomonosuke's mouth hung open in surprise, then clamped shut again. But of course, he was a rōnin with patched, worn-out clothes and his hair growing out on the top of his head.

"I—I have money..." he stuttered, reaching in his obi to pull out a few coins, but knowing as he did so that even having to make such an appeal meant it was too late; they would never be allowed in. Even a run-down place like this could afford to be discerning about its clientele.

"Get out," the madame hissed at them, "before I send for the police."

Already Ichi was pulling silently on his arm. Tomonosuke led him back out to the street, humiliation burning in his belly.

Neither of them said anything as they walked at random through the unfamiliar streets in the long summer twilight. Their wandering path at last took them to the banks of the Hirose River, lined with cherry trees and tall waving grasses. On the opposite shore in the distance, Tomonosuke could see the curved eaves of Aoba Castle, as it watched the city from its hill.

They sat down heavily on the grassy bank, listening to the rushing water. The river was startlingly clear and full of fish.

Tomonosuke lay back with a groan, covering his face with one arm. "I'm sorry!" he burst out, still hiding his face as he spoke. "I should have known."

Ichi lay down next to him, taking Tomonosuke's other hand in his. "It doesn't matter. I'm only sorry for your sake, to receive such rude treatment."

Tomonosuke recalled the first time they met, when Ichi had been turned away in much the same manner at the Peony Pavilion in Sawara. It pained him even more to think that Ichi was accustomed to such cruelty as a matter of course. At the time, he had only spoken up out of mercy, but now he felt acutely the injustice of being branded as a hinin.

"I only wanted to share a private moment with you," Tomonosuke said. "A curse on that old hag for not taking our money."

"Never mind. I find it best not to hold onto resentment," Ichi said gently. Then more playfully, he pressed himself up against Tomonosuke's side. "We can still enjoy ourselves for free."

"No, I won't rut outside like an animal."

"Why not? We did at Toride-juku. And Abiko-juku. And then at Kogane-juku. Shall I go on?"

"No, stop! That was different."

"Different how?"

Tomonosuke could not reply. It was different because he had enjoyed the privilege of his rank, knowing that no matter what he did, no townsman would dare to speak against him, but now he was a non-person, subject to abuse by any passerby. He was ashamed at how hard he was taking this fall, and did not want Ichi to know how much it was affecting him. After all, if Ichi could bear his hinin status with good grace, why couldn't he?

When Tomonosuke did not reply, Ichi pressed himself up against him more urgently, entangling their legs, and breathing in his ear. Ichi's hot breath roused his passion, despite himself. The late summer dusk was falling at last, and they were far down the river bank, surrounded by tall grasses and trees with low hanging branches. There was no one nearby, and it seemed unlikely that anyone might see them, Tomonosuke reasoned with himself. After months of hardship, it was almost irresistibly sweet to surrender to Ichi's advances.

Tomonosuke turned so that he embraced Ichi from behind, wrapping his arms around his chest and pressing his cock up against Ichi's ass. He felt a jolt of heat even though the layers of clothing. How he longed to enter him, to see Ichi's face twisted in ecstasy. But they had no oil of cloves nor any way to easily obtain some, and he did not want to hurt him by being too rough.

Suddenly, a loud crashing noise in the reeds made them both start up guiltily and pull apart.

"Is someone there?" Ichi asked anxiously, in a low voice.

Tomonosuke scanned the gloomy shadows. "A dog just ran down the bank and startled a night heron." He watched the black and white bird fly up into the air. He was about to reassure Ichi that there were no people about, when he turned to watch the dog run back up the bank. A group of boys, intending to do some night fishing for whitebait, judging by their nets and buckets, followed as the dog bounded back down the bank to the river.

"It's getting dark. We should get back to the inn," Tomonosuke said, standing abruptly.

"Anma-saaaaaaan," the boys called in a taunting tone as their paths crossed briefly.

Ichi ignored them, holding tight to Tomonosuke's arm and feeling carefully with his cane through the long grasses as they walked up the bank.

Without breaking his stride, Tomonosuke turned to scold the boys for their rudeness, but before the words left his lips, beside him he felt Ichi jerk back suddenly and fall to the ground.

Instantly forgetting the boys, Tomonosuke turned to Ichi and discovered to his mortification that he had accidentally guided him directly under a low-hanging cherry tree branch, which had struck him full on the forehead. Exclaiming anxious apologies, Tomonosuke helped Ichi to his feet. He brushed anxiously at Ichi's forehead, removing bits of tree bark from his skin. Luckily the abrasions appeared to be minor, only a few small scratches, but already a red knot was forming. The sight of the few drops of blood beading on Ichi's forehead filled Tomonosuke with unspeakable guilt and remorse. His stomach lurched and his heart raced with dread.

"Ichi! I'm so sorry! Are you all right?" he choked out.

Ichi rubbed his head, seeming slightly dazed. "Yes, I'm fine. What was that, a tree branch?"

"Yes, it's my fault. I should have been paying attention."

"Never mind, these things happen. As they say, 'even monkeys fall from trees.'" Ichi smiled wanly and they continued walking, but Tomonosuke was sure he detected a note of resignation in Ichi's voice. Or was it resentment? Ichi would have every right to be angry at Tomonosuke for his carelessness.

As they walked back to the inn in silence, Tomonosuke tortured himself with recriminations. He had only wanted a moment of pleasure together, but instead he had caused Ichi to be injured. Ichi, who was so gentle and kind and trusting, who had entrusted his well-being to him. Tomonosuke felt somehow that this moment was the culmination of their entire relationship, that through his own carelessness and inattention, he had led Ichi into danger over and over again. What kind of elder brother was he? A man was supposed to be the support of his family, like the main beam holding up a house, but he had failed even at that.

When they returned to the inn, Rin exclaimed over Ichi's injury, and ran to find a clean cloth and to draw water from the well to wash his forehead.

Okyō looked sharply at Tomonosuke. "What happened?"

Oblivious to the look that passed between them, Ichi only smiled good-naturedly and rubbed at his shaved head in embarrassment. "I had an unfortunate encounter with a tree, but really, it's nothing. It's an occupational hazard of being a zatō." He smiled at his own joke, but the others did not join in.

As Rin returned and dabbed at his forehead, Okyō glared reproachfully at Tomonosuke.

"Take better care, husband, or you'll spoil his beauty," she said drily.

"No, I told you, please don't blame yourself, aniki."

But Tomonosuke could not forgive himself so easily.

22

The Row House

That year, the rainy season was shorter than usual. The Katsumata troupe passed the time in Sendai, waiting out the hot humid days and endless drizzle in the city, where they might at least make a little money performing at banquets. But when after only fifteen days, the clouds parted and the sun shone bright and hot, Gonzaemon announced they were going back to his hometown in Dewa province.

Somehow, without discussing it or making a plan, Tomonosuke, Okyō, Ichi, and Rin found themselves following along on the long trip far to the north. Tomonosuke had grown increasingly withdrawn. Okyō watched him critically, but she was content to keep traveling with the troupe for now, so as Gonza and the others readied the cart, she made certain their few items were included.

The journey took them away from the eastern coast of Honshū, on a track through the ridge of mountains rising along the center of the island. As they left behind the city and even the post towns, they were obliged to beg for accommodation in farm houses and sometimes sleep outdoors, but the weather was fine, so this was not such a great hardship. They skirted the mountains, keeping to the most populated areas, performing as they went, sometimes for no more than a handful of farmers for a few cups of uncooked rice.

All along the narrow track north, the pine trees grew tall and lush on each side, the hills rising all around them. Dragonflies buzzed overhead and the cicadas screamed in the trees. At night they heard the cries of foxes, a sound that made the hairs rise on the backs of their necks.

They reached Dewa province on the western side of Honshū just before the Obon festival, at the hinge between late summer and early autumn. Their destination was Kubota castle town, the seat of the Satake clan in Akita domain, on the shores of the Sea of Japan. After so many days in the wilderness, Kubota seemed dizzyingly crowded, although it was much smaller than Sendai.

"You lot can stay with Oboro and me," Gen said casually to Ichi as they approached the edge of town.

"What?" Ichi was holding onto the cart as Tomonosuke pulled it.

"We live here," Gen explained. "We ain't staying at an inn. Gonza and the others are going to their house, but it's very crowded. Oboro and I have our own place. You can stay with us."

"Oh no, we wouldn't want to put you out," said Okyō from the other side of the cart, before Ichi could answer. "We can find an inn on our own."

Gen waved a hand at her. "Don't be so proud. I know you ain't got two coins to rub together. Come on, it's all right."

Okyō glanced guiltily at Tomonosuke, who did not take his eyes off the road ahead of him. She should have known this would happen. They had already imposed far too much, and now they were pushing Gen out of her own home.

Okyō's guilt increased when they arrived at the tiny row house that Gen and Oboro shared. They would all have to sleep in one small room together. Tired out from the long journey, and with many practical household chores to attend to, for once Gen stopped flirting and teasing with her. We will stay here only one night, Okyō promised herself, as they all lay down together on bare wooden boards.

The next morning, however, they all arose before the sun and met up with the rest of the troupe, who lived further down in the same row house, then rushed off to a small temple not far from Kubota Castle. The troupe spent the entire day performing, taking advantage of the Obon festival when the temple was crowded with visitors. It was good they arrived early, because the grounds of the temple were soon filled with other performers, all competing for the attention and coins of the festival-goers. Gonza shouted tirelessly, proclaiming the skill and endurance of the tumblers. Tomonosuke did his quick draw three times, as Okyō watched and reset the dummy for him. Not bad, she thought. His technique had progressed from embarrassing to moderately competent.

On the other side of the temple grounds, Gen sang while Oboro and Ichi plucked the strings of the shamisen in unison. Even Rin sang a short song, coached by Oboro.

By evening, they were all so exhausted, it was all they could do to grab some toasted mochi from the vendors in the temple grounds then return home and fall asleep. They repeated this every day, so that there was no time to even consider moving somewhere else.

"Gotta strike while the iron is hot," Gen said as they rose each morning. "Good fortune is fleeting, and winter comes early in Dewa."

Okyō was intimately familiar with the harsh northern winters and the tremendous snowfall in the provinces facing the Sea of Japan. By Shimotsuki, the month of frost, there would be six feet or more, and the only way to get about would be tunnels in the snow. The troupe had to earn as much as they could before the snows began and they could no longer perform outdoors.

After half a month of this grueling but lucrative routine, Gen announced one morning that the Obon festivities at the temple had ended.

"Now what?" Okyō asked as she poured green tea over her tiny bowl of rice mixed with millet. She was already calculating if she might have time to go searching for some other rooms to rent, now that they had earned a little cash.

"Now the real fun begins!" Gen announced with a gleam in her eye.

"Gonza has arranged for me to give a gidayū performance at a yose tonight."

"What?" Ichi set his empty bowl on the floor carefully, his brow creased with concern. "Isn't that very dangerous? Remember what happened in Edo. And if the theater is unlicensed..."

Gen waved one hand dismissively, handing her empty bowl to Rin with the other. "It'll be fine," she said, then thanked Rin who picked up all the empty bowls and took them down to the kitchen to wash. "It's been too long since we gave a real performance, and I'm itching to do it again."

"Aniki?" Ichi turned to Tomonosuke, but if he was hoping they might convince her not to perform, he was disappointed.

"She knows her business," Tomonosuke said with a shrug.

As soon as the morning meal was finished, Gen and Oboro left with Gonza to pass out handbills and sell tickets for the evening's performance. The four of them, who would not be part of the performance, remained behind.

"We can't stay here," Okyō said, with a pointed look at Tomonosuke. "We have to find our own place."

Tomonosuke nodded slowly. "I suppose."

Okyō suppressed her irritation at how passive he had become. Somehow, losing his status and wandering on the road had made him even more willing to cede all decisions to her. While she liked having her own way, it angered her that he was not behaving as the head of the household.

"All right, then you go out and find something suitable," she prodded him. "Rin and I will take care of the washing and cleaning, and pack up our things." There was precious little to pack, but in the months of travel all their possessions had become jumbled together.

"Ichi?" Tomonosuke turned to him solicitously. "Will you remain here, or come with me to search for a room?"

Ichi rubbed his head, his hair grown out several inches now. "Oboro said I might use her spare shamisen, so I thought I would go back to the temple to perform. Even if the festival is over, there might still be a few visitors."

"Very well, suit yourself. You remember the way?"

"Yes, but..." Ichi paused, ducking his head shyly.

"What is it?"

"I-I would very much like to hear the performance tonight. Would you mind taking me there?"

Tomonosuke smiled fondly at him. "Of course not. I'll come find you on the temple grounds in the afternoon."

They walked the familiar route to the temple grounds together. Tomonosuke helped Ichi to find a good location and set out the straw mat. Ichi sat down and tuned up the three strings. He began to play as he heard the sound of Tomonosuke's departing footsteps. There were far fewer visitors to the shrine than before, but by the shuffling and murmuring he guessed that two or three people might be standing before him, listening.

With a flourish and a practiced smile, he launched into some local tunes he had heard Oboro play, doing his best to imitate her quick fingering. This rough style of playing was far different from the elegant classical ballads he had been taught by the Tōdōza, but he found he enjoyed it far more. He had never taken his own playing that seriously. Before meeting Gen and Oboro, he had been content to pluck out well-worn classics on occasion for a few extra coins. But after playing with them, he found in himself a desire to give a really virtuoso performance.

He screwed up his features, his face pointing upwards in concentration as he played. Were there more people listening now? He pushed himself to go faster, to put more spirit into plucking the strings, but he could still feel very keenly the gap between his playing and Oboro's.

When he finished one song, the applause was louder than he expected. The number of coins he gathered up with carefully searching fingers suggested more than a few listeners. He bowed with polite expressions of thanks, then started the next song.

As Ichi played on, his thoughts ran toward Tomonosuke. He was overjoyed that they had at last become pledged brothers, that as Matsuichi kengyō had promised, Tomonosuke seemed to be opening his mind and understanding him, even though that understanding had come at a terrible cost. But if Ichi was honest with himself, he did not truly regret Tomonosuke's loss of status. To the contrary, now they had more freedom than ever before, even if that meant some financial hardship.

Ichi felt he could be happy forever living on the road like this, traveling from place to place with the Katsumata troupe. Even now, Tomonosuke was searching for a neat little row house for all four of them to live together. Ichi could think of nothing that would make his heart gladder. Tomonosuke had been so quiet and withdrawn lately, but surely that would change once they had their own place. And this evening they would go together to hear Gen give a real gidayū performance, just as they had in Edo. He could hardly wait.

* * *

At the hour of the dog, Tomonosuke found his way back to the temple grounds. He was feeling sweaty and dusty and thoroughly discouraged. His attempt to find them a place to live was a humiliating failure. Rooms he considered suitable, even very small rooms in a row house, were far more than what they could afford, and the landlords regarded him with cold suspicion, turning him away when they saw in his traveling papers that he was an itinerant performer. The only landlords that would consider renting to him offered miserable cramped rooms in houses that were falling apart, with holes in the roof and insects crawling on the floor, or next door to teahouses, noisy with customers all night long. He would sooner sleep in a field than force Ichi and Okyō to live in such places.

With every step, he felt as if he were dragging his feet through deep mud. His body felt heavy and lifeless, his mind unable to form a plan of action. He should be thinking up some solution; he knew Okyō expected it of him, yet he could not formulate a coherent thought. In any case, he had promised to take Ichi to the theater, and so he pushed aside all other considerations for the moment. They had already stayed with Gen for days, surely one more night would not make a difference.

His heart felt lighter as soon as he caught sight of Ichi, sitting on a mat in a corner of the temple grounds, in the shade of a crooked dwarf pine tree. A few women with children on their backs were listening to him sing a nagauta, a lyrical ballad on the flowers of autumn. Tomonosuke hung back and watched him play. Ichi had certainly increased his skill dramatically during his time performing with Gen and Oboro. He moved easily from fast to slow passages, his left hand flying up and down the neck of the instrument, as his right hand struck confidently against the strings with the triangular plectrum. The richness of his voice had deepened. He paused at a dramatic moment in the song and the women leaned forward, holding their breath, until he ended with a bravura run of notes and they burst into applause. Tomonosuke felt a surge of happiness in his breast to see the look of pleasure on Ichi's face, although the coins the women threw onto his mat were few.

The song ended, Tomonosuke approached him at last. "Ichi, very well done."

Ichi turned toward the sound of his voice, his face shining. "Aniki! Thank you for coming to get me. That was nothing. Let's go and hear some real music. It's been so long since Gen gave a full-length gidayū performance, not just these common ballads or folk songs. I'm longing to hear it."

As he spoke, Ichi felt methodically for the coins, dividing the mat into sections and running his fingers lightly over every inch. When he was satisfied that he had found them all, Ichi tucked the coins into his sleeve, then wrapped the borrowed shamisen in a green cloth with an arabesque pattern and slung it over his back. Tomonosuke rolled up the mat as Ichi retrieved his cane, and they walked arm in arm out of the temple and toward the theater.

"So have you found us a place to live?" Ichi asked hopefully.

Tomonosuke sighed.

"That bad?" Ichi's face fell for a moment before he disguised his disappointment behind the impassive mask.

"Perhaps it would be easier if we split up, and I found my own place," Ichi said stiffly.

"No!" Tomonosuke surprised himself with the vehemence of his response, temporarily lifted out of his torpor. "No, as we promised, we all four stay together. I'll try again tomorrow."

They did not speak of this any further, but walked the rest of the way to the theater in silence.

The theater was crowded despite the last-minute ticket sales. Evidently the people of Kubota were eager for entertainment, and Shirataki Gen was well known. Gonza greeted them at the door with a smile and waved them in.

The yose or unlicensed theater was even more disreputable and run down than the one in Edo. The floor was nothing more than rush mats over packed earth, and the crowd, mostly men, squeezed in tightly around the stage were townspeople and laborers with kerchiefs tied around their heads, many still wearing aprons printed with the name or crest of their employers. When Gen and Oboro strode onto the stage from behind a hastily hung striped curtain, the crowd erupted in rough cheers and catcalling.

Gen greeted them with a swagger, answering their heckling with a laugh and a few rude suggestions, before sitting down and launching directly into the song, a fight scene from the kabuki play *Sukeroku*, with Oboro playing impassively beside her.

Instead of the show, Tomonosuke watched Ichi sitting beside him, his eyes closed and ear turned toward the stage, taking in each percussive beat of the strings, each expressive turn of phrase. Tomonosuke still felt as if he were not hearing every detail of the music the way Ichi did, but witnessing Ichi's pure enjoyment was pleasure in itself. For a moment, he put aside all cares about the future and reveled in this moment of shared happiness.

Gen was well into her second straight hour of singing when without warning, the curtain behind her rippled then parted, and five or six samurai burst onto the stage behind her.

"A raid!" The crowd screamed and surged to their feet, but in the confined space it was difficult to move.

"Not again! I told her!" Ichi cried, leaping to his feet. Tomonosuke put his arms around him protectively, straining to see the stage from their seats at the back of the theater. He could make out the black lacquer hats bearing the folding fan crest of the Satake clan.

"This is an illegal performance!" one of the samurai shouted. "Shirataki Gen, you're under arrest!"

As he was speaking, without a single backward glance, both Gen and Oboro dove straight into the crowd. The daimyō's men shouted insults at them as they disappeared into the writhing mass of people, all struggling for the door.

Tomonosuke stood with one arm around Ichi's shoulders, hugging him close, the other hand on his katana and wakizashi at his waist, to keep them from becoming entangled in the bodies pressing up against them on all sides. Luckily, they had been seated far from the stage, nearer to the door. With his arm clamped to Ichi's shoulder to prevent them from becoming separated, he inched through the crowd to the door.

Just as they were about to slip outside, Tomonosuke turned back in time to see Gen and Oboro slip out through a window at the side of the theater. The samurai shouted at them. The crowd gave a rough cheer, as the samurai struggled in vain to reach them. Then Tomonosuke and Ichi were carried out into the street by the force of the people behind them, and he lost sight of the two women.

"Gen-san!" Ichi cried as they stumbled away from the theater. Miraculously, the shamisen was still strapped to his back, and he had not lost his grip on his cane.

"She ran off," Tomonosuke explained, hurrying him down the darkened street. "They'll be looking for her at home. We've got to get back quickly!"

Ichi clung to Tomonosuke's sleeve as they hurried through the streets, his regret over the interrupted performance wiped away by fear and concern for Gen's safety. What if she was arrested? He longed to help her, but what could he do?

Tomonosuke led him away from the main road into what he could sense was a narrow alley, which he knew was the entrance to the row house. But rather than going straight up to Gen's front door, Tomonosuke stopped so suddenly that Ichi collided with him slightly. Ichi was about to ask what he was doing, but Tomonosuke hastily shushed him and pushed him back against the wall.

As they shrank back into the entryway of an empty house across the way, Ichi could hear a samurai shouting and rapping at Gen's door—it must be another of the daimyō's men. Ichi prayed that they were sufficiently hidden from view, and that the owners of the empty house would not return at that moment.

"Shirataki Gen!" the samurai shouted. "Open up by order of the Akita daimyō! I know you're in there!"

Okyō slid the door open and regarded him with a sneer. "There's no one here by that name."

"You bitch! Where is she? Don't try to hide her!"

Okyō gave a cold laugh and pushed both shōji open all the way, revealing the single tiny room in its entirety. Apart from Rin kneeling in a corner, the room was empty. Okyō stomped to the closet and slid open the door with a bang, revealing a jumble of bedding and clothing, which she began to heave onto the floor.

"Look! There's no one here! Are you satisfied?"

The samurai did not answer.

"Maybe you'd like to search under the floorboards?" Okyō continued, reaching down by the entryway and pulling one up. The samurai leaned forward, making a great show of searching under the house, but did not see anything.

"Well, if she isn't here yet, I'll just have to wait for her then," he declared, sitting down on the stoop with his legs spread wide, his katana and wakizashi resting upwards by his side.

"Do whatever you like," Okyō sneered at him. "I won't stop you from wasting your time." She shut both shōji with a snap.

Trying his best to look as if he had just emerged from the house across the alley, Tomonosuke went back out to the main road, with Ichi at his side. The samurai did not seem to take notice of them in the dark.

They hurried around to the other side of the house, where a large window swinging open from the bottom faced the back alley. Tomonosuke peered up into the room, waving to catch Okyō's attention. She gave a slow nod without the least surprise, as if this were a plan they had worked out in advance, then held her finger to her lips, glancing at the door. They could see the man's outline against the thin white paper shōji, and there was no question that he could hear every movement, every breath inside the room, as if there were no doors at all.

Casually, as if she were just doing housework, Okyō fetched the large bundle of all their clothes and possessions and placed it under the window, along with two extra pairs of straw sandals that she had just purchased and luckily placed in the closet, not in the entryway. She waited a bit longer, until a family in one of the adjoining rooms returned home, children clattering and calling noisily in the alley.

In one quick movement, Okyō heaved the bundle and sandals out the window, then helped Rin to squeeze through before following herself. Tomonosuke caught first Rin then Okyō, helping them to hastily step into their sandals. He shouldered the bundle, took Ichi by the hand, and they set off down the alley, just as they heard the man at the front of the house shouting again and opening the shōji.

Tomonosuke led them down the dark alley as fast as he dared to go, but when he reached the main road and saw they were not being pursued, he slowed to a deliberately casual pace. They wandered at random, putting distance between themselves and Gen's house, until they were certain they were no longer in danger.

The hour was growing late, the night air slightly chilly. The large clear autumn moon hung in the sky, giving the shadowed trees a silvery glow. As they came upon a small shrine, a rare open area dotted with only a few pine trees, Tomonosuke halted and dropped the heavy bundle to the ground.

"Now what?" He stared at them. Ichi and Rin looked pale and

worried in the moonlight, but Okyō was as impassive as a statue. He couldn't help but admire her in that moment. He would never say so, but he was deeply impressed by how calm and quick-thinking she was when confronted with the daimyō's police. The woman had ice in her veins.

"It's late," she said.

"I know. I'm sorry, but I was unable to find us a place to stay today. We can rest here, and I'll try again tomorrow."

"But what about Gen-san and the others?" Ichi asked anxiously. "We should look for them."

"No," Okyō said decisively. "Gen can take care of herself. This is her hometown, and she's been performing since long before we met her. She'll be fine. We've imposed too much on her already. We'll just be creating more trouble for her if we search her out."

Ichi hung his head unhappily.

"I agree. We should find our own house," Tomonosuke said.

"No," Okyō replied. "People here know we're with her. It's too dangerous. If we're arrested, they'll find out your true identity and send you back to Omigawa. There's no reason for us to stay in Kubota. It's time to return home to Echigo."

"You can't be serious," Rin whispered.

At the same moment, Tomonosuke said more loudly, "What, right now?"

"Yes, now," she said grimly.

"No, it's too dangerous." Tomonosuke spoke more firmly than he had in months. "Once we leave the city, there could be wild animals on the road at night." When Okyō did not reply, he continued, "Come, we can rest here under the trees for a few hours without being noticed. We'll leave before dawn, before the shrine maidens come to sweep the grounds in the morning, then depart for Echigo."

23

Bosama

Ichi sat back against the rough bark of the dwarf pine, but sleep did not come. The promise of sharing a neat little row house, of himself and Tomonosuke living together as townspeople, had vanished like a dream on a spring night. Now they were to depart Kubota for Echigo? And for what? He had no desire to live among samurai again, but Tomonosuke had made the decision without consulting him, and he had no choice but to go along.

The longer he sat on the cold, hard ground, the more his legs and bottom ached. He shifted onto his side, and as he did so, he felt Rin, who was seated beside him, place her bony hand on his.

"You don't have to go with us," she whispered.

"What?"

Ichi was not sure if the others could hear them. Tomonosuke sat nearer to the main gates to the shrine, to guard against any unexpected disturbance. As for Okyō, he was not sure if she was awake or asleep.

"To Echigo," Rin said, still in a hoarse whisper. "My lady would never agree to go there unless she was truly desperate. It won't be good. You don't have to go. You could stay here in Kubota, or go back to Edo, or do whatever you want."

Ichi did not admit as much to Rin, but he had just been thinking this himself. He was not in danger; the daimyō could not arrest him. He was worried for Gen and Oboro, and concerned that without intending to, he had stolen Oboro's shamisen, which was still strapped to his back. He felt guilty for taking it, even if it was a spare. If he stayed, he could return the shamisen and perhaps help Gen, or at least ensure her safety. But if he did so, he might be parted from Tomonosuke forever. How could he abandon his sworn brother? And he realized, as he sat listening to the hooting owls and rustling of his companions, that his playing on Oboro's shamisen would likely be their only source of income on the road to Echigo.

Ichi grasped her hand. "No. I am pledged to my elder brother, and we promised never to part. Whatever awaits us in Echigo, I will face it with all of you."

"You don't know...I can't..." Rin broke off, her voice ragged.

"I'm sure Okyō-dono is not the only ones with bad memories there," he said gently.

"I was ten when my father sold me," she whispered. "They make you do housework until you're old enough to..."

She broke off, but Ichi knew very well what her fate would have been, and it was not at all that of the high-class oiran like Hana-ogi. Rin would not have been trained in music, dancing and flirtatious games. No, her lot would have been drudgery as a maid until she was fourteen or fifteen, then turned out to sit before the lattice all night, waiting for any customer to point a long, thin tobacco pipe at her, and bring her to a back room to serve him sake before sating his carnal desires. All her fine clothing, every bite of food she ate would increase her debt to the brothel, and no matter how much she earned, she would have little chance of buying out her contract.

"Okyō-dono rescued me, paid off the brothel and took me to live with her," Rin whispered. "When she was wed to Uchida-dono and we left for Omigawa, she swore no matter what, we would never, ever go back."

Ichi grasped her hand in both of his. "We are going to Okyō-dono's home. No matter what happens, you will never go back to that brothel, or any other, I promise. When I pledged to aniki, I made him swear never to abandon Okyō-dono, nor you, Rin. We will protect you no matter what. I think of you as my own younger sister."

Rin sniffled and gave a slight laugh. "Younger sister? I do believe I'm older than you by a year or two at least."

"Is that so?" Ichi feigned ignorance. "I wouldn't be so rude as to ask your age. In my mind's eye, you are a dainty girl with a figure like the willow tree, no older than 'two eights' as the poets say."

That provoked more laughter from her, and he was relieved to hear it sounded heartier. He patted her hand and settled back against the tree again.

"Come, let's try to get some rest," he said. Somehow, reassuring her also set his own mind at ease.

She sighed and leaned her head on his shoulder. Ichi was certain that he would not sleep at all, but the next thing he knew, Tomonosuke was shaking his shoulder and saying it was time for them to leave, before the priests or shrine maidens arrived.

* * *

In the early dawn hours under a grey, chilly sky they departed Kubota without ceremony and headed south along the Hokuriku Road. Although they had learned from the Katsumata troupe how to travel on almost no money at all, this journey on their own was much more arduous, not least because there were no post towns. This was not a well-traveled route to Edo furnished with amenities for processions of daimyō and their retinues, but a narrow track with nothing for miles but rice fields surrounded by mountains in the distance.

Ichi knew that the farmers they passed would have no interest in his services as a masseur, and without the tumblers and other musicians, he and Tomonosuke alone could never draw a big enough crowd to be worth their time and effort performing, even in the few towns they passed through. Mostly they went from one remote farmhouse to the next. Without discussing it, Ichi fell into the role of bosama, a common practice in the northern provinces, for a blind man to go from house to house, playing the shamisen outside the gate in exchange for food.

At each farmhouse, while Okyō and Tomonosuke hung back at the road, Rin led Ichi to the main entrance, where he played a song or two until one of the inhabitants poured a ladle of uncooked rice into the cup fastened to his belt. It was usually the wife or a female servant who did this, often without speaking. He tried to train himself not to startle at this unfamiliar, unannounced touch, but to nod his head in thanks and continue playing, but it was difficult not to jump when his concentration was suddenly broken by a tug at his waist.

The people they encountered were taciturn and aloof, usually only saying a few words in their lilting rural dialect, but they seemed glad for some rare entertainment. Ichi played folk tunes in a new style he had learned from Gen and Oboro, a fast, rough style of playing, without singing. The tunes started by going up and down the scale, up-down, up-down, up-down, before quickly progressing to faster and faster plucking and fingering in ornate arabesques. Even without words, Ichi made the shamisen speak of the harsh northern winters, the wind whistling down the mountains covered in pines, the grains of rice ripening in the summer heat.

The weather was turning colder, but it was still too early for snow. Here and there an early maple stood out in a blaze of red or orange against the lush green of the pines in the mountains. They were lucky to be traveling after the rice harvest was more or less complete, or they would have found the houses empty, with the farmers sleeping in the fields in their rush to bring in the crop. The road was lined with golden sheaves of rice hung upside down to dry on large triangular frames.

The rice Ichi earned as a bosama comprised most of their food, supplemented by the occasional loach Tomonosuke caught if they passed a river or stream. They did not have a rice cooking pot, nor did they care to carry such a large, heavy item. At the end of each day, they combined all the rice and begged one of the farm wives to cook it for them. The kinder households gave them a side dish to go with it, miso soup with tofu and dried seaweed, or chopped braised burdock root, then allowed them to spend the night in the barn or shed.

Many of the farmers grumbled about a poor rice harvest, but they did not listen too closely, being more attuned to the rigors of the road.

Despite the weariness of travel, and the uncertainty at their destination, Ichi found he enjoyed being a bosama. The music was challenging to play, and more exciting than the sedate concert pieces he had learned from the Tōdōza. It was gratifying to have an appreciative, uncritical audience, even if the only sign they gave was the occasional sigh or murmured thanks. He could hear the sincerity in their voices.

As they continued south, they skirted the western edge of Mount Bandai, which they had seen in the distance on the opposite side from the east on their previous journey with Gen. The afternoon sun beat down from a high cloudless sky, warming the cool autumn air. Their straw sandals kicked up small clouds of dust as they walked along, Ichi with his hand on Tomonosuke's arm, Okyō and Rin somewhat behind them.

"Can you see the mountain?" Ichi asked. He was listening for the cries of the deer, but so far all he heard were the clear voices of the bell crickets hidden in the grass by the side of the road.

"Yes, just there, in the distance," Tomonosuke replied, pointing with the arm Ichi held so he could feel the direction. "There are two peaks, one higher and the other lower, and just a bit of snow at the very top."

"And are the leaves turning yet?"

"Only a few, a spot here and there among the green. In a few days it will be more."

Ichi tipped his head back, letting the sun warm his face. "I'm sure it's very beautiful."

"I suppose it is." Tomonosuke's voice was flat and dull.

"You don't like it?"

"This is a rough, wild country."

"Do you wish you were back in Edo?"

"Don't you?"

Ichi sighed. He wished Tomonosuke could enjoy their freedom as he did.

"Not entirely," Ichi said carefully. "In Edo, there were always people standing in our way, but here on the road we can be together as we like."

"I am glad to be with you," Tomonosuke admitted.

Ichi smiled up at him hopefully. "You see, life on the road isn't all bad."

"The journey would have been much more difficult without you, bosama," Tomonosuke said with a slightly lighter tone.

"It is more pleasant to travel with companions," Ichi replied modestly.

"I can still hardly believe you walked from Edo to Sawara on your own."

"That was nothing. If I were a true bosama, I would be traveling all around Dewa and Tsugaru on my own."

Tomonosuke was silent for a time before speaking again.

"When we first met, I thought you were in need of my protection and guidance, but as it turned out, that wasn't true at all, and now you have become the support pillar for all of us."

"A slender support, providing just barely enough to keep us from starvation," Ichi said, although in truth he was glowing inside at these words.

"Still more than any of the rest of us. I'm always pleased to watch you perform these lively northern tunes."

"It's you I think of when I play," Ichi said softly, his heart full at the thought of Tomonosuke's admiration of his skill. But more than that, he felt pride at being the one providing for the others. They were all depending on him, he realized, with a surge of happiness. He thought of what Hanawa Hokiichi sōkengyō had told him, to never let anyone tell him what he could or could not do.

He wished the road might go on forever, that they might pass straight through Echigo and continue on forever as vagabonds.

24

Winter Beyond the Barrier

At the port city of Niigata, they briefly resumed their former roles, with Ichi walking the streets in the evenings with his whistle, as the merchants and townspeople were eager for a massage after visiting the public bath. Tomonosuke picked up a little more cash with his quick-draw demonstration. Okyō tied pampas grass to the dummy, and the crowd cheered when the gauzy fronds fluttered to the ground.

Whatever coins they could possibly spare Okyō used to buy more cold weather gear—padded short jackets called hanten, straw raincoats, more underclothing. When Tomonosuke complained of having to carry it all, she gave him a scornful look.

"You have no idea what's coming," she declared.

The weather was turning, with more and more trees changing color every day. Life in Niigata was easier than on the road, but this was not their destination, so as soon as they had rested and provisioned themselves, they pressed on south along the Hokuriku Road. Once again, Ichi played in exchange for rice as they went house to house through the countryside. The harvest was now long over.

At last, just as the nights were becoming truly cold, they reached Jōetsu, the capital of Echigo province. The name Echigo, meaning beyond the barrier, hinted at how remote this region was in ancient times. But now Jōetsu was the seat of the Takada domain, under the daimyō Sakakibara Masachika, who commanded 150,000 koku of rice a year.

Okyō led them away from the crowded merchant class center of town, past Takada Castle with its curving tile roofs and high stone walls, to the district where the vassals of the Sakakibara clan had their gated residences. They walked in silence down a broad avenue lined with delicate maple and weeping cherry trees, the last of their colorful leaves waving elegantly in the breeze. On either side of the avenue, high smooth walls of dark wood protected the residences from the outside, and imposing gates announced to the world the status of those within.

Okyō paused before the largest gate. The roof of the gate was heavy with thatch, and the transom was carved with the Sakakibara crest, the wheel of an ox cart. In an earlier martial age, the gate might have been barred and guarded, but after centuries of peace, such precautions hardly seemed necessary. As it was daytime, the doors of the gate stood open.

Looking grimly straight ahead, Okyō marched through the gate, her straw sandals crunching on the gravel, and up to the front door of the main house. While small in comparison to the daimyō's Edo residence, the house was impressive for a single family. The thatched roof had been replaced with elegant wood shingles, and the carvings over the front door depicted a mighty carp ploughing the waves.

Without pausing, Okyō slid the wooden outer door open with a sharp bang and strode into the small entryway, purposely built narrow and with a low ceiling to prevent a visiting enemy from raising his sword, although such a thing had never come to pass. In a loud voice, she called out, "I'm hooome!"

A plain-faced girl in a striped cotton kimono slid open the shōji curiously, then upon seeing who it was, slammed it shut again. Some minutes later, the maid slid the door open again, only a crack, peering out at them with wide eyes.

"I'm sorry, young miss, but my lord says you cannot use the main entrance. If you could go around to the side..."

Okyō stiffened in anger but did not reply. With a decisive sniff, she turned on her heel and marched back outside, then around to another door directly to the right, with the others following after. Rin shot her a worried look. It was a very bad sign that Okyō's father would not allow her to enter by the main door as a member of the family, but forced her to the side entrance, which was for servants and tradesmen.

The outer door was so low they had to duck down to enter. Tomonosuke put Ichi's hand on the crossbeam so he would know it and not hit his head. They stepped inside to a much larger entryway with a packed earth floor leading into the same foyer as the main door, but here the inner doors stood open, revealing the six-mat room within. The maid hovered nervously and did not invite them to step up into the house.

A moment later, an inner door slid open and closed, and they were joined by an older man in a black silk kimono bearing the Sakakibara crest. He had a pinched, thin face and his topknot was scanty.

"Honored father," Okyō said, bowing as she stood in the entryway.

"How dare you show your face here, you trollop," Sakakibara Masahiro replied with a sneer. "What are you thinking, showing up unannounced like a beggar? And who are these vagabonds you've brought with you? I assume this is your good-for-nothing husband. And look, you've brought back that whore you rescued like a stray cat. Well, none of you are staying here, I can tell you that much."

Okyō stared at her father without flinching throughout this barrage of abuse. Looking him straight in the eye, she boldly kicked off her sandals, stepped up into the house and sat herself down in the middle of the foyer.

"We're not leaving," she declared. "If you try to throw me out, I'll scream so loud all the neighbors will come running."

With a look of bewildered admiration, Tomonosuke followed her up into the house and knelt beside her. He was deeply ashamed to appear at his father-in-law's house in such a condition, as a fugitive with his hair grown out and dirty from the road, but he could not allow Okyō to be the only one with courage.

"Honored father, I am Uchida Tomonosuke, husband of your daughter. I am at your service." Summoning as much dignity as he was able, he gave a three-finger bow, his hands flat on the tatami, thumbs and fingertips making a triangle.

Tugging on Ichi's hand, Rin led him up into the house as well to sit behind Tomonosuke and Okyō, the four of them silently daring her father to have them dragged bodily from the house.

Masahiro regarded them with disdain, then without further argument, slid open the inner door with a bang and left, followed by the maid, who shut the door with a snap.

The four of them sat rigidly for some time, but as the minutes dragged on to hours, they sagged into more comfortable poses. When they had waited for what felt like two hours, Tomonosuke at last broke the silence.

"Now what?" he asked, looking at Okyō.

She shrugged with an air of unconcern, although her face was drawn and pale with tension.

"Okyō-dono, that was very brave," said Ichi in an undertone.

"I've had a lot of experience," she said bitterly. "I'm sure he means it when he says he will throw us out, but I don't intend to make it easy for him. He cares too much for what the neighbors think to risk a big scene."

A third hour dragged by, when without warning the inner door opened again and a different man entered, somewhat younger, and with a softer face. As soon as she saw him, the rigid tension in Okyō's back seemed to release, and she gave the three-finger bow.

"Uncle," she said. "It's been a long time since last I saw you."

The man sat before her, snapping his hakama smartly as he knelt, and inclined his head slightly. "Kyō-chan," he said familiarly, with a slight sigh. "What have you done now?"

She raised her head and stared him down, her eyes snapping furiously. "Uncle, I have done nothing wrong. Circumstances have driven us back home. Would you turn out your own family to starve in the street?"

He gave a bitter, short laugh. "Of course not. Your father refuses to take you in because of your scandalous behavior, but I, Hotta Yoshito, will allow you to stay with me."

Okyō's gaze did not waver. "I and my husband and our servants," she said.

He raised an eyebrow. "You keep your own personal masseur?"

"All four of us or I'm not leaving this room," she insisted.

He stared back at her for several long, silent moments, then shrugged. "Come, let's go." He stood and without a backwards glance strode out the front door, pausing only to step into his wooden sandals.

Okyō and the others scrambled to retrieve their sandals and other belongings from the side entrance and follow Hotta Yoshito out the gate. As they walked down the street, Tomonosuke gave Okyō a searching stare.

"He's the head of our branch family," she whispered, her eyes fixed on the back of the man walking several paces ahead of them. He too was wearing a black silk kimono with the Sakakibara crest on the back. "He has four daughters, all married out. The daimyō would not allow him to adopt a son-in-law so he has no heir and lives alone with his wife. I suppose that's why my father forced him to take us in. His house has extra space, while my two brothers and their wives and children live in my father's house."

She did not mention anything about the scandal Yoshito referred to, and Tomonosuke assumed he meant their unannounced arrival and his own obvious status as a rōnin.

"A branch family? So he's not your father's brother?"

"No. We're only distantly related, but he's always been kind to me."

"Well, that's a bit of luck then, right?"

Okyō settled her lips in a line. "We shall see."

Yoshito's house was not far, only a short walk away, but the residences were progressively less grand as they went along. He led them through a much more modest gate, to a house with a thatched roof and cracks in the clay walls. The door rattled loudly as he opened it and shouted, "I'm hooome!"

A small woman in late middle age with a pinched face and perpetual frown greeted them in the entryway. As they slid off their sandals and stepped up into the house, he introduced her as his wife, Osono. She regarded them with suspicion.

"We agreed to take in the daughter, not the whole lot of followers and hangers-on," she muttered, then more loudly to her husband, "I don't suppose Masahiro gave you any provisions or allowance for them?"

Yoshito shook his head silently.

"We have money," Okyō lied. Their carefully saved stash of coins was not large, certainly not enough to provision four people for the entire winter.

"All right then." Osono gave her a critical look. "You can use the kitchen but you'll have to buy your own food. And we only have one room to spare."

Okyō gave her a deep bow. "Thank you, aunt. We are indebted to you."

Yoshito showed them to an eight-mat room that evidently had been used by his daughters before they married into other families. A few peeling woodblock prints and shrine tags were still stuck to the wood beams. The tatami mats were lumpy and musty, and the paper of the fusuma had holes, only a few of which were haphazardly patched. The open closet revealed several futons, hard and stiff as crackers. It was an interior room with no windows, only unadorned fusuma on all four sides. The side opposite the hall let into a larger room with a view of the garden, but that would not be for their use.

At Osono's direction, a maid provided them with an andon and a plain ceramic brazier, with a small lump of coal sitting atop the pile of ash.

"Begging your pardon, but my lady says she ain't giving you no more charcoal," the maid said apologetically in her thick northern dialect as she lit it. "You'll have to buy more on your own, miss."

As soon as they were alone, Okyō sank down to the floor, all the fight gone out of her at last. She sat in a daze as Rin unpacked their few possessions, and Tomonosuke showed Ichi around the room. It only took Ichi a few moments to run his fingers over each partition, to situate the fusuma leading to the hall and the closet. Feeling emboldened by his mission to assist Ichi, Tomonosuke led him to the other parts of the house they might use.

The house was not very large. The kitchen was just beyond the main entrance, no more than an alcove with dishes and trays stacked up along the walls to the ceiling, and a cookstove with two iron pots standing beside the alcove in the entryway. A service door led to the back garden.

Ichi allowed Tomonosuke to guide him down to put his feet in the extra wooden sandals provided, and they went out the side door. A few paces away, they found the well, and beyond that in a corner of the garden was the privy. As they went, Tomonosuke was careful to guide Ichi's hands to the landmarks that might be most useful to him, to warn him of uneven ground, and to describe their surroundings in as much detail as he could. Ichi ran his sensitive fingers along the side of the wall, the door jamb, the rough stones of the well, cataloging each detail.

Ichi often found himself led by strangers as a matter of necessity, but they usually grasped his cane and remained at a distance. He avoided allowing anyone to move his hands about. His hands were his livelihood and he tried to take care what he might touch, as even a minor injury could put him out of work for days. But he trusted Tomonosuke, who guided him now with much greater skill and gentleness than he had shown previously. The thought that Tomonosuke was finally learning his ways made Ichi's heart glow.

"Now where are we?" Ichi asked, as Tomonosuke led him on what seemed to be a gravel path surrounded by shrubbery.

"We are going around the back of the house. To the left is a shed. Oh, I see the storehouse, only it's not a freestanding building, but connected to the main house."

"Yes, Rin mentioned that they build them that way in the north because of all the snow."

"How curious. Oh!"

"What is it?"

"We've come around the other side of the house. I can see a small formal garden. This must be directly off Hotta-san's private rooms."

Ichi paused. "We'd better go back then."

"Yes, let's go back. It wouldn't do for the lady of the house to look outside and see us poking about her garden."

They hastily retreated to their room. The first night they went to sleep hungry, too exhausted to do anything else.

The next morning, Okyō sent Rin to the market with a few coins. She returned a few hours later with supply of charcoal, a chunk of dried, smoked bonito, and nothing else.

"What is this?" Okyō ordinarily never spoke a harsh word to Rin, but hunger and frustration got the better of her.

"I'm sorry, my lady, but there's precious little food at the market," Rin whispered, her head down.

"How can that be?" Okyō snapped. "You don't know how to ask. Why do I have to do everything?" Snatching up the purse Rin proffered, Okyō stomped off angrily.

Not knowing what else to do, Tomonosuke leaned against a beam between the fusuma with a sigh. Ichi felt for Rin's hand.

"She didn't mean it," he whispered to her, squeezing her hand. She squeezed him back.

Okyō returned an hour later, with a small measure of unpolished rice, mixed with barley and millet.

"I'm sorry I scolded you, sweetheart," she said wearily. "You were right. The harvest this year has been very bad."

Tomonosuke sat up straight, looking at her in alarm. "How did we not notice? Every farmer we stayed with complained about the lack of rain. I had no idea it was so bad." His mind was racing—if there was already so little food, what would things be like after several months of snow?

"Well, at least we're not homeless, with winter coming," Ichi said, attempting to sound hopeful.

Okyō's head came up, her eyes snapping. "We may yet freeze or starve," she retorted. "How are we to earn money? My uncle won't countenance any bosama or entertainers living here. If he finds out we're performing in the streets, we'll all be thrown out."

"I can still give massages," Ichi offered. "No one will take notice of one more anma walking the streets, whistling for customers, especially if it's a neighborhood far from here. In any case, the best-paying clients are in the licensed quarter."

"And how are you to find your way there in an unfamiliar city?" Tomonosuke asked uneasily. He knew Ichi was eager to resume his role as sole supporter of their family, but it still seemed dangerous, at least on his own.

They all fell silent. If he or Okyō were seen in the licensed quarter, it might be another excuse for Yoshito to throw them out.

"I'll take you," Rin said in a small, uncertain voice.

"No! Absolutely not!" Ichi cried in indignation, red blotches standing out on his cheeks.

"Well..." Tomonosuke drawled.

"No!" Ichi turned in the direction of his voice, frowning. "Aniki, how can you be so cruel? I promised her she would never have to go back there, not even to walk nearby."

They all fell silent again for a few moments.

"I will go with you," Tomonosuke said at last. "We'll take precautions, and hope that no one recognizes us, or at least no one who might carry tales back to Hotta-san."

Those precautions meant changing out of his worn, much patched kimono and back into the cotton trousers and jacket, the peasant clothes that Gonza had given him, and more importantly, laying aside his katana and wakizashi. Six months ago, he would never even have considered doing so, but now it seemed so obvious, the only course of action. Even on a less perilous errand, he had no desire to encounter other samurai in the street.

They waited until dark. Rin silently retrieved their sandals from the front entrance, then they slipped unnoticed out the side door.

"You're very kind to Rin," Tomonosuke remarked, as he led Ichi away from the samurai neighborhood to the less reputable side of town.

"You should be too," Ichi scolded him. "You know how much she's suffered, don't you?"

"I know Okyō bought her contract from a brothel, but I never really thought about it."

Ichi sighed. "You don't have to risk this, you know. I could have found my own way there eventually."

"And you were just telling me not to be so thoughtless and unkind."

The clear, bright autumn moon shone down on them from a sky as black and brittle as obsidian. Their breath came in clouds; surely the snow would begin to fall soon. Ichi's face stood out in the moonlight, pale and lovely. Tomonosuke felt worn and ragged from the road, but Ichi looked as graceful and beautiful as ever. He knew Ichi was enjoying the leveling of rank between them. While Tomonosuke still felt very keenly his loss of status, he could not begrudge Ichi this pride. Rather, he was pleased to see his younger brother so competent and resourceful.

"Well, in any case, you only need to accompany me this once," Ichi said. "After today, I can remember the way."

"Oh! But I haven't been showing you the landmarks!" Tomonosuke was stricken with remorse for being too caught up in his own thoughts and not guiding more efficiently.

Ichi laughed. "I already know we've walked four blocks straight, then turned left and walked one more block, and the houses have become smaller and closer together, with fewer trees among them."

"What? You can tell all that just by listening?"

"Yes, of course, and you could too if you paid attention. Now we're crossing a small stream, right?"

Tomonosuke walked more slowly, pointing out the route. They had passed the licensed quarter on their way into the city, and he recalled the way without much difficulty. He paused at the corners and mile markers to let Ichi find them with his cane.

When they reached the narrow streets lined with teahouses and brothels, their lanterns shining and shouts and cries echoing, another short argument ensued. Tomonosuke still hesitated to leave Ichi on his own, but Ichi insisted that he could take care of himself, and besides, customers would not want to hire a masseur who had a companion to stare at them. At last Tomonosuke conceded the point and found a darkened corner to wait.

He watched Ichi tapping his way along the street, blowing his whistle, until a maid plucked at his sleeve and led him inside a teahouse. Tomonosuke leaned back into the shadows. He was squatting in the doorway of a toothbrush shop that had closed for the day, judging by the sign beside the door. He intended to keep a sharp eye out for when Ichi emerged back into the street to seek his next customer, but soon exhaustion got the better of him and he dozed, squatting with his back braced against the shop entrance. Confused images raced through his mind, of himself and Ichi walking along the road, endlessly walking.

A few hours later, Tomonosuke startled awake to the sound of Ichi's voice. "Aniki?"

"I'm here," he said groggily, struggling to his feet.

"I thought I heard the temple bell. Is it the hour of the ox already?"

Tomonosuke had no idea, but it felt very late. The paper lanterns were mostly out, and the street had gone quiet.

"Come, let's go home."

* * *

This became their daily routine. Ichi went out each night in secret on his own, and for a month or so he did quite well. The money he earned should have been enough to buy some rice and a few vegetables, but each time Rin went to the market, there was less and less to buy, and the price was higher and higher. Charcoal at least was still plentiful and cheap, and they laid in as much as they could. Ichi remarked cheerfully that the interior room held the warmth better than a room facing the outside.

One of Osono's maids took pity on them, and when Rin prepared their meager stores in the kitchen, she silently slipped them some dried sardines or toasted soybeans or pickled daikon when she thought the mistress might not notice. But it was still not enough.

Tomonosuke went down to the stream and caught a few small sweetfish, while Rin and Okyō scoured the hills for mushrooms and bracken.

But then the snow began to fall, sporadically at first, then every day, giant fat snowflakes falling so fast that the world turned white. The stream froze over, and the hills became impassable.

The snow in the yard piled up two feet, then three. From the shed, Okyō fetched large, cylindrical straw boots with rope handles to hold them on. She showed the others how to use these to stomp down the snow to clear a path from the kitchen to the well and the privy. This had to be done at least once a day, sometimes twice, and Osono's maids were happy to let someone else do it.

Ichi stopped going out to give massages. The snow obliterated all landmarks and muffled the echoes, tripped up his feet and froze his fingers. Even if he could make the trip, there were hardly any customers.

By the end of Shiwasu, the last month of the year, the snow reached the eaves of the house, and the road was a dark tunnel. For a few days, the weather turned unexpectedly warm, and some of the snow melted rapidly, then the next morning the skies darkened and eight feet of snow fell in a single day. There was no question of going out.

They passed a subdued New Year's holiday, with only a few pine boughs and a cake of mochi, a gift from their hosts, to mark the occasion. As Yoshito shared the mochi with them, he solemnly wished them good fortune in the coming year.

25

The Storehouse

Mutsuki, the first month of the new year, was dire. One snowy morning, Rin came back from market still clutching the unopened purse. The stalls were all closed. There was no more food to buy, and nothing more would come in until the spring harvest.

Yoshito prevailed on Osono to show them mercy, but by then there was precious little rice in the storehouse to share. The famine had come for all of them.

Reluctantly, Osono cracked open the thick, fireproof door to the storehouse, but Okyō refused to go inside, her face white. Rin went in her place, receiving a strainer full of uncooked rice, but reported back that the number of bales in the storehouse was not so great.

Tomonosuke did a quick calculation in his head. The household held ten people: himself, Ichi, Okyō, Rin, Yoshito, Osono, and their four servants. The rice would have to last all of them until the spring crop could be harvested, if the weather was favorable. It would not be enough. They could eke out a bit more with barley and millet, but a body could starve from eating only millet.

"I suppose the storehouse at your father's house has more bales of rice," Tomonosuke observed over their meager evening meal.

Okyō glared at him angrily. "If you're so certain, go beg from him yourself," she shot back. "But I tell you now, he'd sooner see me in my grave than give us any."

Tomonosuke did not reply, but still he felt that Sakakibara Masahiro would not allow his only daughter to starve, much less the head of the branch family. Masahiro was a high-ranking bannerman to the Takada daimyō, and a direct relation. Failing to provide for his dependents would dishonor him as head of the family. Surely if he only knew how desperate their circumstances were, he would help them.

In the middle of the month, Tomonosuke chose a sunny day for the short walk to Sakakibara Masahiro's residence. The piles of snow glittering in the sunshine on either side of the road reached above his head. He squinted his eyes against the glare, sharp as a knife. Not for the first time, he felt grateful to Okyō for equipping them all with winter clothing. He tucked his hands up inside the spacious sleeves of his padded hanten jacket.

Masahiro was not pleased to see him. Once again, Tomonosuke was not admitted beyond the six-mat room at the front entrance, and made to wait a very long time before Masahiro emerged from within, scowling at him.

"I don't recall inviting you to call on me here," he snapped.

Tomonosuke gave a low three-finger bow. "Honored father," he said, straightening. "Begging your pardon, but I have come to inform you that Hotta-san has insufficient stores to last until the next harvest, and your daughter—"

"What's it to me?" Masahiro cut him off.

"But I, that is..."

"That whore! Did she put you up to this? Well, she's your problem now. After the shame she brought on our family, you were the only one foolish enough to wed her, but that's your misfortune."

Tomonosuke tried not to let his surprise show on his face, but he must have failed, because Masahiro immediately narrowed his eyes and shifted his tone.

"Oho! You didn't know!" he smirked. "She damaged her reputation with her scandalous behavior, and no one in Echigo would have her. Only the far away Uchida clan was so desperate for her dowry that they agreed to the match without asking questions. Well, much good it's done you, I see."

"But the rice—"

"I have two sons and their families living here in this household to provide for. Okyō is no longer my dependent. As for Hotta-san, he shall make do with what he has, as we all must. It's your responsibility to provide for your family, Uchida-san." His voice dripped with sarcasm. "And what are you doing here anyway, so far from Omigawa, and looking like a fugitive? Perhaps I should send word to Lady Chacha...?"

Tomonosuke felt the blood drain from his head. "N-no, that won't be necessary."

"Good." Masahiro gave menacing smile. "Take care of your own family, Uchida-san."

Tomonosuke walked home through the snow with his head spinning. Privately, he had always thought Okyō was exaggerating her father's cruelty. His family could also be severe and demanding, but he could not imagine even Lady Chacha would be so heartless. And what was this scandal? It was the first he had heard of it.

* * *

"I told you it would be a waste of time," Okyō declared, reading Tomonosuke's face immediately as he came in.

"What would be a waste of time? Aniki, where were you?" Ichi sat up, his face creased in a frown.

Tomonosuke methodically peeled off his hanten and scarf and placed them in the closet without answering. He was never so glad to return to this rundown, cramped room.

"He went to beg my father for food, but he was turned away, as I said he would be," Okyō explained, never taking her eyes off Tomonosuke. He sat down heavily before the brazier, warming his hands above the charcoal. How he longed for his tobacco pipe.

"At least he isn't turning you over to the Omigawa daimyō," Okyō continued. Tomonosuke met her eyes for a second, then looked away. "Oh gods!" she cried. "What have you done?"

"Nothing!" Tomonosuke shifted to a more comfortable cross-legged position. Rin served him a cup of tea. The green leaves had been brewed so often the tea was little more than hot water, but he was grateful for it. "I doubt your father will go to so much trouble just for us." He took a long sip, feeling warmer at last.

Okyō sniffed and turned away.

They were all weary with boredom and inactivity, and being stuck together in this tiny room with nowhere else to go and nothing to do was very trying. Osono did not even allow Ichi to practice the shamisen in the house, saying it was a low-class instrument and the noise would disturb the neighbors.

"What did he say?" Okyō asked after a time.

Tomonosuke stared into his empty teacup. "He said he might write to my mother, but I don't think he will."

"You sound very certain. What else?"

"Well..." he paused uneasily. "He said you dishonored the family."

"He's a beast!" Rin burst out.

"What did he do to you?" Tomonosuke asked. He was trying to be gentle, but his voice sounded harsh even to his own ears.

Okyō turned to face the wall, but Ichi reached out and found her hand. "Did he lock you in the storehouse?" he asked, in the softer tone Tomonosuke had failed to achieve.

She nodded, then glanced at his waiting face and added, "Yes."

Tomonosuke shuddered. That explained why Okyō never went to fetch the rice from the storehouse, but always made Rin go instead. He felt a pang of sympathy for her, shut in the cold windowless building with stone walls a foot thick, for who knows how long.

"I'm the first born," she said in a low voice. "You know how it is. He was forever complaining that I was not born a boy. Then when my brothers were born, I was ignored completely. When I came of age, he tried to marry me to Kaminoue Naonaka, a high-ranking bannerman, but I refused. Kaminoue was an old man, with a reputation for cruelty. I would have been his third wife, after the first two died.

"So I said no. I said no daughter in Japan can be forced to marry against her will. He locked me in the storehouse and said I could stay there until I changed my mind."

"I'm so sorry," Ichi said, rubbing her shoulder.

"No, don't." Okyō shook him off. "I don't want your pity. You wanted to hear the story, so here it is. I stayed in that storehouse for days and days, until I couldn't stand it anymore. I pretended to be sick, and when they let me out to use the privy, I ran away. I ran to the licensed quarter, thinking maybe I could find work as a maid, but of course everyone saw right through me and no one would talk to me.

"Then I saw Rin being beaten by a brothel owner for refusing a customer, and I helped her run away too. I couldn't let her go back, and I didn't know what else do to, so I went back home and took her with me. I told my father I would marry Kaminoue Naonaka if only he let me keep Rin as my maid.

"But it was too late. I had been gone for two days, and had been seen all around the licensed quarter. Kaminoue Naonaka wouldn't have me, and neither would anyone else in Takada domain. They said I should go back and be a prostitute, since that was what I wanted. Gossip got around that I was so sex-crazed, I had run off just to steal customers from the honest whores. That's why I had to be given to the third son in a domain far enough away not to have heard, and too poor to ask questions."

She turned and glared at Tomonosuke, daring him to take offence at her words, but he only looked on her with sympathy.

"I had no idea how much you had suffered," he said softly. "You could have told me. I would not have judged you harshly for it."

She turned away from him again, tears streaming down her face. Tomonosuke felt a twisting stab of guilt deep in his gut as he witnessed her anguish. He longed to comfort her, but everything in her posture said *don't touch me*.

"I'm sorry my failures have caused you to return to this place," he said.

"It wasn't your fault," she choked out. "Your only crime was trusting too much."

"You're a better wife to me than I deserve," he replied. Then because he could not think if anything else to do, he put on his padded jacket again and went out to the back garden, leaving Ichi and Rin to embrace and comfort her. He could not help but think she would prefer their attentions more than his.

The garden was buried in snow. Even the tracks from the house to the well, the privy, and the shed were covered again. Taking the large circular boots from the shed, he stomped about in the snow at random, clearing his mind of all thought. A brittle crust had formed on top of the drifts, and the crunching sound as he broke through to the powder below was oddly satisfying. His breath hung in the air.

Masahiro was right, he realized. He had a responsibility to Okyō, Ichi, and Rin. For too long he had simply drifted along, letting others make decisions for him, allowing them all to be buffeted by circumstance.

No more.

He would not let them all stay here to slowly waste away. They had all grown thin from months on the road, and now they were becoming gaunt, emaciated. Ichi most of all, who had always been lean. His eyes and cheeks had become hollow, sunken. It pained Tomonosuke deeply to see him sitting listlessly in their run-down room.

Tomonosuke thought of how fearlessly, cheerfully Ichi took to the road, even in unfamiliar places, how he never hesitated to strike out for somewhere new, and always expected to be met with kindness. He was ashamed to think how cowardly he had been by comparison.

His heart beating faster after the unaccustomed exercise, Tomonosuke returned the boots to the shed and went back inside, brushing the snow from his clothing. With more conviction than he had felt in months, he borrowed paper and an inkstone from Yoshito and penned a letter to Lady Chacha.

26

Grey Starlings

Every day was filled with the sound of trickling water as the snows melted. Still they passed the time in the same way, lying about the cramped room, eating the rapidly dwindling store of rice, the portions growing smaller each day.

In the entryway by the kitchen was an enormous wooden barrel, as high as a man's waist, covered with a lid and weighted with rocks. Inside, it was filled with salted, fermented rice bran, used to pickle vegetables. Every day, the maids removed the lid and plunged their hands and arms in to the elbow, turning the bran to prevent it from spoiling, filling the air with the acrid, sour smell. Daikon, carrots, cabbage, and cucumbers that had been kept cool in the storehouse were rotated through, but now there were almost none left.

When the maids were not looking, Rin, with Ichi by her side, shifted the stones off the lid and slipped her hands in, feeling about for bits of cabbage leaves that might have been forgotten. On finding one, she could not help but put it directly into her mouth, without even rinsing it. The taste was almost unbearably salty.

"What are you doing!" Ichi poked her in the ribs. "Don't eat that!"

But a moment later, he had his hands in the bran as well. The taste was awful, and the texture was like wet sand, but they were so hungry they could not stop themselves.

"Someone's coming!" Ichi hissed at her, his sharp ears picking up the footfalls before she did. They hastily replaced the lid and hurried outside to the well to wash the tell-tale crumbs of bran off their hands.

A few hours later, they were writhing on the floor, clutching their bellies and moaning.

Tomonosuke looked at them in alarm. "What's wrong? Are you ill?"

"They've been eating the rice bran out of the pickle barrel again," Okyō said with contempt. To Rin she said, "I told you not to do that."

Rin squeezed her eyes shut and did not answer. It was only wind, but it was very painful. Suddenly, she let out a tremendous fart. They all giggled despite themselves. Rin turned red and rushed out to the privy, with Ichi following behind her.

It was quite a long time before they returned, their faces drawn and greenish.

"We're leaving," Tomonosuke declared with a sudden resolve.

"What, just like that?" Okyō stared at him in surprise.

"We can't remain here in Jōetsu to slowly starve to death. Now that the snow is melting and the roads are beginning to open, we have to go, before we're too weak to walk."

"And go where?"

Tomonosuke pursed his lips. He was hoping that perhaps in some other domain, the famine would not be as severe, but he had no clear plan in mind.

Ichi sat leaning against a beam in the wall, his gaunt features still pale. "Still no word from Omigawa?"

"No."

"Well, it's yet early in the season," Ichi offered hopefully. "Surely if we can only return to Edo, there will be more food and a way to earn money."

"You have no idea how hard the road to Edo is," Okyō snapped.

Edo was not so far, only about fifty miles or so, but in between lay the Chichibu mountain range, a steep, unfamiliar territory. Tomonosuke felt trapped in this remote town, far from home and without any way to easily return.

"In any case, if we cross the mountains, we should continue on to Omigawa and try to get you a pardon, rather than attempting to get by in Edo under false papers like fugitives," Okyō said.

"A pardon is not at all certain," Tomonosuke said morosely, "even if my mother sees fit to intervene, which is even less certain."

"Even if you had an heir at last?" Ichi said. They all turned to stare at him. Even Rin straightened up in surprise.

Okyō laughed incredulously. "Don't be ridiculous!" Since they had all come to live in this tiny room together, Ichi slept beside Tomonosuke and Okyō slept beside Rin, but none of them had indulged in carnal relations of any kind. Proximity, modesty, and privation had robbed them all of any feelings of lust.

"Well..." said Ichi slowly, "perhaps it would be time now to consummate the arrangement from earlier."

"What arrangement?" Tomonosuke asked suspiciously.

Ichi could not see the murderous look Okyō was shooting him and blundered on unaware. "You know. That I, ah, would help Okyō-dono to conceive an heir. You said—"

"What?!"

"Ichi, be silent!"

Okyō was standing before him, her face red, her hands curled into fists.

Ichi's mouth fell open, a small *o* of confusion.

"Aniki, you didn't know? But you said..."

"You fool! Why must you say such things out loud?" Okyō sat down again and turned her face to the wall.

Tomonosuke felt anger rising in his breast. Just when he was at last feeling greater sympathy for Okyō—how could she manipulate him like this? The thought of her conspiring with Ichi filled him with resentment. Now more than ever, he felt trapped in this tiny room with the two of them, and nowhere to go.

"Aniki?"

Tomonosuke felt a pang at Ichi's hurt, lost expression, but he was not yet ready to put his anger aside. Even though he was certain this was Okyō's idea, he was displeased to think that Ichi had gone along with it.

"Aniki, please! Don't be angry! I thought you knew! Okyō-dono was afraid that if she didn't have a child, her father would divorce you two and bring her back here to marry someone else."

And yet here they were anyway, living under the shadow of her father, for all the good it did them, Tomonosuke thought bitterly.

"Aniki? Please say something."

Tomonosuke felt a twisting stab of pain in his gut to realize that as long as he remained silent, Ichi had no way to know what he was thinking or feeling. Yet he did not want to give voice to the furious jumble of his thoughts and say something intemperate that he might regret.

"I...I do not consent to such an arrangement," he said at last, holding his voice steady with a great effort.

Tomonosuke half expected Ichi to bump his forehead to the floor and beg for forgiveness, but instead he merely nodded and said, "I understand. It was my fault for misapprehending."

Ichi stood and felt about in the closet for his padded jacket.

"Wait, are you going out? Where are you going?" Rin asked in alarm. She had been watching this exchange with wide eyes.

"Yes, now that the roads are clear, I'm going back to the licensed quarter to look for massage customers," he said wearily. "If we're to travel to Edo, we'll need more cash."

Tomonosuke watched him go with hooded eyes. Earlier, he might have tried to stop him, insisting that he was too weak from hunger, that the roads were not clear enough yet. But now he said nothing.

* * *

Much later, past the hour of the rat, Ichi returned, his mood utterly altered. He rapped lightly at the fusuma before entering the room, unsure if the others were awake or asleep, if the andon was lit or extinguished.

"Ichi! You're back!" Tomonosuke's voice was troubled. "Come in. Wait, Rin is lighting the andon."

"What for?"

Ichi smiled as he sat down, reaching his frozen fingers toward the brazier. He could hear Rin striking a flake of quartz against a metal bar embedded in a small block of wood to light the lamp wick. This seemed to him a waste of lamp oil, as they could just as easily converse in the dark, but sighted people had their peculiar habits.

"Ichi, we were worried about you!" Tomonosuke said as the andon sparked to life with a fizzing sound.

Ichi waved a hand, still smiling. "I told you, I'm perfectly fine. I didn't make much money, but it was no trouble at all to find my way. But listen, I figured out how we can get to Edo."

"What is it?" Tomonosuke sounded wary. Ichi could hear rustling and shifting, as Okyō sat up from the futon. He felt badly for awakening them, but he was bubbling over with good news.

"I fell in with a company of linen merchants who are traveling to Edo tomorrow. They want to be the first to arrive in the city with their stocks. They're certain the mountain passes are all open by now. There's to be a very large group departing at dawn from Naoetsu. They're going to float down the Hokura River on a barge, then pick up the Mikuni Road to Edo."

"Oh, it's the grey starlings," said Okyō.

"The what?"

"Every spring, so many people go to Edo, they call them grey starlings. Not just the merchants, but laborers going to look for work. Ichi is correct, there will be a big crowd. It will be safer if we go with them rather than on our own."

"So we leave with them at daybreak?" Ichi asked hopefully, pleased to be the one who solved their dilemma.

"Yes," Tomonosuke said decisively. "There's no reason to stay here."

"Without notifying Sakakibara-sama?" Ichi asked.

"Yes. He will only try to interfere. I'll leave a note for Hotta-san, but I'm sure he and his wife will be glad to be rid of us."

"I agree," Okyō said, jumping up to collect their few possessions.

* * *

In the hour of the tiger, long before the rest of the household arose, they crept silently out the front door. Tomonosuke and Okyō carried the bundles, while Rin guided Ichi by holding one end of his bamboo cane. He carried Oboro's shamisen on his back wrapped in the green arabesque cloth.

As they hastened along the deserted road, Rin took several bites of something then pressed it into Ichi's hand. It was a long piece of smoked, pickled daikon, he realized. He ate part of it, enjoying the salty, crunchy sensation, before stopping to think.

"Wait, Rin, where did you get this?"

"I took it from the kitchen as we were leaving," she said carelessly.

"Rin! That's stealing!"

"We need it more than they do. Anyway it's too late now."

Ichi held out the daikon for her to take. "Please, give the rest to aniki and Okyō-dono."

Ichi was unhappy with Rin's casual theft but the aching hunger in the pit of his stomach was a constant companion, obliterating all other concerns. He was even more unhappy to think that Tomonosuke might still be angry with him, but now that they had embarked on the course he suggested, there was nothing to do but put one foot in front of the other. The breeze on his face warmed very slightly and he heard a few reluctant birds, telling him the sun was rising.

At Naoetsu, near the port, they found the grey starlings, a group of nearly a hundred men and women—laborers, townspeople, and merchants—gathered on the banks of the Hokura River, slowly loading their possessions onto a series of large, flat barges. They would have to pay ferrymen to drag them against the current with a long pole, as they were heading inland, into the mountains, but still it was faster than walking.

Ichi, Rin, and Okyō crouched on the pebbly riverbank while Tomonosuke went to negotiate with a group of linen merchants and a ferryman to secure their passage. The wife of one of the merchants had lit a small fire and was roasting sweetfish on skewers while they waited. A fishy, oily smell floated in the air, making Ichi's stomach contract painfully.

To distract himself and pass the time, Ichi unslung the shamisen and began to play. His fingers were stiff and slow after months without practicing, but he pushed himself to go faster, playing one of the northern folk tunes he had learned from Gen. Soon he could sense that a small crowd had gathered, and he poured even more of the wild, rural north into his performance. He thought of the deer calling from the mountains, the swish of the wind over the wide rice paddies, the cries of the birds in the tall pine trees.

As he plucked the last notes, the crowd applauded, an appreciative audience. The merchant's wife pressed two skewers into his hand and he thanked her profusely. He gave one of the fish to Okyō and Rin, and shared the other with Tomonsuke.

Tomonosuke ate gratefully, but would not say anything, except that they had a place on one of the barges. Ichi wondered anxiously if he was still angry, but now was not the time to ask him.

As they floated up the river, away from Jōetsu, Okyō stood up to watch the houses slipping past, Takada Castle in the distance. Angrily, she threw the empty skewer she still held into the river.

"Good riddance!" she shouted.

Tomonosuke tugged at her sleeve. "Sit down! People are staring at you," he whispered.

She sat down heavily. "I don't care! I'm never going back, never! I thought it would be better to come here than to die, but now I don't care. I'll die before I ever go back."

"Let's hope it doesn't come to that," Tomonosuke said grimly.

* * *

The journey from Jōetsu was not easy, but at least they were in good company. The grey starlings, like their namesake, were a rowdy, dirty, raucous bunch, in high spirits and eager to begin their seasonal migration, despite the lack of food. They shared what little they had, supplemented as best they could with river fish, bracken, and mushrooms.

A few adventurous souls even hunted some rabbits when they camped for the night on the river bank, then roasted them before the fire on spits. Out of curiosity, Ichi tasted a bit, but the unfamiliar greasy, gamey taste turned his stomach. He had heard of wild men in the mountains eating the flesh of animals, but it seemed very uncivilized to him.

They continued up the river for several days, as far as possible, but as they entered more deeply into the mountain range at Matsunoyama they were at last obliged to bid farewell to the ferrymen and continue on foot. The weather was chilly as they trudged along the muddy track, still lined with piles of snow, skirting the edge of Mount Naeba until they came to Shiozawa, a post town along the Mikuni Road that connected Echigo to Edo.

On the Mikuni Road, they traveled from post town to post town, each one about a day's walk apart. The linen merchants took a shine to Ichi, and in exchange for entertaining them in the evenings, they allowed him and his companions to stay with them at the inns. Ichi was very grateful not to have to sleep outside, but even in the towns there was very little food to be had, and walking all day made him hungrier than ever. He could barely summon the energy to pluck the shamisen strings, but urged himself on with the knowledge that Tomonosuke, Okyō, and Rin were depending on him.

Each night, they fell into an exhausted sleep, and each morning arose early to begin the journey again. Still Tomonosuke did not speak to him, but whether from anger or weariness Ichi could not tell. The thought weighed on his spirits and made the journey seem even more arduous.

The road turned due south, up into the mountains, until they came to Mikuni Pass, the highest point of the journey. Although it was well-traveled, the track through the pass was steep and treacherous with mud and tree roots and low-hanging branches. Rin guided him as usual by holding one end of his cane, but walking in this manner was much more difficult on the rough, uneven path than on a city street. Ichi tripped and fell several times on the way up, and each time Rin apologized profusely, although he assured her it was not her fault.

After a tree branch caught him full in the face and knocked him backward, Ichi heard Tomonosuke tell Rin to take the bundle, then felt him grasp his arm. Ichi rearranged their grip so he was resting his hand on Tomonosuke's elbow, the two walking very close together. With this closer contact, and his cane in his other hand, Ichi had a much clearer concept of his surroundings, and proceeded with more confidence and fewer mishaps.

"Thank you, aniki."

Tomonosuke merely grunted.

When they reached the top of the pass, the company paused to rest and take in the view. The area was called Mikuni (Three Province) Pass because it commanded a view of three provinces: Echigo, Shinano, and Kōzuke. The travelers all remarked to one another on the view.

The ground was too muddy and wet to sit, so Ichi leaned against Tomonosuke. He did not pull away from this intimate pose, which Ichi took as a hopeful sign.

"Tell me, aniki, is the view very beautiful?"

"It is."

"What does it look like?"

Tomonosuke paused. "The mountain peaks are still snowy and white, but in the valleys the light green leaves of the trees and grasses are already springing up. It's like in the poem." He recited:

> *yuki no uchi ni*
> *haru wa kinikeri*
>> Even amid the snow,
>> the spring has come.

Ichi completed the lines:

> *uguisu no*

kōreru namida
ima ya tokuramu
The nightingale's frozen tears
now flow at last

As he spoke, Ichi felt his own tears start in his eyes. "Aniki, please forgive me!"

Tomonosuke's voice was even lower and rougher than usual. "You conspired against me with my own wife."

"No! Not against you! And I tell you, I thought you knew! You are my sworn elder brother. I would never, ever betray you. I would sooner cut out my own heart and replace it with a stone." He paused uncertainly when there was no reply. "Please, aniki! If you can't forgive me, then leave me here on the mountain. I don't wish to go down the other side unless it's with you."

Tomonosuke gazed down at Ichi's anguished face as the younger man clung to him, his arm draped over Ichi's shoulders. Tears rolled down Ichi's face from his perpetually half-closed eyes, and Tomonosuke felt his throat constrict and his own eyes burn with tears. Ichi's face was gaunt with hunger, his cheekbones standing out sharply and his ruined eyes even more sunken than before. He looked haggard and wan.

They were all hungry and thin, but Ichi, who had been more than lean even before the famine, seemed the worst affected. As he huddled under his arm, Tomonosuke could feel his shoulder bones and ribs jutting painfully. He realized how far Ichi had been pushing himself, not only to walk all day but to perform far into the night, so they might all have shelter and at least a little food.

How could he ever doubt Ichi's devotion to him? He felt humbled by Ichi's generosity and bravery, the way he never hesitated or complained but always pressed on hopefully. Staring into Ichi's face, even though he could not return his gaze, Tomonosuke felt deeply moved. This one flaw somehow made his grace and allure more profound, more affecting. Did not the greatest beauty also contain a trace of sadness? As in the poems of the *Kokinshū* they recited to each other on the day they first met, and again just now, the images of sublime elegance and desire were threaded through with melancholy at the fragility, the transience of all things. Tomonosuke felt a sudden powerful rush of emotion at the thought of the gaze not returned, the sympathy and desire he felt for him.

Rather than answering Ichi directly, Tomonosuke recited another poem, the line springing forth from his lips unawares.

haru no yo no
yami wa ayanashi
ume no hana
iro koso miene
ka ya wa kakururu
In the darkness of a spring night,
I may not see the alluring plum blossoms,
yet how could I fail to notice their scent?

Tomonosuke felt another pang as he watched Ichi's features convulse with uncertainty and anxiety. Surely he understood the poem? But perhaps it would be best to speak more plainly. He found it unexpectedly difficult to find the right words.

"Forgive me for being angry and causing you to worry," he said at last. "I understand why you and Okyō acted as you did. I will not continue this journey unless it's with you."

"And the scent of the plums?"

"We need not rely on sight to know beauty. There are other ways in which we recognize each other. I have learned that from you."

"Aniki!" Ichi's still wet face was transformed with smiles. Again Tomonosuke felt his chest constrict, but the sensation was pleasing. He would dedicate his life to ensuring he always saw that look of happiness on Ichi's face, he thought. He was slightly surprised to discover so much emotion conveyed despite Ichi's cloudy, half-closed eyes, in the hands clutching his arm, in that shining, guileless smile.

Tomonosuke embraced him tightly but only for a moment. The top of a mountain on a public road was no place for intimacy.

"Come," he said roughly. "The others have nearly all begun the descent. We must hurry if we don't want to be left behind. It's still a long way to the next post town."

Ichi nodded, apparently too overcome to speak, and fell into step half a pace behind him, holding tightly to his arm with one hand, and feeling along the uneven track with the cane in his other hand. Tomonosuke walked carefully, keenly aware of his responsibility to guide him safely, and of the tremendous trust that Ichi was placing in him. Yet his heart felt lighter than it had for many days.

27

The Letter

The travelers slowly descended from the mountain pass. At last they drew away from the mountains to easier terrain, yet still food was in short supply. After many days of walking, they reached the end of the Mikuni Road in Takasaki-juku. This was a large, prosperous post town, yet the grey starlings did not linger.

They took one short night's rest, then set out before dawn the next morning on the Nakasendō, which would bring them to Edo. Unlike the roads they had walked previously, the Nakasendō was one of the five official routes, a broad, well-traveled road with fine stone paving. After Takasaki, there were only twelve more stations until they reached Edo, and the merchants and laborers were eager to arrive.

Although the road was much easier, Tomonosuke felt almost unbearably weary, and looking at the others' gaunt faces, he knew they felt the same. At each post town, there was no rice to be had, but only millet and brayed soybeans. Rin and Ichi had taken to chewing on grass as they walked along; she passed to him the tender green shoots just now springing up in the warmer weather, but this did little to sustain them.

At Urawa-juku, as they sat at yet another tavern that had nothing to offer beside strips of dried daikon, without even soy sauce to dip it in,

Tomonosuke was gripped by the certainty that they could go no further. There were only two more stations before they reached Edo, but what would happen then? The merchants had linen to sell and would not support them any longer. The laborers could find work, but as a samurai, even a rōnin, Tomonosuke was forbidden from day labor, and no boss would dare hire him. Ichi could go back to the Tōdōza, but Tomonosuke, Okyō, and Rin could not follow him there.

He watched Ichi downing cup after cup of watery barley tea in a vain attempt to fill his stomach. Tomonosuke knew Ichi would never consent to go live at the Tōdōza residence again if he knew that Tomonosuke did not have a home or income, not even to save his own life.

So what then? They were not far from Omigawa. Perhaps they should return to Sawara. Even if he were arrested, perhaps he could secure clemency for the others.

"What do you mean there's no sake?"

Tomonosuke raised his gaze as a haughty voice rang out across the tavern, then immediately ducked his head again. He recognized the man—it was Inō Tadanobu, a low-ranking retainer of the Omigawa daimyō. Tomonosuke had no wish to speak to him, and listening to the man remonstrate with the serving girl, he felt ashamed on his behalf. Of course if there was no rice, there could be no sake either. How could he not understand that? It was sickening the way he carried on as if he expected the sake to appear if only he shouted loudly enough. The poor serving girl could only bow her head and apologize over and over.

To Tomonosuke's horror, as this was going on, Ichi strode confidently to Inō's side and interceded.

"My lord," Ichi said boldly, bowing low, "it is indeed a shame there is no sake to be had here or anywhere in this miserable town, but perhaps you might pass the weary evening with some music? I can play any song, old or new."

Inō turned his attention from the serving girl to Ichi, but the curl of his lip remained unchanged. "No charm in listening to you pluck the strings without a cup in my hand."

Ichi bowed even lower. "Then perhaps a massage, my lord?"

Inō paused for a long moment, in which Tomonosuke feared he might strike Ichi, but at last he dropped his angry look and rolled his shoulders with a sigh. "Very well then, why not? I've been traveling hard. I deserve a bit of rest and relaxation."

Tomonosuke was still apprehensive, until he saw Ichi straighten again and noticed a hint of a smile on his lips as he followed Inō out of the tavern. Ichi knew what he was doing, Tomonosuke realized.

An hour later, Ichi returned to the room at the inn they were sharing with a triumphant grin on his face.

"I'm back!" he announced cheerfully.

"Ichi!" Rin cried out, rising up to take his hand as he opened the shōji. "Welcome back."

"Did he pay you?" Okyō asked.

"Do you know who that was?" Tomonosuke asked at the same time.

Ichi laughed as he knelt down and tossed a few coins onto the floor.

"Of course I know who it was! I have often massaged Inō-sama in Sawara, although he didn't recognize me. He underpaid me too, the beast, but it doesn't matter. What I learned from him more than made up for it."

"What?" This from Okyō, although the others were just as eager to hear.

"He's been dispatched by the daimyō himself to carry a letter to Jōetsu addressed to you, aniki, from your mother."

"What!" Tomonosuke started up in surprise. He had given up hope of receiving a reply to his letter months ago. He began to pace around the tiny room.

"Go talk to him," Okyō said.

"No!"

"Aniki, you can't let him travel all the way to Jōetsu in vain," Ichi added.

"Why not?"

"Don't you at least want to know the contents of the letter and how things lie before we return to Sawara?" Okyō asked.

Tomonosuke ceased pacing and stared at her. He had not even spoken aloud his decision to return home rather than continue to Edo. How did she know?

"Come, aniki, Inō-sama is in no hurry to depart tomorrow morning, I assure you. Let us pass by his inn at the hour of the dragon, and he'll be overjoyed to deliver the letter to you here in Urawa and save himself the weary journey north."

"Yes," Okyō agreed. "Surely the letter contains good news, otherwise the daimyō would be sending retainers to arrest you, not just one man to hand you a note."

Tomonosuke at last consented to this plan, although he had very little sleep that night. He could not admit that he was deeply ashamed to appear before that boor Inō Tadanobu in his current state, with his hair grown out and wearing patched peasant clothes. But Ichi and Okyō were correct, he had to face him if he planned to return home at all.

The next morning was warm and sunny. Tomonosuke had no excuse not to set out on the path Ichi instructed, although he insisted on going alone. Ichi had a peculiar way of giving directions: turn left at the milestone set at the corner, go past the soy sauce brewery with the sour smell, turn left onto the largest street with many trees overhead. He wasn't sure of the name of the inn, being unable to read the sign, but it was a large, expensive one with a stone horse trough in front.

Tomonosuke found it surprisingly easy to find his way, and felt renewed respect for Ichi's ability to navigate and memorize city streets on his own. There before him, as Ichi had said, was a large inn with a narrow rectangular horse trough in front. The noren curtain fluttering in the morning breeze announced the name Kinotokiya.

He loitered uncertainly as a maid came out to splash water on the street to keep the dust down. She gave him a sidelong look, the bamboo ladle in one hand and the wooden bucket in the other, but did not say anything to him. He stood aside as a groom led two horses from the stable around the corner and tied them to the hitching post in front of the inn. Another groom followed with two more horses, obscuring the entrance. Tomonosuke gave the horses a wide berth.

He waited as guests departed one after another, some on foot, some on horseback. A palanquin arrived, carried by two young men with arms covered in tattoos, and bore away a lady in a hat and veil.

At last, only one horse remained, and then Inō Tadanobu emerged from the noren, stretching and blinking in the morning sunlight with a scowl. Feeling as artificial as an actor on a stage, Tomonosuke passed in front of him, trying to make it seem as if he were simply walking down the street. Inō's gaze passed right over him as if he did not exist.

With an inward sigh, Tomonosuke interceded himself between Inō and his horse and locked eyes with the man.

"Is that Inō-san?" he said, with a show of surprise, feeling even more like a talentless actor.

Inō narrowed his eyes, his scowl deepening.

"Don't you recognize me?" Then, scraping up what felt like the very last of his dignity, he said, "It is I, Uchida Tomonosuke."

Inō's eyebrows shot upward. "You! It can't be!"

"Unfortunately yes." Tomonosuke twisted his mouth down at the corners, enduring Inō's gaze that swept his shameful appearance from his unshaven head to his worn straw sandals.

"Well, well, well." Inō sucked air noisily between his teeth as he rocked back on his high wooden sandals and shrugged an arm up inside his kimono, stroking his chin as he stared at Tomonosuke with open contempt. "Fancy seeing you here. As it happens, I was just on my way back to Omigawa. Perhaps I could take you with me, if you're willing to ease our travel expenses."

Tomonosuke stiffened, meeting the man's gaze boldly. Like a flash of enlightenment, he suddenly realized he had no cause to feel ashamed. Rather, it was Inō, attempting to cheat him, who should feel shame. Was there no end to the duplicity of his fellow samurai? Where was their much-vaunted honor? He felt deeply grateful to Ichi for so skillfully uncovering the truth for him.

He held out a hand imperiously. "The letter, if you please."

Inō blinked in surprise, pulling his arm back through his sleeve. "What?"

"I know you bear a letter addressed to me. Hand it over now, or I will inform the daimyō of how you failed to discharge your duty."

Inō's disposition changed in an instant. "Of course, sir. I have it here." He reached into the fold of his kimono and drew out a long thin paper folded vertically.

Tomonosuke recognized his name written on the front in his mother's bold hand. He took it without a word.

"If I might be of service on your return to Omigawa...?" Inō offered in an ingratiating tone, but Tomonosuke had already turned his back and was striding away.

"No need," he said without looking back. "I will return in my own time and make a full report to the daimyō."

*　*　*

"Oho, I wish I had been there to hear it!" Ichi crowed when Tomonosuke related his encounter. Even Okyō gave a little smirk of satisfaction.

"But come now," she prompted. "Read the letter!"

Tomonosuke broke the seal and unfolded the paper to the left. The letter was not long, only a single sheet. Lady Chacha began with a formal salutation, poetic reference to the spring weather and how the plum blossoms had already faded but the cherries were not yet in bloom, and a perfunctory inquiry into the state of his health.

"'I received your letter with concern,'" Tomonosuke read aloud. "'It was thought that you had perished in the earthquake. However, since the honored daimyō's return to Omigawa, the irregularities in the office of the exchequer increased, and further inquiry found that Matsudaira Sadahide had been engaging in questionable practices. In his wisdom, the daimyō removed him from office.'" Tomonosuke paused and looked up at his audience, to see his own look of surprise mirrored on their faces.

"'I trust you will make all haste to return,'" he continued. "'I informed the daimyō that you had traveled to Echigo to attend to an urgent matter concerning your wife's family. He is willing to allow it for a brief time only. If you do not return as soon as possible, you will be guilty of the offense of leaving the domain without permission.

'I await your return,'" the letter concluded. "'In haste, your mother, &c.'" Her signature was starkly refined. There followed the date, the tenth day of the month of Yayoi, the tenth year of the Bunsei era (1827), his name, and a brief postscript.

"'Postscript: Doubtless you have already been notified, but the honored daimyō passed away shortly after the New Year and has been succeeded by the young Lord Kiyochika, now titled the honored daimyō Lord Uchida Masamichi, styled Bungo-no-kami.'"

28

The Return

They departed the inn immediately, not even pausing to bid farewell to the grey starlings, or to search out Inō Tadanobu, the bearer of the letter. As he was on horseback, presumably he was already far ahead of them on the road.

Tomonosuke felt the need to return urgently. His shock at no longer being considered a rōnin was replaced with anxiety over his status as absent from the domain without leave. This was a serious offense, and he had no wish to be cleared of one charge, only to be stripped of his status for yet another.

The journey to Sawara was short but difficult. There was no official road in the direction they wished to go. They walked through small villages, not even proper post towns. As they went east, the effects of the famine seemed less severe, but while there was somewhat more food to be had, they had almost no cash left to buy any, nor did Tomonosuke wish to tarry long enough that they might earn more.

For three days they hurried along, sleeping rough, eating no more than a few sweetfish roasted on skewers, until at last they came to Toride. At Okyō's insistence, Tomonosuke used nearly the last of their cash to visit a barber to have his face and the crown of his head shaved and his hair cut, oiled and tied in a proper topknot. He had been unwilling to waste money on vanity, but dressed in his old crested kimono, even if it was patched and worn, he felt returned to the world, no longer a vagabond or fugitive.

While he was doing this, Rin and Okyō visited the public bath. They combed each other's hair and tied it in the best approximation of the marumage chignon they could manage on their own. There was no more money for them to visit a hairdresser. Okyō's appearance was also greatly altered by their time as fugitives, as her shaved eyebrows had grown in and the toothblack had chipped off, giving her a somewhat ghoulish appearance. Tomonosuke knew she felt as ashamed of her appearance as he did of his, but there was nothing they could do about it until they had more cash.

Ichi waited for them by the docks. "Well?" he asked with a wan smile when he heard Tomonosuke call to him. "Are you very handsome now? I'm sure I'm the only disreputable looking one." He rubbed a hand over his head. His hair had grown out several inches and stood out in all directions, and yet the effect only offset his delicate features and made him look more lovely than ever.

Tomonosuke draped an affectionate arm over his shoulders. "I don't know how you manage it, but you are still more beautiful than the rest of us put together."

* * *

Tomonosuke used the very last of their coins to hire a barge to take them down the Tone River, and even then, the ferryman would only consent on the promise of further payment after they arrived. Eager to reach Sawara and secure this additional cash, the ferryman pushed on with remarkable speed. Unlike when they left Jōetsu, this time they were traveling with the current, which was swift as the mighty Tone was swollen with the melting snow from the far-off mountains and the spring rains. The ferryman guided the tiny boat along at a brisk clip, weaving around the barges laden with goods from Edo.

When night fell, the ferryman anchored the boat along the shore, but as they had no more money, they slept as best they could inside it, and set out again early the next morning. Tomonosuke was feeling light-headed from hunger, and the others appeared limp and listless in the rocking boat. The ferryman munched methodically on strips of dried squid, but he did not offer to share, and they did not ask.

Tomonosuke watched as the low rolling hills of Shimōsa Province slid by to his right, to his left the endless flat plains divided neatly into rice paddies. The flooded fields reflected the blue sky and white clouds like a series of gigantic mirrors, dotted all over in perfectly straight rows with the tiny rice seedlings. At last the rice paddies gave way to more and more houses, first with thatched roofs then tiles, as they arrived in Sawara. The river banks were lined with weeping willow trees, the new leaves a pale green.

Home, he thought, viewing the houses and trees as familiar as his worn-out robes, yet it did not feel like home. All around him, the city was bustling with traffic, on the road and in the river, goods plying to and fro, laborers pulling carts or carrying boxes, men and women rushing off in every direction, dogs barking, samurai on horseback pushing through the crowd and ignoring who might be underfoot. He felt oddly detached from it all.

* * *

Ichi felt the boat bump up against the dock, then Tomonosuke's hands helping him from the boat. He was very unsteady, and sat down hard as soon as he felt the dock beneath his feet. It was as if he had used the very last of his energy to reach Sawara, and now had nothing at all left.

The next few hours were a blur. Ichi was only vaguely aware as Tomonosuke sent to Lady Chacha for money to pay the ferryman and a palanquin to carry them to the Uchida family residence. The air in Sawara smelled familiar, Ichi thought faintly as he bumped along, squeezed inside the palanquin with Okyō, while Rin and Tomonosuke walked along beside it. The smell of cedar from the buildings, mingling with the murky canal, the breeze filtering through the new leaves of the trees, and far off the faint scent of the sea, all combined to remind him that he had returned. But it did not feel like home, exactly. He was too tired and hungry to form any further coherent thoughts.

The noise of the merchant district at the center of town fell away, and the sound of the palanquin bearers' grunts and feet crunching on gravel was much louder as they entered the quieter samurai neighborhood. At an unfamiliar residence that he sensed was quite large, Ichi allowed himself to be led from the palanquin by unknown hands, taken to a bath, and given a change of clothes. After the bath he fell into an uneasy sleep and awoke with a start, uncertain if it was day or night.

"It's all right, we're at Uchida-dono's family estate," Rin whispered, and he felt her small bony hand grasp his reassuringly. "Sit up, it's breakfast time," she added.

His head swam as he sat up and pushed aside the futon, realizing that it was the smell of rice that had awakened him.

"Ichi, this is for you." He was very relieved to hear Tomonosuke's voice, and feel his hand pressing a small warm bowl of rice into his, followed by chopsticks. Nothing had ever smelled so good, yet he could hardly taste it.

"Slow down! Don't eat so fast," Tomonosuke warned him, but Ichi could not help himself. He gulped down the entire bowl in less than a minute, and heard Rin beside him doing the same. A few minutes later, it all came back up again, both of them taking turns retching into a bucket.

Okyō opened the shōji along two sides of the room to let in the fresh air, while Tomonosuke sent to the kitchen to ask them to prepare okayu rice porridge.

Ichi passed the day like an invalid, resting and slowly eating plain rice porridge, but by the second day, he felt much recovered.

"Was there no famine here?" he asked, working on his second bowl of rice for his morning meal.

"It was not as severe in this region," Tomonosuke said, then added uncomfortably, "and it seems my family has been hoarding rice."

No one said anything. It was shameful to think that his family might be allowing people to die in order to have more for themselves.

"They say the spring harvest will be better," he offered hopefully.

* * *

On the third day, Tomonosuke was summoned to an audience with the daimyō. He thought to go alone, but Okyō and Ichi insisted on accompanying him, and Rin added that she must attend to her lady. He gave up arguing with them, seeming slightly relieved not to have to go on his own.

Still somewhat shaky, Ichi leaned on Tomonosuke's arm for the short walk to the daimyō's residence. No one spoke; the only sound was the slapping of their sandals as they walked along the dirt road. Tomonosuke had greeted his mother and elder brother upon their return but the others had been too unwell to do so, and in any case, he had only spoken a few words to them. He had no idea what the daimyō would say to him. It seemed unlikely he would be executed—if that was the daimyō's intention, he would have arrested him already. But he could still be disciplined or even stripped of his rank.

Tomonosuke was wearing a formal crested kimono loaned to him by his brother, and plain grey hakama, with his katana and wakizashi at his side. He did not feel like his former self, exactly, but he was more self-assured than he had been in months. It was not for his own self that he wished to have his rank reinstated, he realized, but that he might provide for Ichi and Okyō.

It was strange to see the young lord sitting at the head of the great hall, surrounded by the same senior counselor and other high-ranking advisors and bannermen who had served his father. Kiyochika, now renamed Masamichi, seemed to find it strange as well, perhaps because he had spent his entire life until his succession living in Edo. He seemed ill at ease as he acknowledged Tomonosuke's formal greeting with a nod.

Tomonosuke was slightly alarmed to see his mother and elder brother already seated in the hall, below the senior counselor to the left.

When had they arrived? It made him uneasy to think they had been talking about him in his absence.

Lady Chacha was a striking figure, remarkably youthful and vigorous for her age, which was past sixty. Her back was straight, and the high bridge of her nose and clear, sharp eyes gave her a penetrating, severe look. She did not wear her hair long, tied in a high round marumage chignon like most women, but cut to shoulder length, parted straight down the middle and hanging loose, like a medieval nun. It was a rather eccentric affectation that nevertheless made her seem even more formidable. The color was a steely grey. Beside her, his eldest brother seemed small and unassuming, with his plain square face.

Tomonosuke knelt at the far end of the hall, directly opposite the daimyō. The brocade edges of the tatami mats were arranged to form parallel lines drawing the eye to where the daimyō was seated on a slightly raised platform at the head of the room, before a decorative alcove adorned with a stark arrangement of a few white narcissus flowers.

Okyō knelt to his right. Somehow in the short time, Okyō had managed to set her appearance to rights, having her hair oiled and neatly if plainly dressed, her eyebrows shaved, and her teeth again properly blacked, as befit a married woman. Her white skin, of which she had been so proud, was now much darker. She still only had her patched old kimono to wear, and he felt badly for her that she had not been loaned a new kimono as he had. But as always, she comported herself with as much dignity as if she were wearing the latest Edo fashion. Far behind her, near the door, Rin hovered, her toes curled beneath her as she knelt, as if she were ready to spring up again at any moment.

Ichi knelt to his left, still looking gaunt, but at least the color had returned to his cheeks. Like Okyō, he held himself with perfect grace and confidence, as if he had no doubt that he belonged at this audience.

The young daimyō, never skilled at concealing his thoughts, blinked in surprise to see Tomonosuke with this retinue, instead of appearing alone, but he did not say anything aloud. Instead, he said, "I am glad to see you returned to the domain. It was feared you had perished in the earthquake."

Tomonosuke gave a three-finger bow but did not dare reply beyond a formulaic polite greeting.

"I understand you were attending to an urgent matter involving your wife's family?" the daimyo continued.

"My father fell ill, my lord," Okyō lied without the slightest hesitation, also bowing beside Tomonosuke.

"I'm very sorry to hear that. I trust he has recovered?"

"Yes, my lord," she murmured. Tomonosuke prayed the daimyō would not dispatch a letter to her family.

"Very good. We shall overlook this breach in light of your service to the domain."

Tomonosuke glanced up in surprise.

"It was due to your intervention that Matsudaira Sadahide's embezzlement came to light. I apologize for not heeding your warning earlier. After you, ah, departed and he returned to the domain, he became bolder in his crimes, until the senior counselor investigated and found he had been falsifying the records. This was just after my honored father passed on. I realized then what you had been trying to tell me so many months ago. I am sorry I aided him in falsely accusing you."

Tomonosuke bowed again. "My lord, I am grateful."

"In any case, he has been dismissed, and Matsuoka Toshizo has been appointed the head of the office of the exchequer. Your post in the office has been reinstated and your salary increased to ten koku per annum."

"Thank you, my lord!" This was double what he had received before. Tomonosuke could hardly believe his good fortune.

"I trust we can rely on your loyal service henceforth. You will remain here in Sawara at the residence of your elder brother, at least until your wife bears you an heir. Is that understood?"

"Yes, my lord."

"And the reason you are accompanied by this anma is...?" Evidently he could stay silent on the topic of Ichi's presence no longer.

Tomonosuke sat up, his back straight as a board and his hands clenched into fists on his thighs. For a moment, he considered dissembling, but then he realized, what is the worst they would do? Throw him out of the domain? Strip him of his rank? Those threats no longer held any weight. He spoke with surprising calm and assurance.

"My lord, the zatō here before you is my sworn brother. We have pledged to each other an oath of loyalty, and as such he is now a member of my household."

"Indeed?" For the first time, the daimyō seemed truly surprised. He glanced at Okyō, but she returned his gaze calmly, daring him to question her. He did not.

"Well," the daimyō continued, "two pledged brothers, what chivalry! Such loyalty among men is admirable. Just be sure not to neglect your duty to produce an heir. That is all. You are dismissed."

"Thank you, my lord."

Tomonosuke bowed low again, breathing a sigh of relief. The daimyō could have forbidden him from pledging himself to a non-person. It was quite benevolent of him not to mention the disparity in their ranks. But as Tomonosuke raised his head, he caught sight of his elder brother staring at Ichi with an appalled expression, and his mother openly seething. He would hear about this at home, he was certain.

Then he turned to take Ichi's hand and help him to his feet. The look of pure, artless happiness on Ichi's face made whatever awaited him at home seem more than worthwhile.

29

Flower Viewing

"Really, Tomo? A non-person, and a blind man, at that? What are you thinking?"

Tomonosuke's eldest brother did not even wait until they returned home, but began censuring him as soon as they exited the gates of the daimyō's residence. Lady Chacha, walking beside them, chose to allow her eldest son to speak for her.

By force of will, Tomonosuke kept his eyes trained on the road ahead, not looking behind him several paces to where Ichi was walking with Rin holding one end of his cane, and Okyō beside them.

"I won't have this anma in the house," his brother continued imperiously, when he did not reply.

Tomonosuke slid his eyes over to his brother. "You will," he said. He had never spoken out against his elder brother before, and his brother stared at him in surprise. "Our lord has ordered it, did you not hear?" Tomonosuke continued. "He ordered my household to stay at the family residence, and that includes all my dependents. He even deigned to favor me with words of praise. I'd say that's a high honor, wouldn't you?"

His brother pressed his lips into a thin line and changed the subject. "You know, Matsudaira Sadahide made a dreadful scene as he was being dismissed. Blamed you for his downfall. I would watch my back if I were you," he said vindictively.

"What, is he still here in Omigawa?"

His elder brother only shrugged, unconcerned. "He's a penniless rōnin. Who knows where he went?"

* * *

Tomonosuke settled into the Uchida residence as the cherry trees were in bloom. Although the house and outbuildings were in far better repair than anywhere they had been staying previously, the family was not well off commensurate with their rank, and with his two elder brothers and their wives and children also in residence, there was precious little space. Tomonosuke and Okyō were given a single six-mat room at the far end of a long corridor, while Rin was assigned to the servants' quarters in the second floor of the largest shed and set to work in the kitchen.

Ichi was not given any particular place, nor even any bedding. In the evening, Tomonosuke himself marched out to the storehouse to retrieve a spare futon and set it between his and Okyō's, which a maid had previously spread out. He then found that he had to do this every night. Even when Tomonosuke himself placed Ichi's futon in the closet in the morning, by evening, he found it returned to the storehouse. When he tried to have the duties reassigned so that Rin could take care of their room and bedding, the senior maid informed him tonelessly and without looking him in the eye that this would not be possible.

At mealtimes, the maids set out small trays for Tomonosuke and Okyō in their room, and served their food, but Ichi was only given what Rin managed to secret out of the kitchen by walking around the back and scratching at the shōji facing the garden.

This was the house in which Tomonosuke had grown up, and although his elder brother was now officially the head of household following the death of their father many years previous, it was still very much his mother's house. He recognized Lady Chacha's hand in this and a dozen other insults, letting them know that Ichi was not welcome in the house, regardless of what the daimyō had said.

His work rota was delivered, a vertically folded letter requiring him to report to the office of the exchequer five times each month. Matsuoka Toshizo was competent if unremarkable, and Tomonosuke found it a relief to be working for an honest man.

Yet he could not be easy. He should be happy, he reflected as he walked home along the canal, watching the pink cherry blossoms scatter in the breeze. He had been reinstated and his name cleared, and they at last had enough food to eat. They were all four becoming less emaciated and pale. But enduring his mother's critical eye at every turn was wearing on his spirits.

* * *

Ichi as well was painfully aware of Lady Chacha's censure, even if she had not yet spoked it aloud. He was accustomed to the highborn considering him below contempt, and he had no intention of attempting to change her opinion of him. But it galled him that she had the power to torment him in this way. Was this to be his reward for his loyalty to his elder brother?

The situation was even more unbearable because Ichi had nothing to do. Tomonosuke had his work rota and other domanial and familial duties, Okyō was obliged to assist her sisters-in-law with household chores, and of course Rin was kept busy morning until night in the kitchen. Only Ichi was left idling in their room all day, unable even to read or write to pass the time. He did not dare to go out and seek massage customers, nor to play the shamisen, as these low-class pursuits would give Tomonosuke's family an excuse to throw him out. He could always go back to the Tōdōza if he wished, but that would mean parting from Tomonosuke.

He thought again on what Matsuichi kengyō had said about attempting to live among sighted people as one of them. Although he had not dared to speak his desires aloud, at the time Ichi had been privately hopeful that he could gain Tomonosuke's regard, and not just his baser desires. And he had—the memory of how the others relied on him still warmed his heart. But now he was reduced to miserable dependency, and the thought of trying to win the respect of every sighted person in this household depressed him extremely.

* * *

"The cherry blossoms are looking particularly fine today," Tomonosuke remarked as he returned home to once again find Ichi sitting alone in the darkened room. He flung open the shōji along the outside wall, allowing in the cool spring breeze.

"Oh, indeed?" Ichi smiled wanly, turning his face to the outside.

Tomonosuke sat down heavily beside him. It pained him to see Ichi like this, even more so knowing he would never complain.

"Yes, but the blossoms are almost finished," Tomonosuke said. "I'm sorry I didn't have a chance to take you to a flower viewing party."

The town had been alive the past several days with raucous gatherings along the riverbank under the trees. The flower viewing parties were supposed to be about appreciating the beauty of transience, marked with poetry recitation, but most people took the event as an excuse for excessive drinking in public.

Ichi shrugged. "Not much point to flower viewing for one who cannot see."

Tomonosuke was shocked. This was something he himself might have said out of ignorance a year or more ago, but the Ichi he had come to know did not indulge in self-pity, nor did he reflexively deny himself the pleasures of the sighted world. He castigated himself for not noticing how low in spirits Ichi had sunk.

"That's not true!" Tomonosuke jumped to his feet again and tugged Ichi by the hand. "Come, let's go right now."

"What? Isn't it nearly evening?"

It would be dark in an hour or two, but Tomonosuke insisted that hardly mattered. He stopped by the kitchen to receive from Rin a few rice balls with okaka wrapped in a dry bamboo leaf, as none of them could bear to skip a meal, even now. With the packet of rice balls dangling from one hand by a string and Ichi holding his elbow, he led the way at a brisk pace to the riverbank, lined with rows of cherry trees with their pink blossoms and green leaves.

The parties had mostly ended as the blossoms scattered, and now only a few people were out, but Tomonosuke felt the quiet was preferable. As they ate their rice, he tried his best to describe the scene.

"The sun is just setting, and the sky is a brilliant orange," he began uncertainly. "There are not many blossoms left on the branches, but the few pink flowers here and there are quite lovely. On the ground there are great drifts of petals, almost like snow." He recited:

koto naraba
sakazu ya wa aranu
sakurabana
miru ware sae ni
shizugokoro nashi
Why does the cherry not fail to blossom even now?
Even I, upon seeing them, cannot be at ease in my heart.

"Ichi, I'm sorry!" he burst out.

Ichi's brow wrinkled in surprise, his opaque eyes rolling as if he were trying in vain to meet Tomonosuke's gaze. "Sorry for what?"

"For how unkindly my family treats you, for how unhappy you are in my home."

"No, I'm very grateful—"

Tomonosuke grasped Ichi's hands, desperate for some connection between them to compensate for the unreturned gaze. "Please don't feel you have to hide it from me. I feel the same way. The thought of leaving you idle and alone day after day pains me. Will you not return to the Tōdōza in Edo?"

"I confess I have thought on it. Is that what you desire?" Ichi hung his head to the side diffidently.

"No—I mean, I want you to be happy, but I should be grieved to part from you."

"I as well," Ichi replied softly. "I am pledged to you, aniki."

Tomonosuke sighed. He wished he had at least asked Ichi to bring his shamisen with them to the riverbank. He missed hearing those wild northern tunes, and even more missed the look of happiness on Ichi's face as he played.

The current situation was untenable, Tomonosuke realized as they returned home in the dark, the blowing petals ghostly in the moonlight. If he could not persuade Ichi to leave, then he must change the conditions at home himself.

* * *

Several days later, he lingered over his morning meal rather than rushing off to the daimyō's residence, as it was an assigned work day.

"Why haven't you left yet?" Okyō asked pointedly, sharp-eyed as ever.

"I, ah, have to speak to my mother before I go," he said, trying to be a vague as possible.

"You're going to confront her about how she's been treating Ichi," Okyō stated flatly.

Tomonosuke's heart sank. How did she always know what was in his mind?

"Aniki, no!" Ichi cried in distress, setting aside his rice bowl.

Okyō spat the pit of a pickled plum into her empty rice bowl with a clink and set it down decisively. "I'm going with you."

"And I!" added Ichi.

Tomonosuke sighed, not bothering to argue with them. Propriety demanded he speak to his mother in private, but secretly he was glad to have the two of them with him.

Lady Chacha was seated at a small desk in her room, the shōji open to the garden on two sides. She had not ceded to her eldest son upon her husband's death, but still occupied the largest rooms in the residence, with a view into a stark but tastefully arranged rock garden. A more conventional samurai widow might have been reading poetry or arranging flowers on a spring morning, but Lady Chacha was going over the household accounts and triple checking each line, as she did every day. She would follow this with two hours of copying sutras, then inspecting every corner of the residence and scrutinizing the work of each servant.

She cocked an eyebrow as a maid announced Tomonosuke, indicating that she was not pleased at this interruption to her daily routine.

Tomonosuke knelt down and gave a three-finger bow, followed by Okyō and Ichi. "Honored mother, good morning."

"Yes?" She swept aside the ledgers with irritation. "Please be quick. I'm very busy."

Tomonosuke raised his head from the bow, making his back as straight as hers. "Honored mother, please forgive the intrusion. I will get straight to the point." He had told himself not to flinch, but still he could not prevent himself from taking a deep breath before saying what he had planned so carefully in his mind. "Our lord Masamichi has ordered me to reside here, and I do so willingly, but all the members of my household must be allowed to live here as well. I—"

"Is that not so?" she said coolly, cutting him off.

"This treatment of Ichi cannot stand," he snapped, feeling his control starting to slip.

"All the *persons* in your household have a place commensurate with their rank," his mother said, turning her attention back to the ledger. "I'm sure I don't know about non-persons."

"Ichi is an accomplished musician," Tomonosuke plowed on, clenching his fists against his thighs and leaning forward slightly. "The daimyō recognized our pledge to each other, and you must as well."

She snapped the ledger shut again. "Really? You listen to me. Who do you think rescued you from vagrancy and starvation? I was the one who delayed your execution long enough for you to escape. I was the one who interceded with the daimyō to clear your name, who found evidence of Matsudaira Sadahide's duplicity, who convinced the daimyō not to punish you for your absence from the domain. And this is how you repay me—bringing shame on the family by contracting an intimacy with a beggar! A wretch blinded by his own bad karma, despised by heaven. Was there ever a son so unfilial?"

Tomonosuke felt the a stab of ice in his belly. He could bear her insults himself, but he hated that Ichi had to hear such spiteful words.

"The Buddha preaches compassion for all beings," he said through clenched teeth, about to argue further, but he felt his courage wither as his mother fixed him with her searing gaze.

"The blind are of no benefit to others, but only waste the world's resources. Why should I welcome such a one in my house?"

"Honored mother, if I may," Okyō added in honeyed tones, bowing again with perfect precision. "Ichi was the one who saved my husband's katana and wakizashi when the row house fell down on us in the earthquake. Surely for that he deserves our gratitude?"

Lady Chacha regarded Okyō with disdain but did not speak. She had not forgotten for a moment how much money Okyō had brought to their family.

"Ichi has been loyal to me through all my troubles," Tomonosuke continued with more confidence. "What kind of man would I be if I broke my pledge of brotherhood to him?" His mother seemed about to argue, but he continued on. "His blindness is not punishment for his misdeeds in this life nor in a previous one. He fell ill as a child—is that not a misfortune that might happen to anyone? My own troubles have been the result of my poor judgment, yet I have been forgiven and even rewarded. How can we condemn him for an accident that might have befallen anyone?"

Still she did not seem persuaded, although Tomonosuke knew her to be of an intellectual bent, and not ordinarily one to ignore reasoned argument.

"My lady," Ichi said, bowing then straightening again. Everyone turned to stare at him, not expecting him to speak on his own behalf. "My lady," he continued, "it is an honor to meet you. You must be very proud to have raised such an admirable son. Even if I were a samurai of the highest rank, I would feel unworthy of him. How much more so that I am only a lowly zatō. I am aware how the sighted world thinks of me, but I endeavor to live a righteous life, and I think there is no shame in it."

Tomonosuke felt a warm glow in his chest, watching Ichi lift his chin proudly, daring her to speak against him again. If she had expected him to grovel or back down, surely she must be surprised. He thought again of Hanawa Hokiichi, his confidence and accomplishments. What Ichi had learned from the Tōdōza was far more than merely a trade.

His mother did not deign to reply to Ichi, but turned her attention back to Tomonosuke. "Did you come here merely to berate me? What is it you want?"

He met her gaze steadily this time, without looking away or hesitating. He had hoped that this conversation might go differently, but he realized now that forcing her to admit defeat would only end badly for everyone. And besides, he had a different plan, one he had held out as a last resort, but which now seemed not only inevitable, but preferable.

"I had a private audience with the daimyō yesterday," he said, enjoying the look of surprise on both his mother's and his wife's faces. "He has agreed to post me permanently to Edo once more. We depart tomorrow. I will trouble you here no longer. I am very grateful for all you have done for me, and I shall do my best to bring honor to the family through my service to the daimyō at his Edo residence."

30

The Reunion

"Aniki, how did you convince the daimyō to grant your request?" Ichi lay back in the barge, leaning against a bale of rice as the ferryman poled the boat up the Tone River. It was a beautiful late spring day, and he closed his eyes, enjoying the warm sun on his face.

They had not departed for Edo the day after informing his mother as Tomonosuke had threatened. It had taken many more days for the senior counselor to draw up the official paperwork and advance his salary, and for them to outfit themselves and arrange the trip, but at last they were on their way, back along the Tone River, headed to Abiko-juku where they would meet the Mito Road to Edo.

They were all feeling like seasoned travelers by now, although the way was much easier now that they had sufficient money and food. And unlike when they had traveled the same route with the daimyō's retinue, now they could do as they pleased and not have to wait for hours at the checkpoints. They were all four in high spirits.

Tomonosuke smiled down at Ichi, pleased to see his cheerful nature returned.

"It was very easy," he said. "All I told him was that my previous post had been in Edo, and it seemed only right that I should be returned to it, if the domain was in need of my service there. My only regret is not asking as soon as we returned to Sawara."

"Never mind, we're on the way to Edo now," Okyō said. She was sitting beside Ichi, with Rin's head resting on her shoulder. She smiled at Tomonosuke.

Something about her looks different, he thought. It was a moment before he realized he had never seen her so relaxed and happy. He was so accustomed to her watching him with hooded, critical eyes that it was a surprise to see her let her guard down like this.

"My salary is still not so great," he warned them. "I've heard there is a housing shortage after the earthquake and fire, and the rents are shockingly high. We shall have to make do with a small room in a row house again."

"I don't care, as long as we all can live together," Ichi declared.

"Of course, why else did we leave Sawara?" He paused then added, "I apologize for my mother's rudeness to you."

Ichi frowned slightly. "It was no worse than I've heard before."

"Still, it grieves me that you had to hear it from her. I was so proud of how you defended yourself." He did not add, he had been slightly worried that Ichi might choose a self-sacrificing path and force Tomonosuke to choose his family rather than him. He was deeply grateful Ichi had instead stood up to her.

Ichi shrugged and gave a hollow laugh. "I lied when I said I was honored to meet her. Forgive me for saying so, but your best qualities are despite her, not because of her."

Tomonosuke did not know what to say to this. He had always found her difficult, but it had never before now occurred to him that she might be in the wrong about anything. It was a strangely freeing realization.

"And so," said Okyō with a smirk, holding Rin even closer, "now we have all four been rejected by our families and must make our own way in the world. I too was proud of how you spoke to her, Tomo. You've changed."

"Have I?" He still felt like the same person. But Okyō was right as usual. He would never have spoken like that a year ago. "But as you say, we must make our own way in Edo."

"What does that mean?"

He looked at Ichi, looking lovely in the summer sun. His face had filled out again, his even, delicate features glowing with good health. "I mean, Matsuichi kengyō mentioned to me that you might rise in rank if you study music more seriously and pass the exam."

"Oh, that." He rubbed a hand over his face.

"Yes that. You don't want to? Why not? I saw how happy you were when you were performing with Shirataki Gen. Don't you want to do that more?"

"I'll think about it."

* * *

They passed through the post towns on the Mito Road without incident. The weather was fine, the spring harvest was coming in, and food was at last more readily available. The inns they stayed at were not the most luxurious, yet they felt lucky to be sleeping indoors in their own rooms.

Before long, they were crossing the curved Nihonbashi Bridge, their high wooden sandals echoing on the wood planks as they hurried across the entrance to Edo. The great city still bore traces of the earthquake and fire of the previous year, with some lots standing empty, but new buildings were going up as fast as the construction crews could knock them together. Everywhere teams of tattooed men stripped to the waist with towels wrapped around their heads shouted and chanted in unison as they heaved the heavy beams in place.

Disdaining the hilly Yamanote neighborhood favored by upper-class samurai, Tomonosuke wanted to find accommodation downtown among the Edokko, but those were the areas hardest hit by the fire and houses were in short supply. He compromised by renting rooms in a row house in Ochanomizu along the banks of the Kanda River, close enough to downtown that they could go out to the theater whenever they pleased. Compared to the places they had stayed recently, the row house was very noisy—the voices of the neighbors, doors and wooden sandals clattering in the alley at all hours, the whistles of anma in the evening and the tofu vendors in the morning, the wooden clappers of the neighborhood watch striking at all hours with shouted reminders to be careful of fire. But Ichi welcomed this noise as a part of the excitement of city life. He had no desire to move back to the provinces.

On the second day in their new home, Ichi found himself alone with Tomonosuke after the morning meal, as Okyō and Rin departed together for the market.

Somewhere along the Mito Road, in one of the post towns, Tomonosuke had acquired a long thin metal pipe and a small pouch of tobacco. Now the sweet smoke wafted through the room. Ichi found the scent made him nostalgic for when they first met.

Smiling to himself, Ichi felt for his tray, checking the position of his empty dishes, then reached across with the backs of his hands for Tomonosuke's bowl and cup and began methodically stacking them on his own tray.

"What are you doing?" Tomonosuke's voice sounded more relaxed than he had in months.

"I'm going to wash the dishes, what else?"

"You?"

"What do you mean me? In Sawara, I had to do the washing up until we could afford a maid."

"I'm sorry. I mean, of course I know you can do it, but Rin will be back soon. Just leave it for her."

"Aniki, that's not very kind of you. If we are to live together, I should contribute to the household."

"Then do as you did in Jōetsu, and contribute by earning money. If you would only study..."

Tomonosuke trailed off as he saw Ichi's face close, the inexpressive mask in place again. Moving slowly and deliberately, Ichi held the tray in one hand and rose to his feet, holding the other hand before him and reaching out with his fingers until he found the shōji. Craning his head to see out the open door, Tomonosuke watched as Ichi felt his way with his bare feet, stepping carefully down into his sandals, moving his hand in circles until he found the shared kitchen in the alley.

It took Ichi quite some time to fetch water from the well, then return and scrub each dish with a hemp palm bristle brush. He ran his fingers over and over the inside of every one to be sure they were clean.

"I do apologize," Tomonosuke said again as Ichi stepped back inside and stacked the dishes on a small shelf along the wall. "I didn't mean to imply that you can't take care of household chores. Of course you can. I only meant that as my work rota has not yet been assigned, we might take our leisure today."

Ichi, seated on his knees, turned in the direction of Tomonosuke's voice. "It's all right."

"And you don't mind that I gave Okyō and Rin the larger room to sleep in? I'm sorry, I should have asked you."

Ichi shook his head, smiling. "Of course I don't mind. I would have offered it to them myself."

"I know this house is cramped for four people. If you would rather stay at the Sōroku yashiki..."

"No! I told you, living here with you is the greatest happiness. Although perhaps we might call on Matsuichi kengyō tomorrow, to let him know we have returned to Edo."

"Yes, by all means."

"Then perhaps now..." Ichi, suddenly shy, hung his head to the side as he reached out with tentative fingers. "if it will be some time before Okyō-dono and Rin return..." He found the rough fabric covering Tomonosuke's knee as he sat on the floor. They did not even have cushions or a hibachi; presumably these were among the items Okyō would have delivered later in the day.

Ichi felt Tomonosuke's large hand grasp his with sudden intensity, pulling him into a rough embrace. Then Tomonosuke's lips were on his, and Ichi's own lips curved up in a grin even as he returned the kiss. Here was the passion he had longed to feel, the ardor Tomonosuke had been repressing throughout their many hardships, expressed openly at last.

He returned the embrace with equal abandon, giving himself wholly to his elder brother.

Tomonosuke trailed hot kisses along his jawline and down his neck as Ichi's breath came faster. There was a rustling and shifting as Tomonosuke searched about for something with one hand, never breaking their embrace. A moment later, the pungent scent of clove oil filled the air.

Ichi loosened the twisted knot of his loincloth and settled back with a sigh of anticipation. How sweet, he thought, to give himself entirely to his elder brother, to trust that they understood each other even without words. They lay on their sides, Tomonosuke pressing up against Ichi's back and embracing him about the middle. Tomonosuke's body was leaner, more muscular than before. Ichi wriggled against him, enjoying the sensation of their two bodies fitting together perfectly and breathed deeply, the scent of tobacco and cypress layered under the distinctive cloves.

The hot and cool sensation of the clove oil sent shivers along his spine, and he breathed deeply. Tomonosuke was gentle as always, slowly helping him to open, knowing just how to touch him. Tomonosuke pushed his hips against him, and Ichi groaned as their cocks slid together.

Ichi reached around behind himself and grasped Tomonosuke's cock, enjoying the little gasp he gave as his fingers tightened. Ichi guided him in, letting him know he had enough of waiting. Tomonosuke began with only the slightest movement, increasing the rhythm only slowly, but soon enough he worked up to surging thrusts, until Ichi was moaning with delight, each guttural cry nearly forced out of him as they rocked together.

Just as Ichi felt he could not wait a moment longer, Tomonosuke reached forward to wrap his fingers around his cock, and they both finished at the same moment, their bodies bathed in sweat heaving together.

Spent, Ichi dropped his head back, nestling against Tomonosuke's neck, feeling his hot breath washing over his face. He gave a little sigh of contentment.

* * *

As the days passed, they fell into a routine, with Tomonosuke going out for his work rota at the Omigawa daimyō's Edo residence, Ichi giving massages, and Okyō and Rin taking care of the house. Tomonosuke wished that Ichi would turn his attention to his music but although he practiced from time to time, he seemed in no hurry to do more.

As Ichi had requested, they visited to the Sōroku yashiki to pay their respects to Matsuichi kengyō and the other members in residence. The old man listened in wonder to their tale, but Ichi did not mention studying for a higher rank, and Tomonosuke did not want to press him.

High summer brought the festivals and street performers, theater performances of all kinds, and fireworks in the evening along the river.

One afternoon, Tomonosuke rushed home, banging open the shōji in his haste.

"I'm home! Where is everyone?" He was pleased to see that Ichi had not yet left for his evening rounds, but was still getting ready, tying on his indigo trousers. He raised his head in surprise when he heard Tomonosuke clattering in the entryway.

Okyō and Rin had just returned from the bath house and were sitting in the adjoining room combing each other's hair, but opened the sliding door when they heard him come in.

"What is it?" Okyō asked.

Tomonosuke waved the piece of paper he clutched in his hand excitedly. It was a handbill, printed with bold characters and featuring a colorful woodblock image.

"It's Shirataki Gen!" he cried, giving the handbill to Okyō. "She's back in Edo, with the Katsumata troupe."

Okyō looked at the handbill, which bore the image of a beautiful woman striking a swaggering, masculine pose like a kabuki actor, fingers extended and arms at sharp angles.

"Oh! Oh!" Ichi sat down again, seemingly overcome. "Are they truly here? I've been so worried about them. I was going to ask if we could send them a letter, but I didn't know where to address it. We must go see them!"

"It appears they will be performing in a yose tonight," Okyō said, reading the handbill.

At Ichi's insistence, they all headed out to the theater in Kanda well before the performance time stated in the handbill. There just outside the theater was Katsumata Gonzaemon, supervising two laborers in hanging vertical banners announcing the name of the troupe in bold, stylish characters.

"Ichi! Kyō-chan!" Gonza greeted them familiarly, with a wide grin on his broad, ruddy face. "It's been so long! Gen will be pleased to see you."

Ichi bowed formally. "Katsumata-sama, I'm glad you're well. I was so worried about all of you."

Gonza gave a hearty laugh. "No need to worry on our account. It's all just business." He paused and looked at them again. "Oho, if that isn't Tomo! You have come up in the world, samurai-san."

Tomonosuke gave a brief, precise bow. "Thanks to your assistance, I was reinstated by the Omigawa daimyō. I'm no longer a rōnin."

"Is that so? Well, come inside, the others will want to offer their congratulations."

Gonza's wife Osan, their children and the other tumblers greeted them noisily, leaving off their rehearsals on the stage to rush over to them as they entered the theater. Gen and Oboro followed a few moments later, emerging from backstage.

Gen greeted Ichi like a younger brother, crushing him in an embrace, then offered Okyō a sly wink. She demanded to hear the whole story of how they had returned to Edo, and Tomonosuke gave a brief account.

"I'm very sorry I never sent you a letter," Ichi said when he had finished. "I've been thinking of you all every day and wondering how you fared."

"Ha, a letter!" Gen laughed. "And send it where? We've been on the road since we ran from that raid in Akita."

"And was the famine very terrible further north?" Okyō asked with concern. They all looked thinner, although not dangerously so.

Gen shrugged. "We got through it. I heard Echigo had it the worst. But never mind, that's behind us now. Come, we'll find you the best seats for the show."

She took Ichi's hand gently, but he tugged back, hesitating. "Oboro-sama, I must apologize for leaving with your shamisen. I never meant to take it from you. I've been very careful with it. I'll return it to you tonight after the show."

Oboro put her arm around his shoulders. "Think nothing of it. I'm sure you've put it to good use. Promise me you'll practice every day, and you may keep it."

Still Ichi would not hear of accepting such a valuable item as a gift, but insisted that he pay her for it. She only laughed and patted his arm, telling him there was no rush. The Katsumata troupe planned to stay in Edo through the end of the year at least.

"That's right," said Gen, as the two women guided him to a seat at the very front before the stage, one on each side, squeezing him between them. "Business is booming! After the earthquake and the fire and the food shortages, the people are wanting to enjoy themselves."

When Gen and the others departed backstage again, Okyō leaned over to Ichi as they all sat together on cushions on the floor and whispered, "You'll never be able to pay for that shamisen by giving massages."

Tomonosuke looked daggers at her, appalled at her bluntness, but Ichi did not seem to mind.

"I suppose you're right," he said with a smile, turning his face slightly in the direction of her voice. "Maybe I should try performing more seriously."

Tomonosuke did not say anything, stifling his slight chagrin that Okyō might succeed where he had failed at encouraging Ichi.

Soon the theater filled with the usual raucous crowd of townspeople and the tumbling began. As always, Gen took the stage last. She performed her most popular piece, the death of Atsumori from *The Tale of the Heike*. She was in rare form. The crowd shouted encouragement, calling out at the moments of the highest tension, as she strained and stretched her voice to depict the pathos of the beautiful boy Atsumori cut down in his prime, and the regret of the grizzled old warrior Kumagai.

Ichi listened with rapt attention, his head bowed and an ear turned toward the stage. When Gen described Kumagai finding the flute that Atsumori had carried with him into battle, Ichi raised his head, his cheeks wet with tears. Impulsively, Tomonosuke reached for his hand, and Ichi squeezed it tightly.

After the show, they joined the troupe at a yatai for broiled eel and sake. Perched on tiny stools around the outdoor stall, they drank straight from the ceramic bottles and listened to Gen and Gonza tell tales of near escapes and life on the road. After they had finished eating, Oboro and Gen brought out their shamisen and played some popular tunes while the others sang along.

Then Gen pushed her shamisen into Ichi's hands, and he played duets with Oboro, more of the northern tunes, the ones that had kept them from starving on the road. As they raced through the complex fingering, going faster and faster, he matched her note for note so that the two shamisen spoke with one voice. Then she paused and let him go on his own, even faster. The others applauded.

"My goodness, Ichi, you've improved," Gen said. Her face was flushed a dark red from the sake and she wobbled a bit on her stool, but the admiration in her voice was sincere.

"Yes, I said so too!" Tomonosuke added, lunging toward her, his words slightly slurred. "Isn't he good? We've been telling him to give up massage and perform professionally, but he won't do it."

"Hmmm." Gen stared at Ichi until he squirmed in embarrassment, conscious of her gaze, even if he could not see it.

"Is that something you want to do?" she asked him at last.

"I, uh, I mean..."

"Yes he does," said Rin, "more than anything, even if he's too modest to say so himself." The sake was making even her more outspoken than usual.

"There's no room for bashfulness if you want to play on stage," Gen declared. "So do you want to or not?"

"Yes!" Ichi said, sitting up straighter, his eyes blinking reflexively. "Yes, I do!"

"Then why won't you take the exam in the Tōdōza?" Tomonosuke burst out with the question that had been on his mind for days.

"You don't understand. That training is so strict—just copy the master, play exactly the way he does. And the sound is so boring. There's no room for expression. I can't play like I did just now and pass the exam."

Gen guffawed. "That's how it is, my lad! Look, if you want to be taken seriously as more than just a street performer, first you have to be certified, and to do that you must pass the exam. Besides, you can't improvise until you have mastered the form first. You have a good technique and a good ear, but I can tell your form is unstudied. Learn it first, then you can do as you please."

"Is that how it is," Ichi muttered, hanging his head.

"That is the way of the world," Oboro affirmed, patting his back. "We had to do so too."

"I will speak to Matsuichi kengyō," he promised.

31

The Five-Story Pagoda

The season turned from late summer to early autumn, although the weather remained hot. The month of Hazuki brought typhoons, and the rain fell incessantly, turning the streets to mud and blowing across the fields. But the storms were relatively mild, and the rice harvest was good enough that people could declare the famine was truly over.

The Obon festival came and went for Tomonosuke's household with less fanfare than usual. Not only were all four of them far from the graves of their ancestors and unable to pay their respects, but the holiday was a reminder of how they had been forced to sever ties with their living family. Rin and Ichi had long ago become inured to being cast out, but for Tomonosuke the wound was still raw.

He fretted for days over whether or not to send his mother a letter. He had not done so since his departure.

"A letter won't make any difference," Okyō observed, finding him seated before a small table with inkstone and brush before him, staring at a blank sheet of paper.

"I always thought of myself as a filial son," he said stiffly, not looking up.

"You can write the most filial letter in the world, it won't change her."

He looked up at her in anguish.

She sat down beside him and took his hand. "I know. Having to endure cruelty from a parent makes one feel as if the world is out of proper order. All you can do is be brave and try your best to be virtuous despite them."

He looked deeply into her eyes for perhaps the first time, for once seeing kindness and sympathy, rather than impatience and judgment. "Okyō, I'm glad you are my wife."

She turned away in embarrassment, dropping his hand. "Stop! I won't share a bed with you, if that's what you mean."

Since moving into the row house in Ochanomizu, Okyō slept beside Rin in one room and Tomonosuke slept beside Ichi in the other room. As they kept no other servants besides Rin, there was no one to condemn them.

Seeing that she was more embarrassed than angry, Tomonosuke gave a small grin. "Anyway," he said as he gathered up the unused writing things and put them away, "perhaps it is time to think about an heir at last."

"I—" Okyō's mouth gaped open in surprise, and she was clearly about to object.

Tomonosuke cut her off. "The arrangement you made with Ichi was not, upon reflection, such a bad idea. I apologize for my hasty reaction. If you wish to put the idea to him again, I don't mind."

Okyō blinked at him in surprise. "I'll see what he has to say," she replied slowly.

* * *

Ichi walked home from the Sōroku yashiki where he had been taking his shamisen lesson with Matsuichi kengyō, in preparation to pass the exam. Not wanting to draw attention to his decision, he had not mentioned anything to Tomonosuke, but surely he noticed that Ichi was out more often in the earlier part of the day.

The walk from Ryōgoku to Ochanomizu took nearly an hour, but Ichi found his way quite easily. He had only to cross the Ryōgoku Bridge over the mighty Sumida River, located right at the spot where the smaller Kanda River branched off to the west. Then it was merely a matter of following the road beside the Kanda River until he reached the row house in Ochanomizu.

The road home was lined with merchants' shops: wholesalers of pottery, umbrellas, sandals, lacquerware, paper, brooms and brushes; makers of incense, medicine, and cosmetics; greengrocers and confectioners. Often one of the merchant houses would send a child or servant to request Ichi's services within. The merchants enjoyed gossip and conversation with an anma almost as much as the massage itself. Ordinarily Ichi was happy to oblige, and to make a profit on the return trip from his lesson.

But today he brushed off the maids who tugged at his sleeve and pretended not to hear the shouted greetings as he hurried along, his head awhirl. He had scarcely attended to his lesson either, and Matsuichi kengyō had scolded him for his careless missed notes. He could not stop thinking about Okyō's proposition.

Unlike last time, she had not attempted to trick him or shock him or play games. After Tomonosuke departed for the upper residence, and while Rin was washing the dishes from the morning meal, Okyō laid a gentle hand on his arm and whispered in his ear that Tomonosuke had reconsidered, and was amenable to their prior arrangement to produce an heir, if Ichi consented.

"You don't have to answer now," she said. "Take some time to think it over." And then she was gone, clattering out the front door to the communal kitchen area.

Ichi was stunned. He had never heard her address him so kindly before—this was the tone of voice she normally used only when speaking to Rin, when she thought no one else was about. Somehow he felt that this was her true self, the tender heart she kept hidden behind her usual bluster and irascibility.

As he walked along, however, Ichi could not come to a decision, and in any case, his entire attention was taken up in searching out landmarks with the tip of his cane, listening carefully to ensure he did not get run down by a horse or ox, or wander off course. He counted each bridge he passed to his right, listening for the distinctive clop of wooden sandals on the curved wood planks of the bridges. After passing the ninth bridge, he turned to the left down a narrow alley that led to the entrance to the row house.

"I'm hooome!" he called as he stepped out of his sandals in the entryway and slid open the shōji leading directly to the main room.

"Welcome home." He was never so glad to hear Tomonosuke's deep masculine voice greeting him.

"Aniki! Is Okyō-dono at home?"

"No, she went with Rin to the bath house. Why? Is something wrong? You look distressed."

Ichi removed Oboro's shamisen from his back and laid it in the closet, feeling with wary fingers to be certain he did not bump it in the doorframe. Turning about with his hands before him, he knelt down, facing where he guessed Tomonosuke to be.

"Aniki, is it true? You wish me to father your heir?" He forced himself to be bold, to speak the words without shame. Unnecessary modesty and failure to speak plainly had caused misunderstanding between them, and he would not repeat the same mistake. Tomonosuke was his sworn brother. Ichi reminded himself not to hide his true feelings as he would with a customer.

"If you wish to," Tomonosuke said solemnly. "I would not compel you."

"But is this truly what you want?" Ichi insisted.

"It is."

"Then I consent." His fingers reached out along the floor until they found the edge of Tomonosuke's kimono and tugged at it shyly. His head drifted down and to the side. "I never thought I would father children," he said in a low voice, running his other hand over his freshly shaved head.

Tomonosuke immediately apprehended the meaning behind this

gesture. Tōdōza members were considered as monks, although not ordained; the tonsure was one sign of that status. "But surely there are some in the Tōdōza who marry and have children?" he asked.

"Well, yes. Hanawa sōkengyō has a wife and three sons."

"So it's not forbidden?"

"No, but it's not so common."

"Well, in any case, legally the child will be mine."

"Yes, of course." Ichi withdrew his hand from Tomonosuke's knee.

"You don't mind it?"

Ichi raised his head, showing Tomonosuke his smiling face, his expression open and without artifice. "No! I can think of no better way to bind all of us together forever."

He was surprised a moment later to feel himself in Tomonosuke's crushing embrace.

"Thank you," Tomonosuke whispered in his ear. Was he crying? Ichi wrapped his arms around him, breathing in deeply his masculine scent of cypress and tobacco, pressing up against his larger, muscled frame.

"Now when I grow old, you can't just discard me for a younger beautiful boy," Ichi said in a teasing tone.

"Never," Tomonosuke replied huskily, returning his embrace with equal ardor.

* * *

The last typhoon blew itself out, and the clouds parted to reveal a brilliantly blue autumn sky. Rin brought home persimmons from the market, and after the evening meal, they all enjoyed the crisp, sweet fruit.

"Tomorrow I believe I'll go to the Sensōji Temple in Asakusa to pray to Kannon," Okyō said, not directing this announcement to anyone in particular.

Tomonosuke only raised an eyebrow at her. She looked away, crunching a slice of bright orange persimmon. Ichi's cheeks turned slightly pink.

"It seems only fitting that we all go together," he said. Okyō rolled her eyes at him, as Ichi blushed harder.

"This is, after all, a family matter," Tomonosuke continued, amused at their embarrassment.

"Aniki!" Ichi looked mortified.

"Really, danna, are you trying to make this more difficult?" Okyō snapped, but she gave him a tiny smirk and he knew she was not truly angry.

As it was nearing the autumnal equinox, the temple grounds were crowded with people buying good luck charms. The most popular charms were in the shape of small bamboo rakes, so heavily decorated with auspicious symbols made of paper—gold coins, smiling masks, ears of ripened rice, calligraphy—that their shape was nearly obscured. Along with the stalls selling the charms were others selling buckwheat noodles, colored balls of mochi on skewers, broiled eel and other street food.

Okyō ignored all the vendors and shouldered her way through the crowd to the temple at the end of the row of stalls. Rin followed after her, holding Ichi's bamboo cane.

Leaving them to pray on their own, Tomonosuke wandered the grounds of the temple. Somehow the crowd made him uneasy, a prickling feeling at the back of his neck.

To the right of the main temple building was a path lined with dwarf pines. He walked along it a short distance and came to the five-story pagoda. He had often seen it from a distance but never up close, so he strolled around the outside, admiring the red and white painted beams. It was by far one of the tallest buildings in Edo, and standing beneath it, he was duly impressed to see the spire reaching to the sky.

Having completed a circuit around the pagoda, he continued on the path until he came to a smaller shrine. He was still so close to the main temple that he could hear the chatter of the crowd, but the area between the stone guardian lions and the offertory box at the front of the shrine was completely deserted.

He was pleased to find this moment of calm after the press of the crowd, and this seemed as good a spot as any to make his offering. Tomonosuke shook the bell on its thick braided rope, tossed a coin in the box, bowed, then clapped his hands twice. Still holding his hands pressed together before his face, he made a vague, brief, silent request to Kannon for good fortune, then bowed once more.

When he straightened and turned to leave, he was taken aback to see another man standing directly before him.

"Uchida Tomonosuke, you dog."

It was Matsudaira Sadahide. Tomonosuke felt the hairs rise on the back of his neck, wondering how long he had been followed. Sadahide was the one who now looked like a rōnin, with his hair grown out, the hem of his hakama stained with mud. Slowly, Tomonosuke slid one foot in front of the other, taking his long-practiced stance, although Sadahide still kept his hands at his side, not yet reaching for his sword.

"Prepare yourself!" Sadahide shouted, his eyes wild. "I have come to take blood revenge on you!"

Still Tomonosuke kept his arms at his side. Drawing his katana even three inches was a capital offence, and gave Sadahide the right to kill him and have samurai status stripped from his family. But as long as Tomonosuke did not draw first, Sadahide had no right to attack him. This talk of blood revenge was laughable.

"I haven't killed anyone in your family," Tomonosuke replied coolly. Even if he had, Sadahide would still have to apply for permission with the daimyō to carry out the vendetta, and it had to be registered with the shogunate. There was no way Sadahide had done this, and dueling without permission was illegal. Tomonosuke forced himself to remain calm. Sadahide was no master swordsman any more than the rest of the officials of the exchequer. Had he even been inside a dōjō since he was a youth?

Sadahide spat at his feet. "You may as well have killed me. Why can't I take revenge on my own behalf?"

Tomonosuke did not answer, or even look him in the eye, instead allowing his gaze to go soft, taking in the whole scene by allowing his focus to drift somewhat over Sadahide's head.

"And anyway you're the one who should have been stripped of your status for running away!" Sadahide ranted on, his voice rising. "So I should be allowed to kill you for disrespecting me." It was true that samurai were allowed to kill a commoner for any perceived slight.

"The daimyō reinstated me," Tomonosuke said quietly. He could see the five-story pagoda looming behind Sadahide, the brilliant orange shining in the sunlight against the bright blue sky. As the silence between them stretched on, he could hear the cries of the turtle doves roosting in the nearby pine trees, their distinctive low hooting incongruously peaceful compared to the murderous intentions of the man before him. Sadahide was no more than an indistinct grey form before him, in his dirty, worn kimono, with hair at the sides of his head coming loose from the topknot. The breeze lifted his disheveled hair slightly.

In the next moment, out of the corner of his eye, far more perceptive than the center of vision, Tomonosuke saw the movement of Sadahide's hand reaching for his katana. Without waiting to see if he drew the requisite three inches, in an instant Tomonosuke had his own sword out of the sheath.

As he had practiced so many times on the road, he lunged forward on one foot with a shout, slicing upwards from below. A second later, trying his best to see the practice dummy before him, he slashed sideways high in the air.

Another second later, Tomonosuke was already returning his katana to its sheath as Sadahide howled in pain. Sadahide's katana clattered on the stone paving as he clutched his bloody hand. His fingers were still intact, but the tendons at the base of his thumb had been severed. He could not pick up the katana with that hand, nor draw his wakizashi. His hair hung down the sides of his head—Tomonosuke had also cut off his topknot, which now lay on the ground not far from his katana.

"Aniki!"

Tomonosuke turned to see Ichi, Okyō, and Rin standing on the path from the main temple, looking ashen faced.

"I'm all right," he called to them.

Sadahide, holding his injured hand against his chest, awkwardly picked up his katana with his left hand, a loud groan escaping his lips. Without looking at them, he fled, leaving his topknot behind.

Ichi rushed towards him, stumbling slightly on the uneven paving stones, his hand reaching out uncertainly. Seeing his distress, Tomonosuke felt a dizzying rush of emotion. He had not been so concerned on his own behalf, but now seeing how much he had upset Ichi, he was nearly overcome. The distance between them seemed to close unbearably slowly.

Tomonosuke grasped Ichi's searching hand. The moment Ichi felt the connection between them, the color returned to his cheeks and he smiled with relief. Then just to be certain, he embraced Tomonosuke tightly, wrapping both arms around him.

"Thank goodness!"

Tomonosuke blushed at this public display, glad that Okyō and Rin were the only witnesses.

"We almost couldn't find you," Okyō scolded, her face pinched with concern. "It was Ichi who heard the sound of your voice."

He extricated himself from Ichi's arms, while still retaining a tight grip on Ichi's hand. Tomonosuke was suddenly overcome with exhaustion so profound he felt he might sag to the ground.

"It's all right," he said faintly. "I'm all right." It was all he could say.

32

One Year Later

In the eleventh year of the Bunsei era (1828), on the third day of the month Nagatsuki, as the peaches and apples ripened and the rice was harvested, Okyō gave birth to a healthy baby boy.

Throughout her pregnancy, Okyō religiously followed the advice in *The Women's Great Treasury*, eating only barley or millet mixed with rice, and daikon, burdock root, jellyfish, carp or other bland foods, avoiding anything sweet or spicy.

From her fifth month onward, she wore a special maternity obi, which Rin sewed for her with great dedication, vigorously bending the stiff, unrefined silk backwards and forwards with one hand as she held the needle steady with the other. She glanced up at Okyō, who was sitting beside the hibachi, studying the almanac to determine the most auspicious day for tying on the obi.

"Do you think the baby will be blind?" Rin blurted out suddenly.

Okyō only smiled. "Of course not, silly. You know he lost his sight due to an illness, right? It's not hereditary."

"And so what if it was?" Tomonosuke, seated on the other side of the hibachi, set down the book he was reading, the latest installment of *The Legend of Eight Dogs*. Ichi was at the Sōroku yashiki, and Tomonosuke felt obliged to defend him in his absence. "Would we love the child any less?"

"No, my lord. Please forgive me." Rin's ears burned and she dropped her gaze back to the obi.

Tomonosuke felt a pang of regret. After their many hardships, Rin had at last lost some of her fear of him, but it still returned from time to time. Again he promised himself to treat her more gently.

"The obi is looking very fine," Tomonosuke said kindly. "If Okyō does not object, I was thinking that all three of us might take turns handing it to her."

The first time the pregnancy obi was tied on was occasion for an elaborate celebratory ritual within the family, although usually it was the husband alone who handed it over.

Rin looked up again with shining eyes. "Might I?"

Okyō set down the almanac and favored her with a look of unalloyed affection. "Of course, sweetheart, I should like nothing better."

* * *

Not long after they held the obi ritual, Tomonosuke heard surprising news from one of the busybodies in the office of the exchequer. In the past, he most likely would have kept this news to himself, but now it never even occurred to him not to share it with his household. As they finished the evening meal, Tomonosuke cleared his throat somewhat self-consciously and placed his empty rice bowl on the small tray before him.

"They say that a body was fished out of the Sumida River a few days ago that looks like Matsudaira Sadahide."

Ichi turned pale, while Rin and Okyō exchanged a look of satisfaction.

"Do you really suppose it could be him?" Ichi asked anxiously, feeling for the edge of his tray with one hand and setting down his teacup with the other.

Tomonosuke shrugged. "There's no way to know for certain. The body has already been interred in the Ekōin temple in the grave for unknown persons. But they said it seemed to be a rōnin wearing a kimono with the Uchida clan crest."

"Ekōin, but that's in Ryōgoku!" Ichi exclaimed. "I know that temple very well. I shall go there tomorrow and pray for his rebirth as a bodhisattva."

"Why?" Okyō huffed. "All these months, I have been worried that he might return. It's a relief to know he's gone from this world, now especially with the baby on the way."

Ichi turned to face her. "The Buddha teaches compassion for all people," he said, frowning. "In any case, I am deeply grateful that is was not aniki who killed him."

Tomonosuke sighed. He too was relieved that Sadahide had run off after his humiliating defeat and not come at him again. He would be within his rights, legally speaking, to kill a man in self-defense, but the thought of taking a life filled him with horror, which was why he had purposely aimed only to disarm him during the duel. But now that he had a child to protect, he shuddered to think what he might do.

"I will go with you to Ekōin," he said.

* * *

Some days later, just as Tomonosuke was about to depart for the upper residence, Okyō laid aside her bowl of rice and announced, "It's time."

"What?" Tomonosuke stared at her, uncomprehending.

"It's time," she said again. "Rin, go fetch the midwives." Her voice was even, if a trifle annoyed at having to repeat herself, but her face was pale and her mouth tight.

In the next moment, the household broke into an uproar as the others fussed over her, but soon enough, Rin was sent out the door on her errand. While they awaited her return, Tomonosuke, with some difficulty, suspended a rope from a beam in the ceiling of the larger room.

Okyō sat calmly, flipping back and forth between two string-bound volumes as she consulted her almanac and *The Women's Great Treasury*. "Today is the day of the dragon, so I shall face to the southwest," she declared, orienting herself under the rope Tomonosuke had just suspended. She would hold onto it to keep herself upright during her labor. She glanced up from the two books in irritation. "Ichi, stop pacing! It's annoying."

Ichi sat down abruptly but could not stop wringing his hands. "I'm sorry! Isn't there anything I can do?"

Okyō only snorted. She did not desire his assistance, nor anyone else's. As soon as the two midwives arrived, she banished Ichi, Tomonosuke, and even Rin to the smaller room. Rin was not pleased, but Okyō insisted. *The Women's Great Treasury* was very clear on this point—only the midwives were allowed to attend her.

No doubt due to her meticulous adherence to these instructions, including facing in a lucky direction as she labored, she had a relatively easy delivery, although it still took many weary hours, as Tomonosuke, Ichi and Rin fretted in the next room. To pass the time, Rin worked on refashioning the pregnancy obi, now no longer needed, into baby clothes.

Rin put aside her resentment, however, the moment the baby was born, caring for mother and baby with tender devotion as Okyō spent the requisite twenty days in bed.

"He looks like a little frog," Okyō said as she and Rin lay on their futons, with the baby sleeping between them. There was something vaguely frog-shaped about the way he held his little arms and legs bent, like all newborns.

"How can you say that!" Rin whispered, not wanting to wake him. "He's the most beautiful baby in the whole world." She gazed at him with an adoring look on her sharp, kittenish features.

Okyō did not reply, but only watched Rin watching the baby sleep. It was not in her nature to make sentimental proclamations or boast of her own family. But the sight of both of them lying beside her filled her with the greatest, inexpressible happiness.

* * *

They named the child Uchida Hiroichi and registered him with the clan as Tomonosuke's heir. They told no one of their arrangement or how the child was conceived.

When the baby was thirty-two days old, as was the custom, they presented him at the shrine to Kosodate Kannon, and when he was one hundred and twenty days old, they held the ritual of the first meal. Ordinarily this would be a lavish affair, but neither Okyō nor Tomonosuke wished to be with their family. Indeed, since they had at last successfully produced an heir, the estrangement only deepened, to their mutual relief. Tomonosuke received a formal letter from Lady Chacha congratulating him, but then nothing more.

They held the ritual of the first meal at home, each taking a turn to hold the baby on a knee and pretend to feed him specially prepared rice balls and roast fish. The only guests were Shirataki Gen and Oboro. It was a joyous occasion, and Gen provided a steady stream of jokes. The baby did not seem to mind being passed from lap to lap, but smiled up at each of them.

He eventually tired of the pretend feeding, however. When he began to fuss, Okyō picked him up, loosened the front of her kimono and gave him her breast, as the others turned to the food. Rin sat beside her, stroking the child's foot lovingly, looking deeply content.

"He's a beautiful child, and born on an auspicious day," Gen said, toasting them with a cup of sake, far from her first. "But Tomo," she added, leaning towards him a bit unsteadily with a conspiratorial wink, "it doesn't bother you that he looks so much like Ichi?"

On the opposite side of the table, Ichi choked on his sake, his face, already red from drink, going several shades darker until he was nearly purple.

"Gen!" Oboro scolded.

Okyō continued gazing down at the infant beatifically, completely unconcerned.

But Gen kept elbowing Tomonosuke in the ribs suggestively. He only shrugged.

"I suppose if the Shining Prince Genji can bear it, I can too," he said. Gen nodded sagely. Tomonosuke thought of the scene in *The Tale of Genji* when Genji formally recognizes the Third Princess's baby, even knowing that the true father is the much younger Kashiwagi. But that was in no other way similar, as it was a sad event for Genji, whereas Tomonosuke felt only gratitude and joy at how his family had expanded, even if it was unconventional.

"Besides, families adopt heirs all the time," he added. "What does it matter how a child came into the world, so long as he is loved by his family?" He stared at Okyō as he spoke, and she gave a tiny smile.

"That's the spirit!" Gen cried, thumping him on the back.

"Oh, how can you be so uncouth?" Oboro scolded. "Such things need not be spoken aloud."

"Why not!" Gen laughed. "How can it be a secret when they even gave him Ichi's name!"

Tomonosuke cleared his throat. "The kanji character is not the same." Gen only rolled her eyes at him.

"Stop, you're embarrassing poor Ichi," Oboro chided her. As Ichi was seated beside her, she took his hand. "Ichi, I've been meaning to congratulate you on your promotion. Well done!"

Ichi ducked his head, murmuring thanks. He had at last passed the exam and been promoted to the rank of bettō. It was as Oboro had said—now that he had the title, the invitations to perform professionally began to come in, and he was starting to make a name for himself. And even better, he had the freedom when he performed to play as he liked, not only the old standards, but the wild, improvisational style he had learned in the north. The Edo audiences loved this new sound.

"I'm sure you'll be a kengyō before you know it," Oboro added.

"Yes, congratulations!" Gen slurred. "I knew you could do it. But are you sure you want to stay in Edo? Don't you all want to go back north with us? You might learn some new tunes."

"No!" All four of them answered at the same time, then burst out laughing.

"It's very kind of you," Ichi said, "but our time in the deep north was not the happiest."

"Oh come on, we can travel together!" she said, waggling her eyebrows suggestively, even though he could not see it. "Don't you miss walking the great highways?"

"Not particularly, no. I do prefer to sleep in a bed, in a house with fewer mosquitoes and fleas."

"You know what they say, if you live in Edo, you can expect to be burned out of your house three times," she replied.

"Well," said Tomonosuke, "we've already been burned out once, so that's only two more times to go."

Okyō, at last finished with the baby, handed him to Rin, then helped herself to some rice and fish. "There will almost certainly be more earthquakes and fires," she said with equanimity. "But Edo is the greatest city in the world. Why would I want to live anywhere else?"

"Hear, hear!" Ichi concurred vigorously, lifting his sake cup in a toast. "Besides, if I am to pass for kōtō and then kengyō, I must remain here for now, right?"

Gen only laughed. "I'm certain you will pass very soon, then you will be plagued with apprentices and come begging to join me on the road again."

"Ha! If anyone wants to apprentice with me, I'll send them to you," Ichi replied with a smile.

* * *

Much later that night, after Gen and Oboro had at last departed, the household retired in their usual arrangement, with Okyō and Rin in the larger room and the baby on a futon in between them. Tomonosuke and Ichi lay with their futons pushed together in the smaller room, with the fusuma between the two rooms shut.

Tomonosuke did not douse the andon, even though the hour was very late. Perhaps it was a bit strange, but he very much liked to gaze on Ichi's face as they lay in bed together. Although Ichi's features had filled out somewhat, he still retained an appealingly boyish look, at the moment slightly marred by the frown that creased his forehead.

Tomonosuke rubbed his finger along the crease until it cleared.

"What is troubling you?" he asked gently.

Ichi sighed. "Do you truly not mind what Gen said to you?"

Tomonosuke wrapped his arms around him, squeezing, and laying his head on his shoulder. "I said no."

"But does the baby really resemble me so closely?"

"He does."

"And you don't mind that people will guess?"

Tomonosuke pulled away to look him more squarely in the face. Even though it was not necessary, it was a habit that had only strengthened over time. He felt he would never grow tired of gazing on such striking, arresting features.

"Why should I mind? After all that has happened, do you think I still care what the world thinks of me? If the child is as beautiful and clever as his parents, he will be fortunate indeed."

"Stop! You're flattering me." But he seemed pleased nonetheless.

"I tell you sincerely," Tomonosuke continued, "I would not have consented if I did not truly desire it. It gives me the greatest pleasure to see you holding our child, and him looking up at you."

"It's not exactly Shino and Gakuzo, is it?" Ichi said with a wry smile. *The Legend of Eight Dogs* was still far from complete, but it did seem unlikely to end with the two fierce warriors raising a child together.

Tomonosuke laughed. "I'm very glad we live in more peaceful times. If I never again have to draw my sword in a duel, I shall consider myself fortunate."

"And I as well," Ichi said fervently. "So how do you suppose Takizawa-san will end *The Legend of Eight Dogs*?"

"Oh, I imagine it must conclude with the dog warriors reinstating the Satomi clan somehow," Tomonosuke said, yawning. The hour was growing quite late. Although he still read each new chapter aloud to Ichi, and they enjoyed the adventure, he found he no longer cared so much about the fate of the clan.

"Medetashi medetashi," Ichi recited, making Tomonosuke snort with laughter at the thought of the novel concluding with the well-worn phrase used by storytellers at the end of a fairy tale. At last he blew out the light and wrapped his arms around Ichi with a contented sigh, in anticipation of many happy days together.

Author's Note

Male homosexuality in Japan of the Edo period (1600-1868) was considered normal, but the culture of male-male relationships was obliterated when the country modernized after 1868, to comply with European ideas of morality. Military propaganda during WWII suppressed knowledge of this history even more, and contorted the image of the samurai to fit the war effort. This is why portrayals of samurai today rarely show homosexual relationships, even though they were extremely common at the time. Most men in the Edo period were what we term bisexual today, although some referred to themselves as woman-haters, meaning they chose to have sex only with men. Female homosexuality is not as well-documented but does appear in some fiction and art. Androgyny in both sexes was a source of much fascination and appears repeatedly in novels and on stage.

The collection of short stories *The Great Mirror of Male Love* (*Nanshoku ōkagami*, 1687) by Ihara Saikaku (1642-1693) is one of the best known contemporary sources on male homosexuality in the Edo period. There are thousands of woodblock prints depicting men having sex with each other, but as one partner is usually wearing female clothes, these are often mistaken today for heterosexual couples. The most detailed source in English on this culture is *Male Colors: The Construction of Homosexuality in Tokugawa Japan* by Gary Leupp.

All the occupations of blind people mentioned in the novel are real: the biwa hōshi, bosama, goze, and anma. The Tōdōza was a real institution, although as they did not keep written records, we have relatively little information about them. The most detailed source on the Tōdōza in English comes from an article by Gerald Groemer titled "The Guild of the Blind in Tokugawa Japan." Although the Tōdōza offered only a few career paths for blind men, it was self-governing and far more self-directed than education for the blind in Europe at the same time. The Tōdōza was disbanded in 1871 as Japan modernized, but the connection between blind people and a career in massage or acupuncture remains strong even today. An early twentieth century version of the anma can be seen in the film *The Masseurs and a Woman* (*Anma to onna*, 1938) or the remake, *My Darling of the Mountains* (*Yama no anata*, 2008).

The Tōdōza were reviled by the samurai class because they served as moneylenders at a time when the samurai suffered severe economic hardship. Having to borrow money from their social inferiors caused a great deal of resentment. One of the most detailed contemporary accounts of the Tōdōza comes from *Matters of the World: An Account of What I Have Seen and Heard* (*Seji kenbunroku*), written in 1816 by a samurai using the pseudonym Buyō Inshi, meaning "a retired gentleman of Edo." The book is translated into English under the title *Lust, Commerce, and Corruption* by

Mark Teeuwen, et. al. Buyō Inshi is an elitist who airs his complaints about many examples of what he considers social disorder, and he is particularly prejudiced against the Tōdōza because of this practice of moneylending. Most of the negative comments about blind people in the novel come directly from him.

By contrast, Isabella Bird in her 1878 travelogue *Unbeaten Tracks in Japan* found that blind people enjoyed far higher social status than in Europe of the nineteenth century. She writes, "...a blind beggar is never seen throughout Japan, and the blind are an independent, respected and well-to-do class..." (337). On the following page, she notes, "The number of the blind is very great, and it is very interesting to find that, without either asylums or charity, they can make an independent living" (338).

Hanawa Hokiichi (1746-1821) was a real person, although I adjusted the dates of his life slightly to bring him into the novel. His 670 volume history of Japan is a remarkable achievement given that there was no reading or writing system for the blind equivalent to Braille at the time. His scholarly work was recognized and held in high regard by the shogunate, and today the Onko Academic Society is dedicated to preserving his memory. There is a memorial museum dedicated to him in Tokyo which is open to the public.

The Legend of Eight Dogs (*Hakkenden*) has unfortunately not been translated into English in its entirety, but a few short passages translated by Chris Drake can be found in *Early Modern Japanese Literature: An Anthology, 1600-1900*. In total there are 106 volumes, published from 1814 to 1842. It was one of the most popular novels of the late Edo period. The author, Kyokutei Bakin, born Takizawa Okikuni (1767-1848) really did become blind late in life, and dictated the later chapters of the novel to his daughter-in-law. There is no record of whether or not Bakin and Hanawa might have met, but they were contemporaries living in Edo.

The type of music that Ichi learns to play in the northern provinces is called tsugaru-jamisen, which is still quite popular today. It was almost certainly developed by blind itinerant musicians in the mid nineteenth century. The creation of this style is credited to a bosama called Akimoto Nitarō, nicknamed Nitabō. Although he lived about fifty years later than the setting of this novel, it's not unlikely that this style of playing started to emerge somewhat earlier. There is an animated film about him titled *Nitaboh The Shamisen Master* (*Nitabō: Tsugaru shamisen shiso gaibun*, 2004). One of the last traditional bosama, Takahashi Chikuzan (1910-1998), record many albums which can be easily found online.

The description of the Yoshiwara is taken from *The Sexual Life of Japan* by J. E. de Becker (1863-1929), originally published in 1899, republished under the title *The Nightless City*.

The Women's Great Treasury (*Onna chōhōki*) was originally published in 1692 but remained in print and widely read throughout the Edo period. It consists of five volumes of advice on every aspect of daily life. Volume three on childbirth has been translated by Reiko Tanimura and Richard Chart.

All poems come from the *Kokinshū* collection of poems, compiled sometime in the tenth century. *The Tale of the Heike* is an epic poem describing a twelfth century civil war. It emerged in the oral tradition in recitations by biwa hōshi in the fourteenth century and was written down later. The most recent English translation is by Royall Tyler.

Glossary

andon: oil lamp with a rectangular shade covered with paper

aniki: elder brother

anma: professional masseur, almost always a blind man

bettō: middle rank in the Tōdōza

biwa: a large stringed instrument similar to a lute

biwa hōshi: blind itinerant monks trained to recite epic poetry and accompany themselves on the biwa

bosama: blind itinerant musicians in northern Japan, playing door to door for food handouts

-chan: childish form of -san, most often attached to girls' names

daimyō: feudal lord, in charge of the domain

danna: master, husband

-dono: respectful term of address to a superior, similar to Lord or Lady

Edokko: child of Edo; commoners born in Edo who take great pride in their distinctive urban culture, perceived as fashionable and chic even by the higher classes

fundoshi: loincloth made of a single strip of fabric twisted like a cord, looped around the groin and between the buttocks

fusuma: interior sliding doors that serve as room partitions

gidayū: long-form narrative chanting accompanied by shamisen, usually performed by men in a heroic style, but sometimes also by women, called onna (women's) gidayū

goze: a blind woman itinerant musician

hakama: loose trousers worn by men over a kimono

hatamoto: bannerman, a high ranking samurai, although there are many grades within that rank

hibachi: brazier; a large box or bowl filled with charcoal, usually the only heat source in a room

hinin: non-person, outcaste or beggar

-juku: a post town along major roads connecting Edo with the provinces, set about a day's walk apart, featuring inns, restaurants and other amenities for travelers

hōkan: buffoon or clown, male comic entertainers in the Yoshiwara pleasure quarter

kagema: teenage boy prostitutes catering to adult men

kataginu: samurai's formal vest with extended shoulders, worn over a kimono

katana: long sword; as only samurai may carry a sword, it is the mark of their status

kengyō: the highest rank in the Tōdōza

koku: a bale of rice, used as the standard system of payment for samurai

kōtō: second lowest rank in the Tōdōza

matoi: a standard or banner made up of long white streamers attached to a long pole, topped with a large geometric figure or insignia, used by firefighter gangs to warn of a fire by waving it from a nearby roof

mochi: sweet sticky rice pounded to a thick paste and shaped into a ball

momohiki: peasant trousers, tight at the calf and secured by tying around the waist

nagaya: row house, single story apartment or tenements

nagauta: ballad

noren: divided short curtain hung at the entrance a business or restaurant

obi: sash tied around the waist to hold a kimono closed

oiran: courtesan or high-class prostitute, trained in poetry, music and dance, known for distinctive, elaborate headdress and costume

okaka: dried fish flakes seasoned with soy sauce

omikuji: a fortune written on a small slip of paper, sold at Shinto shrines

onēsan: elder sister

osechi: special feast for the New Year's celebration

rōnin: masterless samurai

-sama: polite term of address, similar to Mr., Ms., or Mrs.

-san: shortened form of -sama

shakuhachi: large bamboo flute with seven holes, played by blowing into one end

shamisen: a three-stringed instrument somewhat similar to a banjo, played by plucking the strings with a large triangular plectrum

shōgi: board game similar to chess

shōji: sliding doors faced with translucent white paper

sensei: teacher, also used as a respectful term of address

sōkengyō: grand master; the head of the Tōdōza

tatami: thick woven rush mats in standard rectangular size (approx. 1 x 2 meters or 3 x 6 feet), built into the floor; the number of mats is a measure of the size of the room, usually three, six or eight mats

Tōdōza: the guild of blind men

wakizashi: short sword; along with the longer katana, the mark of a samurai's status

yashiki: residence, estate, or mansion. Daimyō were required to keep at least two residences in Edo, the upper residence (kami-yashiki) and lower residence (shimo-yashiki)

yatai: outdoor stall selling food and drinks, with some seating in front

yose: an unlicensed theater

zatō: the lowest rank in the Todoza

Time Keeping

In premodern Japan, the day was divided into twelve units of two hours. There were several methods of keeping time; one of the simplest is based on the animals of the Chinese zodiac. Hours were not absolute but were timed to the sunrise and sunset, so the length of each interval varied throughout the year.

Rabbit 5AM - 7AM
Dragon 7AM - 9AM
Snake   9AM - 11AM
Horse   11AM - 1PM
Ram   1PM - 3PM
Monkey 3PM - 5PM
Rooster 5PM - 7PM
Dog   7PM - 9PM
Boar   9PM - 11PM
Rat   11PM - 1AM
Ox   1AM - 3AM
Tiger   3AM - 5AM

The calendar followed the lunar year, which began in late January/early February. Although the name of each month is usually translated to follow the Western calendar, starting with January in the first month, in fact it usually fell one month later. There was no concept of weeks or days of the week; each day was referred to by number only.

January Mutsuki
February Kisaragi
March Yayoi
April Uzuki
May Satsuki
June Minazuki
July Fumizuki
August Hazuki
September Nagatsuki
October Kannazuki
November Shimotsuki
December Shiwasu

Numbering of years was not consecutive but tied to the reign of an emperor, although the name might be changed following a disaster. This novel takes place in the Bunsei era (1818-1830).